Pra

"This sweet, slice-of-life romance from Walsh (*The Happy Life of Isadora Bentley*) kicks off when overworked associate book editor Kelsey Worthington is hit by a curb-hopping car and taken to the hospital, where she meets Georgina Tate, the formidable owner of Tate Cosmetics . . . Walsh delivers just enough introspection to make her heroines' journeys believable without slowing the pace. The romance, when it comes, is gentle and sincere rather than steamy. Readers looking for G-rated love stories will want to snap this up."

—*PUBLISHERS WEEKLY* FOR *THE SUMMER OF YES*

"Courtney Walsh is an incredible storyteller. She has a magical way of weaving hope and happiness into every story she writes. If you love books by Denise Hunter and Rachel Linden, then say yes to *The Summer of Yes!*"

—MELISSA FERGUSON, BESTSELLING AUTHOR OF *HOW TO PLOT A PAYBACK*

"Two unlikely women come together for a summer that will change their lives in Courtney Walsh's latest perfect page-turner. Full of heart, humor, and, oh yes, a happy ending, *The Summer of Yes* reaffirms why Walsh is one of my favorite writers. This feel-good novel is her absolute best yet—and the beach read that everyone will be talking about!"

—KRISTY WOODSON HARVEY, *NEW YORK TIMES* BESTSELLING AUTHOR OF *A HAPPIER LIFE*

EVERYTHING'S COMING UP ROSIE

Also by Courtney Walsh

STAND-ALONE NOVELS

The Summer of Yes

The Happy Life of Isadora Bentley

Things Left Unsaid

Hometown Girl

Merry Ex-Mas

ROAD TRIP ROMANCES

A Cross-Country Christmas

A Cross-Country Wedding

NANTUCKET LOVE STORIES

If for Any Reason

Is It Any Wonder

A Match Made at Christmas

What Matters Most

HARBOR POINTE NOVELS

Just Look Up

Just Let Go

Just One Kiss

Just Like Home

PAPER HEARTS NOVELS

Paper Hearts

Change of Heart

SWEETHAVEN CIRCLE NOVELS

A Sweethaven Summer

A Sweethaven Homecoming

A Sweethaven Christmas

A Sweethaven Romance (a novella)

EVERYTHING'S COMING UP ROSIE

A NOVEL

Courtney Walsh

THOMAS NELSON
Since 1798

Everything's Coming Up Rosie

Published in Nashville, Tennessee, by Thomas Nelson. Thomas Nelson is a registered trademark of HarperCollins Christian Publishing, Inc.

Thomas Nelson titles may be purchased in bulk for educational, business, fundraising, or sales promotional use. For information, please email SpecialMarkets@ThomasNelson.com.

Library of Congress Cataloging-in-Publication Data

Names: Walsh, Courtney, 1975- author.
Title: Everything's coming up Rosie: a novel / Courtney Walsh.
Other titles: Everything is coming up Rosie
Description: Nashville, Tennessee: Thomas Nelson, 2025. | Summary: "Sometimes what you think you want and what you actually want turn out to be different things . . ."—Provided by publisher.
Identifiers: LCCN 2025000803 (print) | LCCN 2025000804 (ebook) | ISBN 9780840713858 (trade paperback) | ISBN 9780840714053 | ISBN 9780840714008 (epub)
Subjects: LCGFT: Christian fiction. | Novels.
Classification: LCC PS3623.A4455 E94 2025 (print) | LCC PS3623.A4455 (ebook) | DDC 813/.6—dc23/eng/20250113
LC record available at https://lccn.loc.gov/2025000803
LC ebook record available at https://lccn.loc.gov/2025000804

Printed in the United States of America

25 26 27 28 29 LBC 5 4 3 2 1

For Professor Alan Langdon
Seeker of Joy
Proof that length of time spent with a person does not determine the impact on a life

PROLOGUE

WELL, SHOOT. THIS ISN'T HOW my life is supposed to go.

On the day I graduated from Northwestern with a BA in musical theatre, diploma in hand and stars in my eyes, I told myself I wouldn't give up until I made my dream come true.

I also pledged never to do Amish theatre, but as it turns out, it pays really well. Beggars can't choose and all that.

Back then, in those idealistic years postgraduation and pre–real world, I turned up my nose at the idea of a plan B because "they" said that if I had a plan B, I'd be more likely to use it. And I didn't want to use it. Because I was going to make it.

I held my future in my own two hands, which meant, according to Eleanor Roosevelt and Timbuk 3, that the future belonged to me and I needed to have a pair of shades ready.

It all seems so naive now.

It's amazing how seven years can change everything. Seven years of auditions, callbacks, rejections. Seven years of temp jobs and ushering patrons to their seats and getting very good at making fancy coffee drinks. Seven years of what is starting to feel like wasted time.

I randomly think how change must be *way* faster for dogs.

I'm glad I don't have a dog. If I did, that would mean that both of us were about to become homeless.

Because today, standing in the hallway of my soon-to-be-ex

three-story walk-up in Brooklyn, I mindlessly wonder if someone is trying to tell me that dreams like mine are for fools.

There's a yellow envelope stuck to the front door and a suitcase—my suitcase—propped in the corner of the hallway.

I stare at the envelope, and the envelope stares right back.

I groan. This is not my day. Apparently this isn't my year either.

After months, the play I've been rehearsing finally opened in a tiny black box theatre in the Village. Yes, it was an original, but the playwright had some other successes and the script wasn't half bad.

It seemed the critics solely focused on the part of the script that wasn't half good.

They hated it. One of them wrote, "The redhead playing Julietta couldn't be more wrong for the role. Her stilted delivery and understated reactions reminded me of the time I made the mistake of letting artificial intelligence try to narrate a book for me. This calls into question the ability of this director—everyone knows if you get the cast wrong, you get the whole show wrong."

What I took away from that review, of course, is that *I* ruined the whole show. The miscast redhead playing Julietta was me. Never mind that the director actually *wanted* the stilted delivery and understated reactions. That I did what I'd been directed to do.

The show closed after only two performances.

I huff as I open the envelope that someone—I'm assuming one of my roommates, Ellen, whose name is on the lease—taped there. I pull out a handwritten note telling me she's found someone else to rent my room. Someone who can pay.

This is not unexpected.

> The timing is better this way since you're heading home tonight for that baby shower, but I've given up ever seeing the last four months' rent from you. I packed your things to make it easier because Trinity is

moving in tonight. I'm sorry this didn't work out, and I really do wish you luck, Rosie.

Ellen

I crumple the paper and throw it on the floor. Then I rush over, pick it up, and try to smooth it out. I'm angry, but I don't want to have anyone else *see* I'm angry. I stuff the paper into my bag, grab my suitcase, and head downstairs, the whole time thinking, *So this is what rock bottom feels like.*

If this isn't rock bottom, it's rock-bottom adjacent.

And now, I'm going home.

Home. For the first time in years.

Home. To reunite with all of my old high school friends, the same people who voted me Best Actress and Bravest Grad for the senior class. Never mind I've done a terrible job of staying in touch.

Home. To desperately try to hide the truth. There's no way I'm letting people see that I'm a failure.

I'm an actor.

Time for the role of my life.

CHAPTER 1

I HAVE THAT FEELING YOU get when you're next in line for a roller coaster.

A little bouncy, a little anxious, and so excited that I might wet my pants.

"Rosie?! I can't believe you're actually here!"

My best friends, Taylor, Marnie, and Maya, all rush toward me, and for a few moments it's like the rest of the room fades away. I'm seventeen again, getting ready for homecoming with the three people I love most in the world, aside from my family. We all try to talk at the same time, succeed for a solid thirty seconds, and then stop and laugh.

It's like we never left each other and all of my hesitation about being here melts away.

Our friend group is a sitcom.

Taylor—the chipper one. Class president. Head cheerleader. Currently pregnant.

Marnie—the studious one. Speech team champion and National Merit Scholar. Currently crushing it as the anchor for the local news.

Maya—the wild one. Rebellious party girl who hid her intelligence behind blue hair and piercings, both of which, I now see, are gone, making her currently look beautiful and grown-up.

I step back and look at Taylor's belly. My gorgeous friend is tiny, so the baby bump looks like someone stuck a basketball to her midsection.

My hand hovers over it. "Can I . . . ?"

Taylor takes my hand and pulls it toward her belly. "Of course! All aunties have full access."

Maya and Marnie and I each put a hand on Taylor's stomach, like the last ones to leave wins the car, and I grin. It's been too long since I saw them, too long since I've been home, too long for all the things. I'm so out of the loop, and I swear to myself not to let it happen again.

"Taylor, honey, come say hi to your Aunt Janet!" Taylor's mom gives us a wave, then ushers her daughter to the opposite side of the room.

"Where do I put this?" I give the card I brought a little shake.

"Oh! Over here," Maya says. "And make sure to sign the guest book."

I set the envelope down, grateful my mom offered to go in on a gift card together. It's impersonal, and I do plan to buy something for the baby once she arrives, but right now, I just can't swing anything extra. The Cheez-Its I bought at the airport just about did me in.

Thankfully the Bank of Mom doesn't charge interest.

"So you're doing a movie?" Marnie asks, a wide smile on her face.

"And you work in a Broadway theatre?" Maya grins. "Oh my gosh, you have the best life."

They each loop an arm through mine and lead me we're-off-to-see-the-Wizard style, over to an empty table.

"Oh yeah, things are good," I say brightly as we sit. "I mean, I don't know about 'the best life,' but . . . it's good. It's, you know, different every day. It definitely has its challenges."

I don't want to lie to them.

But I also don't want to tell them the whole truth.

"Have you met anyone famous?" Maya asks. "Please tell me you know Timothée Chalamet."

"Better yet, please tell us you're *dating* Timothée Chalamet."

I look around for some water. My throat is dry. "Sadly, no. He's . . . uh . . . in a bit of a different . . . league than I am. "

"Okay, so tell us all your news," Marnie says.

"Is there water?" I ask. You'd think being an actor would make these kinds of situations easier, but I've always been better with a script to memorize. "Actually, I'm going to run to the bathroom quickly."

"You okay?"

I wave Maya off in what I hope is a nonchalant tone. "Yeah, I just feel like I'm still on the plane." I swallow and wince. "Motion sickness or something . . ." My voice trails off as I set out to find the restroom.

I can't keep this up, of course, but how do I tell them the truth? They want all the details of what's supposed to be—but absolutely isn't—an exciting life.

After college, I booked a few jobs right away. I got a small role in a cop show filming in Chicago before I even graduated, and I took it as a sign that yes, I was on the right track. After that, I joined the national tour of *Oklahoma!*, which closed after only a month and a half, thanks to the director's odd, dark, and very disconcerting burlesque interpretation of the classic. And even though I was only in the ensemble, a part of me knew it wasn't a good production, but it was a job, and that meant that I was *making it*.

That all changed really fast. Like a carp in the desert . . . things dried up.

And every time I'm about ready to quit in favor of a more stable job that actually pays the bills, I'll book something small—a one-liner in a TV show, or a walk-on role in a movie, or a named part in a small, experimental play that's being produced off-off-*off*-Broadway. Like so far off it's in Ohio.

Those are the dangling carrots that keep me stretching my neck out and biting for more, even though I'm beginning to regret all of my life choices.

I look at my reflection in the mirror, aware that this baby shower might require the most acting of anything I've done in the last seven years. This is Taylor's day. I'm not going to ruin it. I've gotten very good at keeping any uncomfortable feelings to myself.

Depressed loser is not a role I want to play.

I splash cold water on my cheeks, then pat them dry. "You can do this," I whisper to my reflection, wishing for the ten thousandth time that I didn't have freckles.

Would I book more jobs if I didn't have freckles?

"Rosie Waterman? I can't believe you're here!"

I turn and see Ireland Abbot standing in the bathroom behind me. She must've slithered in when I wasn't looking.

Taylor and Maya were the more popular ones in our group, and unlike in all the teen movies, they didn't ditch Marnie or me when we got into high school. We became an eclectic foursome that had each other's backs.

But that didn't mean everyone else understood our friendship. More than once, Ireland had humiliated me in high school, and more than once, she tried to convince Taylor that I was ruining her social status.

Mean girls don't always outgrow their meanness, it seems.

"Hi, Ireland." I smile at her through the reflection in the mirror as I avoid looking at my own eyes. She looks great, darn it.

I know I'm not classically beautiful. I often rely on my wit to set me apart. I decided I could make a go of this acting thing if I was fun and funny and interesting to look at, but standing next to Ireland, I feel less *interesting* and more *rough and ready*.

"I keep waiting for another update about your big, fancy acting career." Ireland moves to the sink next to mine and admires herself in the mirror.

Our eyes meet in the glass, and I paint on a smile. I feel heat rise, and I try hard not to use my years of improv to roast her here in the ladies' bathroom.

"I'm just living my life," I say. "I don't see the need to report home every time I book a job. That would get tedious." I laugh to try and cover my annoyance, but I'm sure it doesn't work. I flip on the water and stick my hands under the stream, mostly because I need something to do with my hands.

She lifts her chin, I assume so she can look down her nose at me. "You're adorable, Rosie. Still out there trying to make it after all this time. Does waiting tables pay well these days?"

It's so cliché—actors waiting tables. I haven't worked in a restaurant in two years. Temp work proved to be much more my style. And I typically don't spill drinks on anyone in an office.

Although, there was that one time . . . I feel heat on my neck, the kind that rushes when you're in a scene and the other person forgets their lines. So many digs flit in and out of my mind, but then, like a person about to enter into an online argument with a troll, I hit Delete, paste on a smile, and flick the water off.

"I need to get back to my friends," I say. "It was great running into you." I don't even bother drying my hands as I rush out of the bathroom before I say something I'll regret. I wish I could say she has no effect on me, but even I note the way the run-in has unsteadied me. As if that one encounter could transport me back to high school.

I'm not that girl anymore.

My mom emails me updates about my former classmates, and I happen to know that Ireland Abbot is a lawyer at some big, fancy firm in Chicago because in real life, mean girls do *not* finish last.

I hurry back to the table, decorated with a white tablecloth and the most adorable pink mason jar centerpiece with sprigs of greenery inside and try to put Ireland out of my mind. I bet she bought Taylor the stroller / car seat combo she had on her registry without any help from her mother.

I plop down in the chair next to Maya.

"You good?" she asks.

"Great," I say. "Just a little woozy I think." And tired from hauling every single thing I own all over Brooklyn, to the airport, and then to Pleasant Valley, the small town in Illinois where I grew up.

"So?" Marnie is smiling at me, as expectant as Taylor's stomach. "Tell us about this movie! What's it about? When can we see it?"

I force a smile. Thanks to the many, many phone calls from my perpetually worried mother, I've perfected the fine art of making my life sound shinier than it is.

I call it . . . creative storytelling.

It's not lying *exactly*. I'm telling my mom and stepdad that their daughter is doing just fine, despite a few challenges.

But honestly . . . I can't bear to say the truth out loud. What would everyone think if they knew?

"Well . . . my mom might have exaggerated a little about the movie gig." I don't have the heart to tell them my mom made that movie sound cooler than it was because *I* made it sound cooler than it was.

I absently wonder if there's a special place in hell for people who turn their mothers into liars.

"Where is your mom?" Marnie asks.

"She and John are on a cruise," I say, secretly thankful I don't have to contend with their worry as my life implodes.

I look around the restored loft right in the heart of downtown Pleasant Valley, searching for inspiration to change the subject. "Was this building always here?"

"It was the gum factory," Marnie says. "Remember?"

"Wait, it was?" I frown, trying to remember, which I don't.

"The *mayor* is really pushing the downtown beautification plan,"

Maya says, weirdly emphasizing the word *mayor*. The others react to it too, which makes me feel like I'm on the outside of an inside joke. "Twenty-five by '25. It's this whole campaign to try to be a Top 25 city by 2025. Murals, new lampposts, refurbishing buildings to try to attract more businesses . . ."

"Can we really call Pleasant Valley a 'city'?" Marnie shakes her head. "More of a glorified rest stop." We all laugh—me a bit longer and louder—and I know I'm working overtime to sell my own happiness, and I beg myself to stop being so obvious.

Marnie brings the attention back to me. "So! What's next for you? Are you sticking around for a while? Can we at least get brunch in the morning?"

My heart aches.

I want to tell them the truth so badly.

I want to give up and admit that my life is in the toilet, that I'm virtually homeless, and that I'm very close to quitting on the only dream I've ever had.

And also? That I miss them.

But I can't say any of it. The fear of disappointing them is too great.

I mentally stiffen. I'm an actor. I can get through one baby shower, right?

I force a smile. "Oh, I had a bunch of auditions last week, so I'm just waiting. That's the hardest part of this whole thing . . . the waiting." The image of the frantic self-taping, uploading, and résumé-submitting bender I'd gone on last week washes over me.

Like a woman possessed, I'd submitted myself for at least two dozen jobs, some of them I'm probably not even right for. Some acting jobs, some directing jobs—even one for a script doctor. And with every Send button I hit, I'd say a silent prayer that *this* could be the one that would change my life.

I go on these panic-induced submission benders sometimes, usually right around the time rent is due.

"It sounds wild," Marnie says. "I could never do that. Not knowing what your next job will be or who you'll be working with, or—"

"Uh, it sounds *exciting*," Maya cuts in. "And it's perfect for you, Rosie, since you're such a people person."

I smile. I am a people person. I do really well ushering people to their seats at the Winter Garden Theatre, which is the steadiest of all of my jobs but keeps me watching the stage instead of performing on it.

"What about you guys?" I ask, really wanting to stop talking about me.

Maya reaches over and squeezes Marnie's arm. "Tell her your news!"

My eyes go wide. "What news?"

Marnie tosses a quick glance around the room and settles on Taylor, who is stuck in conversation with Mrs. Copecki. The only effective way to get out of a Mrs. Copecki conversation is to gnaw one of your own limbs off.

"It's not a big deal," Marnie says.

"Uh, it's a *huge* deal." Maya pushes her shoulder into Marnie's. "Tell her, or I'm going to."

"I got a new job," Marnie says a bit shyly.

"She's burying the lede. Come *on*, Mar, it's in *Milwaukee*." Maya's eyes go wide. "And she's the morning anchor!"

"Whoa!" My heart is instantly confused, and I hate it. I'm genuinely excited for Marnie, but her news makes me feel left out and somehow . . . small. I shove the thought aside because I want to be nothing but thrilled for her. She's one of my very best friends, but I feel like I should've known this news already.

The fact that I don't is my own fault.

"That's amazing, Mar!" I say, meaning it. "So, wait. You're moving?"

She nods. "I've already started hauling some of my stuff to my new apartment. I have a view of the lake right from my living room! I mean, you have to sort of crane your neck and look around a building, but it's there, I promise."

"I knew it was just a matter of time," I tell her. "You're so talented. And *such* a good reporter. I'd definitely want to have my morning coffee while you tell me what's going on in the world."

"You'd have to start watching the news to do that." Marnie smiles.

"Oof. Yeah." I shudder, then grin at her. In college, Marnie continued with the speech team and discovered she was really good at public speaking. Natural. Honest. And incredibly witty. She became a broadcast journalism major and got a job in a small market right after college. And now, an anchor in Milwaukee.

Her life is going according to plan.

"Maya has news too," Marnie says. "You next. Tell her."

Maya rolls her eyes, like she doesn't want to brag on herself, but we all know better. She holds out her perfectly manicured left hand and wiggles her fingers. It's the first time I notice the giant engagement ring she's wearing.

"Holy heck, Maya!" I grab her hand for a closer look at the ring. "You're *engaged*? Gil finally proposed?"

Maya's face falls. "Not Gil, Rosie. Matty."

"Wait. Matty?" I give my head a quick shake, trying to locate details I've obviously deleted from my mental hard drive. "Have I been living under a rock? Matty *Banks*?"

"Yes!" she gushes. "He's the mayor." She grins, and now I make the connection to the lilt on his title earlier. She lifts her hand, admiring her ring. "I can't believe it. I'm going to be a politician's wife."

"And she bought the salon," Marnie says, giving our friend a squeeze.

"You *bought* the salon?" I can't hide the surprise in my voice. Or the tears that spring to my eyes. "Oh my gosh, Maya! You're a business owner?"

Maya was not the one who was supposed to have her life together at this point.

As an actor, you're taught to tap into feelings and emotions—to use them to make scenes more honest and believable. But one of the most difficult parts of acting is that you have to portray your character's emotions while burying your own contradictory emotions at the same time.

This is what's happening to me right now.

Thrilled for my friends. Guilty for lying. Embarrassed about my life.

"What is it?" Maya leans forward and lowers her voice. "Are you okay?"

I sniff and try to shake the tears away. "I'm just . . ." I take a breath. "I'm so happy for you guys." I bring my attention back to my two friends. "I really, really am."

Maya lets out an "awww," but Marnie only stares. She squints at me. "Spill it."

I sniff again. "There's nothing to spill," I say. "I just miss you all. That's it, I promise."

She's not buying it.

Act better, Rosie.

I shake my head and give her hand a squeeze. "I'm fine. I just need to get home more, that's all." That isn't a lie. I do need to get home more. I need the three of them in my life.

How I'd survived this long without them is a mystery.

I glance over in time to see Taylor's pained look in our direction. As predicted, Mrs. Copecki is still gabbing, only now she's using her hands, which means she's moved on to the "armchair medical advice" portion of her diatribe.

I nod at Taylor. "I think she needs a swoop and save."

We all stand, silently and in unison, like we're soldiers just called into battle, and I don't miss how good it feels to be a part of this group again. To have people I fit in with. These three always accepted me, weirdness and all.

And they never, ever made me feel ridiculous for dreaming big dreams.

I make acquaintances easily, but friends are harder to find. There are always people to go out and do things with, but they're nothing like these three are to me. It's tiring to be in a world where every friend is potential competition and no one is ever telling the truth.

We all walk over to Taylor, each of us chatting very loudly about a random topic in voices that make what we're saying sound *very important*. I quickly realize we should've chosen a single topic to focus on because when Maya says, "I think he choked on a chicken bone. You have to come immediately," I start giggling.

Taylor tries to extract herself from a confused-looking Mrs. Copecki, who stops her with a hand on her arm and says, "Cabbage leaves are the only thing that are going to help with your sore boobs, but don't let that scare you off of breastfeeding. You need to find the nice big ones, ones that cover the whole—"

"Whoa, Mrs. Copecki!" I say, placing a hand on her shoulder. "It's fantastic advice, but I read that, uh, peanut butter is way better . . . for the skin. Right, Mar?" I widen my eyes, hoping for a "yes, and . . ."

She doesn't disappoint. "Oh yes, it's all the rage with our generation. You can even add jelly on the other one." And with divine timing that can only happen in the spur of the moment, we look at each other and simultaneously say, "PB&J boobs!"

This makes Maya laugh, which makes Taylor laugh, and leaves Mrs. Copecki stunned into silence (an achievement not seen since Reagan was president). We rush Taylor out of the room and onto the rooftop terrace, where we all collapse into each other in a fit of laughter. The kind that really makes no sense but somehow doesn't have to.

Oh, how I've missed this. I ache from the laughing and the distance.

Maya can't breathe. Taylor has tears streaming down her face. Marnie is doubled over, desperately clinging to me for support. I know I'm going to spend the rest of the day coughing and clearing my throat because that's what happens when I laugh this hard.

Honestly, I'm probably laughing more than the situation calls for just because I need to laugh.

A stray thought hits me.

What if I tell them what the last seven years have really been like? They might have advice. They might not think I'm a disaster.

It might be just fine.

Then, another thought.

Their plans are working out brilliantly.

Mine are rife with rejections. They think I'm doing fantastic—and I can't stand the thought of letting them down. Or of being the one they have to worry about. Or of being the failure.

So I stay quiet. Today isn't about me anyway.

"PB&J? Did you two plan that?" Taylor shakes her head, still wiping tears from her cheeks.

"Hey, she stopped talking about cabbage leaves," I say. "And, Mar, way to go all-in there. Impromptu speaking for the win!" I offer her a fist, and still bent over, she reaches up and bumps it.

Taylor giggles, then scans our little circle. "I wish we could ditch this shower and go hang out. We have so much to catch up on."

"Marnie and Maya told me their big news," I say. "Everyone is doing so, so great." The tears are back, clouding my vision. I blink a million times to keep them from falling.

"Yeah, but you've told us almost nothing about what you're

doing, Rosie," Marnie says. "Is there a show coming up? Should we get tickets? Or set our DVRs so we don't miss some big debut?"

I push a hand through my hair, feeling like everything is about to come crashing down.

And I'm not about to be the sob story that ruins this shower.

I deflect. "Oh, there's plenty of time to catch up on all of that." I wave a hand in the air. "Today is about you." I take a step toward Taylor. "I'm so happy for you, Tay. And Aaron too." I pull her into a tight hug, and after a few minutes, Maya and Marnie join in. We stand like that for at least thirty seconds—enough time for the hug to affect me, and when I pull away, I'm wiping tears from my cheeks.

"You're crying." Taylor reaches over and wipes my cheeks dry.

I point a finger at myself. "*Actor.* I can cry on cue," I say through a wonky smile. "This is just for effect." I push the emotions away. Like usual.

It doesn't seem to be working right now, though, which means I'm on shaky ground.

I do my best to get through the rest of the afternoon, like I'm performing a Saturday matinee of *Cat on a Hot Tin Roof*, the sixth show of eight, acting for a sea of blue hair in a three-hundred-seat auditorium.

And while I love seeing my friends and catching up with everyone, by the time I'm back in my parents' house that evening, all I want to do is hide.

I'm not thriving. I'm barely surviving.

This isn't how it was supposed to go.

And I have no idea how to fix it.

CHAPTER 2

THE NEXT DAY I MEET my friends for brunch.

Taylor and Marnie are brunch people, which is to say they do things before eleven in the morning, like eat avocado toast and talk to people who also eat avocado toast.

Maya and me? Not so much.

At least Maya didn't used to be. When I pull up to Harold's in the Square, the only restaurant that serves brunch in Pleasant Valley, I see her standing outside on her phone. She's impeccably dressed, hair pulled back into a slick ponytail, expensive bag hanging off her shoulder.

She looks so . . . grown-up. And so . . . put together. I don't see a trace of the rebellious Maya I used to know. The girl with the dark, thick eyeliner and black nail polish is gone, and in her place is this gorgeous, refined . . . adult . . . woman.

And she owns a business.

And she's marrying a mayor.

It's like I'm in some weird, twisted version of *Freaky Friday*, but all my friends have switched places with new, fancy, successful people, and I've stayed exactly the same.

Marnie appears on the sidewalk next to her, and suddenly I'm self-conscious about my outfit. The pink joggers and thrifted bright-yellow sweatshirt seemed like a good idea—I'm one for comfort over style, for sure—but there's no way to hide in a neon sweater.

I glance up at the rearview mirror and blink three times. "They love you, Rosie. They aren't going to think less of you if you tell them the truth. Just be honest—"

I gasp at the knock on the window of my mom's minivan and turn to see Taylor standing in the street, frowning. "What are you doing?" she shouts through the window, over-miming with her hands to indicate that I'm nuts.

I open the car door and get out. "You scared me to death."

"It's nice to see you still talk to yourself." She smiles.

"Beats paying for therapy," I quip, knowing that it doesn't—it's only cheaper.

I grab my bag and close the car door, clicking the button on the key fob to lock it.

"And you still carry a gigantic bag." She tosses me a sideways grin.

"Hey," I protest, "I seem to remember my gigantic bag saving you more than once."

"Fair point." She nods. "I could always count on you for an Advil or a sewing kit or a burrito—"

"That was one time," I say. "And it was an emergency."

"Emergency Burrito." Taylor says this like it's an official thing, and smiles as we cross the street toward the restaurant. "Do you know how many times during this pregnancy I wished I had a whole jar of Jif and one of those chocolate pudding Snack Packs?"

"As a matter of fact . . ." I start to dig through my bag.

"You don't have a—" She gasps before she can complete the thought as I pull out a chocolate Snack Pack.

"Oh. My. *Gosh*, Rosie!" We practically collapse into each other, laughing so hard we can't get words out. People walking by probably think we're deranged or drunk or both, but at this moment, I don't care.

Marnie walks over to us and starts to say, "What is wrong with . . ." And before she finishes, I toss the Snack Pack in her direction, which she swats out of the air with a "What the . . . ?" like it's a large bee made of pudding. It rockets straight into a guy's arm who was walking past, and he startles with a, "Hey, watch it!"

This sends us into near-hysterical asphyxiation. Taylor grabs her stomach and wheezes, "Stop it, stop it, I'm going to have the baby right here!" I can't breathe, and I'm going to die happy.

Taylor finally gathers enough air to gasp, "What the heck, you Snack Pack lunatic," which sends us laughing again.

We come to our senses, shaking heads and wiping tears, and she wraps an arm around me. "Whew. I needed that. Oh my gosh."

I glance around and notice a few side-eyes tossed our way. "We must look crazy."

She laughs and points a don't-get-me-started-again finger at me. "I know. You're the only friend I have who is willing to make a fool of herself on my behalf."

I grin and bend over to pick up the pudding. "I make a fool of myself as a job."

Maya spots us from down the block and storms toward us. "Finally!" She lifts her arms, and her diamond catches the sunlight, a reminder that her life—like everyone else's—is right on track. "I'm starving."

Marnie smiles. "I'm so glad we're all together again."

"And we have so much to celebrate!" Taylor says.

Maya opens the door to the restaurant. "We can be sappy later. *After* I get my avocado toast."

"She's still mean when she's hungry," Marnie says in a low whisper as we walk inside.

"And she eats avocado toast. What's next, lemongrass bagels?" I whisper back. Taylor stifles a laugh and gives me a gentle elbow to the ribs. Maya was always a little like a tiny garbage disposal. It was impressive how much food she could put away for being such a small human.

We're seated at a table in the back, and after the waitress brings us our drinks and takes our orders, I feel a shift in the mood. It's like a dark cloud just covered the sun, save for the spotlight that just flicked on in my face.

And, yep. They're all looking at me.

My smile is weak. I'd decided I need to come clean with them on the drive over. After all, if I don't go home tomorrow, which was my original plan, they're going to figure out the truth. That I don't have any idea what comes next.

Still, now that I'm sitting here, under the weighty glares of three people who probably know me better than anyone, my courage slinks out the back door.

"You haven't been straight with us," Marnie says.

Uh-oh.

"Yeah," Taylor chimes in. "We're trying to live vicariously through our friend who lives in New York City, but *she* won't tell us *anything* about what it's like."

My heart drops, hopefully not too noticeably. "Right. I was going to, I just—"

"We saw the video, Rosie. It's amazing!" Maya practically squeals.

"The . . . what? What video?"

"The one where you're like, mean." Maya shimmies her shoulders.

Mean? What are they . . . ?

Oh, wait.

The low-budget—but yes, professional—training video I did for future veterinarians. I portrayed the "what not to do" in three different scenarios, and the whole behind-the-scenes experience was a bit humiliating. The kind of video that would resurface if someone ever hosted a "Roast of Rosie Waterman" because it would provide so many opportunities for mockery.

But it was work. And it paid. So I took it.

I just didn't know anyone I knew would see it.

"It was so fun to see you being, you know, completely different than the way you really are," Taylor says.

My cheeks are hot. "How did you see it?"

"Your mom sent out a mass email," Maya says, and then, pointedly, "Otherwise, we never would've known."

The words *mass* and *email* land with a thud.

I try to regroup as I stammer, "Ugh, sh-she did? I mean, I should've . . . ugh . . . I'm sorry about that. It was a small thing, just for an industry training video, not like, you know, *Broadway* or anything."

If my mom and stepdad weren't on their Alaskan cruise right now, I would definitely have a few choice words for my mother.

"Why didn't you tell us?" Marnie asks. "We would've celebrated with you."

I shrug. "It's really not a big deal."

"It's a *huge* deal," Taylor says. "Every bit of work matters, right?"

They care. It's so obvious. Why not let them in?

What are you so afraid of?

I hope my laugh doesn't sound nervous. "I mean, yeah. Totally. Working actors work, so it doesn't really matter sometimes what the work is, right? *That* one, though . . ." I don't want to go into the details of how the director spoke to me, like I was hardly worthy of breathing the same air as him. And the script? I shudder remembering how terrible it was.

I should be thankful they're excited about this, but it just widens the divide between them wanting to celebrate the little things and me not wanting to talk about them at all.

"Can we talk about something else?" I ask.

Taylor's frown deepens. "Rosie, are you okay?"

I feel my smile give and I beg it to stay put. "I'm great." I take a sip of my iced tea and look away.

"She's not great," Maya says to the others like I'm not here.

"She's obviously not great," Marnie says.

"Ohh. Guy trouble?" Taylor asks.

Marnie sighs. "Not all of us are dying to get married, Taylor."

"No, but Rosie would be *such* a good girlfriend," Taylor says. "Any guy would be lucky to have her. She's so fun and happy."

My insides roll. I feel neither of those things.

"When was the last time you went on a date, Ro?" Maya picks up a piece of bread from the basket at the center of the table and tears off a chunk. "Have you gone out with anyone since Peter?"

"Uh, it's been a while," I say.

"See?" Taylor reaches over and touches my shoulder. "You need to get out there. We aren't getting any younger." She rubs her belly.

"Are you on any of the apps?" Maya asks. "I could make you a profile while you're home."

Marnie levels my gaze. "Unless you don't want to get married and have kids, which is a totally cool choice too."

"How am I still the center of this conversation?" I ask.

"You're the most interesting." Marnie shrugs.

"I promise you I'm not."

I point at Marnie. "New job."

I point at Taylor. "Brunching for two. Maybe three, who knows."

She snorts and tosses a piece of bread at me.

I point at Maya. "Shacking up with a mayor."

Taylor snorts again as the other two shake their heads at me.

"You're living in *New York*, Rosie," Maya says. "It may as well be another planet. We all still live here."

"Not for long." Marnie tips her glass at us and sips her drink through a smile.

Maya sulks. "I always thought I'd be the one to get out of here."

"If you marry the mayor, you could be here forever." Taylor takes a sip of her tomato juice because apparently she had a craving.

I turn to Marnie, hoping that this will be an acceptable change of subject. "When do you move?"

"She moves in two weeks," Maya says. "We know all of Marnie's news. You are the mystery."

So much for that plan.

"Agree," Taylor says, then adds, "no offense, Marnie."

Marnie holds up a dismissive hand as Taylor turns back to me, talking with her hands: "We want to hear about your big, amazing life. We definitely want to come see one of your shows—anything you're in, really—but the only time we hear about them is from your mom."

"After they're over." Marnie picks up a mini muffin from a basket at the center of the table. "I can't keep doing this no-carb thing. It's killing me. Can I . . . just . . ." She takes two more muffins.

"Carbs are amazing." Maya picks up a muffin and shoves the whole thing in her mouth. She practically moans as she chews, so loudly she draws attention from an elderly woman at the next table. She grins at her. "It's so good!"

The woman frowns and turns away. I smile to discover there is still a trace of the Maya I knew in this well-manicured, pristine package.

Marnie pushes the muffins away and takes a sip of her mimosa. I pause to admire her for a second. She's dressed in all black with black sunglasses propped on top of her head, perfectly straight, shiny brown hair cut into a very professional shoulder-length bob. She looks like a reporter.

"Rosie, what is going on with you?" Taylor asks. "I find out all your updates from social media. Do you even read our group chat anymore?"

"Of course I do," I say. "I just don't text in there because . . ."

I stop myself from saying, "*Because I have zero news and my life sucks,*" and instead complete the thought with, "Because sometimes the updates just aren't that exciting. You know, little things. Not the *really* big thing."

"*Yet,*" Marnie says.

Yeah, I think. Yet *will forever be tomorrow or next week or next month.*

Or never.

"I won't lie," I say, knowing that's all I'm doing. "It's not easy. Lots of auditioning and waiting. Lots of prepping and preparing and recording and refreshing your email. It's just not, you know, exciting all the time."

My updates would be things like: *"Got a temp job in an office. I'll be here three days, which is, apparently, long enough for me to spill coffee on three different people and screw up the bagel order for the entire office."*

Nobody wants to hear these kinds of things. I'd be the lead in a new play called *Head Above Water: Barely*.

"So?" Taylor says, but they're all looking at me now.

My phone buzzes in my pocket, and I ignore it for a moment.

"So . . ." This is the point in movies where the leading lady tells some outlandish lie that always, always comes back to bite her. Like, *"I'm secretly a princess hiding my identity by living this very mundane life."* Or, *"I'm talking to this big Broadway director, and it's only a matter of time, really, before I go on for the lead in* Mamma Mia!*"*

But these are my friends.

And friends don't lie to each other.

Which is why I've been distant.

Because if I'm not texting or calling, I'm not lying. They all still believe I'm living the shiny life I set out to live.

The waitress appears at the table, along with a man who is carrying two trays. They arrange our meals in front of us, and when they walk away, we all have to switch plates because they mixed up each of our orders. I glance up. My friends are now occupied with their food, and something inside me squeezes at the sight of them.

I have to come clean. I have to tell them what life has been like for me.

I need one of them to tell me it's okay to quit. Because I think that's what I need to hear.

I say a silent prayer. *Lord, please. Give me the strength to give up on this dream. And look, if You've got something out there for me, give me a si—*

My phone buzzes again. I pull it out and see a new email notification.

"How does everything look?" The waitress is back.

"Actually, I ordered the *fiesta* potato platter," Taylor says. "I think this might be the *siesta* potato platter."

"She's here to party, not to nap," Maya quips as she shakes an insane amount of salt onto her avocado toast.

The waitress laughs, and they all start chatting, diverting everyone's attention away from me long enough that I can skim the email:

Dear Miss Waterman,

We received your application for employment for our summer theatre program at Sunset Players. After careful consideration, we feel like you would be an excellent fit to join the creative team for our upcoming production of Rodgers & Hammerstein's *Cinderella*. Attached, you'll find the payment package, which does include room and board. Please look it over, and let us know as soon as possible if you're still interested in the job.

Auditions are next week, so we'll need to get you here this Friday for a tour of the grounds and to get you all settled into your living quarters right away.

We have a vibrant theatre arts program in Door County, Wisconsin, and we're thrilled to welcome you to the family!

Because of the quick turnaround and preparation required, we will need your answer by this Tuesday. We apologize for the last-minute request. We had some staffing changes, and here we are. We look forward to hearing from you soon.

Sincerely,
Connie Spencer
Human Resources Director

I reread the email, more carefully this time, trying to remember whether I applied for this job during one of my panicked root-beer-float benders. It seems like this would be one of the many jobs I clicked on, even though I have no memory of doing so.

I click the attachment and open the payment package details.

Um. It pays.

Whoa.

Really, *really* well.

Not only does this job include room and board for the entire summer, but it also pays better than any acting job I've had in my entire career. While it's a little unnerving that this is all happening so quickly—plus being on the creative team rather than on the stage, which suggests someone bailed on the job at the last minute—I just have to wonder.

Don't give up yet, Rosie.

I navigate over to the Sunset Playhouse website and see that they are, in fact, a legitimate organization, so having money to pay the creative team makes sense. I click around for a few minutes, looking for information on this particular production of *Cinderella*, but I come up empty. So the website is a little outdated . . . not a big deal. If they've had staffing issues, it makes sense. Maybe I can help.

And let's be real, I don't have any other options right now.

The timing of this isn't lost on me. I was about to unload the truth about the last seven years, hoping one of my friends would tell me to quit. It wasn't what I signed up for. It didn't pan out, and that's okay.

But now this. An out-of-the-blue job I never could've seen coming.

I click back over to the email and type out a reply, half listening to the conversation that has now turned to the dating lives of the waitstaff in this restaurant, because there is a story about every one of them and Maya knows them all.

Ms. Spencer,

It is wonderful to hear from you with such excellent news! I've looked over the materials, and I would love to officially accept the job. I can be in Door County by Friday, and I'm excited to begin.

Sincerely,
Rosie Waterman

I hit Send and watch as the email disappears, noting the slightly giddy feeling rising up inside me.

I got a job. In a theatre. And it doesn't involve showing anyone to their seats.

My mother's words rush back. *"Promise me you won't let anyone steal your dreams, Rosie."* And I absently wonder if "anyone" includes me.

"So . . ." I interrupt their conversation now that I have actual news, which feels good. Especially since I'm telling the truth.

"I wanted to let you know I'm going to be part of the creative team for a production of *Cinderella.*" I realize as I say it that I know very little about what this job entails.

They collectively gasp, wide-eyed.

Dropped silverware, hands raised, there's overlapping, "Like, directing? Have you done that?" with "I knew you were keeping something from us!" and "Where? When can we come see it? I love *Cinderella*!"

And as I smile—and as they genuinely are happy for me—my reservations fall away, and I can't help but wonder if *this* is the one.

Is this the job that's going to change my life?

CHAPTER 3

THURSDAY MORNING, ALL THREE OF my friends insist on driving me, en masse, to the bus station, which is about a half hour away.

We all pile into Taylor's SUV because it's the biggest, and my heart breaks yet again at the realization that I'm not ready to leave.

Over the last several days, I've helped Marnie pack up her apartment, gone cake tasting with Maya, and helped Taylor address the thank-you cards from her shower.

To some, boring and mundane.

To me? Brilliant and special.

A stark reminder of what's been missing.

When I told them I'd taken the job in Wisconsin, they were so genuinely excited for me. It made the whole thing seem important. I got a job! No, it's not New York, but it's a professional job in the theatre, which Taylor was quick to point out.

To them, that was a very big deal. Maybe a little celebrating was in order.

Their support buoyed me. It made me feel like I wasn't totally crazy for quickly replying yes and hitting Send.

However, now that the bus station is getting closer and the job is somehow getting more real, a wave of worry washes over me.

What if I'm making a terrible mistake? What exactly will they want me to do on a creative team? Yeah, I took directing classes in college, but I've never actually done it. Assisting someone could be a great learning experience, though. Maybe that's my new job. Why didn't I ask more questions?

Oh, right. Because I'm desperate.

Maya leans her face forward between the front seats of the SUV and smiles at me. "I made you a dating profile."

I spin around and look at her. "You did what?"

"I don't like the thought of you being alone in Door County," she says, sitting back. "Or in New York. Or anywhere, for that matter."

"And you think I need a guy?" I fake scoff. "I'm a strong, fierce, independent woman."

"Right, but you're not getting any younger, so I made you a dating profile." She reaches forward and clicks her perfectly manicured nail on my phone three times.

"Again with this," Marnie groans. "We're not old, Maya." She pushes Maya out of the way and sticks her face between the seats. "Ever since she and Matty started dating, she's convinced that nobody can be truly happy if they're not in a relationship. I tried to tell her that I'm a career girl and I'm perfectly content, but guess what?"

I wince. "She made you a profile too?"

"She made me a profile too." Marnie rolls her eyes and slumps back in her seat.

Maya swipes around on her phone, then hands it to me, revealing Marnie's profile. "I'm very good at making them. And since I'm officially off the market, it's my job."

"Well, in that case, you're fired," I quip.

I click through the photos Maya has added to the profile. "Marnie, you look hot! What is this picture from?"

"Class reunion," Maya says, then teasing, she adds, "The one you didn't come home for."

Now I'm the one who groans. I'd bailed on them.

"The life of a career girl," Marnie says sympathetically.

More like the life of a broke girl, I think but don't say.

"I did switch your location to Milwaukee, Mar." Maya takes the phone back from me. "You might want to give the most recent matches a look before you just write them off. I mean, do you really want to miss out on this?" She holds up the phone to reveal the photo of a very attractive, outdoorsy-looking man.

My eyes widen. "Whoa. How is that man single? He looks like if Old Spice were a person."

Taylor and I both laugh, but Marnie doesn't crack a smile. "I think dating apps are stupid," she says. "And sleazy."

"I met Matty on an app," Maya says.

"We went to high school with Matty," Taylor says, not turning back to look at her.

Maya shakes her head. "I mean I *re*-met him on an app. We didn't really know each other in high school. He was older, and I was—"

"Dating Troy," I say in a singsong.

After a beat, there's a collective "*Troyyyy . . . !*" from all of us at the memory of Maya's high school boyfriend, the one who didn't seem to believe in bathing or washing his hair.

Maya rolls her eyes. "It was a phase."

"He smelled like a boy's dorm room." I scrunch my face. "Dirty clothes and . . ."

"Weed," Taylor supplies.

"Whatever!" Maya protests. "I thought he was hot. He was in a band."

"What was the name of his band?" Taylor asks over her shoulder.

The three of us in unison shout "Stiff Kitty!" and then laugh.

"How can you not remember that?" I ask Taylor. "Their logo was a cat face with X's for eyes, stuck to the grill of a car."

"Say what you want, I don't care." Maya fakes getting defensive, then looks at me. "I didn't have as much to go on for your profile,

Rosie, but I still think it came together. You'll need to download the app, and all the notifications will come right to your inbox. I texted you the log-in info."

"Maya, I'm even less interested in dating than Marnie is," I tell her.

"Why? Don't you want to meet some drummer in a band and live happily ever after?" Maya teases.

"Aren't those two things mutually exclusive?" I ask.

She makes a face. "Good men are out there. Look at Aaron"—she motions to Taylor—"and Matty." She smiles a little to herself. "You two both deserve to be as happy as we are."

"Aaron leaves his underwear on the bathroom floor, and he still plays video games until 2:00 a.m." Taylor sighs. "So you actually might be a little happier than I am right now."

When she realizes we're all looking at her, she scrunches her face and quickly adds, "I'm sorry. I'm just hormonal."

Maya shrugs this off like she's used to it. "I have a good feeling about this summer, Ro."

"I'm still struggling with your use of the word *men*." I groan. "Are we old enough to be dating men?"

"Heck yeah," Maya says. "And don't settle for dating some boy. You deserve to be dating a man."

Maya takes my phone out of the drink holder, sticks it in front of my face to use facial recognition to open it and starts clicking. "I'm just going to download the app . . . right . . . there." She flips it around and points to a hot-pink square with a red heart in the middle. "This is it. Love Match. I set up push notifications so anytime someone likes your profile or leaves a message, you get a text."

"Oh no," I say. "No notifications. Take that off."

She mockingly shrugs. "I'm sorry, I forgot how to do that."

I narrow my eyes playfully. "You're the worst."

"I look forward to hearing you take that back when you find the love of your life," she says, her tone wistful. "You can thank me later."

"I'm not a casual dater, Maya, you know that. I'm not even a biannual dater." I drop my phone back in my giant bag. It'll sink down into the abyss, and I'll have to dump everything out to find it, but at least it's safe from Maya's impending matchmaking.

"I don't see the point in dating people I have no interest in marrying," I continue. "Isn't that the whole reason people go on dates? Find the match, walk the aisle, pump out two point five kids?"

"Rosie, I swear, you're an eighty-seven-year-old woman trapped in a hot, twenty-nine-year-old body."

"Actually, I am," I quip. "Get off my lawn."

She laughs and sits back.

I muse, "I like people, but I like to be home too. Honestly, my idea of a perfect date would be, like, making dinner at home and binge-watching *The Office*." I shrug. "Too much going out is exhausting."

"Maybe that's why you're still single," Taylor pipes in.

I point a finger at her in agreement. "Maybe that *is* why I'm still single."

"Well, if you and Marnie don't start putting yourselves out there, you're going to end up like Miss Bates." She puckers her lips in what I can only assume is supposed to be an old-spinster expression, or her impersonation of one of the actresses who played Miss Bates in one of the many *Emma* adaptations.

"I happen to *like* Miss Bates," I say. "She's the underdog."

"There's just one problem, Ro." Maya peers at me, like she's about to say something important. "The underdog doesn't usually win."

Before my mind can process that, Taylor pulls the car into an empty parking space in front of the bus station. "We're here!"

We get out of the car and walk around the back. I open the hatch and pull out my suitcase, and after I've closed the trunk, I turn and face them.

Taylor's already wiping tears from her cheeks, Maya's wearing a pouty expression, and Marnie's just staring at me.

"Promise you're going to be better about staying in touch," Taylor says.

"I promise," I say, meaning it.

"Promise me you're going to at least pay some attention to those dating app notifications," Maya says.

I smirk. "I promise I will think about maybe trying to remember once in a while to at least pay some attention periodically."

Marnie reaches out and hugs me. "Don't let her make you think you need a man."

I hug her back. "Fierce independent woman," I say.

I move to Maya, who squeezes me hard, then makes a pouty face. "You can be independent and still be in love."

I nod, smiling at her, and glance over at Taylor, whose face is a patchwork of emotions.

"I'll miss you," she says.

I pull her into a hug. "I'll miss you too," I say. "But I'm coming back when Baby Rosie is born."

"Uh, her name's Maya," Maya says.

"Marnie is more original." Marnie hitches her purse up on her shoulder, disinterested in having an emotional goodbye.

I smile at Taylor. And I pause. Almost long enough to define it as lingering. "I don't want to leave you guys."

"Good, it's important for you to remember you've got people. And we love you," Taylor says.

"I know." I give a definitive nod, determined in this moment to be a better friend. "I'll let you guys know when I get there."

I pull the handle up on the suitcase and balance my bag on top. Most of what I own is in this suitcase. Most of what I had back in

New York belonged to my roommates or wasn't worth keeping, which is why I didn't put up a fight when Ellen packed me up and sent me on my way.

My whole life is in this bag. I look up at my three best friends.

Or maybe my whole life is in this parking lot.

CHAPTER 4

AFTER HOURS ON THE ROAD, the bus finally pulls into a station in town.

Sturgeon Bay. Huh. Sounds fishy.

I chuckle at my dad joke as I scroll to Connie's reply to my email. She said there would be someone here to meet me and drive me to my cottage.

When I first read that, all I could think was, *I have a whole cottage?*

I haven't even had my own bedroom since I left my parents' house.

Rent is ridiculously expensive in New York. Obscenely so. A six-hundred-square-foot apartment needs at least three roommates. And a loan.

A cottage? Are you kidding? Heck, even a small one—even a *room* in a small one—will feel like a palatial estate.

I get off the bus and wait for the driver to pull my suitcase from the compartment underneath, and once he does, I take it, avoiding eye contact because I'm cashless and not sure of the tip situation. I could tell him to keep company with great people, invest early in life, or get seven to eight hours of sleep at night, but I don't think those are the kind of tips he's looking for.

I wheel the suitcase away from the bus and see a tall man, probably a couple of years older than me, leaning against a dark blue pickup truck. He's wearing a ball cap, a red vintage-wash T-shirt, work boots, and a pair of well-worn jeans. Handsome, but not like he's trying to be.

He's watching me, and because I know what I look like, I know he's not checking me out—he's probably my ride.

Maya's clichéd *"you're not getting any younger"* speech comes rushing back to my mind as I start off in his direction. I tell my mind to can it—I'm not looking for love in Wisconsin.

He shifts, angling toward me a bit, and I think . . . but then again . . .

He's like a cross between Scott Eastwood and Glen Powell. But with darker hair. I involuntarily cast him in a movie in my brain, playing opposite me, of course—him, a loner with a past, me a bright spark of a girl, home for the holidays but not interested in romance. Our paths cross at the local bus station and . . .

I click off my mental TV and start in his direction. I'm about to reach him when it occurs to me that he might not actually be my ride. He caught my attention so quickly, I didn't bother to look around.

This guy could be waiting here for anyone.

My eyes dart to the right, where a smallish muffin of a man with a mustache is standing next to a beat-up sedan. He's wearing a Hawaiian shirt, a pair of long khaki shorts, and tall socks with sandals.

Oh yeah. *He's* my ride. No doubt.

I toss Scott/Glen a slight smile and keep walking, as if I'd always meant to walk in a straight line toward him only to make an abrupt turn at the last minute.

I smile at my ride, and he smiles back, wide and excited.

"You need a ride?" he asks, his accent thick.

"Are you . . ."—I open my phone and glance down at the email Connie sent me with the name of the man who is picking me up—"Booker?"

Without breaking the smile, the guy shakes his head and points behind me. I don't have to turn to know where he's pointing.

I smile, but I'm guessing it looks more like a wince. "Awesome. Thanks."

I do my best to act unbothered as I spin on my heel to find the guy, still in the same spot he was before, only now, he's looking at me sideways instead of straight on.

It's no less unnerving.

I take a few steps toward him. "Are you . . . Booker?"

"In the flesh."

I try not to think about his flesh. Or my flesh, which is currently overheating. I squeeze the handle of my suitcase, aware that my palm, like my knee pits, is sweating. "I'm Rosie."

"I figured."

I frown. "Why?"

"Because you asked Roberto if his name was Booker."

"Ah. Ha. Yes," I say. "I did do that. You were there." I try to save the moment. "You still are. Here."

He doesn't respond.

His silence is unnerving, and I wonder if there's a rock big enough for me to crawl under. Or maybe I could empty the contents of my suitcase and zip myself inside. But then my underwear would be strewn around on the sidewalk, and considering the fact that they are all granny panties, I tuck that idea right back in my brain.

I draw in a breath, quietly righting myself. I'm being ridiculous. He's just a guy.

I'll think of him like I would a new scene partner. Easy.

He raises an eyebrow and nods down to my side. "That your bag?"

"Uh, sorry, yes." I drag the suitcase closer.

He reaches for the suitcase, and as he grabs it, our hands touch, and for some reason, my heart knocks around in my rib cage like a pair of wet tennis shoes in a dryer. The metaphorical shoes launch from the imaginary dryer and hit me in the mouth, which starts saying things again.

"Oh, look, our hands," I say, and then, to make absolutely sure he (and Roberto, for good measure) knows what a complete weirdo I am, I start singing, "Oh yes, oh yes, we both reached for the case, the case, oh yes, the case," to the tune of "We Both Reached for the Gun" from the musical *Chicago* while shimmying my hips and shoulders in an embarrassing little dance.

In my defense, I completely sell out to the bit.

After I finish, I look up at Booker, stick one foot behind the other, and dip into a slight bow.

He only stares.

I put my hands on my hips. "Oh come on, nothing? No smile?" It's like trying to banter with a TSA agent who has six more hours on their shift.

His smile is, at best, half-hearted.

"Yeesh," I say. "Tough crowd." I wipe my hands down my pants, as if smoothing my outfit will tamp down my musical lunacy.

His smile changes to polite, and he reaches again but stops short.

"I'm going in now," he says like a hostage negotiator instructed to keep everyone calm. "Can I get this for you, or . . . ?"

I release my death grip on the suitcase. "No encore. I promise. I would love you—I would love *for* you to—it would be good. Great." I snap my jaw shut and draw in a quick breath, letting go of the suitcase. "Here."

What is wrong with me? I can perform in front of hundreds of people—why has this audience of one turned me into a gibbering weirdo?

The corner of his mouth lifts, and I try not to notice how bright his eyes are.

I take a step back as he wheels the suitcase over to the bed of his truck, then tosses it inside.

He then opens the passenger side door of the truck and looks at me. "You coming?"

"Right!" I point at him. "Yes." I move past him, and as I do, I take a chance and start to hum a little tune as if I'm going to sing again.

He chuckles, shakes his head, and motions for me to hop in.

"Okay, okay, I'm going." I smirk, and I'm ecstatic when I see him try—fail—to hide a smile.

Making people laugh is one of my favorite things.

I step up quickly, grab the oh-crap handle inside the truck, and hoist myself up. Once I'm in, he takes the door, and after making sure I'm inside, closes it for me, then makes his way around to the driver's side.

This is not the kind of guy I'm used to being around. I have a lot of friends, but they're all actors. While it may seem like all actors look like they should be movie stars, that's not actually true.

Most of my friends are, like me, ordinary people. Many of them have an insane amount of talent. But there hasn't been a single one who's turned my head since I moved to New York.

Partly because I was still dating Peter for the first two years I lived there, but mostly because I'm a very determined person. And my goals have always been about my work.

Which is pathetically ironic, considering that even with 100 percent of my focus, I'm still a solid professional failure.

Booker is now talking to Roberto, in Spanish, no less, which gives me a second to glance around his truck. You can learn a lot about a person based on their living spaces.

For example, me. I don't currently have a living space.

The inside is clean—something I didn't expect. I don't know what I was expecting since I don't have a lot of experience being in guys' trucks, thank goodness, but I just thought it'd be messier.

It's vacuumed, wiped down, and smells masculine. Like he drove it through a forest with the windows down.

He opens the driver's side door and effortlessly hops in. I offer a smile, then turn to stare out the window. Once he's buckled in, he starts the engine and I feel him glance my way.

Not so much with my peripheral vision, but some other sense is picking up that he's looking at me.

"You good?" he asks.

"*So* good." Still not looking at him.

"You're the theatre person, right?"

"Aw, what gave it away?" I glance over and smile.

I see a twinge of amusement on his face. It's as if me being a theatre person tells him all he needs to know about me.

"I am," I say. "Hopefully you don't have anything against"—I speak as if my words have air quotes— "'theatre people.'"

He shifts the truck into Reverse and pulls away from the curb. "Not at all. I haven't really known many." He pauses, then adds, "Do you all spontaneously burst into song?"

I frown and give a semiserious, "Maybe."

He banters right back. "So I should expect more of that?"

"If you're lucky."

He chuckles. "Might be entertaining. We'll see."

We drive in silence for several minutes, and Booker doesn't seem to mind. I am not that calm. I'm a space filler, but for the life of me, I can't think of anything to say.

I look out the window as the trees pass by, marveling at the shades of green. "I'm sure it seems sort of ridiculous," I say.

"Does it?" he asks, as if it's perfectly normal for me to pick up our conversation from ten minutes ago. "I think it's cool that you do it, you know, for fun."

I look at him. "Well, it's my career, so it's not exactly 'for fun.'" I try to keep my tone light, but I'm afraid it's still coming across snarky.

I glance at him as he tosses me a quick look. I feel myself deflate a bit as I look away. I've always been overly sensitive about my chosen career path. It's such a long shot for anyone to actually *make it* as an actor, and pursuing it, especially as a woman pushing thirty, sometimes feels frivolous and misguided.

Thirty for a female actress may as well be fifty-eight.

He looks confused. "Can't your career be fun?" He slows down for an upcoming stop sign, signaling to turn onto a frontage road.

Fun. Psh. Clearly he doesn't have a clue about what a soul-sucking career acting is.

"Well, yeah. It can be. I mean . . . it *is*, at times, fun, but . . ." I trail off.

"But?" he asks.

I shake my head. "Nothing."

And we're back to silence. Except for a very loud and demanding question racing through my mind: *When was the last time I had fun?*

CHAPTER 5

I'M NOT USUALLY A CONVERSATION killer. But I'm doing a bang-up job here.

Finally, when I can't take another second of silence, I say, "You really think that?"

He leans his head slightly but doesn't take his eyes off the road. "Think what?"

I look down. "That it's, you know, cool? That I do theatre?"

He gives me a quick side-eye. "I really do."

"Thanks," I say quietly. "That's . . ." I pause. "People don't usually think so." I try to laugh off the pathetic honesty of what I just said.

I think of my friends. Now *they're* cool. It's a wonder they let me in their group at all.

I pull my phone out and text our group chat to let them know I arrived safe and sound. I do not, however, tell them I'm currently riding in a truck with the most beautiful human I've ever laid eyes on.

I immediately receive three text replies, and I tuck my phone away, still thinking about my friends. Not even one week at home, and it was like no time had ever passed at all. Maybe that's how it is with people you grew up with.

People who helped you become who you were going to be.

In high school, Maya made my slightly outdated fashion preferences cool with three simple words: *"Audrey Freaking Hepburn."* We were freshmen, and she came over to my house, pulled me into my bedroom and said, "You've got this great artistic vibe going on, but"—she waved a hand in my general direction and scrunched up her nose—"it needs to be edited."

"Edited?" I'd been confused. I wasn't trying to have a vibe. I was just wearing what was on the top of the pile.

That's when Maya pulled out a bunch of photos and taped them to my mirror. They were all of Audrey. "From now on, you channel *her*."

I stood and walked over to the mirror. "I don't think I can pull this off."

Maya took me by the arms and looked me straight in the eye. "From now on, you aren't just a mousy girl who likes to pretend to be other people for fun. You're Rosie Freaking Waterman. Serious Actress. And you've got style."

"I really don't."

"You're right." She squinted. "But you will."

Maya took me shopping, invited Marnie and Taylor over for makeovers, and by the second week of ninth grade, I had an identity that actually suited me. Pixie pants and belted dresses and headbands and ballet flats. She took the fact that I never really fit in and made it my trademark. It didn't make me cool, exactly, especially not to people like Ireland Abbot, but it helped shape my identity.

After spending some time in that memory, another thought hits me.

I really should thank her for that.

My eyes scan the dashboard, eventually making their way to Booker. "So . . . what do you do?"

"Physical therapist," he says.

"Really?" I'm hoping my reaction doesn't read as big as I think it does. I look at his work boots. "You don't look like a physical therapist."

He chuckles and the corner of his mouth lifts. "And what does a physical therapist look like?"

I frown, holding up my hands and moving them in front of me as if I'm picturing the architecture of a building that's not there. After a moment, I slump them to my lap. "I don't know actually."

Then, after a pause, I ask, "Don't you have, like, way too much of an education to pick people up from the bus station?"

"I do whatever's needed," he says. "Rehab an injury, help out around the cottages, or"—he tilts his head at me—"run a taxi service."

"Impressive." A physical therapist who volunteers for a theatre community? Not typical.

"Where are you from?" he asks.

I smile. "Normally I just say Chicago because it's easier for people to find on a map than the small town no one's ever heard of. It's about an hour outside of Chicago," I say. "Like a suburb of a suburb."

"And that's where you do theatre?"

Do theatre. Cute.

"Oh no, I moved to New York after college." It always sounds cooler than it is.

"New York? Whoa. You're, like, legit."

I suck in air through my teeth and shake my head, "Ohh, I wouldn't go that far." If only he knew how many nonworking actors there are in New York. Living there isn't the impressive part.

I keep my insight to myself. "I'm guessing this job will be a little different than other ones I've had, though."

He chuckles like he knows something I don't. "Uh, *yeah.* Safe to say it'll be a bit different."

His reaction strikes me as a bit odd, but I just chalk it up to him probably thinking I'm a long way from New York. "I just mean because I'm on the creative team." I look at him. "Not on the stage."

He pulls off the highway and turns onto a more rural road. "Normally you're on the stage?" he asks.

"Normally, yes," I say, "or on the screen."

"Like movies?"

I hesitate. I don't want to start this off with a bunch of half-truths—but something within me only wants to bring home the A papers and leave the D's and F's in the desk drawer.

"More TV than movies, but yeah, I've done a few." Not in a while but not a lie.

"Have you been in anything I would've seen?" he asks.

"Um . . . I did an episode of *Law & Order*," I say, not admitting that it was six years ago or that I played a dead body on a slab in the morgue. "But mostly I work in the theatre."

I think of my jobs as usher and coat check and security, and since those were technically inside a building that was known as a theatre, I decide this isn't a lie either.

Another lull.

Again, he seems unfazed by the silence, and in that silence I start to feel an unfamiliar feeling—I feel myself relax. We drive for about half an hour, and I let my stress drift away as I watch the green hills of Wisconsin out the window.

The rhythmic bump of the road under the tires, the warm sun through the window, the smell of his truck, and . . .

"Rosie?"

My eyes flutter open, and it takes me a few seconds to figure out where I am. Door County. Theatre job.

I glance over. *Hot guy.*

"You fell asleep." Booker's smile is kind.

"Oh geez. Sorry." I sit up. I immediately raise my hand to my mouth to make sure I didn't drool.

"It's fine," he says. "I'm a big fan of rest."

"Hopefully not when you're driving," I quip.

He laughs, and I don't hate it.

I stretch, slightly embarrassed that I fell asleep. I only sleep because my body forces it, but rest isn't something I seek out.

I look around and see that we're parked in front of a very large, very fancy building with a sign out front that says Sunset Hills Clubhouse.

"This is it," he says.

We both get out of the truck, and he crosses around to the sidewalk to meet me.

I look around, searching for the theatre building, but I'm not seeing one. Normally you can pick out a theatre from a whole row of buildings because you can see the fly system sticking up another twenty feet from the roof.

I don't see anything like that.

Only this huge clubhouse, a few other buildings, and a golf course. In the distance, I see tennis courts and a pool, and farther away, a lake.

Is it . . . outdoor theatre? Theatre in the round, maybe? Theatre in a park could be cool, though the website didn't say anything about that.

Booker is now standing at the door of the clubhouse, staring at me. He doesn't say anything, just gestures toward the door, as if to question whether or not I'm coming with him for the second time in the less than sixty minutes I've known him.

To counter, I feign looking around, give a big oversized stretch, and put my hands on my hips, smacking my lips. Then, with what I hope is great comedic timing, I glance at a nonexistent watch on my wrist, physically react with a "Well, shoot!" and rush over to his side.

He takes a breath and nods. "Yeah. You're a theatre person."

"I'm not apologizing for it," I banter, mock flexing. "That was comedy gold right there." It wasn't, but he doesn't say so.

When I walk inside the clubhouse, I go silent. It's massive. And ornate. And not what I was expecting. Finally, after gawking for what feels like three acts, I look at Booker. "What is this place?"

"This is Clubhouse Village," he says. "It's sort of the social epicenter of Sunset."

"The theatre has an epicenter?"

"No, the theatre is just one part of this place." I can hear his confusion as he frowns. "Didn't you look it up when you applied for this job?"

I don't even remember applying for the job, but in my desperation, I'm sure I didn't read closely. I'm a skimmer on a good day, so at best I looked it over like it was the seventeenth page of mortgage paperwork.

"Uh, *yeah.* Of course. Yes, I . . . totally did that." I hitch my bag up on my shoulder and push a hand through my hair, knocking my sunglasses off the top of my head. They clatter to the ground, and Booker and I both bend over to pick them up at the same time.

On the way down, a vision flashes—we're two cartoon characters about to bonk heads.

Thankfully, the vision is just my overactive imagination and not a premonition, and we're both quick enough to react before we knock into each other.

However, this results in us both stopping short of picking up the glasses but looking up simultaneously, faces—and lips—inches away.

He doesn't move, and of course neither do I. Mostly because my heart is caught in my throat. He slowly reaches down and picks up my sunglasses, handing them to me before I breathlessly stand back up.

In my mind, this all looked like a romantic meet-cute, even though it was neither romantic nor cute.

"Well, *that* was close," he says lightly.

Yes. It was. Can we do it one more time from the top, please? I need another take.

"Thanks," I say, finding my breath and my footing. I gather myself and look around. This *epicenter* is huge. "This place reminds me of the kind of fancy vacation resort I've never been able to afford."

He smirks. I bet his full smile is nice. I bet it crinkles the skin around his eyes just a tiny bit. I look away before I say something stupid like, *"I can't wait to see your eye crinkles."*

"Yeah, it's nice," Booker says. "There's a golf course, tennis courts, now pickleball courts—seems like that's the sport of choice. Those are all out back." He walks over to the opposite side of this lobby/atrium area we're in, then points out the giant floor-to-ceiling windows. Sure enough, I can see everything he said I would and more. Pools. Hot tubs. A large wraparound patio on the opposite side of this clubhouse that's lined with exercise machines, and I really start to wonder what I've signed up for.

Is this theatre at a country club? For rich lonely women and their tennis pros?

"There's also a restaurant, a pavilion for weddings and parties, a full gym on the lower level with yoga, Zumba, step aerobics, the works. It's really important for the members to keep moving. That's sort of my domain down there. I'm the resident physical therapist, but I'm also the head of health and wellness. The facilities are all open to staff too, so you're more than welcome to work out if you want."

I glance over at him. Important for the members to keep moving? Health and wellness? "I'm so confused—where is the theatre?"

"Booker! You're back!" A woman's voice, complete with a pronounced Southern lilt, turns us both around.

Rushing toward us is a short older woman with dyed blond hair and a full face of makeup. *Rushing* is a bit of a stretch. She's definitely in the third act of her life.

When she meets my eyes, she smiles. "You must be Rosie!" She pulls me into a tight hug and claps her hand on my back. "I'm Connie! We exchanged emails! Oh my word! You are just the *cutest* thing." She stands back and looks me over. "The cutest." Then, to Booker. "Isn't she the cutest?"

He appears to think for a second, then says, "I mean, for a theatre person, she's not bad." Totally deadpan, perfect delivery.

I'm simultaneously insulted and impressed.

Wait. Is he flirting? Should I flirt back?

I raise my eyebrows. "Not bad?"

He crosses his arms over his chest, and I swear I see the hint of a smile behind his eyes. "You know. For a theatre person."

"So a compliment then?" I ask lightly.

"If that's how you want to take it," he says.

"Is that how you meant it?" I ask. "Because I wouldn't want to assume you're being kind when you're really insulting me." I quirk a brow.

He shrugs, the corner of his mouth pulling up slightly.

"Uh . . ." It's Connie, and she sounds confused. "Do you two know each other already?"

"Oh yeah, Rosie and I go way back," Booker says, smirking.

"About sixty-ish minutes," I add. "And yet, I don't even know his last name."

"Hayes."

Booker Hayes.

His eyes latch on to mine like Velcro, as if he's daring me to look away. But I refuse to lose this impromptu staring contest.

"Oookay," the woman says. "Should I wait, or . . . ?"

My cheeks flush with a rush of heat.

Finally, I look away, hoping this unexpected exchange doesn't result in me spontaneously combusting. I'm certain it's a million degrees in this air-conditioned clubhouse.

Booker is still watching me. Still smirking, like this is all amusing to him, like maybe my oddness actually makes me more interesting.

It's wishful thinking, and I know it. Not that I'm wishing for anything with someone who lives in Wisconsin. I meant what I said to Maya. I'm not into casual flings. Even if Booker does melt me from the inside out.

"You okay, honey?"

Am I sweating?

Booker just nods in Connie's direction, indicating I should probably answer her.

"I'm great," I say, turning away from him.

"Booker has this effect on all of us, dear," Connie says—and not quietly. "I would say you'll get used to it, but I'd be lying." She giggles, like none of this is mortifying.

Booker chuckles to himself smugly, and I straighten. "Nope. No effects. I'm just . . ." Hot. Bothered. "Can I get a bottle of water?"

She giggles again, as if I'm just being silly, when really I feel like I've been chewing on cotton balls and could really use a drink.

"Well, I doubt you're the only one immune to his charms." Connie winks at me, and then her face turns pouty. "But of course he's not interested in dating anyone around here."

He smirks. "Well, you're already taken, Connie."

She lets out something that might be described as a titter and squeezes his bicep. "Oh, you. Such a tease." Then to me: "Can't blame you for getting all gooey around him."

"I'm not gooey," I say.

"Oh, sure you are," Connie says. "And just you watch out for this one. He doesn't like to mix business with pleasure. In case you're single and looking." She pauses, then adds, "Are you single? Are you looking?"

Booker's face is unflinching, like he's used to this, but I'm so surprised by the blunt question, sandwiched between humiliating commentary disguised as sweetness, that I can't respond.

She picks up my left hand. "Huh. Not married." She turns it toward Booker. "You two would be *adorable* together, what with your"—she waves a hand from his neck to his hips and back again—"all of this." She turns to me. "And you, with this quirky, adorable thing you've got going on. Your eyes are just the brightest blue! Big too. And those lashes." She tuts as she shakes her head. "My eyelashes are blond, so without my face on, I look like something from *Night of the Living Dead.*" A pause. "You're probably too young to know what that is. It's a zombie movie."

"Mrs. Spencer," a young woman wearing a Sunset Hills polo and a pair of khakis calls over from behind a desk. "The computer just shut down again."

"Oh, for the love." Connie shakes her head. "They sure make this place look nice, but they're so cheap when it comes to the computers." She looks at me and breathes a smile. "I want to get you settled, but—" She breaks off and looks at Booker. "Oh! You don't have any patients this afternoon, right?"

"No, it's my day off," he says, as if reminding her.

"Perfect." She claps her hands together. "Then *you* can be on Rosie duty."

Rosie duty? Is this going to be a permanent assignment or . . . ?

"Take her over to the staff cottages—she's in Dahlia." She turns her attention back to me. "The on-site staff live in the same little pod, two staff members to each cottage. They're all named after flowers. The cottages, not the staff members." She giggles. "You'll be living with our events coordinator, Daisy." She scrunches her nose. "Well, shoot. This staff member *is* named after a flower." Then her eyes go wide, as if she's just realized. "Daisy and Rosie! *Two* flowers! It's practically perfect."

"In every way," I answer in a British accent, finishing the *Mary Poppins* lyric that I'm sure no one will catch on to.

Connie giggles again, and I decide she's a character I'd like to play someday.

"Uh, I'm so sorry. Mrs. Spencer?" the girl calls out again, this time a little more desperately as she's trying to help an older man wearing a sun visor and a scowl.

"I have to run, but we'll have your suitcase delivered to your cottage, and tomorrow we'll get you squared away, okay?" She starts walking away, then calls back over her shoulder, "Booker, tell her about family dinner!"

I turn back to Booker.

He looks at me.

I wince dramatically. "Guess you're stuck with me."

"Guess so," he says. "Should be entertaining."

"Or annoying," I say.

He raises a brow.

"Give it a day."

He shakes his head. "Nah. You're harmless. Honestly, a breath of fresh air."

Me? A breath of fresh air?

He starts back in the direction of the door but makes a turn toward the elevator. "We'll go downstairs first. Are you into fitness?"

I think about this. He probably likes women who hike trails and play mixed doubles . . . whatever they are. Which is probably why I blurt out, "Oh yeah. I'm *very* into fitness. I'm like . . . Ms. Peloton."

The elevator opens, and he steps inside.

The words "That's a lie" splutter out. I always make things sound better than they are—I know this about myself, and I hate it—but I'm strangely okay with the truth being enough at this moment. Here, I don't have to pretend. At the end of the summer, I'll never see any of these people again.

A strange feeling overwhelms me at that realization. I'm free here. I can be whoever I want to be. I can workshop a new personality for myself.

Or what if I was just myself?

I cling to that thought with both hands.

But then a new thought slips in its place—I'm not sure I know who that is anymore.

I meet his eyes. "I'm not into fitness. Or golf. I don't really understand it. Or pickleball."

"It's the fastest growing sport in America," he offers. "It's pretty popular and easy to get the hang of. It's like oversized Ping-Pong. You might like it."

"Eh . . . I don't think I will."

"Have you ever played?"

"Not once."

"Then how do you know you won't like it?" The elevator doors start to close, and he lifts a hand to stop them. They brake and reopen. He leans his head out of the elevator because I'm still standing in the hallway, unsure I want to be in such a small space with him. "Are you going to stand out there, or are we going to tour this place?"

"Yep. I'm . . . yep." I step inside, and he hits the button to close the doors, and I do everything I can think of to slow my breathing.

My phone buzzes. Then buzzes again.

I pull it out and look at the notification lighting my screen: "You have a possible love match" it screams at me in an obnoxious pink font.

The words are unbearably large and sent with confetti, and I glance over to see that Booker has, in fact, seen the notification over my shoulder. I click the button and toss my phone in the oversized bag.

"You, uh, sure you don't want to get that?" he asks, a bit of a tease in his voice. "A possible love match sounds important."

"Do you always read other people's texts?" I ask.

"Not my fault." He leans back against the wall of the elevator, hands up in surrender. "That font is huge." After a pause, he quips, "Is that so you don't miss any love matches?"

"It's not huge," I say. "And I'm not—it's nothing. My friend set that up. I don't even . . ." I smile in spite of myself. "Oh, just shut up."

Thankfully, he laughs. Because my flustered "*shut up*" might've come off snotty.

I glance over at him and find him smirking. "What?"

A shrug. "Nothing. I just think you're going to be fun to have around."

I catch my breath.

He thinks I'm fun to have around.

The elevator dings, and the doors open. Metaphorically, so does my heart.

He steps out. "You ready for this?"

My brain answers the question the only way it knows how: *Nope.*

CHAPTER 6

BOOKER SMELLS GOOD. DARN IT.

There's no way to think that and *not* feel like a creeper.

Plus, it's making it very hard to concentrate on anything he's saying, especially because I'm trying to place what it is he smells like. The woods? Leather? Caramel? I'm coming up empty.

The lower level of the clubhouse is as he described—full of physical therapy machines and exercise studios with glass walls. We stop outside a Zumba class for senior citizens, and I can't help but smile as I watch. They're uninhibited, hooting and hollering and dancing and punching, and it makes me want to join them.

I used to be more uninhibited, but the more the rejections piled up, the more closed off I've become. It's hard to give 100 percent of yourself all the time. Every time. Only to be told you're not what they're looking for.

I zero in on a man, front and center in the Zumba class, wearing a headband, tank top, and a pair of short black shorts. He's so into it, he looks like he's auditioning for a J.Lo music video. If he was, I think he'd have a shot. He's actually not half bad.

Booker keeps walking. "The pool is also really popular here—water aerobics, lap swim, community swim lessons."

He leads me through the space and out onto the lower deck, which has a patio that opens out to the golf course, and points over to a row of parked golf carts. "We'll take one of the golf carts. It's easier."

I frown. "Is this like a compound?"

"Kind of, I guess." He sits behind the steering wheel of one of the carts.

"Oh my gosh. This is a cult. You're in a cult." I start dramatically looking around, as if clocking the exits and waiting for the right time to make a break for it. "Did I get hired to teach theatre to a cult? Are you their leader?" Then, under my breath, I add, "Ugh. The good-looking one is always the leader."

He laughs. "Will you just get in?"

I slide into the passenger seat and the cart lurches forward as he steps on the accelerator, pressing me into the cushion.

"Have you driven one of these before?" I tease.

"Have you?" He rests his hand on the steering wheel like he's out for an evening cruise. Somehow, he even manages to make driving a golf cart look cool.

I scoff. "No." I point at myself. "Not a golfer, remember?"

"Ah, right. Well, it's easy to learn," he says, then clarifies, "the cart, not the golf. Golf will take a lot longer to learn."

"Do I need to learn?"

"What, golf?"

I make a face. "No. Driving this cart."

"You don't have a car in your suitcase, right?"

Shoot. No. In New York I didn't need a car, but here? Add that to the growing list of things I didn't think about before I took this job.

Two old men walk by as we pull away from the row of parked carts. "Booker! Nice score!" He nods at me, wags his eyebrows, and I frown.

"*New employee*, Dennis," he says, correcting him. "You doing your exercises?"

Dennis waves him off, and Booker shakes his head as he presses on the accelerator. "He's a salty one. Harmless, but he likes to flirt."

"Is he around a lot?" I ask as Booker drives us away from the clubhouse, past the tennis and pickleball courts.

"He lives on the property, so yes," he says. "Most of the people you'll work with live here, but some of the amenities are open to the community, so it's a little bit of a mix."

Lives on the property? Something's niggling at the back of my brain about this place, but I can't quite put my finger on it.

I agree with Luke Skywalker . . . I have a bad feeling about this. Especially considering how little research I did before applying *and* before taking this job.

He slows the cart to a stop in front of a building with a sign outside that says Community Center.

"Every weekend, they do events here. Cooking classes. Bingo. Mixers for the people on-site to get out and be social. There are book clubs, knitting clubs, swing dance lessons—"

"Swing dance? *Definitely* a cult."

"I'm pretty sure cults don't have event planners." He presses the accelerator, waving to an older couple in a golf cart as it passes. "The Abernathys," he says. "They're new here."

As we drive down the wide sidewalk, he points out the Sunset dining hall up ahead and explains how my employee meal swipes work. "Basically, you'll have plenty of food. Sunset is great about taking care of their employees. It's honestly a great place to work." As we pass by the building, he adds, "Oh, and you've *got* to try the frozen custard in there. Hot fudge, marshmallow, and a sprinkle of nuts . . ." He presses his fingers to his lips and does a pronounced chef's kiss.

Two women wave at him as they walk past. "Morning, Booker!"

"Do you know everyone here?" I ask.

"It's like a small town, and I work with pretty much everyone at some point," he says. "You'll see."

"Very different from New York," I say absently.

"Couldn't be more different, actually." He looks at me. "Are you going to be okay with that?"

"Me? Yeah, totally." Which I hope is true but might not be.

He quirks a brow and nods at my small suitcase. "Because you're holding on to your bag like it's a life preserver."

I relax my grip. "I'll be fine." My laugh sounds nervous in my own ears, so I fill the space with an obvious observation. "It's so . . . green here."

His eyes are back on the road, but I still feel his attention as if they're fixed on me. "That's what we call 'nature.'"

"Har, har."

He smiles. "You'll love it."

"I don't have a great track record with nature," I say.

"Too much of a city girl?"

"Yeah, maybe. I'm more accustomed to the concrete jungle."

He leans across the cart and points to something in the distance. "Over there, there's a bike path and a walking trail that span the entire perimeter of the grounds. An early morning walk outside every morning would be a great way to start your day."

"Is that your professional opinion?" I deadpan.

He tosses me a sideways glance. "Why, yes, it is."

He drives us over to the opposite side of the compound, where the grounds become a neighborhood, and he stops in front of a rounded building. "And that"—he points to the building—"is your theatre."

I stare at it. It's unassuming, almost like a converted barn, but like the rest of the buildings, this one seems to have been well maintained.

I feel a familiar pull, an excited flicker, like . . . coming home, somehow.

"They do some art classes and dance classes in this building," he says. "But you'll mostly have free rein of the place."

His phone buzzes, and he gets out of the cart to answer the call. I sit, staring at the building in front of me, and after a few seconds, Booker is back.

"Sorry," he says. "Pickleball injury. I'm going to have to cut this short."

"Oh, it's fine," I tell him, not wanting to be a burden. "If you point me toward my digs, I can walk."

He pulls away from the theatre building, steering the cart back onto the path. "No, I'll drive you over, and tomorrow I can take you inside the theatre."

"You don't have to do that," I tell him.

"Not a problem," he says. "I don't like to leave a job undone."

I nod, my eyes scanning the landscape in front of us,

I laugh to myself. "I have a feeling this isn't actually your job."

He shrugs. "Keeps it interesting."

CHAPTER 7

WE CONTINUE ALONG THE PATH, and at this point I've completely lost all sense of direction. I'm not sure I could even find my way back to the clubhouse.

"This place is huge," I say, mostly to myself.

"You'll learn your way around." He veers off to the left. "These are the staff cottages." And then he brings the cart to a stop. "This is it. Your cottage for the summer."

I glance up at the most adorable sage-green cottage with an oversized porch, wide pillars, and white trim. "Really?"

"Yep," he says.

My cottage. I look at the mailbox—it looks handcrafted of wood painted white—and I think, that's *my* mailbox. "I've never had my own mailbox," I say on a sigh.

Those are *my* shutters. That's *my* hanging plant. *My* porch swing.

And though I know I don't actually own this place, I get to live here. For a whole summer.

Still hasn't sunk in yet.

Booker hands me a key and gestures toward the handle, indicating I should get out of the golf cart and go check out my cottage.

I take the key and hold it, feeling a little like an impostor.

Maybe I can get through this like any other role. But then it hits me—I get through other roles by pretending.

"All yours, Rosie."

Well, crud. I like how he says my name too.

But it really does make me want to drop the act. All of it. Is he right? Is it safe to be myself here? To admit all the things I never say out loud?

The truth is, I like Booker. Right off the bat.

I want to know him. His story. Part of that is probably the actor in me, but seriously—why is he still single? What does he want out of life? Is this his big dream? Doing physical therapy at . . . whatever this place is?

I want to know the answers to all of these questions.

I want to know Booker Hayes.

But do I want him to know me? That's the kicker.

I pause. Maybe I *do* want someone to see all of it. All of me.

My hand is trembling as I slide the key in the handle and turn it.

And maybe I want it to be a guy I just met today.

I stop short because I vaguely remember Connie telling me I have a housemate.

"Wait. Doesn't someone live here? I mean, don't I have a . . . ?"

"Daisy? Oh yes, she's your housemate, but she's still at work. We're good to go in and take a look around."

I open the door, step inside, and am immediately met with a clean, fresh, floral, open, inviting atmosphere. It's like if *cozy* had a smell.

Anyone who's ever been to New York knows none of those adjectives are ever in the same sentence as "New York."

Sentences about New York usually contain words like *crowded* and *expensive*. And sometimes, *urine*.

Booker steps in after me, and I walk into what looks like an entryway, opening up into a living room, dining room, and kitchen, all open with no walls.

Compared to Ellen's apartment, this place is cavernous.

"Have you ever heard of a pocket neighborhood?" he asks.

I shake my head. As if I could form words right now. I can't believe I get to *live* here.

"It's like a small community of, in this case, cottages, all sharing common space. They're all front-facing, and the sidewalk goes around in an oval with the yard at the center. Take a look out the front window. The independent living cottages are arranged the same way."

I look out the large bay windows to see what Booker just described. Each cottage has its own very small yard with flowers and plants and a few small shrubs, and on the opposite side of the sidewalk is a big oval-shaped grassy area, which, I assume, is the common space he mentioned.

"Geez, the porches are huge."

"That was intentional," Booker says. "The idea was to think of each porch as an extra outdoor living space. It contributes to the sense of community."

"Yeah, this is nothing like New York," I tell him. "Well, Brooklyn, I lived in Brooklyn."

"Lived? Like, past tense?"

Shoot. I can't afford to slip up if I want to keep myself *to* myself. And I do. I totally do.

Right?

A Mark Twain quote pops in my head: "If you tell the truth, you don't have to remember anything."

Shut up, Mark.

"Live," I say quickly and then add, "sorry. I'm not there a ton because, you know, travel and so on."

"Ah." He seems to buy it. "Movies."

"And things." I nod, hoping my horrible poker face doesn't give away that I'm only holding a two and a seven, offsuit.

"You have neighbors, though, right?" He's watching me again. But it's more than watching. It's like he's trying to actually *know* me. And I'm not used to that. The only people who actually know me are my friends from home. And that's only by default because they were there as I was becoming who I am.

In some ways, I've gotten so far away from that girl . . .

"Oh yeah," I say. "I just don't know them very well."

Actually, that's not entirely true. I've used the people in my building for inspiration for characters lots of times.

"I mean, there's Archie, a self-proclaimed 'monster demon,' who everyone avoids at all costs. He's got quite a few . . . er . . . piercings and wide, wild eyes." I picture the floor of our building. "And Mrs. Righetti, whose idea of 'taking out the trash' is setting all of her garbage bags in the hallway. Oh! And there's a guy named Danny who wears a robe. And only a robe. Definitely been arrested for public indecency more than once."

Booker chuckles, folding his arms and leaning against the back of the couch. "It's different here. They want you to get to know people. And everyone's really friendly. I mean, it's all part of the mission," he says. "People living in community."

"I knew this was a cult," I mutter.

He laughs. "The staff does family dinner pretty often in the Commons, which is right"—he walks over to the window and points to the building at the end of the oval—"there."

He's really close to me. Onstage this is hardly an issue, but here, in my real life . . .

I take a step back and try not to let on that I'm a little breathless. "Family dinner? I thought you just ate in the dining hall with everyone else."

"I mean, you can," he says, shrugging. He makes his way back across the room, thank the Lord. "And most of us do, for breakfast and lunch. But the staff lives in this pocket neighborhood, separate from the residents, so it's a chance to, you know, get to know your coworkers away from the job. It's not mandatory, of course. I mean, you can eat frozen pizza in your bedroom if you want." He chuckles at this.

"Frozen pizza?" I scoff. "How do you know I'm not an amazing cook?"

"Are you?"

"No. I'm actually terrible."

"We have cooking classes too," he says. "Daisy sets them up, so you can ask her for all the details."

"That . . . ," I ponder, "could actually be fun."

"See? You fit here already."

I fit here. Huh.

"Do you live in this little . . . pocket neighborhood?" I ask.

He eyes me for a fleeting moment, then quips, "Are you going to stalk me?"

I shrug. "Probably."

"As long as I'm prepared." There's amusement in his tone. "The blue one across the yard is mine." He points toward the front door. "I manage the staff cottages, so one of the perks is I don't have a housemate. Anything that goes wrong, they call me, and I'm the guy who'll fix it."

"Anything?" I ask.

"Sure," he says. "I'm pretty handy."

"So if my sink breaks?"

"That's me."

"Or if my toilet leaks?"

"Also me."

"Cabinet door comes loose?"

"That's also something a handyman would fix, so . . ."

"And if I, like, run out of tampons?"

He looks like I caught him off guard, and I think, *Point for me!*

He winces. "Then you're on your own."

I shake my head. "Chicken."

He feels like a friend I've had for years. How did he do that?

"Actually, I *could* also help with your feminine products, but it would require a trip to the canteen."

"The canteen?" My eyes go wide. "Is this a summer camp cult?"

"Not a cult." Then he narrows his gaze. "Did you go to summer camp?"

"Theatre camp," I tell him.

"Ah, of course."

I mock stretch, as if prepping for the Olympic hammer throw. "Four years in a row. It was more 'theatre' than 'camp,' though."

He laughs, and I like making him laugh.

I notice a bright bag on the kitchen counter. "Does that belong to . . . ?"

He looks over. "Daisy."

I look at him. "Is she nice?"

"Absolutely. She's the special events coordinator," he says. "Super outgoing. She's younger, and a bit of a whirlwind."

"How much younger?"

He shrugs. "Probably your age."

I frown. "How old are you?"

Without a beat, he says, "Thirty-three."

"Oh wow, yeah, you've got one leg in the grave, old man." I laugh. "You're only four years older than me."

"I'm an old soul," he says, brushing it off. "I'd rather stay home watching reruns of *The Office* than go out to the bars on the weekends."

At that, I freeze.

I know that our phones eavesdrop on our conversations because I've said things like, *"Maybe I should start drinking energy drinks,"* in casual conversation only later to be bombarded with ads for Red Bull every time I go on social media.

But there is *no way* Booker could've heard me say this exact thing to my friends before I left for the bus.

"You good?" He gives me a quizzical look.

"Yeah. Yep. All good." I give him a weak thumbs-up, and then, before I can decide if this is a sign from the universe, I say, "Pickleball injury."

He squints, studying me. "Right. I should head out . . . But I'll swing by in the morning to finish your tour," he says. "That'll give you some time to unpack and everything."

"Sounds good." I nod. "Go forth and heal."

He smirks again, and after only a short time of knowing him, I've already decided it's a trademark I could get used to.

He sticks his hand out toward me. "It was good to meet you, Rosie."

I stare at it a beat too long, then slowly slip my hand in his. He squeezes it, and all I can think is that Connie was right.

I'm gooey on the inside, and I don't want to let go. Ever.

CHAPTER 8

BOOKER'S HAND IS STILL WRAPPED around mine when out the front window I see a golf cart come screaming down the sidewalk and skid to a stop directly in front of the cottage.

A blond girl (*definitely* younger than me) jumps out, a wide smile on her face.

I drop Booker's hand. "Is that—?"

He opens the front door, cutting me off midsentence. "Afternoon, Daisy!"

"Why, Booker Hayes," she says, and I instantly detect another Southern accent because it comes out like "*Whah, Book-uh Haize.*" North Carolina. If I had to peg it, I'd say Charlotte. Odd for Wisconsin. "Well, aren't you just as pretty as a pie supper?" She smiles in my direction but reaches for Booker, pulling him into a tight hug.

I make a mental note to tease him for this later.

Tan-skinned Daisy is wearing white denim cut-off shorts and a tight white tank top underneath a red gingham button-down knotted at the waist. She looks like a Fourth of July picnic table.

"Daisy, this is Rosie," Booker says. "Your new housemate."

Daisy looks at me, throws her hands in the air, and lets out a high-pitched scream. And I never thought I was the Elphaba before, but in this situation, I am clearly not the Glinda. "Well, goodness *gracious*! Finally! I've been here all by myself for *weeks*!"

She throws her arms around me and hugs me almost as tightly as she hugged Booker. She smells like strawberries. "Did this absolute *dream*boat give you a tour?"

"The absolute dreamboat did," I say mid-hug, tossing Booker a look over Daisy's shoulder.

He seems amused by this whole fish-out-of-water scenario playing out in front of him.

Daisy gives a final squeeze, then releases me and pulls back. "*Per*fect. You're going to *love* it here." She talks with her hands, all kinds of kinetic energy. "All the residents are so adorable and kind. Well, most of 'em. Arthur is salty, but that's only because his sweet Annie passed away and he's completely lost without her, and Belinda probably won't like you because you're pretty and she likes to be the most beautiful woman in every room. She really likes me, which I'm only just this second realizing is both a compliment *and* an insult." Her smile is wide. "I'm desperate for a friend my age! Do you like to go out? There's this great bar that's mostly locals—I go there almost every weekend." She looks at Booker. "You should come too, Booker. And maybe bring some of the other guys—Louie, maybe?" Back to me: "It'd be fun?"

I scrunch my face. "I'm not really into the bar scene. Or . . . going out."

She scrunches her face right back at me, waving a hand in my general direction. "Well, we'll work on that." Daisy wraps her arm around me. "I'll show you around your new home." She looks at Booker and does a little curtsy. "You're dismissed, handsome."

"Yes, ma'am." He mock salutes, then glances at me. "See you tomorrow."

I don't look away, mostly because I don't feel like I can. But also because I don't want to.

There's something magnetic and mesmerizing about him, something I'm pretty sure I've never felt before.

He lingers for a few extra moments, then backs away, gets into the golf cart, and drives off, leaving me staring after him like I'm a puppy whose person just rode off into the sunset without her.

"Oh-kay-uh," Daisy says, her accent turning the word into a drawn-out, three-syllable word. "*What* was that about?"

I look at her. "What was what about?"

She presses her index fingers to her temples, like she's seeing into the future. "I am sensing . . . a lot of tension. The romantic kind." She flutters her eyelashes.

My laugh is nervous. "What?" I'm usually better at hiding my feelings. It's like this place—or that man—has cast a spell on me, one that makes me super obvious and plows right through all my defenses.

"You and Booker Hayes." She places a hand on my shoulder, as if I'm headed off to war. "Many have tried. Many have failed. Best of luck to ya." She slaps my shoulder once. "But if you're breaking down that wall, I want a front-row seat."

I don't tell her the price I would have to pay to break down that wall. But I do remind myself because I'm in great danger of forgetting.

"I don't know what you're talking about," I say more firmly than I feel. "I just met the guy. He's . . . fine. We're fine. It's fine."

"Fine, *fine*. I can take a hint." She laughs. "My last roommate was the arts and crafts leader. She never talked. She knitted a lot and made these tiny fuzzy animals out of yarn." Her accent makes that last bit sound like three questions. *"She knitted a lot? And made these tiny fuzzy animals? Out of yarn?"*

"She also had a whole book about crafting with cat hair, so you know, *that* was gross." She shuts the front door. "I'm all for hobbies, but most of the time, I felt like I was just walking around the house talking to myself." She looks at me. "I can show you all the ways to get out of wearing the hideous uniforms." She shimmies her shoulders. "Dress-up days go over *really* well here. Or you can just find creative ways to hide from Connie." She laughs. "It'll be nice to have a friend!"

I think of my friends back home with a strange ache I haven't felt in years. I promised them I would be better about staying in touch, and I'm going to keep that promise.

I'd convinced myself I don't need people—but my trip home showed me how much I miss being a part of something.

A *community*.

Would I find that here?

I follow Daisy through the cottage and find myself standing in a small hallway.

Daisy points to the left. "Bedrooms are down the hall here. We do have to share a bathroom, but I promise I'm not too messy. My hair does get in the drain, but when it's clogged, we get to call Booker, so it's really a pro and not a con." She grins as she leads me down the hall and past the bathroom, stopping in front of a door. "This is you."

I flip the light on and walk inside the room.

"There's a door here that opens to the outside." She moves across the room to show me. "Which is why I'm not in this room, even though it's a little bigger than mine. I watch a lot of scary movies."

"So if someone breaks in, you want them to kill me first," I muse aloud.

She scrunches her nose. "Pretty much."

I look around the room. My suitcase is at the end of a metal-framed double bed, as if it appeared by some strange Disney World–type magic. The dark hardwood floors perfectly complement the white shiplap walls, and even though it's bare, it's got a homey feel.

In two seconds, this nearly empty bedroom in the middle of Wisconsin feels more like home than anywhere I've ever been since I was six.

Definitely more like home than my cramped apartment in Brooklyn. That always felt like a place to crash.

Never like home.

I tell myself not to get too attached to any of this because it's a short-term arrangement, but when I open the door out to the patio, I realize that's going to be harder than I thought. The patio itself is small but sweet, and beyond that, there's a slice of the golf course backed by big beautiful trees.

It's stunning.

Despite being in this little pocket neighborhood, it feels quaint and private back here.

"Do you like it?" Daisy asks from her spot in the doorway.

"Are you kidding?" I turn toward her. "This room is bigger than my entire apartment in Brooklyn."

She frowns. "Wow. Really?"

"Real estate is at a premium there," I say. "I had three roommates, so this place makes me feel like I'm living in a palace." And the whole idea of actual *alone time* has me feeling giddy. I was never alone in my apartment. Someone was always home, and we were just piled on top of each other so tightly it was hard to breathe. Worse, the people I lived with weren't my friends.

I glance at Daisy. I like her. She and I could be friends.

I think about Booker. I like him too. He and I are . . . already friends?

I think about the cooking class. The promise of theatre. The room I'm staying in. *My* room I'm staying in. In my summer cottage.

And I'm filled with an emotion I haven't felt in ages.

Excitement.

CHAPTER 9

AFTER FROZEN PIZZA (COURTESY OF Daisy) and the best night of sleep I've had in maybe my entire adult life, I wake up Friday morning to the sound of my housemate singing "Firework" loudly and off-key in the shower. It makes me smile.

I glance at my phone and see new texts in my chat with my friends.

MAYA: You got a love match yesterday, Ro!
MARNIE: How do you know that?
MAYA: I'm logged in to her account.
TAYLOR: Maya! That's a violation of her privacy.
MAYA: There are no secrets among friends.
And he's kind of cute, Rosie. He could be your soulmate.

I read over the conversation and smile, loving that they're in my business again.

ROSIE: I don't believe in soulmates.
And stop reading my messages, creeper!

I freeze at the sound of a knock on the door and then a mix of voices in the living room. After a few seconds, Daisy calls out, "Rosie! Booker's here for you!"

I sit up like a shot and catch an unfortunate glimpse of myself in the mirror above the small vanity on the opposite wall. My red hair is snarled, and my pale face could really benefit from some bronzer.

My door opens, and I instinctively gasp and pull the covers up to my neck, relieved to see Daisy, not Booker, looking at me.

"Just wanted to make sure you're up," she says. "Booker's here for you."

"Yep!" I say. "Just give me a few minutes."

She grins. "You got it!"

I dash down the hall to the bathroom, carrying an armload of clothes, and hurry to make myself presentable.

When I emerge from the bathroom seven minutes later, I find Booker and Daisy in the kitchen.

I walk into the room, and they both stop talking.

"Hey," he says.

"Hey," I say.

And then . . . a five-second pause.

"He-ey," Daisy says, her eyes widening, as if to acknowledge the awkward tension in the room. "Here." She thrusts a to-go cup of coffee at me. "I assume you drink coffee." She nods to the fridge. "Creamer's in there."

I take it. "Thanks." I pour cream and sugar into the cup, and when I turn back around, Booker is standing there and Daisy is . . . gone.

"Sorry I just showed up," he says. "I realized we didn't set a time, and I don't have your number."

"Is that your way of asking for it?" I tease, hoping a playful approach will quell the nerves I feel around him.

He shrugs, the corner of his mouth inching up. "Might be good to have it. That way if I get an emergency request for tampons, I'll know who it's from."

I motion for him to hand over his phone. I take it, put my number into his contacts, and then send myself a text from his phone. I glance up and hand it back. "There. Now we're phone friends."

His eyes narrow. "Great."

"Great."

"Good."

I smile. "Do you want to go?"

"Yep." He walks toward the door, and I follow, grabbing my bag from the hook by the door.

"Bye, Daisy," I holler down the hall.

"Have fun!" she singsongs back.

Seconds later, I'm back in the golf cart, bouncing along, resisting the urge to snap a photo of Booker to send to my friends.

"Did you get your pickleball injury all taken care of?"

He taps his thumb on the steering wheel and waves to another cart as we pass by. "Yep. Got there just in time. Probably saved a life."

"Ah, pickleball. The deadliest of all the sports." I smirk over at him, but he doesn't glance my way.

I smile to myself as he picks up his tour narration where he left off yesterday. And while very little looks familiar, I do recognize the theatre the second it comes into view.

"Can we go in?" I ask, wanting to get a look at the space.

He checks his watch. "Absolutely. Most of the residents are probably still at breakfast, but we might run into a few of them."

Residents, I think. *Not just* people.

"Everyone eats at the same time?" I ask, trying to understand, because I feel like I'm missing something. Like I've just stepped into a twilight zone or joined a commune or something. By all accounts, Booker seems normal, but I bet those cult leaders seemed normal too. That's how they brainwash their members. By being handsome and charming.

And Booker is definitely both of those things.

"No, not necessarily." He steps out of the golf cart. "I mean, most of the residents do. Some people cook their own meals in their cottages, but most choose the clubhouse or the dining hall for their meals. It's one of the benefits of living here."

I hop out and follow Booker up to the entrance. I can't wait to see what it looks like on the inside. I can't remember the last time I was this excited about theatre.

He opens the door, and I walk through, past the box office and into the lobby, stopping in front of two big doors that I assume lead into the auditorium and to the stage.

I look at Booker and motion to the doors. "Can I . . . ?"

"Sure, yeah," he says. "This is your domain now."

I smile at that. I've never had a domain. Especially not a theatrical one. I pull the door open and step inside the space. It's all dark except for what seem to be work lights on over the stage. They cast enough of a glow for me to see that this isn't some tiny, black box theatre. It's a good size—probably seats about four hundred or so.

"How often do they do shows?" I ask.

Booker shrugs. "I'm actually not sure. At least a few times a year. I help out when they need things, but mostly I'm on the other side of the campus."

"It's beautiful." I look up at the theatrical lighting, the fly system, the sound booth.

It's funny. Theatres all smell the same.

The stained wood of the floor, the years of fabrics and costumes, the slight acrid smell of the lighting fixtures, the faint twinge of sawdust from the scene shop—the smell of possibility.

I think about some of the spaces I've performed in over the years. The eighth floor of an office building that had somehow been converted into a performance space. The front window of a former retail shop. A storage unit.

Theatre spaces are insanely expensive to rent, especially in New York, but with a little creativity, I've learned you can perform anywhere.

There's nothing like being on a real stage, in a real show, in front of a real audience.

"Hop on up. Show me something." Booker points to the stage.

"What? Now?" I'm not shy, but for some reason I feel utterly unprepared.

"Come on, I thought performers love to show off," he says.

I lift a finger in a point. "That's a common misconception. *Some* performers are like that, but most actors I know are in it for the craft."

"That sounds very—"

"Hoity-toity?" I say in a snobby tone, then soften. "It is. I don't know why I said it. I love being onstage. But honestly . . ." I pause, noting how comfortable I am being honest with Booker. "I'm never anxious to be the center of attention. I don't need to be the first in the program or the last one to bow. I just . . ." I look back at the stage. "I just love acting."

He moves over into one of the seats in the fourth row, center, and sits, then motions to the stage. "Here's your chance."

I look at the stage, then back at him.

"Don't you have songs and speeches memorized?"

"Hundreds," I admit.

A whole portfolio, in fact. I have several dozen monologues, both comedic and dramatic, two Shakespearean monologues, and a wide variety of songs meant to show off different parts of my voice and the depth of my acting ability, depending on the character I'm auditioning for.

Three binders' worth of material.

But the thought of going up on that stage and actually getting myself into character and performing for this particular audience of one gives me pause. Performing for people I know in real life is one of the most difficult parts of this job, especially without the benefit of theatrical lighting, which turns every face into a blurry shadow.

"Are you scared?" Booker taunts.

"That won't work," I say. "I've never been affected by peer pressure."

"Is that true?"

"No." I shrug and laugh. Because while peer pressure never talked me into doing something I didn't want to do, I know I care too much what people think of me. Which is probably why I didn't tell my three best friends anything honest the entire time I was home. For someone who makes her living "making a fool" of herself, I sure do struggle with it these days. I guess there's a difference between being goofy and being a failure.

I walk up onto the stage. "Can I go backstage?"

"You're really not going to perform?" He actually sounds a little disappointed. "How am I supposed to know if you're any good?"

I chuckle. "Do you need to know if I'm any good?"

"Yes," he says. "Doesn't every physical therapist need to know that the resident theatre director knows what she's doing?"

I raise my eyebrows and wave my hands and arms at him as if casting a spell. "I'm going to have to leave you in suspense."

He shakes his head and smiles, which is currently in the lead of my favorite elicited responses from him. He leans in. "That's a shame." He stands and makes his way up to the stage.

"Are *you* going to perform?" I ask, taking a step back.

He smirks. "I make a point to never put myself on display."

I smirk back. "That's a shame."

He holds my gaze for a few seconds, and when he looks away, I note the disappointment that floods my chest.

I might not like to be the center of attention, but I wouldn't mind being the center of his.

That's not something I've felt in a very long time. Or ever. My relationship with Peter made sense, but it wasn't built on emotion. I liked that it wasn't. I didn't want anything to derail me from my goals. We got along well, so we made sense.

Until we didn't.

"Feel free to look around back here if you want to." He walks over to the stage-right wing. "I think there's a whole crew that handles the sets, and lots of volunteers who come in and paint. They team up with the art students to, you know, make it all look pretty." He motions to a door. "Scene shop back there, just behind the stage, and dressing rooms downstairs."

"It's an amazing space," I say.

"It was a dream of one of the residents," he says. "When she died, she left a huge endowment specifically for the construction and operation of a theatre. Probably why they were able to bring you in and pay your salary."

There's that word again. "One of the residents?" I ask. "Like resident actors?"

"What are you doing in here?" A gruff, gravelly voice calls down from somewhere overhead.

I look up, searching for signs of life, but all I see is blackness.

"Arthur?" Booker calls out, shielding his eyes as he struggles to locate a person in the catwalks above us. "What are you doing in the cats?"

"I asked you first!"

Booker looks at me. "That's Arthur. He knows this place inside and out, but he's a pistol."

"Sound carries on the stage, Book," he says. "Who's your girlfriend?"

"Not his girlfriend." I turn toward the voice and wave. "I'm Rosie Waterman."

"Who?"

"Arthur, will you just come down here?" Booker asks, though it sounds more like a command than a question. "Let me make a proper introduction." Then to me, he adds, "He really shouldn't be up there. He has balance issues."

"Lobby!" Arthur's bark is followed by the slam of a door.

We start down off the stage and make our way to the lobby, my mind buzzing with questions I'm not sure how to ask.

"Whatever he dishes out," Booker says as we come through the dark theatre, "dish it right back."

My eyes need a second to adjust to the bright light of the lobby, and my head needs a year to adjust to this new life in Door County.

A few moments later, a nondescript door opens and a thin, nearly bald man walks out. He's wearing what looks like a work uniform—gray pants and a matching gray button-down—and a pronounced scowl.

He gives me a once-over. "You're a child."

I give him a once-over. "You're an old man."

He squints at me, expression holding steady. "How old are you?"

"I'm twenty-nine."

He scoffs and glares at Booker. "Practically a toddler."

I narrow my eyes. "This from the guy who probably owes Jesus a quarter."

He stiffens. "'Though I look old, yet I am strong and lusty.'"

Interesting. Shakespeare. I mentally roll up my sleeves.

I mock bow and retort, "'Your lordship, though not clean past your youth, have yet some smack of an ague in you, some relish of the saltness of time in you.'"

Oh yeah. Two can play, buddy.

I see a sliver of a glint in his eye, just for a brief moment, and he switches gears.

He starts to circle me, and I counter-cross.

"'To get back my youth I would do anything in the world, except take exercise, get up early, or be respectable.'" It's like he just threw down a challenge and is now waiting to see if I pick it up.

Oscar Wilde. Nice touch. I offer my own Wilde in return.

"Well, 'the old believe everything; the middle-aged suspect everything; the young know everything.'" I pause and then add with a smile, "But I'm not quite young enough to know everything."

He harrumphs. I'll take that as a win.

Booker just stares. "Is this how theatre people fight?"

He abruptly turns his head to Booker. "*This* is who they sent us?"

"This is who they *hired*," Booker says, nodding toward me. "She obviously knows her stuff."

"I have my BA in theatre from Northwestern University," I say, because that really is the only notable thing on my résumé.

"Plus she lives in New York," Booker says.

Arthur waves his bony hands around in circles. "Lah-de-dah." He starts off in the opposite direction, and I glance helplessly at Booker, who glances helplessly back at me.

"I was in an episode of *Law & Order*!" I call after him.

"Everyone's done an episode of *Law & Order*!" he hollers without looking back, and then he disappears behind another slammed door.

I look at Booker. "He's old, but, boy, is he quick."

"But you held your own, I think. I had no idea what you two were talking about."

I shrug. "It's one thing I'm good at. Memorization. I've got a lot of lines from random plays and books I've read stored right up here." I tap on my temple. "Especially the classics."

"He'll warm up to you then," Booker says. "And you want him on your side because he's the guy who knows how this whole place works."

Well, good. Maybe this Arthur guy can shed some light on the question that's been bothering me since I woke up in Booker's truck . . .

What in the world is this place?

CHAPTER 10

WE'RE ABOUT TO LEAVE THE theatre building when a group of women burst down the hall like it's 8:00 a.m. on Black Friday at Target. They're chatting and laughing, and they all look a little sweaty.

At the sight of Booker, their cackling turns to murmuring, and, if I had to guess . . . admiring.

"Booker Hayes," one of the women practically purrs.

"Ladies." Booker smiles and takes his hat off, and it's the first time I notice his messy, wavy, dark blond hair. It's nice. He runs a hand through it, and I swear I can feel the ladies' knees collectively buckle.

Or maybe those are just mine.

"Are you all coming from a class?" Booker asks.

"Tap class with Veronica," one of the women says. "Finally got my time step down." She does a little shuffle that is definitely *not* a time step.

"Who are you?" A short woman who reminds me of Sophia from *The Golden Girls* takes an aggressive step toward me. Then a side-eye to Booker. "Booker, you're not cheating on my Lydia, are you?"

Booker squints over at her. "No, Evelyn, I'm not, since I'm not dating Lydia."

She points at him. "But you should be. She is a catch. You'd be lucky to have her." She steps away from me and turns toward the woman next to her, muttering something along the lines of, "These men today don't know a good thing *something something something*."

Booker leans closer. "Lydia is her daughter. She's eighteen years older than me and lives overseas."

"Oh, Evelyn, don't be ridiculous," one of the other women says, eyes fixed on Booker. "How can he be cheating on Lydia when he's *clearly* hung up on me?" She laughs, her hand lingering on Booker's bicep.

He gives her a very brotherly pat on the shoulder and says sweetly, "Betty, it would never work out. And to think that a woman like you would even want attention from a poor guy like me. You deserve so much better."

She giggles and preens.

What am I even watching right now?

One of the others walks right up to me. "I'm Sadie Sullivan." She sticks her hand out in my direction, and I shake it.

"Rosie Waterman."

"She's the new theatre director," Booker says.

The aggregate gasp and chatter rivals the best chicken coops, as the women all start overlapping their reactions. There's no way for me to make out full sentences in the barrage of comments.

"Oh my goodness, just in time for auditions . . ."

"I would make an *excellent* Cinderella . . ."

". . . Edgar as the prince, then you're crazy . . ."

". . . hope you're better than the last director . . ."

"Belinda's not gonna like this . . ."

I frown. "I'm pretty sure I'm on the creative team, but I don't know if I'm actually the director."

As I say this out loud, yesterday's realization returns: I should've asked more questions before accepting this job.

"Oh, that's adorable," one of the women—Betty maybe?—says. "Sweetheart, you *are* the creative team." She blinks at me.

I stare back blankly. “What do you mean?”

“You do it all!” She waves a hand like it’s a magic wand. “Lights, sets, choreography, music.”

“Well, you and whatever volunteers you can rustle up,” the one with the daughter—Evelyn?—says.

“You tell us where to stand, when to sit, and, oh! You’ll have to meet with Ginny about costumes. She’s really slow and partially deaf and blind in the one eye, so don’t stand to her right. I’d talk to her right away.”

The other women nod as if this is common knowledge about Ginny.

Evelyn starts walking toward the door. “Come on, girls. I’m starving! Let’s go eat.”

“We’ll see you at auditions, Rosie!” one of the women—Sarah? Sheba? Sadie?—says as she walks by.

The others offer various versions of the sentiment as their voices retreat down the hall. Booker seems to notice a stunned expression on my face because there is, in fact, a stunned expression on my face.

“You okay?”

I take a breath, pause, then say, “Are they . . . are they all auditioning for the show?” I ask.

“Oh yeah,” he says enthusiastically. “They’re diehards. They’ll *definitely* be there. But be aware, they’ll boss you around if you let them, so you’ve got to stand up for yourself. Remember, *you’re* the expert.”

A slow, creeping realization starts at the back of my mind and begins the trek toward the front.

I glance at Booker, back to the hallway where the women exited, then back to him. “I’m sorry, I have to ask, because I noticed it yesterday too. Why is everybody here . . . old?”

Booker studies me like he’s trying to decide if I’m joking. “You’re kidding, right?”

"No," I say slowly. The realization is about halfway through my brain, and I can just start to make out its shape. "I don't think we've seen one person under the age of seventy since I got here, except for you and Daisy and that girl in the clubhouse with Connie."

He squints at me like I'm a puzzle he's trying to solve.

I start to panic. And when I panic, I talk. Just open mouth, say stuff, or launch into a song-and-dance number, as evidenced by my previous nervous outbursts.

"In theatre, we call them the 'blue hairs.' They show up for the Saturday matinee because they want to get out in time to eat dinner at four. They're the ones who buy all of the tickets and then complain about not being able to understand what anyone is saying." I look around the empty space. "I love them, don't get me wrong. I just don't usually see so many of them all at once. I mean, I guess if we got here just as a seniors' class was ending or something, it makes sense, but it's not just here—it was also the golf course, the clubhouse, even the tennis courts—all old people."

He's still eyeing me. "Rosie, do you know what this place is?"

My face must've answered before my mouth could, because he continues.

"You don't, do you?" He cocks his head. "When you applied for this job, did you read the listing?"

I wince. "No! No, okay?" I take a breath and spill everything out. "I applied for a ton of jobs—anything having to do with acting, directing, music, or theatre. I also sent out ten times as many self-tapes as I usually do. I needed a job, I didn't know where my next paycheck was coming from, and I was behind on my rent, and I don't even remember applying for half of them. And then Connie's email came, and it looked great, you know? A job at a professional theatre, and . . ." Why am I telling him this? I'm sure it makes me sound every bit as pathetic as I feel.

But there's something about Booker that makes me want to confess things, which I need to put a lid on right this very second.

I snap my jaw shut.

"Oh boy," he says. "Maybe you should sit down."

I don't move. "Just let me have it." I widen my stance, bracing like he's going to sucker punch me.

He lifts his eyebrows as if to ask if I really want the truth.

I make a motion like *bring it on* and close my eyes.

"Sunset Hills is a retirement community," he says.

My eyes pop back open. "I'm sorry, what?"

"Like a very upscale old folks home, but with independent living options," he says. "Everyone who lives on the property is either part of the community or part of the staff."

"Everyone who lives here is . . ."

"Old, yep."

"Old," I echo.

"You really didn't know?"

"So this production . . . it's going to be cast with . . ."

He nods. "Old people."

"And I'm going to be working with . . ." I gesture for him to answer again.

He nods again. "Old people."

"If I ask another question, is there any chance you're not going to say 'old people' again?"

He squints at me. "Now do you want to sit down?"

"But I looked up Sunset Playhouse," I implore, ignoring his question. "It's a legitimate theatre!"

"It is," he says. "But this is Sunset *Players*. I can see how you got the two mixed up."

I point at him with one finger and use the other hand to dig around in my giant bag without breaking eye contact. I pull out a Twix bar, a pair of 3D glasses, and chopsticks before I finally use both hands to find my phone. I pull it out and google Sunset Players.

What comes up is a website with a tagline at the top: "Door County's Premier Theater for the Young at Heart!" Underneath is a photo gallery of past productions—and just like Booker said, all the performers are old.

"They spelled *theatre* like a movie theater," I say, as if *that's* the headline here.

Booker frowns. "Is that a big deal?"

I try not to be truly offended. "Is that a . . . ?" I stop myself. I know it's a hill I'm willing to die on, spelling it *theatre* instead of *theater*, but I don't have the brain power to educate him on why right now. The important note here is that I now live and apparently work in a retirement community.

"They did *Hair*? *Cabaret*? *A Chorus Line*?" I shake my head, trying to picture it while also trying *not* to picture it. "*A Chorus Line*? How did they do a kick line?"

"Probably very slowly."

It's funny. I laugh, but the kind of shocked, unbelieving laugh that happens when you find out you're the director for a production of *Cinderella* at a retirement community.

"You really don't like old people," he says—a statement, not a question.

I'm momentarily taken aback. "No, it's not that!" I'm just trying to compare what I've experienced to what I'm envisioning . . . and it's like trying to do long division with a potted plant as a pencil.

I just can't seem to work it out.

"You sure?"

I feel defensive. "Old people are great. I'm not prejudiced against old people," I say, stopping short of giving the classic and misguided "some of my best friends are old people" excuse. "I just . . . don't understand how to do a show like *Cinderella*—or any musical—with *only* senior citizens." I sigh. "I'm having trouble wrapping my head around this."

"I can see how that could be an issue if you, you know, didn't read your email."

I make a face. "I get that now, thanks."

He shrugs his hands and shoulders. "But hey, maybe this job could be fun."

I slump. "Oh no."

"What?"

"You're one of *those* people."

He raises his eyebrows. "One of what people?"

I cross my arms. "Make the best of it. Silver lining. Lemonade."

He frowns.

"I bet you are a morning person too."

He looks a little crestfallen. "I *am* a morning person," he says, not taking my point.

"I *knew* it." I say this like Seinfeld said "*Newman . . .*"

He appears to be unfazed. "Dunno. Could be fun."

I shake my head. "You actually think this could be fun?"

A shrug. "It will be if you want it to be."

He did pose the question yesterday—"*Can't your career be fun?*"—so I shouldn't be surprised it's resurfaced, even if it's exasperating.

I look away. My job is never fun. Not anymore. It hasn't been for a while, but I never admit it. In college, acting without the pressure of getting hired for a job that would help pay my rent was fun. Daring to fail gloriously. Digging into a character. Taking all the time I needed to figure out what she ate for breakfast, where she shopped for clothes, how she walked, how she talked—it was a luxury, it was *good*, and I took it for granted.

George Bernard Shaw was right when he said that youth is wasted on the young.

Making a career out of the thing you love is tricky. When it's not going your way, joy is hard to hold on to.

I walk over to a little seating area in the lobby and plop down into the small armchair. "I can't believe this." My mind races—I'm more than a bit panicked—like I'm about to go onstage and I forgot to memorize my lines.

My first real job in ages, and it's not at all what I thought. I'm not even sure I can do this. I'm the whole creative team? That is not how Connie made it sound. I can't put an entire show on by myself. I might have a degree in theatre, and yeah, I took directing classes, but this? I'm not qualified for this!

I stop and realize I've said all of this out loud.

And Booker is now standing beside me, staring.

He must think I'm a lunatic. Who applies for a job without carefully reading the description?

But he surprises me when he sits down across from me, nothing but kindness on his face. "Hey. I get it. It's a lot, and maybe it's not what you thought. But these residents? They're all really invested in this theatre thing," he says. "And some of them are actually pretty good. I mean, I'm not a theatre guy, but . . . one lady—Belinda—she was a professional singer. There's another guy who's a really great tap dancer. His muscle memory is incredible, and physically, he's in great shape for his age. Then there's Sal, who refuses to audition but who always somehow ends up in the shows." He looks away. "And for some reason he's always eating onstage."

I try to look at him, but the sun is shining through the windows behind him, and I can't really see his face. "This isn't how it was supposed to go. I don't know if I can do this."

He doesn't move.

Thankfully, he switches to the chair across from me. And though it was appropriate for him to be divinely backlit, this is a much better view. He leans back and props his ankle on his knee. "What's going on in your brain?"

I frown. "What do you mean?"

"I mean, I just met you yesterday, but even I can see the spiral." He stares at me, face welcoming. It's the kind of face that you can't help but talk to about what you just wrote in your diary.

It's unnerving to feel safe.

I'm an actor. I can manufacture feelings in an instant, but I'm having trouble faking it right now. Which is . . . disconcerting.

"No offense, Booker, but I don't even know you." I look away.

"Which makes me the best person to talk to." He holds up his hands. "No judgment."

If I'm a simmering pot, all kinetic bubbles just waiting for a few degrees of heat and pressure to increase before I push my lid off and spill all over the stove, then Booker is more like a serene mountain lake. Calm. Easygoing. Relaxed.

"It's just—" I clamp my jaw shut.

"Not what you expected," he says. "I know."

I shake my head.

"I get it." He pauses. "I was going to work with professional athletes."

I lift my chin to meet his gaze. "You were?"

"I mean, that was my dream," he says, laughing more to himself than at something funny.

"So what changed?"

He shrugs. "My grandma moved here."

I feel the restlessness inside me settle. Booker has a story, and I want to know the rest of it.

But then, everyone has at least one story, right? The old women who just walked out of here? They probably have loads of stories.

"I figured, you know, this was a way for me to keep an eye on her and still make a living doing what I love."

"But . . ." I'm having trouble squaring him giving up on his dream. It's not what I'd do. It's not what I understand. "You still want to work with athletes, right?"

Another shrug. "Honestly, it doesn't really matter. I mean,

I'm doing what I love, and these people are just as important as basketball players. Probably a *lot* easier to deal with too." He frowns. "Well, some of them."

I smile and pause. And after a beat, I ask, "And you don't feel like you gave up on your dream?"

"Nah," he says. "I just got a new one."

"Hmm," I say. "I don't understand that at all."

CHAPTER 11

BOOKER CARTS ME THROUGH THE residential part of the Sunset Hills Retirement Community, which I now know is the official name of this place.

He's narrating the points of interest as I sit in stunned silence.

I'm trying to focus on his commentary and not on the fact that I've been completely blindsided. It's my own fault, which is another awesome realization.

In the middle of my stupor, I also linger on how casually he mentioned finding a new dream.

This place isn't my new dream.

Plus, it's not that easy. Not for me. I've wanted to be an actor since I was twelve. I've dedicated my whole life to this.

To give up before I achieve what I set out to do is failing. Period. Full stop.

I glance over, in awe of his quiet nonchalance. I don't know if I've ever felt as settled or content as he looks right now.

Did he just give up trying for his dream? That's hard to understand.

He tells me that these medium-sized cottages are homes for the residents who live on their own. "It's the best of both worlds," he says. "They don't have to worry about yard care or snow removal, but they still have their own space. Once they're a member of Sunset, they have programming and meals and shared spaces and physical therapy—it's a community, and it's been really good for a lot of them."

"Including your grandma?"

He nods. "She's in one of the apartments on the other side of the clubhouse. She's been on her own for a while now, but the house got to be too much for her to handle."

"She didn't want to move in with your parents?" I ask.

"They're not really in the picture," he says simply. "Haven't been for a long time."

My expression changes, and he must see it because he shakes his head.

"It's not a tragic story. I had a great life with people who loved me," he says. "Doesn't really matter that those people weren't my parents."

I study him for a few long seconds, more interested in what he's not saying than in what he is. "That's really how you feel?"

"It really is." He shrugs. "Not everyone is cut out to raise a kid."

I eye him for a few long seconds, then remember I don't know this man at all. "Sorry. I'm being so nosy."

"It's okay." He smiles. "And I don't mean to be cagey about it, it's just . . . apparently, I'm 'hard to know.'"

"I feel like there's a story there," I say, hopefully lightly, fighting off the desire to prod him with questions so I can learn everything there is to know about him. I put my feet up on the dash of the cart.

He watches the path in front of us. "Ah. Yes. But you'll never know it because—" He lifts his hands as if I'm supposed to finish the sentence.

"Because you're hard to know."

He gives me a pointed nod, as if to say, *"Bingo!"*

If only that didn't make me want to know him more. "If you don't tell me, I'll be forced to fill in the blanks, and I have a very active imagination."

His amused expression shifts.

"So you use humor to cover up your real feelings," I say, sizing him up. "Interesting."

A quick glance at me. "I'm a guy. It's what we do."

I chuckle.

He turns onto a wide sidewalk. "I didn't realize you're a therapist too."

"Theatre is basically psychology," I tell him, watching the houses go by as we drive. "It's studying people. What they do and why they do it. You have to get inside a character's head in order to, you know, figure her out. What makes her tick? Why does she do the things she does? I could probably be a therapist with no additional training."

"Might be a *bit* more schooling to go through, but . . ."

I shrug playfully. "To-may-toe, to-mah-toe."

There's a brief moment of silence, and then he asks, "Do you ever try and psychoanalyze yourself?"

"Ha! No way," I answer. "I'm *way* too complicated to start asking myself questions. I'm like a balled-up wad of Christmas lights."

He half laughs. "Where to begin . . . maybe with why the panic applying for jobs? Why take one in Wisconsin without even checking it out first?" He glances at me.

I narrow my eyes comically. "I am *also* hard to know."

"If you don't tell me, I'll be forced to fill in the blanks," he jokes.

I feel something inside me settle.

There's a lull, and then I say, "I wouldn't have thought you were hard to know. You seem . . . friendly."

He waves to someone in the distance, as if to prove my point. "Being friendly isn't the same as letting people know you."

Don't I know it.

"It's obvious someone has said this to you before." I study his profile. "Ex-girlfriend? The reason you don't date?"

He pulls the cart to a stop, hops out, and with a flourish, says, "Aaand . . . welcome back to your summer home!"

I eye him as I get up and cross around to the front of the golf car. "You deflected."

"I know, right? Dodged it like a champ."

"Well played."

He raises his eyebrows. "Thank you."

There's a beat. A moment of silence. And then I offer, "I don't like to talk about myself either."

"Perfect," he says. "Then the two of us will become great friends who know nothing about each other."

He's quick. My smile widens.

He smiles back.

And I think, for the first time ever, that I might believe in love at first sight. Or at least friendship at first sight. Because there's something about Booker that makes me want to drop the act. To stop pretending.

More and more it's feeling like that is what this summer might be about.

I'm about to exit the cart when Booker says, "So you basically pretend for a living."

I laugh. "I mean . . . I guess that's one way to put it. If you do it right, it's not exactly *pretending*, but close enough." It's not lost on me that this exact thing might be my whole issue when it comes to my career.

You have to be willing to be completely raw, Rosie. You aren't. And it's blocking you.

"So is it hard not to pretend in your real life?" he asks.

Peter always accused me of playing a role. Isn't that what I did at the baby shower?

"I'm not sure I—" My muscles tense, and I feel defensive, but I'm not sure why.

"Oh, I'm not accusing you of anything," he says. "It's just—you seem like you could use a safe person."

I frown. "And that's you? A perfect stranger?"

He shrugs.

There seems to be a fundamental difference between Booker

and me. He seems more open than I am. Like the wall around him is shorter or something. My wall was built by failure, and it's basically a fortress.

He crosses his arms over his chest. "What if we try something different?" He gestures between us on the word *we* and my heart flip-flops.

Are we a *we*?

I toss him a suspicious look. "Different from what?"

His eyes brighten. "Like, what if we answer every question the other one asks. But, you know, honestly."

I don't know what I expected him to suggest, but it wasn't that. I knee-jerk a "No."

He makes a face. "You didn't even think about it."

"I don't need to." Yes, I'm conflicted about this discovery that it's apparently impossible for me to be honest with the people I love, but opening up to *this man* is not the way to change that.

"Like I said, who better to talk to than a perfect stranger?" he says. "It could be therapeutic."

"Therapeutic?"

"Or practice. You know"—a grin spreads across his face—"for all your possible love matches."

"That's . . . I'm not . . ." Now I'm flustered. I shake my head and turn away. "I'm going back to New York at the end of this job. I'm not dumb enough to try and make some kind of love match in Wisconsin."

As if on cue, my phone dings in my pocket.

He opens his eyes and mouth wide, pointing at me as if to say, *"Ohhh!"*

I grit my teeth, pull out the phone, and click the sound off.

"Come on, you have to admit that was perfect timing," he jokes.

I shove my traitorous phone back in my pocket. "I admit nothing."

He holds up his hands. "No stakes, no ties, no baggage. And I promise I'm not trying anything here. Just thought this might be a good detour. Change of scenery." He pauses. "Since no one knows you, you could be yourself here."

Hadn't I thought the exact same thing only yesterday?

He leans back against the seat of the golf cart. "When this job ends, you'll go back to your life, and you'll never have to see me again."

That comment doesn't hit the way it should.

"Just think about it," he says. "And let me know if you want to practice."

"Answering questions," I say.

"Being honest."

I make a display of cringing. "Sounds awful."

He smirks. "Might be good to have a friend here?"

"You think I need a friend?"

"I think everyone needs friends," he says. "And I am one of the few people here who was probably born the same decade as you."

I muse.

He cocks his head slightly. "Could be fun, Rosie."

I definitely like the way he says my name.

With that, he drives off, leaving me standing there, certain that I don't need to think any more about his offer because his offer is about honest sharing.

And the feelings I'm having right now are not ones I would ever volunteer to share.

CHAPTER 12

ANOTHER FANTASTIC NIGHT'S SLEEP.

I wake up refreshed, and now I'm sitting at the kitchen table drinking a cup of coffee and contemplating this whole retirement community debacle when my phone buzzes and I see I've got a new alert from Connie with the subject line: Orientation Meeting.

"Oh, shoot. I guess I'm late for a meeting?" I glance up. "On a Saturday?"

"Let me guess . . . Connie?" Daisy is standing at the counter eating a bowl of Frosted Flakes. To her credit, she only asked me a few questions when I returned from the theatre tour with Booker. I answered none of them, which she decided meant that I'm now carrying a torch for him.

"She hasn't quite got a handle on how to schedule meetings so everyone knows they're happening. Just shoot her a text and tell her you're on the way. I'll drive you over until they assign you your own golf cart."

"I've never driven a golf cart."

She laughs. "You can drive a car, right?"

"Well, yeah," I say, though until I came home, I hadn't in years. In New York you don't need one.

I send the text to Connie and pour the rest of the coffee down the drain.

Despite the fact that I'm internally freaking out about the best job I've gotten in ages being in a retirement community, the whole place is *so* nice. Nicer than anywhere I've ever lived outside of my parents' house. The job isn't at all what I thought I'd agreed to, but it definitely has its perks.

Even though the pros to this job are starting to pile up, the one con is a very big one. I have a flash of a future casting director looking over my résumé and pausing on *Cinderella*.

Still, none of this changes the fact that of all those résumés and auditions I submitted, this is the only offer I got.

"Okay, you ready?" Daisy grabs her bag from the hooks by the front door, interrupting my thought spiral. "I'll drop you off at the clubhouse. I'm sure Connie will let you follow her back. It can be a little confusing at first—it's a pretty big place—but once you drive it a few times, it'll get easy." She holds up two fingers and says, "Promise."

Her accent makes everything she says sound slightly more delightful, and I contemplate asking if I can mimic her just for practice.

I don't, of course, because I've already got my North Carolina accent down. If she were Scottish, well, that would be another story.

As we walk outside, Daisy closes the door behind her, and my phone dings with a text message. I glance down and see a photo of my parents in a boat with a glacier behind them. Mom's text reads:

> We are having so much fun! And we want to get tickets to come see your show in Door County. It'll be like two vacations in one summer! Can't wait! Send me the info! Make sure to send your friends the details too! You're safe and sound, right? You never let me know if you made it.

That's Mom. Well-wishes with a side of guilt.

I text back a quick: I'm good! Will update soon. Then, after a pause, I add: And I'm taking your exclamation point privileges away! and tuck my phone away.

We slide into Daisy's golf cart, and she backs away from the house, driving twice as fast as Booker did around the sidewalk circle. I brace myself by jamming my foot against the floor and grabbing the overhead handle.

I reach down to buckle a seat belt, but there isn't one. If we have to go around a curve, I'm going to fly out of here.

Daisy waves to every single person we see, yelling at them by name or shouting a general, "Hey, y'all!" Like Booker, she narrates the drive, only Daisy doesn't slow down to let me get a good look, and everything whizzes by in a blur.

We drive through the neighborhood adjacent to the staff's pocket neighborhood, and as we round the corner to the main part of the campus, I notice a girl sitting on a bench in a small grassy area off to one side. She glances up and makes eye contact with me, holding it until we pass. Her expression is blank.

"Who's that?" I ask, doing my best to convey who I'm talking about without letting go to point.

Daisy waves, but the girl doesn't wave back. Daisy seems unfazed.

"That's Dylan," she says. "She moved in with her grandma a few months ago. She's quiet and I think a little miserable. I've tried to talk to her, but she hates it here. Maybe you'll have better luck."

Ooh. A story. I want to find out what it is.

Which makes no sense because at this meeting I'm about to have, I may have to tell Connie that I can't stay. I may not have any option but to move home and regroup.

I'm not qualified to do this job.

And that thought is twisting me up inside.

Daisy brings her cart to a screeching halt in front of the clubhouse. Still holding on for dear life, I look down to see that she actually left skid marks on the road.

"I didn't know golf carts could go that fast," I say.

"Oh, sorry." She half smiles, half winces in my direction. "Everyone's so slow around here, and I never have anyone in my cart, so sometimes I just forget!" She bounces out of the golf cart, and I meet her on the sidewalk. "So I work in here—not too shabby—and it's only one floor away from Booker."

I make a face. "You have a thing for Booker?"

"Honey, *everyone* has a thing for Booker." She laughs. "But, truth be told, I've never seen him look at anyone the way he looked at you."

I give her a *whatever* look, hoping it's enough to convince her I haven't been thinking of him nonstop since I got here.

She moves around in front of me and puts a hand on my shoulder, waiting for my full attention. "I can read people," she says matter-of-factly. "And I know Booker. That man is smitten."

My ears perk up.

"He's the *nicest* guy," she says. "It's not an act. He is genuinely so kind."

Yeah. I had a feeling.

"If Booker asks you a question, it's because he wants to know the answer. If he says he'll be there to help you with something, he will always show up." She shifts. "And also—he actually *likes* it here. Came for his grandma out of some sense of duty or something. And I honestly don't think he'll ever leave."

Noted. No plans to fall head-over-anything.

"Plus, everyone's always setting him up with their daughter or granddaughter or niece or friend or whoever because he's just so good. He's just a really good guy." She pauses. "But it never works out."

I shrug. "Maybe he doesn't want to be in love."

"Or maybe he just hasn't found the right woman."

I balk at the word because if she's referring to me, I'm not ready to be called a *woman*.

"Well, I wish him the best," I say.

Daisy considers me and says, "Uh-huh."

A heavyset man wearing a pink golf shirt walks out of the clubhouse and catches my eye.

"Hi, Mr. Samuels!" Daisy says. "We missed you at Thursday night's cooking class. Don't tell me you don't want to learn how to make homemade ravioli!"

"I got stuck at PT," he grunts. "Booker wouldn't let me go until I got in the pool. I *hate* the pool."

"Well, that's a bummer," she says. "You tell him I said you can't stay late on Thursdays because we have to learn to cook!"

"All right, Daisy!" He chuckles and strolls off.

"Does everyone know everyone here?" I ask as Daisy leads me into the clubhouse.

"Well, I do." She beams. "That's kind of my job."

Connie is waiting in the lobby for us, and when she sees me, she rushes over. "Oh good! You're here. Just a few bits of business I forgot to give you, like your golf cart key and your uniform." She giggles at herself and leans in. "Kind of important, wouldn't you say?"

I smile. Connie is kind, and despite the conflict stirring around inside me, this whole fiasco isn't entirely her fault. Yes, she could've been a little clearer in her email, which implied I was part of a team and not the whole team itself, but I'm the one who didn't read the job description.

Daisy turns toward me. "Okay, this is where I leave you." She pulls me into an enormous hug. I'm sensing this is simply who she is. "We're going to have the best summer! Buh-bye!" She squeezes me—hard—and then she walks away.

I'm torn.

I really like her. And our little cottage. And the theatre space.

And Booker.

But I'm the wrong person for this job. So, so wrong.

"That Daisy has never met a stranger," Connie says. "And she's a kindred spirit. I mean, we are both from North Carolina, so how's that for a small world?" She smiles. "That's why I put her with you, you know, to help you get used to things around here. And maybe also because Booker's place is close by. He's one of the good ones."

"So I hear," I say absently, trying not to let myself be swayed.

"And he moved here for Bertie." She motions for me to follow her. "Did he tell you that?"

"That's his grandma, right?"

"Adoptive grandma." She waves a hand. "It's a long story."

I want to ask questions, but she doesn't give me the chance.

"She's a funny one. Feisty. Doesn't put up with any guff from anybody." Connie walks into an office and moves around to the opposite side of the desk, then motions for me to have a seat in the chair across from her.

"Okay, down to business. Sorry to bring you in on a Saturday—it's just so last minute with everything. We had someone all set up to direct the show this summer, but there was a little mutiny from the other residents, and we quickly had to regroup."

I want to ask for additional details, but she doesn't give me the chance.

"So," she says, "you had your tour. Here is your golf cart key"—she pushes a small gold key across the desk—"your mailbox key"—an even smaller key this time—"and your key to the theatre. Cannot *believe* I forgot to give you these before." She giggles to herself. "I'm feeling so scattered today. Now. This is your name badge, and here"—she leans down and picks up a small stack of polo shirts—"are a few uniforms. I know you have your own"—she gives me a quick once-over—"personal style, but when you're on the premises and working, you should be properly dressed."

I muster a thank-you and slip the lanyard over my neck, but the subtext of this whole scene is me trying to find a way to say: *"I don't know if I can stay."*

I cross one leg over the other and mentally prepare myself for a potentially difficult conversation. "Connie, I have to admit, this job isn't exactly what I thought it would be."

Her painted-on eyebrows pop up. "Oh?"

I wince. "I wasn't aware I'd be directing a show all by myself or that the entire cast would be made up of . . . senior citizens."

She looks genuinely shocked. "Oh dear. Was the job description not clear?"

I'm sure the job description was as clear as a Montana sky in summer, but I didn't exactly read it. Admitting that out loud feels like a mistake, so I don't. "Um, somehow, I failed to"—there is no way to make this sound okay—"well, I guess I just missed it."

"So what are you saying?" She blinks a few times, probably trying to balance my feelings while also weighing options in case I quit. "The auditions are on Tuesday."

"I know." My gaze falls to my hands folded in my lap.

Her tone levels. "As in . . . three days from now."

"I know."

She pauses, and I can practically *feel* her panicking. "Well, okay, I could ask Belinda to step in, but of course, she isn't a very good leader, and oh dear." The color drains from her face, but then she seems to get an idea. "You know, you won't be com*plete*ly alone. Arthur has a whole list of volunteers who signed up to help for this one. Everyone just loves *Cinderella*. I'm sure we can get you a crackerjack team of people to help." The panic returns. "The summer musical is one of the most well-loved events here at Sunset. It's been a tradition going on fifteen years now. And the theatre—it's state of the art, really." A pause. "Is it just not what you're used to?"

My throat is dry. My palms are wet. I hate this, I hate this feeling of backing out, of letting people down, of being so totally and completely in over my head and ill-equipped.

But I can't. I can't do it. I don't know how, I . . .

"The space is wonderful, Connie."

"Oh, good," she says, her face searching for some hope here. "Then what's the problem? I'm sure we can work something out."

If I tell her that directing a musical for a non-equity group of senior citizens would make me the laughingstock of pretty much everyone in the professional theatre community, I might actually offend her.

Correction. That *will* offend her.

"I knew she wouldn't stay." The voice comes from the doorway, and when I turn, I see a beautiful older woman with shoulder-length silver hair and legs that God would only give to a dancer.

"Oh, Belinda." Connie tries to conceal a groan. "Can you knock please? This is my office."

"The door is open, Connie." Belinda walks in. The cadence of her voice reminds me of an old-time movie actor—almost that transatlantic accent from the thirties. "I told you it was a mistake hiring someone so young and . . . inexperienced." Belinda doesn't even glance in my direction, but her whole body is looking down its nose at me.

"We didn't have a lot of options," Connie hisses, as if that will keep me from hearing her. She meets my eyes and smiles. "You really are perfect for the job."

"Like I said in the board meeting, the only directing experience she has was in school," Belinda says. "And that is not the same thing as," she pauses and says this with utmost reverence, "professional theatre." She looks at me. "You really do not have what it takes."

All at once I'm transported back to an audition, one of my first in New York.

Every other girl in the waiting room looked a lot like me, and I shrunk under the strange feeling of sameness.

It became instantly clear that girls like me were a dime a dozen, all clamoring for their big break.

The worry that I'd been kidding myself to ever think I could be a professional actor nearly paralyzed me, and when I went in to read, I messed up so badly I had to start over. Twice.

The casting director was a big name, someone who knew what she was talking about. So when she looked at me and said, *"Well, congratulations, Rosie Waterman, you have successfully wasted my time,"* I wanted Dorothy to splash cold water on me so I, too, could melt away.

But then, the kicker. She took off her glasses, waited until she had my full attention, and said, *"You really do not have what it takes."*

And I believed her.

A part of me still believes her.

But deep within me was the desire to prove to her, to everyone, at any cost, that I have what it takes. I can make it. I can be successful.

It's the reason I didn't quit back then, it's a big part of why I can't admit failure to my friends, and it's why I can't quit my dream now—because I would love to prove that woman wrong.

This feels a lot like that.

No. This feels *exactly* like that. And I don't even know who this woman is.

I press my lips together, stiffen my shoulders, and make a decision. "I'm not going anywhere. I'll do it."

Maybe I decide this for the girl in that casting room who couldn't find her voice at the time. Or the girl I'm trying to let myself be. I don't know, but in this moment, I know this is what I need to do.

I can practically feel the *harrumph* bubbling inside Belinda.

Connie's eyes light up. "You'll do it?"

"Yes. I'm sorry I gave you the opposite impression." I turn to face Belinda. "I'll do it."

She scoffs and preens as she walks out of Connie's office.

"Bless your heart, Rosie Waterman," she says. "Let's put on a show!"

And this is when it hits me—as things often do when my pride makes decisions on my behalf—that there's no turning back now.

CHAPTER 13

AS I LEAVE CONNIE'S OFFICE, I walk past Belinda.

She's huddled up with a few of the other residents, a pre-snap huddle of pompous gossip. When they notice me, they stop talking and watch, like I'm Ted Lasso and I just got hired to coach soccer.

Correction. Football.

I tell myself not to let any of this get in my head.

Let's see if I listen to me.

I can do this.

I head outside to the row of numbered golf carts, locate the one with the number that corresponds with the number on my key—118—and sit down behind the steering wheel.

I stare at the panel—is it called a dashboard in a golf cart?—and stick the key in the ignition. It's clearly marked Off, so I turn it to On. Turning the key doesn't make a sound. Are they electric? I turn the key off, then turn the key to On again. Nothing. Weird. I jam my foot on the accelerator to see if anything happens, which sends the cart forward way faster than I expected, throwing me back against the seat in a lurch.

I slam my foot on the brake, dipping the front end of the cart and jolting me forward.

A duo of golfers walking on a nearby path glances my way. "You okay over there?"

I wave. "All good!"

I draw in a deep breath. Electric. Got it. I take my foot off the brake, but for some reason the pedal stays all the way down.

I remind myself that I'm not an idiot. I can figure this out.

After checking that the key is still turned to On, I slowly press down on the accelerator, but I don't move. I just hear a *thunk*, as if I broke something. I look down to see that the brake pedal is now back where it started.

Weird.

I slowly push the accelerator again, and this time the cart obeys, moving out of the space at a pace that won't maim me.

Once I'm on the path, I realize I should've paid more attention when Booker showed me around, or maybe picked up a map from the clubhouse, because I have no idea which way to go. The campus at Sunset Hills is huge and wide and open, with serpentine sidewalks zigzagging over the grounds. Some are for walking, some for biking, and some appear wider—the specific path for golf carts.

Unlike the other times I've been out and about, this time there are no people anywhere. I half expect to see Will Smith with a German shepherd.

It's a zombie wasteland, except, I notice, for Dylan, the teenage girl living in an old folks' home.

It strikes me that her story is incredibly high concept and would make a really fun play.

I see her sitting on the same bench where she was when Daisy drove me over, looking every bit as morose as she did the first time I saw her.

If this *were* a zombie apocalypse, I have a feeling Dylan would be on the front lines.

Either that, or she'd be one of the zombies.

Come to think of it, in a zombie apocalypse *everyone* would either be on the front lines or a zombie. But either way, I think I'd want Dylan on my team.

I can't remember which direction I'm supposed to go, so I bring the cart to a jerky stop in front of her.

"Hey, um . . . you're Dylan, right?" I ask, and then, so I don't sound creepy, I add, "My housemate Daisy told me your name." She's staring at her phone. "Uh, hi, how's it going?"

She looks up. She has a nose piercing and a pink streak in her dark hair. Her black nail polish is chipping, and she's wearing a dark-colored flannel with ripped jeans, even though it's warm enough for shorts and a T-shirt.

She stares, then gives a "Hey?" The subtext I'm getting is, *"Why are you talking to me and could you please leave, and oh, by the way, can you teleport me to literally anywhere but here on your way out?"*

"I'm Rosie," I say. "Rosie Waterman?" I hold up my name badge like an idiot. It's not like she would've heard of me. Then I continue my streak of open-mouth-say-stuff. "I'm new here. Just got in, met some people, found my house. Oh! And I got this really ugly polo shirt I have to wear and my name badge and this golf cart. My first time ever driving one of these babies."

I can practically *hear* her eyes roll. To her credit, her stoic expression doesn't change.

"I'm . . . happy for you?" She looks back down at her phone.

I try not to let her attitude derail me. I actually do need her help. "So . . . um?" She looks up again. "Sorry. Do you know the way to the staff cottages? The pocket? The staff pocket place?" It's like there are a million words out there, and I know none of them.

Without speaking or blinking or appearing to breathe, she points to her right, in the direction of a wide path that looks vaguely familiar. She then looks back down at her phone again.

I briefly worry that it looks familiar because they all look the same.

"Ah. Got it. Thanks." I'm about to pull away when I hear myself say, "Hey, sorry, one more thing."

This time there is a marked pause between the time she's looking at her phone and when she raises her head to look at me. I may as well be a toddler kicking her seat on an eight-hour flight.

"Have you ever done anything in the theatre? Onstage or backstage or anything? Maybe stage managing . . . ?"

Judging by her face, she has an interest in makeup.

When she slowly shakes her head in a winced no, my cheeks flush, but I'm determined to win her over.

"You sure? No interest? I'm heading up a musical here and thought you might want to hang out with someone young and cool."

She stares.

"It's me."

She continues to stare.

"I'm the young and cool . . . You know what, never mind. This way, right?" I point in the direction she pointed.

She scrunches up her face at me.

Solid.

I hesitate a beat too long before finally deciding that Dylan is not going to sign up for the production team, let alone continue being subjected to someone who's upbeat and witty.

I'm about to turn my cart in the direction she pointed and zoom off, Daisy-style, when I hear her say, "I worked backstage at my school once. They did some play called *Newsies.*"

My eyes are wide when I look back at her, and they go wider when I realize she's now looking at me. "Oh, it's a musical."

Her face melts into an annoyed expression. "What?"

"Since there's music, it's a musical," I say. "Plays don't have— It's a common—" I snap my jaw shut. I sound like the theatre people I can't stand to be around. "Did you like it?"

She shrugs, and her expression says it wasn't terrible.

"I love that show. I mean, who doesn't love Jeremy Jordan, am I right? And who can't get behind the rousing call to action of every showstopping number?" I throw a fist in the air in solidarity.

She stares at me blankly, then says, "Who?"

"Uh, never mind," I say. "I just wondered about the theatre thing because, like I said, I'm in charge of a show they're putting on here. *Cinderella*?"

I say it like it's a question. Like she might not know who Cinderella is. I'm internally face-palming because I'm bombing this little interaction worse than I bombed the one with Booker.

"Wow." The word couldn't have been drier.

"Do you, maybe, want to be on my team?" I ask.

She presses her lips together but doesn't say anything.

After a beat, I say, "I like your nose ring," which was a super dumb thing to say. This is worse than a blind first date set up by my mother.

And yet, that doesn't stop me from saying, "I kind of want to get one, but I don't think I can pull it off."

"I don't think you can either."

Ooh, I like this girl.

"We have auditions next week over in that theatre building—do you know the one?"

No response.

"It's—" I go to point, then crane my neck, hoping to catch a glimpse of it because I have no idea where it actually is. "Uh. Well, shoot. Somewhere around here."

She's watching me again.

I know nothing about this girl, only that she lives in a place that is not conducive to being a teenager. I assume the circumstances of her being here aren't great.

Maybe she just needs a friend.

"Well, I'm sure you can find it. Anyway, Monday morning the creative team is meeting, and auditions start at 9:00 a.m. Tuesday, if you want to join me," I say.

"You want me to help with a show that has a bunch of old people in it?" she asks, then drops her head down and looks at me like Wednesday Addams. "For fun?"

I wince. "Weird, right? I thought it was kind of weird too. We've got an ambulance on standby for the tap numbers," I quip.

She half laughs. It's just her breathing air faster through her nose, but it feels like a win.

"Seems lame," she says. "Why are you doing it?"

"I needed the work." I look away. That just popped out. I clamp my jaw shut and try again. "And I'm . . . excited about it."

"Yeah, you look excited."

"Yeah, so do you," I volley back. "You must have tons of stuff to do around here." I pause. "In the old folks' home."

She purses her lips and rolls her eyes, conceding the point.

"Look, I promise it's going to be fun," I tell her, even though I'm not convinced that's true. "I mean, it *could* be fun. We could *make* it fun. You could help backstage again or maybe do hair and makeup? Or run lights? There's tons of places where we need help."

Dylan's stony expression holds, and I decide desperation is not going to win her over.

"If you want to show up, you know where we'll be," I say. "The offer is open; I'd love to have you."

"I'm probably busy."

I nod, even though she's not looking at me, because I recognize a brush-off when I hear one. I do think I made a dent, though.

"Okay, well. See you around." I give a weak wave as I start off in the direction she told me to go. I follow the wide path to a fork and realize I have no clue which way to turn. This place really needs better signage, though I can see why they wouldn't advertise staff housing for their residents. The staff is probably expected to know their way around.

I turn to the right, and after a few minutes I hit a dead end. It takes me several minutes to figure out how to turn my cart around because I couldn't find the lever labeled F and R underneath my seat and between my legs, and then, after driving around for fifteen more minutes, I'm more lost than ever.

Worse, I'm pretty sure I've passed the bench where Dylan had been sitting at least three times. Thankfully, she's gone, and I don't have to feel like the kid who waves to her parents every time they pass by on the merry-go-round.

I do my best to start over, this time turning left where I think I previously turned right, veering off the pavement onto grass and then onto what looks like a dirt path. I can see where I need to go off in the distance past a few holes of the golf course, and even though I'm pretty sure we weren't on dirt before, I think these carts can go anywhere. They drive on golf courses, which is a ton of grass, sometimes even sand, right?

At some point, the hard ground beneath me softens, and the cart slows and starts to make a funny noise—sort of an angry whirring. The front left end of the cart is leaning farther than the other wheels, and when I look down, I see the tires spinning, stuck to the halfway point in mud.

"Oh, come on!" I shout. But a quick glance around tells me I'm shouting into the ether. There's nobody out here.

I'm lost.

And stuck in mud.

How appropriate.

I groan and stupidly try to get out of the golf cart, but when I plant both feet, I'm instantly up to my ankles in mud. My new white shoes are ruined, which is frustrating because the only other shoes I brought are a pair of bright green Crocs.

Also frustrating because I'm not sure how to get my feet out.

I grab on to the overhead bar on the driver's side and pull my whole body up, extracting my feet from the slurping wet ground.

The sound is funny to me, and I actually laugh out loud despite my misery. Immediately after my rueful laughter, though, I start to panic. What if no one finds me?

What if there are animals out here? Like coyotes? Or bears, or wild turkeys? I know this is Wisconsin, but it might as well be the African plains. I'm not built for this.

I once had a run-in with an angry goose in the crosswalk of a city street. It came for me as if I were the one out of place and chased me halfway down the block.

I hold my mud-covered feet up in the air, hanging halfway off the cart, and I try to flick the chunky globs off my shoes. I kick slightly, and a giant pile of dark sludge falls with a splat to the ground. I turn around and try to see where I veered off the path, as if I have any hope of getting back there. The tire tracks are pretty defined, and I can see the spot where I hit this Midwestern swamp. It's only about three big jumps away. Three jumps to solid ground.

Three jumps.

I took dance.

I can do that.

If I can get back to that spot without sinking farther into this mess, I can walk back the way I came and hopefully find someone to help.

I absently brush my hair from my face, and I can feel the giant wet trail of mud left on my cheek.

Fabulous.

I glance down at the large imprints my feet left in the mud. They've filled back up with water already.

This is going to be messy. But it's just mud. And mud washes off, right?

Yeah. Tell that to my shoes.

I strap my bag around my shoulder crossways, pull the key from the ignition (as if anyone could steal the golf cart in its current state), and draw in a breath.

"Mud washes off," I tell myself as I spin sideways and scootch to the passenger side, holding my brown chunky feet up over the dash. Maybe if I go fast, I won't sink. Maybe on the other side of the cart it's not so wet.

I take another breath and, before I can think about it, I jump out of the golf cart, trying to run toward the grassy area with every ounce of strength in my body.

Nope. It's just as wet. And even a little deeper. My feet sink to mid-shin, and because I leapt with Olympic-long-jump fervor, my torso momentum continues as my feet stay firmly planted.

I instantly flop over, hands out, face down.

I gasp, pulling my face up, inhaling a mouth full of thick, wet dirt as I do. I spit and swipe, trying—failing—to clear my eyes and nose with mud-covered hands. I can't see anything, but I can hear rustling to my right. I start shouting, "Stay away from me, coyotes!" while flailing my arms, because somewhere, once upon a time, I saw on a nature documentary that you're supposed to "make yourself big" if confronted by a wild animal.

"You don't want to mess with me!" I yell, but with the mud slathered on my face, it comes out sounding like, *"You don wanf messif me!"* I'm still mostly lying prostrate on the ground when, out of nowhere, I feel myself pulled up out of the muck like a rag doll and placed in an upright position.

I'm verbally protesting—because *what is happening?*—but quickly realize the rustling I heard wasn't El Chupacabra; it was an actual person. Someone must've come to my rescue.

Unless this is the start of a murder-by-opportunity type scenario.

When I shout, "Don't murder me!" (because that's a good deterrent for murderers—they run away for sure when you shout that at them) I get another mouthful of sludge that slid down from my forehead and over my nose, which I spit out directly at the person who pulled me out of the muck.

"What the—? Rosie! Calm down!" the voice says. "It's Booker."

I go still.

Of course. Of course it's Booker.

My hands are caked and useless, so I try to shake the mud from my face—only to succeed in thwapping a mucky slab of hair around and smacking myself in the face with it.

Lying face down in the mud—or a coffin—is preferable to him seeing me like this.

"Don't say anything," he says, and I swear I can hear stifled laughter in his voice. If it's there for real, I'm going to get back in the cart and drive over him.

"Just grab my arm and walk with me. I've got a towel in my cart."

I never thought the words *"I've got a towel in my cart"* could be a turn-on, but here we are.

I let him lead me out of the muddy area and onto firmer ground.

He stops. "Okay, wait here. I'll be right back."

As if I could go anywhere with my eyes burning and my face covered in sludge.

I hold out my hands for the towel when I feel him return, his body close enough for me to reach out and touch, but he steps closer, ignoring my outstretched hands and begins wiping my face with the towel.

"I think it's safe to open your eyes," he says.

I blink them open, and it's like he's an angel, bathed in light as the sun sets behind him. I go to wipe some of the mud from the corner of my mouth, and he stops me.

"Let me get it . . ." He reaches up and wipes a glob away. It falls to the ground with a wet *plop*.

I wince.

"Do I even want to ask?" He glances past me to where my golf cart has sunk even lower in the mud.

I just look up at him, a grotesque mud monster from the depths.

He grins.

"Why are you smiling?" I ask, because honestly, *why* is he smiling?

He raises his eyebrows. "I knew you were going to be fun to have around."

Shut up.

Shut up right now.

Shut up your stupid beautiful stupid face.

CHAPTER 14

HOSE WATER IS COLD. BUT at least the mud is gone.

Thank goodness my shirt isn't white.

I'm not sure I'll ever live this day down, but at least I got the mud out of my ear. Most of it anyway.

I spend most of the afternoon in my room, unpacking and setting everything up. It's nice to have a space of my own, and without much trying, it's already feeling like an escape.

My phone dings with a new possible love match, followed by a text from Maya: This one is a doctor! Go out with him, Rosie.

I send her a thumbs-down emoji and toss my phone on the bed as my stomach growls, reminding me that I haven't eaten today. It's moved past the point of, *"Hey, you should eat,"* into, *"WHY ARE YOU DOING THIS TO ME!?"*

I make a mental note to pick up some snacks as I walk into the kitchen and open the pantry. I wonder if I could steal a bowl of cereal. I could pay her back tomorrow. There are at least five boxes in here—the sugary kind, nothing healthy. Somehow, after meeting Daisy, this doesn't surprise me. And somehow, it makes me love her more.

I reach for a box of Cinnamon Toast Crunch when a voice stops me.

"That's not yours."

I spin around and see her standing in the doorway.

I pull my hand back. "Oh! Sorry, I missed dinner and haven't had a chance to—"

She cracks a smile. "Just kidding. You can eat whatever you want, but you might want to head over to the Commons."

I frown. "I thought it was closed."

"Special circumstances." She leans her head into the room a little more. "*Your* special circumstances," she adds, as if I don't know that my golf cart hijinks are the *circumstances* she's referring to.

When I don't move, she walks over to me, drapes her arm around my shoulder, and gives me a tug toward the door. "You didn't get a proper Sunset Hills welcome. One thing you should know about the staff here, Rosie"—she stops and looks at me—"is that we take care of each other."

The words land. It's like a clenched fist relaxes.

My friends back home take care of each other too, but it's been a long time since I've really been a part of that circle. I miss it. In the past several years, I've found no suitable replacement. I've done the networking and the mingling. I know a lot of people. But I'm not part of a group. There's no one to call when I feel down.

That thought stops me.

"Give me a second."

I head back into my room and find my phone, click open the group text, and start typing. The old Rosie—maybe the real Rosie—would've shared the crazy golf cart story with her friends. And being home made me realize how I've let my so-called failures steal that part of myself. I don't know how to make light of anything because every mess-up feels like proof that I'm a disaster.

But I don't want to keep myself to myself. Not from them. Not anymore.

ROSIE: Hey guys! I'm getting settled. My cottage is amazing! I have my own mailbox! I've got a story for

FaceTime later—it's a doozy! Classic Rosie! 😳 Miss you guys.

TAYLOR: Oh, I LOVE classic Rosie stories!! So glad you're having fun!

MARNIE: Does this story involve wildlife? I swear all classic Rosie stories involve wildlife.

MAYA: I'm not sure anything can top the attack of the killer goose! 😂

ROSIE: Heading out for a bit, but I'll text again soon! 💜

"You ready?" Daisy calls from the other room.

"Yep, coming!"

I tuck my phone in my pocket as I slip the green Crocs on and meet Daisy as she opens the door and walks out onto the porch.

She glances at my feet and grins. "Your shoes were a casualty of the—"

"Yep," I cut her off.

"Well, those are, you know, a statement piece."

I shake my head and follow her down the steps, across the grass, and eventually into the building they call the Commons.

It's basically a large open room with a cement floor and rows of tables with benches for sitting. It's not fancy or grand, but there's something about it that feels homey and nostalgic. Like summer camp, which is a lot how this whole experience feels.

If summer camp had senior citizens and a golf cart–eating sinkhole.

"Come on, we're going this way." Daisy leads me through the Staff Only door and into the kitchen, where Booker is standing at the stove, cooking what looks like an omelet.

Connie is on the other side of a long silver counter, and Daisy walks over to a cupboard and pulls out a plate.

"What's this?" I stare at them—these perfect strangers—and this simple act of kindness overwhelms me.

"You're hungry, right?" Booker looks at me, and I nod. "Hopefully you like omelets."

He's making me an omelet? "You're making me an omelet?" It takes a second for the scene in front of me to register.

A bagel pops up in the toaster, and Connie uses a pair of wooden tongs to pull it out and put it on the plate. "You can doctor that up however you like." She slides it across the counter in my direction. "Jelly and cream cheese and all the fixin's are in the fridge." Her watch beeps. "Oh shoot. That's my cue. I have to skedaddle. My husband is taking me out to the movies. It's one he let me pick—that man might just get lucky tonight!" She waggles her eyebrows.

I let out one loud laugh—more surprise than humor.

Connie does a little shoulder shimmy, then calls out, "Booker, lock up when you leave."

"I always do," he says.

"I'm going to pretend I didn't hear that," she says. "This after-hours smorgasbord is a onetime thing. For Rosie."

Daisy and Booker exchange a knowing look, and for the first time since I got here, I want to be in on their inside jokes.

The door swings open as Connie is about to walk out, and she lets out a dramatic gasp. "What in tarnation?!"

A heavyset man wearing a backward baseball cap lifts his hands and takes a step into the room, away from Connie. "Sorry, Connster."

She swats him on the arm and then eyes him. "Louie, good heavens! What are you doing in here?"

He tosses a quick glance at Booker, then shrugs. "Uh, came to get a snack?"

"The Commons is *closed* after dinner," she says. "Do y'all raid this kitchen regularly?"

They all look away, like they rehearsed it.

"Of course not, Connie," Louie says, then quickly adds, "hardly ever."

She shakes her head and points a finger. "You're lucky I've got a hot date and don't have time to deal with this right now." The door swings closed behind her as she makes her exit, and from outside she shouts again, "Lock up when you leave!"

"You got it, boss!" Louie shouts and then grins as Booker walks over to the counter and expertly flips the omelet onto my plate.

"Man, I thought she was already gone." Louie's eyes are wide.

Booker shakes his head, but he's smiling. "You're going to get us in trouble."

"She said we could be in here!" Louie raises both palms.

"Just this time," Daisy says. "As a welcome to Rosie. She doesn't know about the other times."

"Well, she didn't know," Booker says. "She does now."

"Sorry, man," Louie says. Then he looks at me. "And you are Rosie, I presume?" He does a strange little bow, and I think I've met a kindred spirit.

"I am," I say.

"I'm Louie." His gaze dips to my feet. "Rad shoes!"

In spite of the flush of embarrassment that rushes to my cheeks, I instantly like Louie too. This is starting to be a trend.

Louie glances at Daisy. "Hey."

Her cheeks turn pink, and her face brightens. "Hey, Louie."

Booker and I are both watching them stare at each other for what becomes at least ten seconds, then Louie clears his throat and walks over to the refrigerator. "Did you make me an omelet, Booker?"

"No. Only Rosie."

Only Rosie. Yeah, I'm in trouble.

Booker looks at me and nods toward my plate. "You should eat before it gets cold." He reaches into a drawer, pulls out a fork, and holds it out in my direction.

I take it and smile. "Thank you for making this."

He leans in. "Figured it'd taste better than mud."

"I heard about that!" Louie laughs. "Booker said it was the funniest—" When he turns and sees my face, he snaps his jaw shut and adopts a solemn expression. "I have always said those golf carts can be treacherous." He picks up an empty metal pan and starts pulling stuff from the refrigerator. "I'm making a sandwich. Does anyone want one?"

"Most of us don't eat two dinners," Daisy says.

"Well, then most of you are missing out." He winks at Daisy, and she smiles. It's like watching a strange rom-com from the inside.

"Louie . . . is . . . one of the nurses," she says as a measured introduction. "He's great with the residents."

"That's *head* nurse, ma'am." He piles ham onto a piece of bread, then adds tomatoes, lettuce, cheese, mayo, and mustard as I slowly chew my very tasty omelet. He looks at me. "And Booker told me all about you, so no need to give me your résumé."

"Oh, he did?" I glance at Booker, who is washing the pan he cooked my omelet in. "Funny, because he doesn't know anything about me."

Booker looks at me. "I'm a very patient man."

At the mention of his proposed plan, I stop chewing. Because for some reason, it doesn't seem like such a crazy idea anymore.

Ask questions and answer honestly. I can do that. Right?

Louie interrupts my swooning with a laugh. "Can't believe you didn't know you took a job with a bunch of old people. How did that happen?"

Because I was desperate, I think but don't say.

"But you are going to stay, right, Rosie?" Daisy pulls a carton of ice cream out of the freezer and scoops some into a bowl. "Like, you're not freaked out enough to leave, right?"

"Ooh! Scoop me some!" Louie says.

Daisy pulls out another bowl. "For a health-care professional, you have the worst eating habits I've ever seen."

Louie rubs his ample belly. "I'm built for comfort, not for speed." He sticks out his tongue and gyrates, and she just shakes her head.

Booker leans against the counter and watches me the same way he did at the bus station before we'd ever spoken a word to each other. And as Daisy and Louie continue bantering, we both start to smile, as if we have our own silent conversation happening in the footnotes.

After a beat, Booker asks, "You are staying, right?" It's almost like he hadn't considered I might not until Daisy said something, but now that the question was out there, he needed an answer.

Or maybe he's just making conversation because he's friendly. That's more likely.

Daisy and Louie stop talking and look at me.

I shrug. "I already unpacked my stuff, so now I have to stay."

Daisy's grin is wide. "Oh good! Oh my word, we're going to have the best summer!"

"I'm not so sure," I say. "That Belinda lady doesn't think I can do the job." And I'm afraid she might be right.

There's a collective groan and shift at the mention of her name.

"I'd tell you her nickname, but we just met and I don't know how you feel about swearing," Louie says, fishing a spoon out of a drawer.

I laugh a little to myself. "What's her story? She told me I wasn't cut out for this."

"Who cares what Belinda thinks?" Daisy says with a scoff. "She's been miserable since she got here. She was like, Miss Maryland or something in the 1970s, and she treats everyone like we're all her little minions."

"She was supposed to direct the show this summer," Booker says with less emotion that Daisy.

I frown. "What happened?"

"The residents who do the shows complained," Louie says. "Pretty much all of them."

My eyes go wide. Ouch.

"She's not very nice." Daisy's tone implies she's underselling Belinda's lack of warmth. "So nobody wanted her in charge. She does have sway, though, because people are afraid of her. Everyone who complained did it anonymously."

I groan. "What if they complain about me?"

"Just . . . be yourself." Booker is watching me again, and I wish I knew what he was thinking.

Daisy's eyes widen. "Yeah, Rosie! Just be yourself. You're going to be great."

"Thanks." My smile is lame as I pick up my bagel and take a bite. "Connie said she was going to get me a team, so at least I won't be totally on my own."

I don't miss the crisscrossing oh-crap looks flying around the room.

"What?" I ask nervously.

"Oh, yeah—"

"No, nothing—"

Daisy and Louie are tripping over themselves.

"What is it?" I ask again.

The room goes silent.

"It's *nothing*," Daisy says. "I am sure Connie is going to assemble the Avengers of theatre crew just for this production."

"If she wants to save the theatre, she will." Louie polishes off the first half of his sandwich. He eats like someone is going to take his food away.

I frown. "What do you mean?"

"She didn't tell you?" Louie shakes his head. "That Connster. She's sneaky."

"They're strapped," Booker says. "Funding for Sunset—staff, grounds, upkeep, amenities—is all paid for by the residents, but the theatre isn't part of the overall operating budget. For the last five years they've been trying to keep the theatre going with fewer resources."

"It started with a gift back in the day, and usually it operates from the investments of that grant," Daisy adds. "But unfortunately . . ."

"Old folks theatre doesn't sell that great," Louie says through a new big bite of his sandwich. "Shocker."

"I heard that's part of why they brought you in," Daisy says. "They're hoping a professional can, you know, fix things."

I set my half-eaten bagel back down. "So, wait, they brought me in to try and—"

"Save the theatre," Booker finishes my sentence for me.

"No pressure!" Louie chuckles.

"Save the theatre? What is this, *The Muppets* movie?" I hear the exasperation in my own voice.

Louie points at me. "*Totally* underrated. Jason Segel was hilarious in that."

"Right?!" I agree. I take a risk and bust out the chorus from "Man or Muppet," and before I can even second-guess my decision, Louie joins in without hesitating. We sing loud, off-key, arms out, overdramatic.

After only four lines, we start laughing, and he slings an arm around my neck. "Hey, Book, can we keep her?"

Daisy looks at Booker. "Oh no. There's two of them now."

I wonder if all of the staff is like this. Instant friends.

It's nice. Really nice.

I pat Louie's arm, and he goes back to eating.

"Guys, I'm not sure I can pull this off. I mean, if this is some kind of last-ditch effort, we might actually be in trouble."

"You're a pro, Rosie." Daisy has somehow produced a jar of hot fudge, and she's now drizzling it over the ice cream—and Louie already has his hand out, *gimme* style. "You'll totally figure it out."

"How do you know that?" I ask, half laughing. "I might be terrible."

"Nuh-uh, urr th' bess!" Louie says with a mouth full of food.

Daisy rolls her eyes.

"That needs marshmallow," Louie says with a nod to Daisy's bowl.

"Marshmallows?" She frowns.

"Nah, *marshmallow*. The gooey kind. Back me up, Book." He holds up his hand in a high five. Booker leaves it hanging, so Louie slaps his own hand and gives a thumbs-up.

"Always marshmallow," Booker says coolly.

Louie walks over to a cupboard and pulls down a large canister. I half watch as he opens it, starting a debate with Daisy about the best sundae toppings.

I can't concentrate enough to argue the merit of a simple butterscotch drizzle on vanilla because this is all setting in. The easy way I fit in with these people, juxtaposed against the daunting task of saving a theatre with a cast of elderly performers.

This theatre program was important to somebody—enough that they gifted Sunset Hills with the money for a building and a director and a program.

Have I just walked into an impossible situation? Direct a show? Save the theatre?

I might be freaking out a little bit.

"There are nuts by the soft-serve machine," Louie says.

"Nuts on ice cream is a bad idea," Daisy says.

"Always nuts," Booker says.

She pauses for a few seconds, then relents. "Fine. I'll try anything once."

"Anything?" Louie's eyebrows pop up and he follows her out of the kitchen, prompting an, "Oh, for the love . . ." from Daisy.

And now I'm standing in the room alone with Booker. Thankfully, Booker is not a mind reader, and I am an actor.

I paint on a smile. "Thanks again for the omelet. And for, you know, saving me from the mud pit." I avoid his gaze. "Very . . . heroic."

"You're freaking out right now, aren't you?" His arms are crossed over his chest, and he's still leaning against the counter, still looking at me, making me think maybe he *is* a mind reader.

Or maybe I'm a terrible actor.

"No," I say, keenly aware of the potential spiral. "I'm not. It's a lot, sure, but I'm . . . super great. I'm a first-time director who's been brought in to save a beloved theatre program *practically* by myself, and no matter what I do, my *Cinderella* is going to have one foot in the grave." I let out a loud sigh.

He smirks and rolls his eyes. "Theatre people are so dramatic."

I think about the whole let's-tell-each-other-everything deal he tried to strike with me, and I'm grateful I had the good sense not to shake on that. Because aside from everything I'm thinking about Booker Hayes, there is a lot here that I don't want to confess out loud.

That I'm in over my head.

That they've put their precious theatre in the wrong hands.

That the whole idea of eating contraband omelets in the Commons with Booker, Daisy, and Louie every night for the rest of the summer is oddly comforting in a way I did not expect.

And even though I'm overwhelmed and a little freaked out, I

think I actually want to be here. And that simply does not make sense.

....

TAYLOR: Rosie! Tell us more about your new job!
MAYA: And I see you've been getting lots of messages on Love Match! Have you responded?
MARNIE: We need the update on that story you were going to share.

I hesitate. I planned to tell them all about MudGate, but as my insecurity about this job mounts, I now have to fight the instinct to make it sound great here . . .

Wait. No. I'm not going to do that. I tap out a reply and hit Send.

ROSIE: It's great. :/ Literally drove a golf cart into the mud earlier today.

I send a photo of myself covered in mud, which Booker took while my eyes were closed and without my permission.

MARNIE: Oh. My. GOSH.
MAYA: What in the world??
TAYLOR: Only you, Ro! LOL
ROSIE: It's a long story, but I'm getting settled, and auditions are in three days. Wish me luck!
TAYLOR: Brilliant women make their own luck. <3
MAYA: Go get 'em, queen!

Things I *could* tell my friends but don't:
That I've met some really fun friends.

That the theatre smells familiar.

That I'm helping save elderly theatre. My brain thinks *resuscitate* elderly theatre, but that sounds cruel. And hilarious.

That having my own cottage makes me feel more like an adult.

That I don't need Maya's stupid dating app because there is a *man* here who is making my stomach flutter.

And that I have very mixed feelings about that last one.

CHAPTER 15

MONDAY MORNING, I SIT STRAIGHT up in bed, eyes wide, like someone poked me with a cattle prod.

I also feel like I swallowed a jar of butterflies.

Today I will meet my team, and tomorrow—auditions. Once we start auditions, we're off and running. There's no turning back.

Once I'm showered and ready, I stare at my reflection in the bathroom mirror. "Yep. We're doing this," I say out loud.

"Heck yeah, we are!" Daisy calls from somewhere in the cottage, and I realize I really need to be quieter when pep-talking myself.

She appears in the doorway behind me. "You look a lovely shade of pale green this morning."

I give a double thumbs-up.

"Oh stop, you're going to be so great!" She grins. "Unless you're not, in which case Belinda will eat you alive."

I groan. "Your pep talk needs work."

"But *everyone else* wants you to crush it," Daisy says, wiggling her pointer fingers at herself. "So. You know. Just go do that."

"I guess . . ." I pause, trying to make it make sense. "It's that same feeling I get whenever I get onstage or land a role or stand in front of a crowd. No matter the prep, seconds before it's my line or my solo or my scene, I have no idea what comes next. But then I open my mouth and the right words come out and everything's fine."

"And that'll happen here too. You'll open your mouth, and the right words will come out." She squeezes my shoulder. "Everything will be fine." A little shrug. "Besides, you know way more than anyone else here," she says. "So just fake it till you make it."

I smile as I roll my eyes. "Ooh, such a cliché."

"Hey," she says. "It's cliché because it's true." She narrows her eyes. "Look at me. I can do a better pep talk."

I turn, tilt my head, and brace myself.

"You don't have to have it all figured out today. Just focus on what's in front of you." She takes me by the shoulders. "You're smart and capable and crazy talented at all this acting and dancing and music stuff."

"You know we just met a couple of days ago," I say.

She shakes her head as if to say that's ridiculous. "Pssh . . ." She waves me off. "It's true. You can't go in that room defeated, Rosie. Be the Riveter! Yes, we can!" She makes a muscle like the famous poster in the mirror.

I try to conceal a smile, but I fail, which Daisy is visibly pleased about.

"Do you want to get breakfast before you go?" she asks.

"Nah," I say. "I don't think I can eat. Too nervous."

"You have no reason to be nervous." She pulls a granola bar from a box in the cupboard and tosses it to me. "At least take this. Just in case."

I take it, knowing I'll most likely need it later. "Wish me luck," I say, as she picks up her huge bowl of cereal.

"Avoid the mud, you'll be fine." Daisy grins at me and shovels a bite of Froot Loops into her mouth. "Crush it, Riveter!" She poses again like the wartime hero and sends me on my way, wondering how, in just a short time, Daisy has managed to become someone I think I'd like to have in my life forever.

I arrive at the theatre an hour before the meeting is scheduled to begin and find Connie standing on the sidewalk in front of the theatre. She bustles over as I park my new golf cart.

"Good morning, Rosie!" she says. "I see you got your new golf cart. Stay on the path from here on out. Sound good?" She claps her hands together. "It's a beautiful day, don't you think?"

It is a stunning day. Sunny and temperate with a stunning landscape in the distance behind the building. A few lazy clouds, a gentle breeze, and shockingly few insects.

I spent most of yesterday watching, reading, and listening to all things *Cinderella*, figuring out what I'm ideally looking for in each role.

Difficult, considering the ideal cast will not actually be auditioning today.

I get out of the cart. "Connie, you didn't mention this show is a last-ditch effort to save the Sunset Players."

Her face falls, then tries to make the best of it by picking up its corners, then settles on a pained smile.

I pull my bag out and prop my sunglasses up on my head so Connie can see my serious expression.

"I'm sorry, Rosie. I didn't want to scare you off." A wince. "Are you okay with this?"

"There's just a lot more riding on this show's success than I thought." I sigh. *And I don't need yet another failure on my record.*

A thought hits me, and before I can think about whether it's the right thing to say, I ask, "Although, with all the other programs here, do you really *need* theatre for the senior citizens?"

I try *not* to imply that it's a tiny bit ridiculous—this whole idea that we're about to cast a young and beautiful Cinderella and her stepsisters from the residents here.

I can tell by Connie's reaction that my question hit her the wrong way.

She frowns and looks down, like she wants to say something but she's not sure she should. Finally, she straightens her shoulders and meets my eyes. "Do you know how much joy people have gotten from these shows, Rosie?" Her voice is laced with meaning. "These shows are good for the seniors who participate in them, but also for the community and their families. No, we don't get large crowds, but people do come out and show their support."

She looks off at the theatre building. "Do you know what some of them come in here with?"

She looks back at me. "Nothing."

It dawns on me that I haven't stopped and thought once about the people here as . . . people. With lives and challenges and stories.

She goes on. "Most aren't happy or hopeful. Their lives are . . ." She pauses, appearing to search for the right words. "Not always easy. Some of them don't have visitors. At all. Ever. Some of them feel they don't have anything else to live for. They're just hanging around, waiting to die. And for some of them, the community they build while doing one of these shows literally keeps them alive. And I know that sounds dramatic, but it's the truth."

I nod. "I understand." I instantly feel like a jerk.

Elite theatre people are a dime a dozen—I just never thought I was one of them.

Do better, Rosie.

"This program has been so good for so many people, Rosie," she says. "It's important. And if we can't save it, well"—she looks away—"the impact will be noticeable, that's all."

I'm ashamed and embarrassed that I've made this job all about me. I could argue that I didn't know anyone felt this way, but the truth is, I never even stopped to wonder.

"You're absolutely right. You'll have my best, Connie, I promise."

The weight of Connie's words settle.

Like Louie said, no pressure.

Connie must see this register on my face, and she moves closer. "You're going to be wonderful. *So* good. We have faith in you. *I* have faith in you."

I meet her eyes, and in them I find absolute confidence.

In me.

"You really think I'm the person, don't you?" I say.

Connie pats my shoulder, then turns toward the building and starts walking alongside me. "I don't believe in accidents. So if you're here, then you're here for a reason. And I'm betting there is something here for you too."

"Something for me? Here?" I try not to laugh.

"Maybe so. I can't wait to find out what it is!" She claps her hands together, then reaches out to take mine, leading me toward the theatre. "I've assembled your team. They're waiting for you in the auditorium."

My team. Right.

Because I'm in charge.

When someone has a question about how things are supposed to go, they'll be coming to me. If someone has an issue with the role they got, they'll be coming to me. If someone's costume doesn't fit, if they can't make it to a rehearsal, if they've fallen and they can't get up, they'll be coming to me.

And they'll expect me to have the answers.

Fake it till you make it.

I mean, that's literally the career I've chosen.

Piece of cake.

We walk down to the front of the auditorium, and I get into character. I'm a strong, capable, confident director who knows what she's doing. I'm fearless and ready to take on this project, regardless of what the outcome might be.

But then I see the "team" Connie has assembled. Yet somehow, it's like they've all been studying the script and I'm walking into a cold read.

I look around, reminding myself that I'm good at cold reads. I've got this.

First there's Arthur, the curmudgeonly facilities caretaker who is disinterested and scowling. Then there are two older women, and next to them, I'm stunned to discover, is Booker.

Connie shuffles around me and claps her hands together like the activities director on a cruise ship. "Good morning! I am absolutely thrilled you've all agreed to be a part of Rosie's creative team. Of course, we will need to recruit a few more people, but this is an excellent start."

"Why don't we begin by telling Rosie who you are?" Connie nods at a woman whose hair is pulled up in a loose bun. The woman is pretty in a girl-next-door sort of way, if the girl next door were in her late sixties.

"I'm Veronica," the woman says. "Connie's asked me to work with you on the choreography. I handle the adult tap classes here, so maybe we could throw a tap number into the show?"

"Oh yeah, maybe!" I force a smile. There isn't a tap number in *Cinderella*.

"Maybe we could turn one of the songs into a tap number? Maybe the fairy godmother taps when she sings 'Bibbidi-Bobbidi-Boo'?"

My heart skips. Do the members of my team know this is *not* the Disney version of *Cinderella*? "We can totally talk about it!"

I don't want to crush their creativity right out of the gate.

A stout, elderly woman with short gray hair and a pair of thick horn-rimmed glasses hanging from a chain around her neck steps forward. "I'm Ginny," she says loudly as she puts the glasses on, presumably to inspect me. Which is what she appears to be doing—through a scowl—when she says, "I've been doing the costumes. I don't like people complaining, so we can put Belinda on notice right now. I'm sure you'll want her to be the lead, but she will wear whatever ball gown I give her. I don't care whether it's in 'her color palette' or not."

"Oh, I don't pre-cast," I say. "Belinda isn't promised anything."

She glances at Veronica, raises her eyebrows, and then turns back to me. "You just might be okay."

If I had to guess, Ginny was definitely part of the group that complained about Belinda potentially being in charge.

Before I can formulate a response, Connie steps forward. "I think you already met Arthur?"

Arthur harrumphs. I glare at him, hoping to communicate, *"I'm not scared of you, buddy,"* even though I totally am.

"He'll be your stage manager." Next, Connie motions toward Booker, who is dressed in track pants and a Sunset Hills sweatshirt. "And, of course, Booker is here to help with the sets."

I look at him, shaking my head slightly. "So you're on my team now."

He shrugs. "I can't come to auditions tomorrow, but"—and then he meets my eyes—"yeah, I'm on your team."

"So that means you have to do what I tell you," I playfully jab.

He smiles and looks at Ginny. "Yeah, looks like it."

At that moment, the back door to the auditorium opens. Everyone turns, and their expectant expressions turn to confusion. Because standing there, backlit by the natural light in the lobby, is a dark-haired teenager with chipping black nail polish, wearing ripped jeans and Converse high-top sneakers.

"Is that . . . Dylan?" Connie asks.

"What is she doing here?" Ginny practically shouts.

I smile. "She came."

"But why?" Ginny asks.

I glance at them. "Because I asked her to be on the team."

There's a pause, and then Ginny plops down in her chair. "Well, she's not doing costumes."

I hear the confused murmurs as I step out into the aisle, passing Booker on the way. He gives me a wink of approval. Dylan has stopped moving and is now standing at the back of the auditorium.

I walk up to her and make sure I don't look happy as I say, "You came," as nonchalantly as possible.

Dylan rolls her eyes. "Whatever. I didn't have anything else to do today."

I nod. "Okay, but you came."

Dylan glares at me. "Are you going to make it weird?"

"Do I look like the kind of person who would make it weird?"

A beat. And then, "Yes."

I do my best not to crack a smile. "Listen, you should know, if you're joining the team, you're *joining* the team."

She scowls. "Duh."

"I mean, you can't bail on us." I turn and look at the others. "The show has to be a priority this summer. There's a lot riding on this."

She crosses her arms over her chest and huffs out a sigh. "A lot riding on a performance of *Cinderella* put on by a bunch of old people?"

I put an arm on Dylan's shoulder and turn back to the group. "Everyone, this is Dylan."

They all stare at her as if they're waiting for a punch line that isn't coming.

"She's, uh"—I'm just spitballing now—"she's going to be in charge of hair and makeup."

"A senior Cinderella with black lipstick," Ginny coos.

I give the others a nervous smile. Booker steps out into the aisle and extends a hand toward Dylan. She looks at his hand suspiciously, and then, after a beat, she reaches out and shakes it.

"Welcome to the team," he says.

The team. As I pan across the motley crew assembled here, I have to wonder if Cinderella will ever make it to her ball.

....

ROSIE: Tonight I broke into the Commons and ate grilled cheese with my housemate Daisy and a couple of the guys who work here. It reminded me of the time we had that lock-in at the high school and we caught Maya in the kitchen with the entire tray of brownies. 😂

It made me miss you guys, and I just wanted you to know.

MAYA: If I remember right, you all plopped down on the floor with me and ate your fair share of those brownies.

TAYLOR: Now I want brownies. Think I can send Aaron to the store?

ROSIE: You're pregnant, so yes!

MARNIE: I miss carbs.

CHAPTER 16

IF MY LIFE WERE A movie—and it absolutely should be, and Ellie Kemper should play me—this would be the point in that movie where the viewer gets to watch a montage of old people auditioning for a performance of *Cinderella*.

It would be a comedy. And a tragedy.

From the man who got up and told dirty jokes for five minutes straight, to the woman who did a slow interpretative dance to the song "Defying Gravity" from the musical *Wicked*, to the brother-sister duo who did a magic act that reminded me a lot of a child covering his eyes and shouting, "Can't see me! Can't see me!"

It's almost noon, and I'm hungry *and* discouraged. I didn't expect Broadway-caliber auditions here, but I thought they would at least be able to sing. And, based on the way everyone talked about how well-loved the shows are, I thought there would be more people trying out.

The stage clears, and as a ventriloquist and her inappropriately dressed puppet make their way up the aisle, I slowly put my head in my hands.

Connie bustles in from the back. She leans in and quietly whispers, "So! How's it going?"

Veronica leans in and whisper-yells, "They're terrible. Terrible! Even the best choreographer in the world wouldn't be able to work with this."

"Oh." Connie gives me a desperate look. "Is that true?"

I glance over the list of people who've auditioned. "I mean . . . it's not . . . *not* true."

"Are you ready for me to start?" The woman has set her ventriloquist dummy on a tall stool, and I can't wait to hear what she's going to make this thing say.

I hold up a finger. "One sec!"

Connie takes the list from me and looks it over. "I don't understand. Where are the regulars? Evelyn? Sadie? What about the Margies? They all said they were auditioning."

"Please tell me there are a bunch of women that live here that are all named Margie," I kid.

"Oh, you've met them?" Connie says brightly.

I stifle a laugh. "You're kidding."

Connie continues, almost as an aside. "They formed a little club. It's actually really sweet. They always do the shows." She looks over the list. "But I don't see their names anywhere on here."

"This is all we've got," I say. "I met some of them Friday when Booker showed me around, and they said they'd be here, but so far, we've mostly had—" I motion to the stage, and the woman with the dummy nods as if I've given her the go-ahead to start, and launches into her act.

"Well, hi there, Miss Loretta! How are you today?"

Arthur mutters an "Oh my dear Lord in heaven," just before the woman starts to make the puppet's mouth move, and at least I can claim that he and I have something in common—a disdain for puppets.

"Sexy as ever, Miss Kathleen!"

"You do look awfully sexy, Miss Loretta. Did you dress up for something special?"

"I'm on the prowl," the dummy says. "I'm looking to find me a may-un!"

"A may-un?" The woman repeats in a dramatic and drawn-out voice.

"I've got needs, Miss Kathleen," the dummy says, though it seems Kathleen has given up on not moving her mouth. "A whole list of needs."

Kathleen pulls a small piece of paper from the pocket of the dummy's bikini bottoms as Ginny leans closer to me and barks, "What did she just say?"

I leap to my feet. "Oh my gosh! Yes! No! Great! Thank you! Incredible job. We'll . . . uh, we'll let you know!"

"No. *Shot.*" Dylan gasps and laughs, and I see she filmed the entire thing.

"Dylan! Don't you dare post that," I snap.

She doesn't move. "This one's just for me. That literally made my whole summer."

The old woman looks unfazed. "Do you want me to grab my other puppets? I have a sexy taxi driver, a sexy loan shark, a sexy Bill Gates . . ."

"Oh, wow, okay"—I'm stuttering now—"that's a lot of sexy puppets. You know, I think we're good. We're, you know . . . We'll let you know, okay?"

She grins at me and coos, "We'll be waiting . . ."

I shudder, then slump in my chair.

"Oh my word," Connie breathes.

"Horrible, terrible, awful," Veronica says.

"It's been hilarious." Dylan smirks, tapping on her phone with a wry grin on her face.

Connie slowly hands the paper back to me. "I can see you've . . . *ahem* . . . got your work cut out for you."

I take the paper. "Yeah, it's been interesting, to say the least."

She frowns. "None of the people from the last show are on this list. I don't understand."

"Maybe putting me in charge made them change their mind," I say, thinking I realistically can't handle this. "Maybe they don't want an outsider directing their musical?"

"It's Belinda." Ginny points her finger in my direction.

"I thought nobody liked Belinda," I say dumbly.

"Typical mean girl. Nobody likes her, but everyone fears her," Ginny says. "They're afraid auditioning for your show will make her mad."

"Seriously?" This is more drama than high school. I sigh.

"Maybe you need to show them that you know what you're doing," Veronica says. "Do you have one of those demo reels? We could play it on the TVs all over the campus."

"She doesn't have one," Connie says. "I already looked. She did play a dead body on *Law & Order*, though."

"Cool," Dylan says.

"A dead body?" Arthur scoffs, waving a hand in the air like he can't be bothered with me anymore. "That's the acting equivalent of a garden slug."

I put my hands on my temples and rub slow circles. "I can't even convince a bunch of old people in a retirement community that I know what I'm doing."

"Oh, stop it."

I drop my hands and look up to find Arthur leaning across the table, glaring at me.

"So it's a setback. You've done live theatre, haven't you?" His acerbic tone catches me off guard. "You should know this will be the first of *many* setbacks you're going to have during the course of this show."

I sit straighter. "Yes? And?"

He stands. "You're the director. Suck it up and figure it out. And if that means going door-to-door and inviting people to audition, then that's what it means."

Connie adds, "And if it means going into the cafeteria and singing karaoke in order to convince people you know what you're doing, then *that's* what it means."

"Epic," Dylan says.

Connie brightens, like she's just solved an impossible equation. "Oh my word, yes! This is the best idea!"

"What is? Karaoke?" I protest. "I thought that was just a metaphor."

I can see she's already forming a plan in her head by the way she's talking with her hands, like she's setting the scene. "Auditions continue tomorrow. I say we pack it up today, then make this happen tomorrow at lunch."

I can see this idea is picking up steam.

"We take the portable speaker that Daisy uses for karaoke night and you perform"—a big flourish with the hands now—"right in the middle of the lunch rush. When you finish, you do a plug for auditions!"

"Wait, what?" My heart races.

"It could work," Ginny says, thoughtfully but not quietly.

"Do you want to do a song with a tap solo?" Veronica asks. "We could do a duet!"

Performing on a stage with the lights blurring any actual faces in the audience is one thing. Performing under the flickering fluorescent lighting of a retirement community dining hall is something else entirely.

You can see them. It's not ideal.

"This is a great idea," Connie says. "I can send out a newsletter blast tonight."

"Oh no, don't do that," I say, but nobody hears me.

"Or maybe not," Connie says, but not because I protested. She's deep in thought. "We want the element of surprise."

"Do we, though?" I ask quietly. "Won't that be bad for their hearts or something?"

"I agree," Veronica says, not listening. "Show everyone that Rosie is the person to lead us *and* the show. There's no buy-in because they don't know her."

Ginny harrumphs. "And because Belinda is ruining it for everyone. She's just jealous, Rosie, because nobody wanted her to direct. I swear, that woman is—"

"Do you care about this show, Rosie Waterman?" Arthur cuts her off and is still looking at me. I'm beginning to think the only facial expression he has is a glare.

I casually wonder if he lives in a garbage can next to Mr. Snuffleupagus.

"Of course I do." Right?

He shrugs, but his expression doesn't change. "Then prove it."

"You're on board with this too?" I ask in disbelief. When Arthur doesn't respond, I groan. "So you want me to go interrupt everyone's meal with a performance in the middle of the day. In the dining hall. Tomorrow."

They all look at me, wearing a collective expression that seems to say, *"Yes!"*

I let out a heavy sigh, thankful that at least Booker had patients and isn't here for any of this. "Fine. What song should I sing?"

CHAPTER 17

THE NEXT DAY, AFTER CONNIE worked her magic to get the karaoke machine set up, I'm sitting, then standing, then sitting, then pacing outside the dining hall, wondering if it's too late to walk to the bus station. I don't even need to pack a suitcase. I'll happily abandon everything I own to get out of this.

"I thought you were, like, a professional at this." Dylan is standing next to me, arms folded. "I mean, you *were* a corpse on a major television show."

I shoot her a look. "*Way* different. This isn't my normal audience. Or venue. Or . . . anything. Nothing about this is normal."

"Well, you heard the old guy. Suck it up."

"You say 'the old guy' as if that doesn't describe ninety-five percent of the people here."

"There's also that hot guy you keep staring at," she says. "The one who drove you around the first day you got here."

I glance at her.

Dylan stares back without a hint of expression. Without breaking eye contact, she pulls out her phone, taps a few buttons, and points the camera at me.

"Dylan, if you even think—"

She cuts me off. "Oh, don't worry, this is just for me." I swear that girl doesn't blink.

I grit my teeth and hit the heels of my hands against my thighs. The mere mention of Booker has me even more on edge.

I purposely didn't mention Connie's little plan last night when he and Louie sat down at our table during family dinner. Is it too much to hope he might miss the memo on my performance?

I peek into the dining hall where Connie is tapping on the microphone on one side of the room, scanning the crowd for any sign that the "hot guy" is there, but it's hard to see the whole room from where I'm standing.

This is what I do. It's who I am. Why am I nervous about this? Because there's more riding on it?

"I don't know if I can do this."

I turn to go, but Dylan blocks me, still holding up her phone, still recording me. "Don't be a chicken."

I smile, reach up, and gently place a hand on her phone, covering the camera, and she gives an "Oh, fine," and clicks the phone off.

The door behind her opens and Daisy rushes in. Louie is right behind her. I watch the door for several long seconds and feel myself relax when it slowly closes and Booker isn't with them.

"Oh no. What are you guys doing here?" I ask.

"We heard you're singing," Daisy says. "Connie sent out a mass email and announced it on the intercom in the clubhouse. 'Come see *Law & Order* alum and Sunset Players theatre director Rosie Waterman take the stage in our very own dining hall at lunch today!'" She holds her hands up in the air as she says this, like she's making a grand proclamation.

Strangely, I feel better that they're here.

Like a cheering section.

"You're in for a real treat." I chuckle to myself as I look at Dylan, who gives a thumbs-up without looking away from her phone.

Daisy squeezes my arm. "We're going to go get a good seat."

A good seat. In a cafeteria. Now I've heard everything.

They rush off, leaving me standing there, feeling the same inevitable feeling I experience before every performance.

The countdown has started, the curtain is going to go up, and the show is going to start whether I'm ready or not.

"None of these people will care if you suck," Dylan says. "Half of them won't be able to hear you and the other half of them won't even remember."

I cross my arms and glare at her, not bothering to explain that not everyone who lives here is actually senile. "I don't suck."

She makes a face at me and slowly brings the phone up, pointing it at me again. She shakes the phone at me as if to say, *"Prove it."*

"I know what you're doing, you little goblin." I narrow my eyes. "It won't work."

"Goblin. Huh. Solid choice." And then she smiles in approval. And she looks really pretty. And almost . . . sweet.

I stop short of telling her so because I don't want to make her feel awkward, but I do wish more people could see that side of her.

I start toward the dining hall.

"Hey, uh . . ." she calls after me.

I glance back over my shoulder. "Are you going to tell me you're not posting it and then post it?"

"No, I mean . . ." Her face looks serious. Not the cadaver-serious like normal; this is alive-serious.

She purses her lips for a moment, then says, "This might actually work."

Her words stop me. Her expression is honest. I half laugh. "Do you really care about this show?"

"No." She looks away. "But . . . you're the first person who's said more than, like, three words to me since I got here." Her gaze hits the floor. "And that includes my grandparents, who, like, live here."

"Oh." I go still.

"Whatever," she says. "I'm fine. I just thought you should, you know, make sure we get a cast or whatever."

A moment passes between us.

She said "we."

She brings her phone back up, filming. "At least this will give me something to watch later."

The door to the dining area flings open and Connie appears. "We're ready, Rosie!"

She's entirely too excited about this.

"I loaded up the song you gave me and I tested the volume, so you should be good to go."

I glance back at Dylan, whose face remains chaotic neutral, and I think it must've been really hard for her to admit to me what she did. Maybe not as hard as performing a musical number for a bunch of retirees who just want to enjoy their lunch, but still, pretty difficult.

I draw in a deep breath and stand in the back of the dining hall, realizing it's nothing like a cafeteria. It's more like a buffet-style restaurant, which makes this so much worse. There are people up and about, filling plates at a long counter with a variety of options, and people crowded around tables, eating, playing cards or chess, mingling—not at all asking to be entertained.

Hey, everyone, put down your applesauce and check out this song!

Connie is at the microphone. She taps it three times. "Yoo-hoo! Families and friends of Sunset Hills!"

Nobody stops talking. The clinking of silverware and conversations continue.

Which is embarrassing, not just for Connie but for me, because can we really expect them to stop talking during their lunch?

They didn't buy a ticket for this. There's no theatre etiquette here. Even dinner theatres let people eat in peace.

"People! People!" Connie raises her voice a little louder, pulls away the microphone, and looks at it as if she's not sure it's working.

Still no change in the chatter.

Finally, she reaches down and turns a knob all the way to the right, and much, *much* louder, she shouts, "Everyone! Listen!"

The mic peaks, causing some feedback, as the chatter goes quiet. Connie's face morphs from whatever possessed her in that moment back to her sweet Southern self.

"That's better," she says, reaching down and returning the knob to the middle position. "Y'all sure do love to chat, don't you?" She giggles, as if that could erase her outburst.

Arthur stomps toward me and hands me a second microphone. I start to thank him, but he grunts and walks away.

Connie starts talking about the last show the Sunset Players put on, and I let the ambient noise of the dining hall drown her out as I do my best to relax and remember how it feels to perform. Because if I'm going to do it, I need to really do it.

If we don't get anyone to audition, they'll cancel the show, and I'll have to move into my parents' basement, where I'll reenact my stint as the corpse on *Law & Order*, lying on a couch in a room with no windows.

I close my eyes and draw in a very deep breath, realizing that I'm not ready to leave this place.

"Ladies and gentlemen . . ." Connie pauses, I think for dramatic effect? And then she inhales a sharp breath and continues.

"Picture it—you're up on the stage, under the warmth of the theatre lights, a whole audience full of people who've come out just to see you." She pauses, and I let the words rest on my shoulders. I know exactly the feeling she's describing.

"Maybe you always dreamed of acting. Maybe it's something you did before you found us here at Sunset. Or maybe you want to do something that scares you, something that reminds you that you're *alive*." She holds out that last word on a long, dramatic whisper. "Well, my friends, I'm here to tell you that you are absolutely not too old, not here at Sunset Hills. Here, we want to *celebrate* the life you've already lived and help you enjoy all the many years you have left.

"But let's not take my word for it." Connie smiles brightly. "I want to introduce you all to our brand-new theatre director, who is here this summer straight from New York City and who is holding auditions *this very afternoon* for our next Sunset Players production: *Cinderella*!"

There's a collective *ooh* and a bit of chatter in response to Connie's dramatic speech.

She continues. "I'm going to let our new theatre director tell you all about that, but first we thought we'd give you a little preview of the caliber of performer you're going to be working with if you choose to join us this summer."

Connie looks out over the expectant faces, now visibly interested in the picture she's painted, and I have to hand it to her, she knows how to work a crowd.

"Without further ado, please help me welcome the sensational Rosie Waterman!"

There's a smattering of applause, and then the lights go out, which was Connie's idea that Arthur begrudgingly went along with.

I tell myself it doesn't matter if I'm performing in a dining hall of a retirement community or on the stage of a Broadway theatre—the effort should be the same.

I also say a silent prayer of thanks that my initial perusal of this place turned up no evidence that Booker is here right now.

Never mind that Dylan is still holding her phone up, ready to record.

I've had "Don't Rain on My Parade" from *Funny Girl* in my portfolio since college. And even though I'd never get the part in real life, that isn't going to stop me from performing it now.

I once had an acting professor who, in an attempt to help his students calm their audition nerves, told us not to look at it as a moment of being judged but rather as a chance to perform. For two minutes, I got to be Katherine in *Newsies*, Glinda in *Wicked*, Miss Honey in *Matilda*, whether anyone gave me permission to be or not.

So that's what I do.

The music begins, and as I walk toward the front of the room, I hold the microphone up, and I let myself forget all of it.

The years of rejections.

The circumstances that brought me here.

The fact that I'm homeless and this job is not at all what I thought it would be.

I remember why I picked this profession in the first place.

I just let myself *feel* the character. I let myself *become* the character. All of Fanny's hopes and dreams are mine. And I'll soak up some of her self-confidence too.

The first time I saw *Funny Girl*, I was ten years old. I came home sick from school, and my mom made me chicken soup and served it to me on a TV tray with cinnamon toast and ginger ale, and popped in an old DVD from her collection.

The second I saw the back of Barbra Streisand's leopard-print coat and hat as she stood outside the New Amsterdam Theatre with her name lit up on the marquee, I was hooked. Completely enraptured.

Here was this woman who'd been told her whole life all the reasons why she couldn't make it.

Nobody thought she was pretty enough for the stage.

Yet somehow, her belief in herself was enough, and she proved them all wrong.

That was the day I realized what I wanted to do. The day my own Broadway dreams were born. And every time I got knocked down, I'd rewatch *Funny Girl* and tell myself that nobody believed in Fanny either.

The first notes of "Don't Rain on My Parade" wake up something inside me. I shed every trace of Rosie, and I *become* Fanny. The way I was trained to do.

It doesn't matter that there are no lights blurring out faces. I put myself in the scene, and I sing like this is the performance of my life. Like it really, really matters.

And I let myself get swept away, and even though it's been a few weeks since I've sung anything, my voice feels strong. I feel relaxed. And when I get to the end of the fourth verse, I start to make eye contact with the people in the audience.

It's all smiles. I lean in. I make my way around the room. At one point, I sit down between two old men who were clearly mid-chess game, and I sing right to them. They play along, one hitting the other on the arm, both laughing.

The crowd responds. And their energy fills me up.

And it's *fun.*

It's been so long since it's been fun.

I come up to the big note toward the end, just before the final chorus, and something inside me shifts.

It's like I can see the note ahead of me, and I falter, hearing that snide, *"You really do not have what it takes,"* as it melds with all the other similar rejections I've gotten over the years, and instead of attacking that note, I find a way around it.

My audience—this audience—will never know. I close my eyes and fake that last note, wishing like mad that Fanny's confidence was easier to hold on to, but I quickly brush it off and I finish, holding the microphone up in front of me.

And unlike my big finishes when I'm in an audition room performing for four people who can't be bothered to look up from their phones, this audience responds with cheers and whistles and hollers and applause.

I take a moment and live in it.

This is the one thing in the world that makes me feel alive.

I lower the microphone and smile as Connie bustles over to me, her ample hips swaying as she walks. She pulls me into a tight hug, then draws back and looks at me, a stunned expression on her face.

"Rosie! You're sensational!"

I resist the urge to ask if she noticed I backed off at the end and lift a hand of thanks toward the cheering diners who are shouting, "Encore!" and clinking their glasses with their silverware. As I look around, my eyes are drawn to where Arthur is standing against the back wall.

And I'm certain I see tears streaming down his face.

CHAPTER 18

THE PERFORMANCE IN THE DINING hall worked.

It worked *well.*

After seeing that I'm not a complete fake and that I have no intention of bailing on the show, as Belinda led everyone to believe, the diehards all showed up that afternoon and sang their guts out. Turns out, several people already had audition songs prepared, and some of them were actually incredible.

By the end of the evening, we had more than enough people to fill every role, including Connie, who, it turns out, is actually a decent performer. Her quirkiness instantly made me think she'd be a perfect fairy godmother, and I added her name to the callback list as soon as she walked out the door.

Arthur didn't come back for the afternoon auditions, which was kind of a blessing. But I was oddly concerned. I asked Connie about it, and she seemed to imply this is typical for him. He likes to be by himself. And stage managers aren't typically at auditions anyway.

Everyone has gone, and I'm packing up my things when the door to the auditorium opens, drawing my attention to the back of the space. To my surprise, it's not Connie or Daisy or anyone I expect.

It's Belinda.

She meets my eyes, and for the briefest moment, there's a hitch in her step.

I stop moving and wait until she reaches me, moving down the aisle with the grace and beauty of a trained ballerina.

Once she's standing in front of me, she pushes her hair back from her face, a nervous fidget I recognize immediately from years of studying people.

A surprising sign that she's not sure what to do with her hands.

She clears her throat. "Am I too late?" she asks without looking at me.

I see the olive branch she's extending for what it is and choose to meet it with kindness. "No," I say gently. "Of course not. I'm glad you're here."

She gives me the slightest nod. "Very well. I assume your accompanist has already left for the day, so I'll sing a cappella." She moves up onto the stage, and I sit back down in my chair and pull out my notebook.

It's been a strange experience sitting on this side of the table, one that's helped me understand what directors mean when they say, "You just didn't fit the part."

It doesn't matter how amazing you are—if you're not right for the role, according to that director's vision, you can't change that. It's eye-opening to realize sometimes an actor can be really good but still wrong.

For years, I let every rejection inform the way I felt about myself, as if each one punctured a hole in my self-worth. Now I realize what a waste of time that was.

I settle back and wait.

And the second she opens her mouth, I hear the proof of why people talk about her talent the way they do.

The familiar notes of "Memory" begin, and even though I'm not a huge fan of the musical *Cats*, the way she sings it makes me put down my pencil and just . . . listen.

For about one and a half minutes, Belinda transports me to an entirely different place. The emotion she's able to access is stunning, and the way she carries herself is like a master class in grace and poise.

As she hits the final note, tears sting my eyes, and when she's finished, she drops her hands and looks at me.

It feels wrong to applaud since I'm the only person in here, and yet, how do I properly convey to her how moving that was?

She watches me for a few seconds, then quirks a brow, as if expecting a response.

"That was . . ." I don't even try to assign a single word to her performance. "Thank you."

She gives me a nod, and then, as breezily as she walked in, she comes down from the stage.

"What made you change your mind?" I ask, standing.

She purses her lips. "Despite what you think, I do care about this theatre group, Miss Waterman. I care very much."

"So it wasn't my lunchtime performance?"

She scoffs. "Oh, heavens, no." Then she gives me a quick once-over. "But . . . you weren't half bad."

I try to keep my smile hidden and easily come back with, "Neither were you," while nodding to the stage.

Her lips press, and I can see she's hiding a similar smile. Coming from her, this feels like she just gave me a Tony Award.

She picks up her purse. "I know some people have me pegged as the Evil Stepmother, but in this particular show, I would be a wonderful Cinderella."

And with that, she leaves.

....

Casting a show, I soon discover, is not for the faint of heart.

Emotion doesn't get to sit at the table with you. After a round of callbacks on Thursday, it's obvious that a lot of the auditioners take this whole thing very seriously. It's strangely competitive but in a respectful way. If what Connie said is true, this is more than just a show for many of them. It's the thing they get out of bed for. It gives them purpose—and it's fun.

But more than fun.

Which makes me feel even more pressure to get it right.

As an actor, I take any role very seriously too. I'm diligent when I get a script, and bringing that character to life is something I don't take lightly. An extra, the friend next door, a corpse . . . it's important for me to know the character I'm playing. But I'm well aware that a show comes to life because of the director's vision. Actors have very little say in that, and my job is to try to make the director's vision a reality.

But I'm the director now.

I'm the one who casts the vision.

I tell Ginny how I want the costumes to look.

I tell Booker what to build.

Having that much control over a show is kind of . . . amazing, actually. Now that I've seen that these actors are here to work, that they don't look at this as some light and fluffy production—they look at it as a chance to create something magical—I want to work hard for them. I want to do right by them. My cast.

My cast.

My cottage.

My mailbox.

The reality of that settles on my shoulders as I look over the preliminary cast list we've made. It's just me, Dylan, Veronica, and Arthur at the table, and another encouraging realization I've had is that this team is actually strong.

Veronica's callback dance combo was simple enough for the auditioners to learn and perform, but interesting enough to challenge them. And not a grapevine in sight, which is a big *praise the Lord* in my book.

Arthur said very little throughout the entire process, but

I learned very quickly to listen when he did speak. While I was surprised he showed up for callbacks, it became obvious he isn't just the guy who manages the theatre here—he knows what he's talking about, which makes me wonder why he didn't direct this show.

I find myself mostly wanting to discover a way to make him like me.

The real surprise, though, is Dylan. While I initially put her in charge of hair and makeup, she quickly stepped right into the position of assistant director, taking initiative in areas that I hadn't even thought of. She's organized and detailed and, when she wants to be (and isn't on her phone), she's really pleasant to be around. It's impressive, given her age.

Now, after much debate, I lean back in my seat and look over the names on the whiteboard. Every character name went up on that board with a list of possible performers underneath, and as we discussed and decided, Dylan erased all but one name for each character. Looking it over now, I see that we don't have anyone else to talk about.

"Oh my gosh, we did it," I say. "We have our cast."

"Good, can we go home now?" Arthur says. "You women are so indecisive."

"I feel like I should be offended by that, but since I'm in such a good mood, I'll let it slide," I say.

"Yippee," he says dryly.

We all stand, pushing away from the table.

"I'll type everything up and send it to you to look over," Dylan says. "Is there anything else you want me to do before the first rehearsal? I can come in early and number the scripts for you?"

I can't quite reconcile this girl in front of me with the one I met on the bench only days before. It's like she was just waiting to be noticed, and now that she has been, she couldn't wait to come to life. "That sounds great, Dylan, thank you. For everything—you've been a huge help."

The smile skitters across her face and is gone just as quickly, like she remembered she's decided not to smile today. "Great. I'll see you later."

"Wait, I'll walk with you," Veronica says, following her out. She lifts a hand in a wave. "Have a good day off tomorrow, Rosie. I'll see you Saturday at the first rehearsal!" She singsongs that last bit, and a wave of excitement rushes through me.

I can't believe it, but I'm actually excited to begin.

And I've completely forgotten anyone's age.

Once they're gone, I'm alone on the stage with Arthur, who is holding his keys and staring at me.

After a three-count, he sighs like an automated phone system just asked him to reenter his date of birth again for the fifth time. "I can't leave till you leave."

"Oh! Sorry. Right, I'll just . . ." I hurry and pack up my things, shoving my laptop and notebooks and callback notes haphazardly into my tote bag and slinging it over my shoulder. "Thank you, Arthur, for being here. And for all the insight."

"I didn't do anything," he says, walking toward the stage-right wing. He grabs the ghost light and wheels it out onto the center of the stage.

Most theatres carry on this tradition of keeping an electric light on the stage once all the other lights are out. It's said to act as a guide to the ghosts that surely haunt every theatre.

It's an old tradition, and I don't believe in ghosts, but I do love that the theatre world still holds on to it. And, of course, there are practical reasons to keep a light on a dark stage; otherwise, anyone who wanders in could tumble right off the edge.

Arthur spins the bulb and the dim light appears at the end of the pole.

"I disagree," I say. "You know your stuff."

He huffs.

"I just mean . . ." He *really* sets me on edge. "I didn't know you were more than just a tech guy." A flash of his tearful face at the end of my performance washes over me. I want to ask him why.

"It seems there's a lot you don't know." He turns.

"So tell me."

He stops, and I white-knuckle the strap of my bag, bracing myself for what I fear is coming.

He turns around and meets my eyes, studies me for a beat, like he's not sure I'm worth his time. Or maybe like he's not sure my skin is thick enough to hear what he has to say.

"You didn't give everything you had to that song in the cafeteria."

I start to protest, but he cuts me off.

"I saw it the second you pulled back."

Oh wow. He *knew.*

"Most people wouldn't catch it, but I know that song—intimately." He presses his lips together, and I know there's more to that story. I also know the odds of me ever hearing it are slim, which makes me want to know even more.

"It's like you were afraid to trust yourself in the moment you needed to most." He shakes his head. "Full of doubt."

I steel my jaw, and he seems to notice that too. He seems to notice everything.

He tilts his head, still studying me. "And if I had to guess, I'd say there's a whole part of you that you don't access when you work."

I swallow, and it's so quiet in here that I hear the noise of it in my head like it's a sound effect in a cartoon.

He leans forward. "You're holding back."

My laugh is nervous. "You got all that from one performance?"

He shrugs.

"I must've done something right," I say before I lose my nerve. "It made you cry."

He goes still but doesn't turn back.

I stop breathing in anticipation of whatever he's going to say next, but he starts walking again and calls over his shoulder, "Try not to drive into a ditch on the way home."

And then he's gone, and all that's left on the stage is the dim ghost light and me.

CHAPTER 19

THE NEXT DAY, I WAKE up still thinking about my conversation with Arthur.

I felt that performance in my bones, but he saw that second where the self-doubt creeped in.

It's not the first time someone has told me I'm holding back. But honestly, what do people expect of me? I can't cut myself open and bleed every time I'm on the stage.

Even though I know for a fact that's exactly what I'm supposed to do.

You can't make anyone else feel anything if you aren't willing to feel it yourself.

Had Arthur really picked up on that just from that one performance? Did he see the slight hesitation when I started singing or the one just before the high note?

And if so, how?

I pull out my phone and do a quick search, typing "Arthur Silverman" into the search bar, and I get several hits. Before I can uncover anything juicy, I get a text from Dylan:

> Did you get the cast list email I sent?
>
> ROSIE: Yes. I'll look it over, then get it posted.

I abandon my search and scan the names on the cast list one last time, eyes hovering over Belinda's. Ultimately, we decided that her evil stepmother energy was too spot on for her to play Cinderella.

That honor goes to a newcomer named Grace, who is meek and quiet and has the most beautiful soprano voice.

Hopefully once we start rehearsals, Belinda will agree with me—and everyone else on my team—that she is in the role she's most suited for.

I print the cast list, which I'll hang on the call-board backstage at the theatre, hopefully before anyone else gets there this morning. At the top of the list is the information about our first rehearsal tomorrow, which means that once I'm done with that, I'm going to give myself a much-needed day off.

As I wait for my coffee to brew, I glance outside at Booker's house. I assume he's at work, but then I see him in the yard, taking a bag of trash to a bin around the back. I'm standing by the large picture window in the front room in my pajamas, gawking like a stalker, when he looks up and glances toward my cottage.

I gasp and dart out of the way, tuck-and-roll style—managing to clip an end table on the way down, barking my shin on the corner, and launching a stack of coasters to the floor.

I'm writhing in silent, angry pain when I glance sideways at the kitchen. Since I'm floor level, I can see under the table . . . and I glimpse a small black shadow skitter across the floor.

I go completely still, shin still screaming at me, and do the thing that can only be described as "listening with my eyes"—darting them around, not blinking for fear I'll miss something.

Seconds later, I hear the unmistakable sound of movement in the laundry room, just off the kitchen. It's like a slight clicking on the hardwood floor.

A tingle rushes down my spine, and my imagination kicks into high gear.

"Oh my gosh, oh my gosh . . ." I'm panicking, furiously rubbing my shin, willing the pain away.

Is it an animal? I'm not good with animals.

Once in New York, I saw a cockroach in our apartment, and I slept with the light on for two weeks.

Call it unrealistic, but in addition to my well-earned fear of geese, I'm also terrified of mice, rats, spiders—anything creepy or crawly—and I'm pretty sure something creepy or crawly is currently making a home of our laundry room.

I gently put weight on my leg and find that it's not all that bad, so I half hop over to the front window, my eyes still glued to the laundry room. I chance a quick look outside in the hope that Booker has magically appeared on my porch, like Superman anytime Lois is falling off a building, to handle this problem.

I swear that woman is always falling off something.

Empty porch. No such luck.

I spot my phone on the kitchen table. My eyes jump from it to the door of the laundry room. More clicking. More movement. This time, a shift and a bump.

I picture a large rat, the size of a small dog, phoning his buddies, setting up a canasta table while chewing on my jeans.

Phone or front door? Which one? My life literally hangs in the balance.

Since I'm wearing slightly skimpy pajama bottoms, a tank top, and no bra, I opt for the phone.

But when I start to move, I hear the critter start to move. I freeze on my tiptoes, rigid and unsure if I'm safer where I'm standing or in the kitchen on the table with a flamethrower.

A shadow runs out of the laundry room and into the room where I'm standing. I scream. And then I scream louder, and before I know it—and with no inkling as to how—I am up on top of the kitchen counter. Still screaming.

My heart is clanging around in my chest, and I can't catch a deep breath. The fear *is* ridiculous. Rodents are much, much smaller than humans, and to some people probably considered cute; but to me they're terrifying and creepy and gross and my heart rate is racing like Seabiscuit's.

My phone is on the table, about ten feet from the counter. If I lie down, maybe . . .

But then I hear the front door open. "Rosie? You okay?"

I'm stretched out on the counter, feet under the cabinet to brace myself, and my torso and arms hanging completely off, desperately reaching for the chair to hook the table to drag it closer to get my phone.

To his credit, Booker made quick work of the yard between our two houses. But the panicked expression on his face tells me that my screams made it sound like I was being murdered.

He looks around, but then his gaze settles on me.

Pretty sure he can see down my shirt all the way to my belly button.

I clutch my arms over my shirt, snap my jaw shut, and try not to think about how ridiculous and *unsexy* I look right now.

"I heard screaming." He starts toward me, stopping at my upheld hand. "What's wrong?"

"Mouse," I say, still hanging halfway off the counter.

He blinks. "What?"

"There's. A. Mouse. In. Here," I say, emphasizing each word so there's no confusion.

"A . . . mouse?"

"Or a wombat. Or . . . something! It's huge!"

"All of this"—he motions toward me, I assume to indicate where and how I'm currently sitting—"is because of a mouse?"

"Booker!"

"Right. Sorry."

"Are you here to help me or mock me?"

"I'm trying to decide." He starts looking around the kitchen, and I clamber back farther onto the counter—one part Ninja and one part drunken bear—and furiously jab a finger toward the laundry room.

He smirks and nods toward where I'm pointing. "In there?"

"It's in there!" I hiss through gritted teeth. Why isn't he moving faster? Doesn't he see that my life is in danger?

He walks—no tiptoeing, no goose-stepping, just normal walking—around to the door of the small room and looks inside. I scoot along the edge of the counter, feet still up off the floor, and watch as he leans down to inspect the area. He moves the washer and the dryer, and that's when I hear something scrambling against the wall in the corner.

"Oh my gosh, oh my gosh, oh my gosh!"

"Hey, Rosie," he calls. "It's not a mouse."

I gasp. "Wombat?"

I hear him laugh. "Chipmunk."

"That's so much worse!" I start to panic again. "Chipmunks are definitely bigger than mice!"

"It's terrified," he says. "And kind of cute actually."

Is that somehow supposed to make me sympathetic? I want him to put it in one of those T-shirt cannons.

Okay, that was harsh. And it's not true. I just don't want it in the house or anywhere near *me*.

I can only see Booker's back, but he's grabbed a broom and, I think, he's attempting to coax the animal into an empty cardboard box he pulled from our recycling bin. I can't believe I'm actually grateful to have a housemate who doesn't break down boxes before she puts them in the bin.

A few minutes later, as if it's the easiest thing in the world, he stands and closes the lid of the box. I hear the trapped animal frantically running around inside as Booker walks straight past me, which makes me curl up in a shrunken ball, clutching my knees to my chest.

He stops briefly and says, "Wanna see?"

I kick my legs out at him and say, "Are you nuts?"

He chuckles and takes the box out the front door. I see him walk around to the side of the house, toward the back of the yard, and release the chipmunk into an open grassy area.

He'll have some story to tell Simon and Theodore when he gets back home.

With the coast clear, and while Booker is still outside, I jump down and snag a hoodie from the hooks outside the laundry room. I pull it on over my tank top because this whole debacle has already exposed me more than I'm comfortable with.

My overreaction was pretty stellar, as my rodent overreactions always are.

But when he walks back in, the only expression on his face is concern. "Are you okay?"

I let out a little sigh of relief. "Yeah. I mean, embarrassed . . . but yeah, I'm fine."

"I get it," he says, clearly trying to make me feel like less of a loser. "Some people are afraid of snakes, some people are afraid of bats, and some people are afraid of chipmunks."

"And some people are afraid of all three of those things." I hitch two thumbs back toward my own body. "My snake fears are worse than Indiana Jones's. Plus, I grew up across the street from a guy who got bit by a bat. He thought it was his superhero origin story, but I think all he got was two weeks in the hospital."

Booker smirks. "Well, we all have our fears, I guess."

He throws away what he just said as an aside, but my senses perk up. "Even you?"

A shrug. "Sure."

Now I cross my arms over my chest, thankful for the cover of the oversized hoodie. "Like what? Obviously not chipmunks," I try to say nonchalantly.

He starts to say something but then stops. He eyes me for a few seconds. "Wait. Are you . . . asking me a question?"

Dang it.

He smiles. "Did you really think you could slip that past me?"

"I mean, yeah." He's like a mystery, and I'm Sherlock Holmes.

We've hung out several nights this week, but most of the information I've shared or learned has been surface-level at best.

He did let it slip that he used to have a childhood crush on Stephanie from *LazyTown*, but that's about it.

"I think the only way *that's* going to happen is if, you know—" He motions both hands toward me as if to remind me this deal is not one-sided.

Double dang it.

I look away, thinking about how I keep getting faced with this same issue—chances to be a little more honest than I'm comfortable being—which is causing me to ask myself why I hold back. I never had my diary shared with the entire student body. Nobody ever pantsed me in gym class.

But when it comes to opening up, it's like I walk right up to the line, inch my toe forward, even make the decision to spend the summer being my true, authentic self, but then I dive for the safety and comfort of solid ground.

Arthur saw right through that.

I haven't told my mom or my friends the truth about New York or this job. That it's not at all what I thought.

Do I need to practice telling the truth? The whole truth?

And is Booker a safe person to practice with?

A few years ago, I enrolled in a master class with a renowned acting coach. Her method of creating characters was to name the emotion you needed to portray and then relate it to something in your own life. Your character is feeling alone? Tap into a time when *you* felt alone in your real life, roll around in those memories, and bring that emotion to the present. As you mined that experience for every feeling it produced, you began to get a better understanding of the character.

Unfortunately for me, that *mining* meant a lot of probing questions in front of a group of people. And that whole exercise proved to me that, while I'd spent years studying human nature, I didn't really understand my own.

This particular professor wasn't deterred by that, since these questions were meant to expose our emotional blockages, and eventually, she hit a nerve that brought me to tears.

I still think about that.

I've pushed aside a lot of emotions over the years. Anything uncomfortable or sad or scary. Any movies that don't have a happy ending. Anything that even remotely resembles love or the possibility of love. Anything that might lead to me feeling out of control or like I need another person.

And although I know that professor had a lot to do with exposing this to me, I don't know how to break out of it.

"I'm afraid of small spaces," Booker says now, drawing me back to the present.

I watch him for a long moment. I've made no promise of reciprocation, but he's still answered my question.

"Really?" I ask. Despite his claim, he seems like the kind of person who wouldn't be afraid of anything.

"Yeah. Super claustrophobic. Tunnels, heights—"

"Laundry rooms?" I cross the room to the coffeepot and pull out a mug.

"There's a window in there, plus the door was open, so that one's okay."

"Do you want some?"

He holds up a hand. "I'm good, thanks."

I add cream and a little bit of sugar, then turn and find him watching me.

"And you're obviously afraid of small, cute animals," he says.

"That creature probably wanted to eat my bones."

He laughs. "You're ridiculous."

I nod. "Yeah. I know." I hesitate, then admit, "And . . . also I'm not crazy about flying over water."

"So no trips to England? Don't they have something like Broadway over there?"

"The West End. I mean, that would be amazing," I say. "But they'd have to drug me to get me there." And then I squint over at him.

He watches me, almost like he's trying to solve a mystery too. "Anything else you're afraid of?"

Oh yeah. Lots.

Failing.

Everyone finding out I'm a fraud.

Letting everyone down.

Having to move back home.

Not making it.

I shake away the barrage of unwanted thoughts. "I didn't agree to this whole 'being honest with back-and-forth questions' idea. Plan. Thing." I take a sip of my coffee, mostly to avoid looking at him.

"Yeah, I know," he responds. "It's fine."

I look off to the side. "But . . ."

His head tilts slightly, a clear question waiting there for me. "But . . . ?"

I say in a singsong, "I've been thinking about it."

He seems to be trying not to look smug, but he's failing. "Oh, you have?"

"Yeah, a little. I just . . ." I open the door to my heart a crack. "I have a hard time talking to people in my real life, so I thought this might be different."

He frowns. "Isn't this your real life?"

I half laugh. "No."

The frown deepens, and I worry that I've offended him. This is *his* real life—not just some pit stop on the road to hopefully bigger and better things.

"Sorry," I say. "I didn't mean—" No, I meant it exactly the way it came out. I make a mental note to stop being a big, fat jerk. "I think you made a good point when you said you were safe because after this summer we won't ever see each other again."

At that, his face falters. He quickly recovers. "That's not exactly what I said."

"Well, that's what I heard," I quip. "Don't let your facts get in the way of my argument."

He chuckles.

"Maybe I just—" I look away. "I'm used to, you know. Acting."

He smirks.

"Real-life stuff, emotions, they're . . . messy."

"And that's bad?" he asks.

"Not . . . bad. Just. I don't like to dwell."

"You don't like to feel."

I go still. "I'm an actor. All I do is feel."

And right now, I'm feeling safe and vulnerable at the same time.

CHAPTER 20

LATER THAT DAY, AFTER RECOVERING from the Invasion of the Chipmunk, grabbing a shower, and discovering that I do, in fact, have a gash on my shin in the distinct shape of an end-table leg, I find myself itching to get into the theatre.

There's something about just being there. By myself. Getting used to the space.

It's more so I can prepare and not mentally break down.

Instead of off-roading in my cart, I decide to walk. It's early afternoon, and it's so green here. This place exists on the opposite end of the spectrum in so many ways from New York, including the color wheel.

Not long after I start out, I see Booker standing by his cart up ahead, and I take note of the way my mood changes at the sight of him. He's talking to a few old guys, pointing and laughing. It looks genuine, and I wonder how I can become as well adjusted as he seems to be.

It makes me wonder if we're the same in a way, not exactly being ourselves and holding people at arm's length.

Is he safe? Probably.

Will I be gone at the end of the summer? Yes.

Is there a good chance that if I start discussing *thoughts* and *feelings* that I'll start to fall for him?

I don't answer that.

He sees me from a ways off and gives a single overhead wave. I wave back and watch as he pats one of the guys on the back, hops in his cart, and starts to drive over to me.

I slow my pace as heat rushes to my cheeks. *Be cool, Rosie*, I tell myself.

As he pulls up, I joke, "Wow, twice in one day. I bet the old women are jealous."

He pushes the brake and it clicks. Wait, do all the golf carts . . . ? *Parking brake.*

I'm trying to pay better attention to things that will come in handy later.

"They'll get over it." He smiles. "Where are you headed?"

I shrug my shoulders and breathe in a content breath. "To the theatre. I just want to be there and hang out, to, you know, get used to the place. Before tomorrow."

"Ah. Preparing for the first rehearsal?"

"Yep. That's when the madness *really* begins."

He chuckles. "Need a ride? I'm headed that way. I don't mind."

"Are we friends now? Do we hang out together?"

He plays it cool. "Or not, you weirdo. You can walk."

I scrunch up my nose and pretend to think about it.

He releases the parking brake and presses the accelerator, slowly inching the cart away from me—making a face at me the whole time.

I pretend to capitulate. "Oh, okay. Fine, if you're going that way, I suppose . . ." I hop into the passenger side and put my phone on my lap.

As he hits the accelerator, a thought hits me. "Oh! Sorry—I didn't even thank you. For saving me from the demon chipmunk."

"Hey." He leans toward me, his shoulder brushing mine. "I'm here for ya."

As he grips the steering wheel, I notice how his polo pulls

tighter, showing all the parts of his chest and biceps that he seems to pay attention to at the gym. There are always people who will be attracted to that, and I've never been one of them.

But it certainly doesn't hurt.

"I told you to call when you need anything." He smirks. "Though I thought maybe you'd use a phone and not, you know, scream."

"It worked, so I regret nothing."

He doesn't drive as fast as Daisy, who drives as though at ten thirty the pizza is free and it's ten twenty-nine.

I try to relax in the soft hum of the cart—to just take in the beautiful day and the beautiful driver next to me, but my brain keeps defaulting to the impulse to share with him.

I want to know him, but that means him getting to know me.

Ugh. What is happening to me?

I shut my eyes tight for a moment, then decide just to go for it. "So . . . questions."

He glances my way. "Uh, what?"

I realize that I started talking in the middle of the conversation I've already been having in my head.

"I think I want to try the practicing thing. You know, questions, being honest . . . That. Whole. Thing," I admit without looking at him.

"The practicing thing," he repeats.

"The sharing," I say.

"The . . . what?" He shakes his head like he has no idea what I'm talking about, but when he glances toward me, he smirks.

"You're teasing me," I say dryly. "I'm baring my soul, and you're teasing."

"If you think this is baring your soul, we're in trouble." He laughs to himself.

I go still, except for the gentle bouncing of the cart.

I'm glad when he chooses to keep things light. Keeping things light is my forte. "Is this because it's the only way for you to uncover all my dark secrets?" And I hear flirtation in the question, though maybe that's just wishful thinking.

I laugh. "No, it seems the people around here are more than willing to talk about you."

"Oh, I bet they are," he says, chagrined. "Hopefully you're smart enough not to believe everything you hear."

"I am," I say. "Though separating Booker Hayes fact from fiction is a little tricky without direct access to the source."

"Maybe that's better anyway. I'm not sure anyone really knows what they're talking about," he says lightly.

"I mean, they told me you're a very good person, so you might be right."

He laughs genuinely, then banters back, "No, that part's true."

"And apparently you don't have any interest in dating." I frown. "Or you haven't found the right woman. Or, I don't know, someone said something, and I tuned them out." I keep my tone light, teasing.

He starts to respond but goes silent instead.

"Not that that matters, you know, to me," I say, filling in the space. "Because I'm leaving and you're here, and not that you and I are, you know, *interested* in being more than friends, but we literally can't because I refuse to do long distance, and—"

"I get it," he cuts me off. "You can't fall in love with me."

"Uh, no," I say, all mock defiance. "It's *you* who can't fall in love with *me*."

He presses his lips together and gives me a once-over so quick I almost miss it. "No promises."

Now I'm the one who goes silent.

He reaches for a bottle of water that's in the cup holder and takes a drink. "So have you thought through how this plan is going to go?" He glances at me. "I mean, I'm sure you'll have a list of rules, right? Oh, shoot . . ."

He swerves and narrowly misses a cone that had been set up next to a storm drain, and the turn jolts me toward him. I instinctively grab on to his arm.

It's the first time I've actually put my hands on him, and it's like my skin is plugged into a light socket.

I immediately scoot away, as if the added space between us will make me feel safer somehow. Seconds later, I realize it doesn't. If a simple accidental touch can have that effect on me, I'm doomed.

"Sorry about that," he says.

I wave him off. "No biggie." *You've seen down my shirt already. I might as well spend the rest of this ride on your lap.* "And to answer your question about rules . . . I don't have any, but I'll work on it. We *are* sort of working together, so I want to make sure to keep things professional."

He shoots me a look while simultaneously slowing the cart. "There's nothing professional about feelings, Rosie."

"But we're working together," I say. "On the show."

"I'm volunteering to help with the show," he corrects.

"Right," I say, "volunteering."

"So any, you know, human-resources-type things aren't an issue," he deadpans, but with a glint.

"Right," I say, "because we're not *dating*."

"Right. Just sharing our innermost thoughts." He takes another drink, then caps the bottle, watching the road as he does. "And definitely *not* falling in love."

I shift in my seat as heat rushes to my cheeks. I take a breath and blow it out. "This was a bad idea."

I swear he's enjoying watching me squirm. "Was it?"

My phone, a savior, buzzes in my lap. It's the group chat with my friends back home. I can practically hear Maya's voice in the back of my head saying, *"Girl, go for it, or something is seriously wrong with you."*

Only, her text won't say anything about Booker because I haven't told them about him yet.

I open my phone and see it's just a check-in text from Taylor, along with a photo of her ample—and very round—baby bump.

I smile down at it.

"Another possible love match?" Booker asks lightly, the hint of a smile in his voice.

"It's my friends back home." I click my phone off, and the screen goes dark. "My friend Taylor is going to have a baby."

"Nice! How far along?" He makes the slight turn onto a different road.

"Oh, about this far." I hold out my hands two feet in front of my stomach. "I'm excited for her. All of my friends are sort of crushing it really." I turn and wish I could meet his eyes. I noticed before that they're the most interesting shade of green, so bright they practically gleam.

I clear my throat. "So if you're still up for it, I was thinking that every Friday I'll share one honest thing about myself, and you'll do the same."

"Why Friday?"

"Because today is Friday," I quip, and then after a slight pause, I add, "and I have something I need to say out loud."

"Ah," he says. "And we have to limit it to one day a week?"

"To start," I say. "I'm not well versed in the fine art of sharing feelings."

He smiles. "You're kind of weird, you know that?"

"I do," I say. "That was literally my nickname in high school. Rosie the Weirdo Waterman."

"Was it?" His eyebrows pull downward.

"No," I deadpan.

He laughs, and I love the sound of it.

"I mean, it might as well have been. I didn't fit in with the athletes or brains or any other stereotypical high school kids. Marched to my own drum and all that."

"That's because you keep the sheet music to yourself," he says, and I smile.

It's a simple, casual observation, but it revs my heartbeat.

He slows down as we reach the theatre building, then turns onto the widened sidewalk and clicks the brake.

He turns to face me. "One question—why now?"

I look right into his eyes, and it's a bit unnerving. I'm a master at pretending, at showing only the shiny side of the apple while hiding the rotten part. The truth is, I'm usually afraid to look right into a person's eyes, in case they can see right through me. It leaves me totally vulnerable, and I'm afraid I won't know how to manufacture the right reaction in time, and an honest one will slip out.

"I think maybe I . . ." Am I really going to admit this? I fiddle with my hands and avoid his gaze.

If I look at him, I'll lose my nerve.

"I think maybe I'm having a quarter-life crisis."

He's quiet. And it's the perfect response in this moment.

"I sort of . . . have to rethink everything." I rub my hands on my thighs. "And that apparently includes thinking a *lot* about why I do the things I do."

"You did say that theatre is like psychology," he says.

I nod. "Right. And the last few months have made me even more self-aware than usual, and I don't like it. I'd much rather . . ." I trail off.

"Pretend." He finishes my thought.

I draw in a breath and blow out on a sigh. "Yeah. It's easier. I mean, it sucks because I hate myself for not being honest—but showing those parts are the hardest for me. It's sort of like, if I pretend well enough, even I will start to believe the story I'm telling. And I guess I've always been more comfortable with fiction than with reality."

When he doesn't respond, I dare a quick glance and, yep, he's watching me, like he's trying to hear what I'm not saying. "Why?"

"I'm not sure," I say, trying not to think about the probing questions my professor asked, and the way those questions put me on display, unraveling me in front of the entire class.

She'd asked the same thing. *"Why? Defend your position! What aren't you facing? What aren't you willing to relive? Why are you so afraid of your feelings?"*

And immediately, just like on that master-class stage, the image of my dad walking out the door assaults my memory.

It's followed by a series of other images—my mom, unable to get out of bed. Packing up our house and moving to a small one-bedroom apartment. Eating peanut butter and jelly every night for dinner because it was all I knew how to make, and she was behind the closed door of her bedroom.

It all worked out—my mom met John, who never had kids of his own and who loved me like I was his. I call him Dad because that's what he was—and is—to me. But the in-between time (after my biological dad left and before Mom met John) is like a blur. And somehow also the most vivid few years of my childhood.

A time in history I'd like to erase.

Even if the time between is when I learned to keep my feelings to myself. To tamp them down because Mom couldn't handle any more sadness. That's when I learned that entertainment could be therapeutic. That I didn't need to seek joy; I could *be* joy.

That became my purpose. My identity.

I'm not the sad girl whose dad left when she was six. That story is as old as fathers. And I don't want that to define me.

Never mind that now, thinking through all of it, I'm struck with the fear that in purposely *not* letting it define me, that's exactly what it's done.

Worse, I think about the way Mom let it slip that she'd given my father everything—her very best years. That I wasn't part of the plan. I can still see her tearstained face, streaked with old mascara and sorrow, as she took my hands and said, *"Rosie, promise me you won't let anyone steal your dreams. Promise me you'll dream big enough for the both of us and you won't quit until you make those dreams come true."*

When I didn't respond, she squeezed me tighter. *"Promise me, Rosie. That's what I want for you. That will make everything worth it."*

The memory settles on my shoulders. It's been there, like an unclosed tab in the browser of my brain, all this time. Influencing every single decision I've made.

These are absolutely not the kinds of feelings I want to discuss with Booker or anyone else. These are the things that would make me a total downer—the things nobody needs to know.

"I'm guessing there's a lot to unpack there," Booker says, considering me. "Maybe next Friday?"

"Yeah, or the fifth, or never." I let out a long sigh, anxious to think about anything else.

I glance past Booker at a row of trees behind the theatre building, but I can feel him looking at me. "I feel like you just had a whole conversation with yourself and didn't say a single word out loud," he says.

"I spend a lot of time in my own head." I point at myself. "But honestly, you're right. I need to start approaching things differently. I think this will make me a better actor."

"So this is an acting exercise for you," he says, and it sounds so . . . awful.

"That's not what I meant." I look away. "It came out wrong."

"I'm not offended, Rosie." And when he says my name, he draws my attention back to his eyes, which are earnest and kind. "But I think a *human* exercise would make you a better actor too."

I frown. "A human exercise?"

"You know, like, connecting with humans?"

I don't move.

"So if it's a little bit of both, then great." He shifts. "This is a safe space."

"I know."

He quirks a brow. "Do you?"

I nod again, unable to verbalize it because, yes, I do know. I can tell that *he* is a safe space. And that's what's so terrifying.

Don't let anyone steal your dreams.

"So we make a deal," he says. "Nonfiction Fridays." He sticks a hand out in my direction.

My eyes drop to his outstretched hand, and a peace washes over me. It's premature, of course; I only met him a week ago, but it's like he sees me so clearly already.

I slip my hand in his and stiffen slightly as he gently squeezes. "Nonfiction Fridays it is."

"You look like you want to throw up."

"I do a little." I scrunch my nose. "It's your face. It's horrible to look at."

"Come on," he says, playing along, "I took a shower this week and everything."

Easy. Fun. Pleasant.

"And it's only one question per Friday?" he asks.

I shrug like, *"Sorry, pal, seat's taken, no soup for you, better luck next time."*

"Dang it. I've got one more, and it's a good one."

I think on it. "Fine. One more, but I reserve the right to refuse to answer."

"Deal."

"And I get to ask you as many."

"Totally fair."

I take a breath.

Maybe this will make me feel less alone. After all, I haven't really let anyone know me since I left home. I was so determined to make it, I didn't want anyone to think I hadn't.

Especially, I realize now, my mother. I need to keep my promise to her.

He nods. "Okay, so today we told each other what we're afraid of."

I protest. "Whatever. I didn't tell you anything. You just found out."

"The screaming and hanging off the counter *were* a dead giveaway." A teasing grin plays at the corners of his mouth.

I stare back, incredulous. "I'm never going to live that down, am I?"

"Oh, *heck* no. Between that and the mud bath, I'm racking up all kinds of dirt on you." He shoots me a look. "No pun intended."

"Good one, Dad." My tone is dry, but I have to look away so he doesn't see my smile.

I glance back as he drains his water bottle and puts it back in the cup holder. Then, seemingly with all the time in the world, he kicks his feet up on the dash of the cart, puts his hands behind his head, and says, "So, Rosie Waterman, tell me something no one knows about you."

I press my lips together and pull in as much oxygen as I can in a single breath. This is it. If we're doing this, now is the time.

Nonfiction Friday.

"Okay . . . something no one knows . . ." There are so many things that no one knows about me, but I start with the simplest.

I look up, straight into his eyes, and I say, "The truth is that I am a failure."

And without explanation, context, or another word, I grab my things and head into the theatre, not believing I just said that.

CHAPTER 21

SATURDAY MORNING, BEFORE OUR FIRST rehearsal gets underway in a few hours, I hop in my golf cart and drive toward the dining hall. The staff Commons is only open in the evenings for family dinner, something I can see becoming a fun tradition, even for me.

The few times I've gone, I've already loved the upbeat atmosphere. It's one of my favorite sounds—the murmur of a crowd, sprinkled with intermittent rises and falls, snippets of conversations and stories, bursts of reactions and laughter.

Everyone on staff seems to be here because they love it. And because it's a great place to work. I mean, the perks are next level. For the first time since I graduated college, I've started to wonder if there's more to this life than what I originally thought or planned.

Could I be happy doing anything other than what I've been doing?

Two weeks ago, it was a hard no.

Today, though?

When I was in school, I read an interview with a popular television actor who'd started a theatre company in a small town on the West Coast. I remember the interviewer asked if he had any advice for aspiring actors, and his reply surprised me. He said, in a nutshell, "If you can be happy doing anything else, do it. This life is hard."

I remember thinking, *Well, life is hard for everyone.* But being here now, I think I get what he was trying to say.

I'm so deep in thought as I stand in the buffet line that I don't notice Booker is standing next to me until he bumps my shoulder with his.

I startle, then look up, and at the sight of him, everything inside me settles.

He's like a walking reminder that I don't need to have everything figured out in this moment. I can just be here, waiting for eggs, next to a guy who now knows I'm a failure—but doesn't know why—and still seems to want to be my friend.

"Oh, hey, I almost forgot." He reaches into his pocket and pulls out a penny, holding it out to me. "Here. For your thoughts."

"That's the line you're leading with?"

He winces. "It went better in my head."

"You brought a prop and everything," I tease.

"I'm trying to learn from the *master.*" He lays it on mock thick.

"There are a few things I could teach you," I say, giving it right back.

He turns to me full-on. "Oh, I'll bet there are." He steps forward, leaving me speechless for what seems like the eighteenth time in the last few days.

I gather myself and hold out my hand. "Fine. Give it."

He presses the penny into my palm. "As an actor, you probably need it, huh?"

I tuck the penny into my pocket and sock him on the arm. "I'll remind you that I'm gainfully employed."

We step forward as the line moves.

"I never understood that phrase," he says. "Gainfully? What does that even mean?"

"Seriously?" I glance over at him as three women bustle by, eyeing him shamelessly, and then, as if they'd planned it, they each give me a dirty look.

Booker notices and laughs.

"This is your fault," I say, stifling my own giggle. "They're all going to hate me if I keep spending time with you."

He seems unfazed as he grabs a tray and two plates from the stack.

I nod down at them. "Something I should know? Are you eating for two?"

He grins. "I always get Bertie's breakfast. She saves our table."

My eyes scan over to the seating area, searching for a woman sitting alone. I've been so curious about her. She must be really special if Booker moved here to be close to her.

"She's the one in the"—he nods toward the tables—"purple jacket." He motions toward a woman sitting at a table near the window, staring outside. "She likes to sit by the window, away from people. That way they won't hear her when she talks about them." He chuckles.

I instantly love her, and I can hardly even see her from here.

There's a lull as we step forward again, and then I say, "It's nice you moved here to be close to her."

He shrugs. "Don't get me wrong, it was a big reason, but also this really is a great place to work."

"But are you happy? I mean, do you ever think about doing . . . more?"

He raises his eyebrows, and I hear the question he's not asking.

"I don't mean to put down what you're doing. It's just that this is a long way from, say, a professional sports team."

"You think I've settled," he says.

I shake my head, even though I'm not sure what I think. "No, I just—" Am I in danger of being a jerk again? I decide that no, I'm not judging, I'm genuinely curious. As if Booker has the secret answer to a question I didn't even know I should be asking.

When I go silent, his eyebrows pop up, encouraging me to go on.

"I never thought I could be happy doing anything other than, you know, what I was doing. Or trying to do." I take another step forward. "But I'm not even sure that's made me very happy."

"So," he says, "when are you the happiest?"

I narrow my gaze. "Oh no. Sorry, chief. That feels like a Friday question."

"Did you just call me chief?" The corner of his mouth lifts, but it's our turn to go through the buffet, so his focus shifts onto the food. We pile our plates high with pancakes, bacon, and eggs, then move over to the short line where we swipe our cards.

I can't square the idea that letting go of a big dream could actually make me happier.

"Do you want to come sit with us?" His question silences the noisy voice in my head.

"Are you sure? I don't want to impose . . ."

He hands his card to the woman behind the register. "Totally fine. It'll keep Bertie from hounding me about things I don't want to talk about."

"Oooh . . . what kind of things?"

He takes his card back and picks up his tray. "Sorry, chief. That's a Friday question."

I smirk as I hand my card to the cashier. Once she swipes it and hands it back, I thank her, pick up my tray, and follow Booker to the table where Bertie is sitting, still staring out the window.

Booker sets down the tray, and Bertie looks up. The purple jacket she's wearing, I now see, is crushed velvet over a lime-colored shirt, and she completes the outfit with wild patterned pants. Her white hair is cut into a stylish, short cut, and she's wearing black-rimmed glasses that instantly give her character. At the sight of me, her face brightens.

"Rosie!"

I'm shocked she knows my name. "Yes! How'd you know that?" My gaze flicks to Booker, who doesn't meet my eyes.

She moves the tray closer to her and motions for me to sit. "Booker tells me everything."

He slips into the seat next to her and says, "I told her there was a new theatre director—that's all," downplaying whatever he's mentioned about me.

I sit down across from Bertie.

"Oh, stop it; that's not all." She gives me a pointed look. "But I'm not one to stick my nose where it doesn't belong, so—" She makes a motion like she's zipping her mouth, then takes her plate off the tray. "You cheated me on the pancakes."

I giggle while unfolding the napkin and spreading it across my lap.

"I was in here the day you sang that parade song, missy." Bertie picks up a piece of bacon. "I'm sorry Booker missed it. You are something."

"Something good or . . . ?"

She leans forward. "Something amazing. Quite impressive."

I feel my confidence swell at the compliment, but it's instantly crushed when Arthur walks into the dining hall. I have no idea why, but it's like his eyes are drawn straight to me, and the second we make eye contact, he grimaces and looks away.

"What's that about?" Bertie asks.

"He manages the theatre," I say.

"Yes, Arthur Silverman." She gives him another quick glance.

I frown. "You know him?" This reminds me that I never did finish my internet search on Arthur, and I really need to. Something tells me there are secrets to uncover.

"I know *of* him. It's not a very big place. But I don't think he socializes much." She waves her hand, as if she's brushing that topic aside. "But let's talk about you. Booker says you're from New York?"

We chat for a few minutes, and I tell Bertie a little about myself—only facts, which, I notice, she already seems to know.

Booker's been unusually quiet, and when I pause, he pushes his chair back, picks up his empty cup, and stands. "I'm going to get a refill. Anyone want one?"

"I'm good, thanks," I say as Bertie shakes her head. He pauses, like he's rethinking leaving the two of us alone, but finally walks off.

There's a brief lull, and then Bertie draws in a breath. "It's all so fascinating, isn't it?"

I lean back in my chair. "What is?"

"Life." She waves a hand as if to encompass everything around us. She stops, looks at me, and smiles as she says, "I'm sorry, it's what old people think about."

I laugh, thinking maybe it does make sense that Booker took a job just to be close to her.

"*Fascinating* might not be the word I'd choose to describe life." I take a sip of my orange juice. "Maybe *confusing* or *messy*."

"Oh yes. It's both of those things. Is it that way for you now?"

And when I find her studying me with that same quiet intensity I sometimes see in Booker's eyes, I have to remind myself they're not actually related at all.

My gaze falls to my half-eaten food, and I find myself mentally leaning toward hyperbole, flirting with embellishing the facts, and then realizing I don't want to add anything to the truth.

"I mean . . . yeah, it is, kind of. I'm okay. I'm not in crisis mode or anything. Just have a ton on my mind. First rehearsal, directing a show, working in a new place . . . It's a lot." And for some reason, I add, "And I guess some days I wonder what in the world I'm doing. You know . . . with my life."

She laughs. "Oh, is that all?"

I smile, but I fear it comes out more like a wince.

She reaches over and covers my hand with her own. "Oh, my dear Rosie, you have to lighten up a little." She squeezes my hand. "It's just life."

Just life?

That flies directly in the face of the words I usually live by: "You only get one shot at this life thing, so don't screw it up." Or my mother's directive never to give up until I achieve my goals.

Bertie pats my hand, smiling. It seems that the older people get, the simpler things become. All of the worry and stress and *things* that seem so demanding are filtered out, leaving behind only the most important parts.

"Did Booker tell you we're not really related?" She pulls her hands back and picks up her fork.

I'm still hung up on her casual wisdom drop, but I manage to say, "Uh, no, Connie did."

"Ha. Connie never met butter she didn't like to spread."

I laugh as she glances across the dining hall to where Booker is holding his refilled drink, chatting with one of the residents. "He sometimes says that I saved him, but the truth is, it's the other way around."

I sit up a little in my chair, curious about Booker, of course, but also curious for more of Bertie's story.

She talks like we're casual friends. "I couldn't have kids of my own, and when my best friend's grandson needed somewhere to live, it felt like the miracle we'd been praying for." She watches Booker from across the room, and a wistfulness comes over her. "It's funny how things always seem to work out, isn't it?" Then to me, she says, "It always works out in the end."

Does it?

I push aside all the real questions I want to ask. About Booker's parents. About his grandmother. About his heart.

Those are Friday questions. Ones that he should answer.

"I know he moved here because he's protective of me. Or maybe because he feels like he owes me or some other nonsense." She scoops a bite of egg onto her fork, then adds wryly, "But I've told him a million times he should go live his life." She holds the bite up but pauses before eating it. "This is no place for a young man in his prime."

"You don't think he's happy?"

"Oh, I'm sure he could be happy anywhere—that's just how he is." She picks up her water and takes a drink. "But there's a big wide world out there. Doesn't make sense to waste it playing everything safe, does it?" Her eyes widen. "Take you, for example—"

"Oh, Bertie, I'm not a good visual aid." My mind snagged on the words *playing everything safe*, and I desperately want to steer this conversation back to Booker.

"You are!" She sets her cup down and studies me. "You have a dream, and you're out there working at it. Chipping away to make it happen."

I glance over at Booker, wondering if she's drawing a comparison or simply making conversation.

"But I'm not exactly succeeding," I admit.

She waves me off. "That is *not* what matters."

"It kind of does," I tell her. "I feel like I'm just spinning my wheels. At some point, they'll probably spin right off the car. I probably need to find something more, I don't know, stable."

"You *could* pivot," she says, her tone sounding like that's a perfectly acceptable choice, "if that's what suits you. There's something awfully exciting about a fresh start. Or you could adjust and try a new approach to the old dream. Every life experience teaches us something." She studies me. "Maybe you just need a little shift."

A little shift. Feels like it would be seismic.

"Does it make you happy?"

"What, the acting?"

She nods.

"I mean, it's work," I say. "Most people don't have the luxury of having a fun job."

She shakes her head and waves at me. "I totally disagree."

I stop moving and look at her, remembering Booker's question on the first day I met him: *"Can't your career be fun?"* I guess I know where he got that idea.

"You can find fun anywhere," Bertie says. "It's when you stop looking for it that it disappears."

A regular fortune cookie, this one.

"And life is a wonderful adventure, isn't it?" She smiles.

I don't have the heart to tell her that no, life's not some wonderful adventure. Or fun, for that matter.

I'm still trying to figure out how to reconcile *"It's just life"* and *"wonderful adventure"* and *"Does it make you happy?"* when Bertie changes the subject.

"What about romance?"

Her out-of-left-field question makes me choke on my drink for the second time in ten minutes.

She laughs. "I don't have a lot of young people to talk to around here, so I may as well get to the good stuff while I can."

I set down my drink and let out a big sigh. "I don't really have time for romance."

"Romance is part of the adventure, Rosie." She points her fork at me. "That's why I think it's time for that one"—she now points her fork across the room at Booker, who appears to be deep in conversation with a pink-faced man who keeps rubbing his shoulder—"to move on. He's never going to meet someone and fall in love and give me grandbabies if he doesn't leave this place." She takes another bite of her pancakes. "Not a lot of options here."

I chuckle. "No, there certainly aren't."

"At least that's what I used to think until you came along."

But I don't get a chance to correct her because Booker is back.

And he's not alone.

"Bertie, this is Arthur. Arthur, Bertie," he says, sitting down next to his grandma.

"Arthur Silverman," Bertie says, and it sounds like, *"Finally, we meet."*

He nods shyly and sets his tray down next to mine. My stomach tenses as he sits.

"So you two are working together," Bertie says brightly. "That's nice."

I can't be sure, but I think I hear Arthur grunt.

I cough-laugh and avoid looking at him. "I don't think working with me is Arthur's idea of 'nice.'"

"Oh?" Bertie's eyebrows shoot up, looking at Arthur. "Is that true?"

He shifts in his seat and protests a little, but Bertie isn't having it.

"Whyever not? Rosie is a perfectly delightful girl." And then, pointedly, she asks, "What is it you don't love about our Rosie?"

Our Rosie.

I look at Booker, and he just shrugs, as if to imply that this is just kind of what she does. Just go with it.

Bertie turns to Arthur and doesn't miss a beat: "What is it that's got your face all puckered? Did you eat a lemon?"

Most people seem to handle Arthur with a healthy bit of caution.

But not Bertie.

He doesn't scare her one bit. In fact, I'm starting to think nothing scares her.

She's suddenly the most fascinating person I've ever met. Because how does one become fearless, and where can I get some of that?

Before Arthur can start to mount some kind of defense against Bertie's questions, she makes a kind of announcement.

"I know what the two of you need." She leans back, hands spread, waiting for our attention. "Actually, what all of us need."

Booker starts shaking his head, as if he's seen this before.

"We need a night on the town."

I frown. "Wait. Can you leave?" I turn to Booker. "Can she leave?"

He makes a face and says, "She's not a prisoner. Everyone can come and go, depending on their circumstances."

"That's right, Booker," she says. "I need to get out of this place and eat real food, like chicken fingers and french fries, and be around young people. I can still party." She shakes her shoulders as she says this, and I can't help but laugh.

Booker smirks, almost like he's set this woman loose and makes no apologies.

"Tonight," she says, like she's unfolding the plans to a heist, "we're going to Buster's."

"Buster's," I repeat—both a statement and a question.

"It's a bar. One town over," Booker says. "Daisy's a regular."

"I don't go out after dark," Arthur says, placing a napkin on the table.

"Well, that's ridiculous." Bertie scoffs, matching his delivery almost perfectly. "All the best things that have ever happened to me happened after dark."

"I'm going to need to hear all those stories," I say, my eyes wide.

"Oh, I've got 'em," she says, pushing her chair away from the table. "Let's meet in front of the clubhouse, and Booker will drive us there." She looks at Booker. "We'll take my car."

We all stare.

She looks at us one at a time. "Good? Good? Good? Great. See you all at eight!"

And with that, she's gone.

I slow turn to Booker. "What the heck was that?"

His amused expression holds. "There's no sense arguing with her. When she decides to do something, she just goes right ahead and does it." Then, to Arthur, he says, "And I hate to break it to you, but if you think you can just not show up, rest assured that she will steal the keys, take her car, find you, and put you in the car herself."

"This is your fault," Arthur says. "If you had just left me at my table in peace."

Booker stands. "Come on, you two, it'll be good for us to get out. See the world."

"We're not seeing the world—it's Wisconsin." Arthur glares at Booker.

"And I hope you've got your cowboy boots, because tonight . . ." Booker pauses, as if for dramatic effect. "Is line dancing night."

He flashes that gorgeous smile, picks up the dirty dishes, and strolls off, leaving me and a miserable Arthur sitting awkwardly at the same side of the table.

We share a glance, and for a brief moment, we connect, both hoodwinked and desperate for a way to escape this plan.

CHAPTER 22

THERE IS NO ESCAPING THIS plan.

Arthur learns this the hard way at 8:07 p.m. when, just as Booker predicted, Bertie tracks him down at the theatre while Booker and I wait in her Honda Accord.

It occurs to me that this is the strangest double date I've ever been on, first and foremost because this isn't a date.

It's more like an abduction.

Nothing to see here—just a motley crew of multigenerational, very unlikely friends.

From a retirement community.

Going line dancing.

You know, the usual.

"I'm glad you didn't wear a cowboy hat and boots," I say.

"Why? You have a thing for cowboys?" He gazes at the door of the theatre, nonchalant as ever.

"Cowboys *are* hard to resist," I say, trying desperately to banish the mental picture of him striding out of a saloon saying, *"I'm your huckleberry."*

I see the corners of his eyes crinkle in a slight smile. "Duly noted."

While we wait, he asks about the first rehearsal. I give him a brief overview—we did introductions of the team and the cast, then read through the script.

Twice, our Prince Charming fell asleep at the table, which

doesn't bode well, but it did give me the idea to have as many daytime rehearsals as possible. Apparently, starting at 2:00 p.m. was a cardinal sin.

"Overall, it was good," I tell him. "Maybe even fun." I look away, smiling. Because it was fun. And because I'm already looking forward to the next one.

Bertie busts through the front door of the theatre, followed by a very grumpy-looking Arthur. She rushes over to the car and motions for Booker to roll down the window.

"I'm going to ride with Arthur," she says. "He said he'll only come along if he can drive himself. He also said he's not dancing." She leans in and whispers, "But we'll just see about that."

I have to laugh because as intimidating as Arthur is, Bertie doesn't seem to notice. Or maybe she notices but doesn't care, which sort of makes her my hero.

"Are you sure this is a good idea?" Booker asks. "Some people really do like to be left alone."

She waves him off. "It's not good for anybody to be alone, Book, you know that." She winks at me. "That's for you too."

"I'm not alone," I quip. "I'm here with you jokers."

She turns to Booker. "Oh, I like her. I like her a lot." She hitches her bag up on her shoulder and looks at me. "He likes you too, in case he doesn't say so."

"Bertie." Booker's tone is like a warning.

It's clear by her mischievous grin that Bertie isn't intimidated by him either. "See you there!"

Booker rolls up the window and looks at me. "She's been on this kick about me settling down."

"Would you like me to set you up with a dating profile?" I tease.

He shoots me a look and shakes his head, and only then do I realize that our oddball double date just became a single date, and even though that's not actually what this is, it's definitely what it feels like. I fold my hands in my lap. "I'm in love with your grandma."

"She's the best." He starts the car and backs out of the space. We drive past Arthur and Bertie, him with his arms folded and her pointing at the passenger-side door. We're soon down the curvy road and off the Sunset Hills property.

The sun has begun its grand descent, and with the open fields, the sky looks massive. And beautiful.

"Wow," I say, taking it in. "You don't see sunsets like this in New York."

"It's pretty spectacular, isn't it?" Booker slows the car, stopping at an intersection. He glances at me. "And the way the light comes in . . ." A pause. "You look really pretty right now."

A heat sizzles in my belly from that compliment. I was unprepared to fake a response, and I feel my face flush. "Um, thanks," I sputter. And then add, goofily, "You *do* like me." I waggle my eyebrows, joking, but Booker doesn't deny it. Instead, he smiles and goes back to looking at the road.

I'm not used to this—being open *or* having the attention of a man I find so attractive.

My ex-boyfriend, Peter, was good-looking, sure, but part of the reason I was with him was because he was really the only option. More of a relationship of proximity. Plus, he didn't make demands on me. He didn't lead conversations, and he most certainly didn't ask a bunch of personal questions.

He also didn't make me feel all loopy inside.

"Sorry, I made it weird," I say.

"Well, you're a weirdo," he teases.

I smirk over at him. "I don't know how to accept compliments."

"Then I take it back. You're hideous."

I spin around. "It's out there now. You can't."

"No, forget it, I'm totally taking it back. Words can't describe how pretty you are, but numbers can. Two out of ten."

I laugh and smack him on the arm. "You think I'm pretty. Ha." Maybe I could learn to accept compliments.

I settle in my seat, smiling throughout my whole body. It's fun. Nice. Easy. Safe. And it's totally not a date.

The endorphins racing through my body get the best of me, and I hear myself say, "Do you remember asking me before what makes me happiest?" I don't look at him—I don't want to lose my nerve. It's not Friday, after all. And if I answer the question, it's a freebie, and not part of our deal.

"Hmm. Vaguely." He's still in teasing mode.

"The truth is, when you asked me that, it kind of caught me off guard," I say. Finally, I dare a peek at his profile. He's casually holding on to the steering wheel, looking like he's ready for his close-up, and I feel like more of a mess than ever.

"Bertie talks about adventure and fun and life and all of this stuff like it's just out there—all over—waiting for us to take it, but . . ." I trail off. Because how do I make this make sense?

"But?"

"I thought I knew how to find those things. I followed my passion. I'm doing what I love. Something I think I'm pretty good at." I go still. "I hear *adventure* and I think of jumping out of a plane or snorkeling the coral reef or even just going on an unplanned road trip. Do you think that's what she meant?"

"If that's the kind of adventure your life needs, I guess."

"It's not. None of those things sound fun to me."

Which begs the question—what does? "I don't think I've been happy in a really long time," I say quietly.

"But acting makes you happy, right?"

I think for a second. "Yes. It absolutely does. The work does. Figuring out characters. The craft of it." I shrug. "It just . . . it just got so *hard*. It became about what everyone else thought I should do, or who everyone else expected me to be. My job is contingent on being liked."

"Ooh. Yeah, that would suck," he says. "Some of my patients hate me, but I don't care as long as they do their exercises."

I want to laugh, but I'm stuck in this loop, in the middle of admitting something out loud that's surprising even to me. Because what am I saying? I'm not going to quit acting—I love it too much.

"Auditioning is an endless cycle of judgment, and I'm starting to wonder if I'm cut out for it."

He goes still, the only sound the tires on the seams of the highway.

"It's okay to change direction, you know."

"Bertie said kind of the same thing," I say. "Find a new way to look at the old dream."

He chuckles. "Yeah, that sounds like her."

"But that feels like quitting."

"Quitting something that isn't working for you isn't a bad thing."

I sit with that.

Is that where I'm at? This isn't working for me anymore and I need to change course? Start over and hope it's as exciting as Bertie seems to think it could be?

I don't even know.

I've always approached acting in such a serious way, I wonder if it's possible to find the fun in it again—if I ever found it fun at all.

After my mother made me promise to fight for nothing less than a big dream, I became solely focused on it. This dream of being an actor has been my identity for as long as I can remember; I'm not sure I know what my life looks like without it.

"This is why you feel like a failure," he says. "Not because you are one, but because the thing you've dedicated your life to isn't working out the way you pictured it."

When he says this out loud, it makes so much sense. I stare hard out the window, my vision clouding over with fresh tears.

"What are you afraid of?" he asks. "I mean, besides chipmunks."

"Everything." My slight laugh eases the knot in my throat. "I have three best friends back home. Maya, Marnie, and Taylor. They're all *thriving*. All three of them. Getting married, having babies, getting promoted at work. They have careers and families and—"

"Rosie, you know it's not a competition," he says gently.

"I know." I groan, unable to fully agree. "I know it's not. And I want them to do amazing things and be so happy."

"And I'm sure that's what they want for you too."

I nod. "They do. They're such good friends. They'll be thrilled to hear I'm spending time with someone so attract—" The words are out of my mouth before I can stop them.

He pounces, overly dramatic. "Whoa, whoa, whoa. Slow down, this relationship is going *way* too fast here, geez." He grins over at me.

I smile back in spite of my flushed cheeks. "That just sort of slipped out."

"Uh-huh. I see your marriage-trap plan from a mile away." His tone is flirtatious as he turns his attention back to the road.

All of a sudden I'm keenly aware of exactly how far my body is from his. There's a weird pull to figure out a subtle way to shrink the space between us.

"But your friends know things have been hard, right?" he asks.

I wince, and for a moment I wish I hadn't said anything about feeling like a failure.

"Oh," he says. "They don't?"

"Nobody knows," I say.

"Except me," he says.

I nod. "Except you."

And my short-lived regret in sharing that dissipates. I find I don't mind him knowing.

"Why didn't you tell them?" he asks. "Would they judge you?"

"They've never once made me feel anything other than brilliant and loved." I stare out the window, not sure why this is all hitting me. "And in typical Rosie fashion, I made my life sound like a shiny penny."

"Do you know why?"

Why? There's that question again.

"I mean," he continues, "I usually do things because I'm bored, hungry, or tired. But I'm a simple guy."

"Emphasis on *simple*," I jab.

"Funny." He eyes a sign on the side of the road and slows down to turn as he says, "I don't think anyone actually knows what they're doing. We're all in various stages of making it up as we go."

I know I am. But is he right? Is everyone, to some degree, pretending?

"You know, my friends really thought I would make it," I say. "I thought I would too." My laugh lacks all amusement. "How's that for deluded?"

"A case could be made that you *are* 'making it,'" he says. "I mean, you're working in the theatre. You're being paid to do what you set out to do."

He doesn't understand. "I'm not performing."

"No, you're doing something way harder." He laughs. "You're running everything."

"Not everyone can just get a new dream, Booker," I say, a little more clipped than I mean to. "I've wanted to do one thing my entire life. I can't just swap it out for something else."

"That's not what I meant," he says.

I sigh. "I know. I'm sorry. I think I'm just sensitive."

"Too much sharing?" he quips.

"Way too much," I say.

Booker slows down and turns into the parking lot of what looks like an old roadhouse-type bar with a nearly full gravel parking lot.

"Okay, then let's save all of that for Friday."

I suddenly feel like I'm wearing wool in July, so I change the subject. "Ooh, it looks like they got both kinds of music here. Country *and* western," I muse, desperate to lighten the mood.

He laughs to himself as he drives around for a few seconds, eventually finding a parking place. Once we're stopped, he turns off the engine.

"What if, just for tonight, you stop trying to figure out life and the meaning of everything and commit to one thing only—having fun?"

I cover my face with my hands. "I'm not even sure I know how to do that anymore."

"I'll help," he says. "You can figure out all this life stuff tomorrow."

Lighten up, Rosie. It's just life.

His phone buzzes in one of the drink holders. He picks it up and reads the new text, shaking his head.

"What's wrong?"

"Bertie and Arthur aren't coming." He tosses me a suspicious look. "She said they went for ice cream instead."

"Do you think—?"

"She planned this?" He laughs. "Without a doubt."

CHAPTER 23

I'M ON A DOUBLE DATE that's no longer a double date that wasn't a date in the first place.

We're still sitting in the car, collectively shaking our heads at Bertie's master plan.

I look at the bar. There's a lit-up neon Buster's sign out by the road, and the name is hand-painted on the actual building—and not by an artist.

I smile. "She did seem concerned that you'll never get out there and live your life."

He rolls his eyes. "Oh yeah. I've heard the whole speech. Multiple times."

"You know what this means?" I pump my eyebrows despite his skeptical look, and then, because I don't want to feel vulnerable anymore, I sing: "She thinks I'm good for you."

Without missing a beat, he says, "She's a terrible judge of character."

I smack him across his arm, aware that this has become my go-to when I don't have a good comeback.

"We'll go in, share some wings, and then go home," he says.

"Uh, you skipped right over the line dancing," I say, eyeing him.

"Yeah, I'm not dancing."

"That is not the deal." I turn in my seat. "If I have to be out of the house, then you have to make it worth my while."

"Okay." His eyes lock onto mine. "What did you have in mind?"

There's something slightly suggestive in his tone, and I freeze because the question makes me think about things that I shouldn't be thinking—not if Booker is really just a friend. And for a flicker of a moment, I wonder what it might be like to let myself give in to the *more* that Booker offers. Exciting attraction that needs to be tamed, instead of careful, measured interactions that offer no surprise.

"Rosie?" Booker is watching me, unaware that I've taken his perfectly benign question and turned it into something else entirely.

"Sorry," I say. "I was . . . I just kind of, you know, zoned out for a second."

He smirks. "You do that a lot." He gets out, walks around to my side of the car, and pulls the door open, holding his hand out to me. I take it, and when I get out, he doesn't let go right away.

Instead, he lifts my hand up, and I follow his lead and automatically spin underneath.

"Okay, maybe one dance," he says. "But it's gotta be the right song."

"Ah, so Taylor Swift, right?" I tease because I have to make light of everything or I'm going to linger on what it would be like to have his arms wrapped around me on the dance floor.

When we reach the bar, Booker pulls the door open, and we're met by a loud wave of music and voices. The overhead lights are dim but reveal a big open dance floor full of people, and tables all around the perimeter of the bar.

It's got an interesting mix of smells—grilled food, alcohol, leather, and hardwood.

We shift inside, and I take it all in. It's like a scene straight out of *Footloose*, with lines of people all moving together, stomping their boots on the wood-planked floor, turning in unison, the occasional cheer ringing out over the din.

"Do you want something to drink?" Booker asks, his mouth so

close to my ear I can feel his lips on it. It sends a shiver down my spine.

I turn toward him, and our faces are so close, it would take the slightest shift for our lips to meet. "Just lemonade?"

He gives a thumbs-up and reaches for my hand. When I glance down, he smirks. "So we don't get separated." He gives me a little tug, and I follow him through the crowded space and over to the bar.

As he orders our drinks, I turn and look around, and that's when I see Daisy, right in the heart of the rows of dancers, looking like she was the one who choreographed this dance. I watch her for a moment, in awe of how free she is. Her smile is infectious, her personality seemingly transmittable.

It's been a long, *long* time since I've let loose and danced.

I'm not sure when things changed—when *I* changed. I'm guessing it was a gradual thing, like the frog in the pot of boiling water.

These days, something always holds me back. That fear of being judged, maybe? Which is stupid because the career I've picked is literally based on being judged.

Booker hands me a tall glass of lemonade with ice, and I remember that here, in this bar, at Sunset Hills, in Wisconsin, it really doesn't matter what anyone thinks about me. After all, once the summer ends, I'll never see these people again.

So I can be the girl who drove her golf cart into the mud. Or the girl who jumped on top of her counter because a chipmunk got into her house. Or . . . the girl who let herself stop thinking and has fun just for one night.

Nobody will even remember come fall.

"You're doing that thing again," he says.

I sip my drink and look at him. "What?"

"Thinking." His eyes are so sparkly. A girl could get lost in them.

"Sorry," I say. "I'm not usually like this." I'm really not. I'm the one who *doesn't* dwell on feelings. But the state of my life has me all out of sorts.

I smile. A real one. "I'm here and ready for fun." I throw a fist in the air. "Woo-hoo!"

We're about to go find a table when Louie emerges from the crowd. He spots Booker, wraps an arm around his shoulder, and lets out a cheer. "Yoooo . . . Booker! You're here? You didn't tell me you were going out tonight!"

"Uh, yeah, didn't know myself," Booker says.

Louie looks at me. "No way! You're here too?" He drapes his other arm around my shoulders, and now we're all three standing in an awkward line. Then, as if realizing something, Louie backs away. "Wait. Are you two here . . . ?" His eyes go wide. He points at me, then at Booker, then at me again.

Booker's shrug seems to challenge me to be the one to respond, which makes me curious what his answer would be.

"No," I say. "I was totally abducted by his grandmother, and she's not even here."

"That Bertie," Louie says knowingly. "She's a schemer."

The crowd erupts with a cheer and Louie joins in for a brief second, like he can't help but be a part of the fun. Then, turning back to us, he says, "Bummer. You two would be *awesome* together." Then, without missing a beat, he goes up on his tiptoes and whistles. "Daisy! Daisy!" He waves his arms, then points at Booker and me. "Look! Look who's here!"

Daisy is still making waves on the dance floor, but when she sees us, she shoots her arms in the air with a loud cheer, then leaves her spot in the line and rushes over—as much as she can through this crazy crowd of people.

She throws her sweaty arms around me, and I wonder if maybe my housemate is a little tipsy. "Rosie! You didn't tell me you were coming out tonight."

I start to respond, but she loops her arm through mine and pulls.

"Let's dance!" she says a little louder than she needs to.

Booker reaches over and grabs my glass as Daisy tugs me back through the crowd and onto the dance floor. The song changes, and as the upbeat bass starts, the crowd whoops so loudly it actually startles me.

Daisy takes her spot right at the center of the group, which means I'm also at the center of the group—and I have no idea what this dance is.

I watch for a few seconds as the crowd begins to move, all in unison. Heat rushes to my cheeks, but then I start to get it, reminding myself I only have one goal tonight.

"Just have fun, Rosie," I say under my breath.

I watch Daisy's feet while she calls out the steps for me, and by the time the first verse ends, I've got it down.

I look over at Booker and Louie, leaning on the bar, watching. Louie, the kind of person you'd want cheering for you if you ever ran a marathon, is pointing and whistling loud enough to be heard over the music.

I want to let loose. I want to let go. I want to feel the freedom I felt before the world beat me down.

A country singer's deep voice sings "Country Girl (Shake It for Me)," and I laugh at the absolute ridiculousness of that lyric, and somehow that laugh loosens something inside me. More laughing. More moving. More shaking.

And before long, it hits me. I feel . . . free.

Uninhibited. Like the version of myself that got lost along the way.

I dance with the crowd, who, I notice, gets more and more into the moves as the song goes on, giving me permission to do the same.

Daisy gives me an approving nod. "You're so good at this!" She takes off her cowboy hat and sticks it on my head.

I press it down farther and tip up the brim. I give her a big wink, grab my belt loops like there's a big ol' buckle in 'em, and own it.

It's just life!

The song continues, and as I make the turn toward the bar, my gaze catches Booker's, who is sitting on a stool, listening to Louie prattle on, but watching me.

I tip my hat as if to say, *"Look at me, having fun!"* and he lifts his bottle as if to toast me, and I note that all reason and logic where he is concerned seem to have left my brain.

This is not a date, Rosie.

And I know this. But that doesn't mean I don't want it to be.

The song ends, and Daisy lets out a loud holler. "That was *amazing*! I had no idea you were so much fun, Rosie! I'm starving, let's go get some food."

At that, she pulls me off the dance floor as a slow song comes on over the speakers.

We make our way through the crowd as a booth opens up, and Daisy slides right into it. "Score! I'll text Louie to tell him to grab Booker and come over here." She pulls her phone out of her back pocket, and I sit down across from her. I'm actually a little warm after the dancing, so I pull off my plaid button-down and tie it around my waist.

Daisy finishes her text and looks up at me. "You look hot in that tank top. Are you guys on a date?"

I shake my head. "His grandma sort of tricked us."

She laughs but doesn't seem surprised. "Bertie's a character."

"Are you and Louie on a date?"

Her eyes go wide. "What? No! Why would you even—?"

"Just picking up on a vibe," I say.

She makes a face, seemingly brushing off such a ridiculous idea.

But I've seen the way they look at each other. I didn't imagine it, right?

I glance at Louie, who is a little chubby with a baby face and a golden retriever personality. And I get it. I have no doubt Louie would treat Daisy like royalty. And she deserves to be treated like royalty. He and Booker make their way through the crowd, and my pulse spikes in awareness.

"What kind of vibe?" she asks.

I shrug. "I saw sparks."

Her face brightens. "I feel sparks! I mean, he's . . . *Louie* . . . you know? Not my normal type. But"—she scans the crowd, and when she spots him, her eyes widen—"he's just so sweet to me, Rosie."

"I get it," I say.

"You do?"

"Louie is good and safe and kind," I say. "And guys like that are hard to find."

He's also hilarious. He's strutting, duckwalking, and finger-gunning everyone he passes on his way to where we're sitting.

It's easy to see why Daisy would fall for him.

"He is *so* nice." She glances back in the direction of the two men, who are still working their way over to us, then back to me. "I'm going to tell him I like him. Tonight." She looks like she might burst.

"Shut up!" My eyes go wide. "Just like that?"

She's definitely tipsy—she's using her hands to talk like she's landing a plane. "Life is too short to keep all my feelings to myself. If I like someone, I should tell them, right?"

"What if you try it and it doesn't work? Or . . ." I search my mind for the long list of things that could go wrong and wonder where to start. "What if you get all swept up and it makes you do crazy things?"

Her face lights up and she points at me. "Oooh, that last one. Yes! That's the one I want!"

"You *want* to do crazy things?"

"Don't you?" She grabs both my hands. "That's where the good stuff is, Rosie. That's how we know we're alive!"

I try to protest but say nothing else because Booker and Louie have made it to the table. I slide over to make room, but Daisy does the opposite. She stands up, faces Louie and says, "Louie? I like you."

"You . . . do?" He looks slightly bewildered.

She nods and puts her arms around his neck. "A lot."

"Really?" His mouth curves into a shocked smile, and honestly, it's like watching the end of a rom-com where two very unlikely people realize they might actually be perfect for each other.

Another nod.

"Shut up!" he says. "I like you too!"

"Wanna dance?" she asks.

"Heck yeah!"

He picks her up, and she throws one hand over her head, shouting, "Woo-hoo!" as he moves through the crowd, leaving Booker and me sitting at the table. Alone.

CHAPTER 24

IT SEEMS LIKE THE UNIVERSE—AND everyone in it—has concocted plans for Booker and me to end up alone together.

I'm stunned by how easy it was for Daisy to make that decision—to tell Louie exactly how she feels with no fear of the consequences. She didn't overthink it or make it into something it didn't need to be. She just said it. Out loud.

One glance at Booker, and I'm bombarded with feelings, none of which I can say out loud.

"So . . . ," I say, feeling suddenly awkward. "Apparently, Daisy doesn't need Friday questions."

Booker's eyes flicker. "I don't think most people need Friday questions," he says. "Most people just say how they feel."

I meet his eyes. "What's wrong with us then?" A dry laugh escapes.

"There's a lot of things wrong with me, for sure, but after watching you on that dance floor, I can't think of a single thing wrong with you."

The words stop me. "That sounds like flirting," I say. When he doesn't respond, I add, "Friends don't flirt."

"Say the word, and I'll stop."

Flirting or being friends? I wonder. Because I don't want to stop either.

He takes a drink from his bottle, which I only now look at.

I frown at it. "You're drinking an alcohol-free beer?"

"I'm driving," he says. "No way I'm going to risk not getting you home safe."

And there's that swoop in my stomach again.

"Besides, I want to have all of my senses tonight."

"Why?"

"Because if I only get you for the summer, I want to be fully present for all of it."

Am I imagining this? I've never been great at reading signs, and I don't want to misinterpret, but . . . "Can I confirm that you are, in fact, flirting with me?"

He doesn't even twitch as he says, "I thought that was obvious."

I frown. "I thought you were anti-romance." I stir the ice cubes around in my glass with the straw, only now realizing that Booker must've gotten me a refill before he came to the table.

"Ah," he says, like he knows. "Don't believe everything you hear, Ro."

Ro.

It's what my friends call me.

I like it.

Peter used to call me *baby*, which always made me cringe.

I remind myself of the many reasons I've been cautious where Booker is concerned: (1) He looks like he just stepped off a movie set. (2) He lives in Wisconsin. (3) This is the most important reason. If I give in to the feelings I'm having for him, I will lose control of all my senses. I meet his eyes. "Aren't you?"

He shakes his head. "Did Evelyn tell you that?"

I nod. "She pulled me aside yesterday after rehearsal to make sure I knew you weren't on the market."

He smirks, and then I remember the first time we met Evelyn.

"She's the one with the daughter, isn't she?" I ask, realizing. "So she was—"

"Trying to get you out of the picture," he says. "I'm not sure how much clearer I can be. I mean, do I just say, 'I don't want to date your much-too-old-for-me granddaughter, the accountant, because she looks exactly like your husband'?"

I laugh out loud at that. "Ouch."

"If you saw Alvin Derry, you'd understand."

I giggle, but then his face turns serious.

And I think I *am* reading this right. And he *does* like me. And pretending I don't understand would be dishonest.

He watches me, and I suddenly become very interested in the condensation on the outside of my glass. I turn it around in my hands. "This is a bad idea." I look up. "I'm leaving when the show is over."

He nods. "Yeah. I know."

"So . . . there's no point."

A casual shrug. "Could be fun."

There's that word again.

"If fun is what you're looking for"—I narrow my gaze—"then I'm not your girl."

"I didn't mean—" He looks away. "I mean, I like being around you. I like *you*, Rosie. I think you're . . . interesting."

"I'm really not."

"You really are." He watches me for so many seconds, a quiet intensity behind his green eyes, that I almost believe him.

The music changes, and he says, "Let's dance."

"Uh, I thought you weren't dancing tonight."

"I told you it had to be the right song." He slides out of the booth and holds out a hand.

I listen for a beat but don't recognize the slow melody playing through the speakers. Still, it's not lost on me that his "right song" is slow, the kind that requires touching.

"We'll lose our seats," I say, not because I care about the seats but because I'm nervous. This feels like a moment. A decision that could change everything.

"A price I'm willing to pay." He makes a *come on* gesture with his hand.

I stare at it for a moment, then look back up at him.

Time to take a leap.

I slip my hand in his and stand, facing him, avoiding his eyes but unable to avoid the way his nearness makes me feel.

The heat between us is charged, like there are tiny zaps of electricity no matter which way I move.

He brushes my hair back away from my face, his eyes searching mine. Without permission, my gaze reaches his lips. They're good lips. Full. Soft. And for a fraction of a moment, I'm certain he's going to kiss me.

And I'm certain I'm going to let him.

But then he gives my hand a tug, and we make our way out onto the floor, through the crowd of people around us dancing like no one's watching. They make it look so easy.

And I think about all the moments in my life that have been defined by this overwhelming concern about what other people think.

And tonight, I don't want to care. So I close my eyes, fold into his arms, and start to dance.

CHAPTER 25

"DID YOU KISS HIM?"

I'm staring out the front window, lost in the memory of last night, eating a bowl of cereal in my pajamas when Daisy's voice behind me startles me back to reality. Unfortunately, it startles me so much my spoon goes flying, landing on the hardwood floor yards away from me with a clang.

I spin around and see Daisy standing there, also in her pajamas, the remnants of yesterday's makeup still streaked on her face.

She quirks a brow. "You're jumpy."

"You should wash the makeup off your face at night," I tell her. "You're going to clog your pores."

"Thank you, Mom," she says.

I walk over to my spoon and pick it up, ignoring her question as I walk into the kitchen and get a clean one. "You're up early."

"So are you." She pulls a bagel out of the cupboard, splits it, and sticks it in the toaster. "And you didn't answer my question."

I scoop a bit of Frosted Flakes into my mouth and chew, trying to come up with a way to end this conversation. Because I already know what Daisy will say when I tell her that no, I didn't kiss Booker.

I really wanted to. I think he wanted to kiss me too.

But we didn't.

While it might be fun initially—sharing truths and getting to know each other better—I'm proud of myself for remaining cautious. Because now, in the light of day, without the influence of line dancing and lemonade, all I can do is fast-forward a few months to see how *not* fun it would be to be head over heels and have to say goodbye.

Daisy pulls her bagel from the toaster and slathers it with cream cheese, then takes a bite like she hasn't eaten in days, letting out a slightly inappropriate-sounding moan. "Oh my gosh, this is so good." She's wearing plaid boxers and an oversized sweatshirt that hangs off her shoulder. Her hair is piled in a bun on top of her head, and for some reason I can't figure out, she looks gorgeous.

And then it hits me—she's happy. Genuinely happy.

I study her for a few seconds, the way I often study people, thinking to myself, *So this is what happiness looks like.* No concern for what's up ahead, just a willingness to let go and go along for the ride. I dipped my toe in those waters last night, but today? I'm firmly back on solid ground.

"You good?" Daisy says, her mouth full of bagel.

I eat the last bite of my cereal and rinse out my bowl. "Yeah. I'm good. I need to get to the theatre."

"I want details," she pouts, like a toddler whose parent won't let them have ice cream for dinner.

"There are no details," I say, sticking the bowl and both spoons in the dishwasher. "Booker and I are just friends."

She laughs. "Friends? Girl. Friends do *not* look at each other the way you two look at each other. Or dance the way you two were dancing." She wags her eyebrows. "Did you also carry a watermelon?"

I ignore the *Dirty Dancing* reference and a vivid, pleasant memory assaults my senses—me, standing on the dance floor, Booker's arms around my waist, my hands clasped behind his neck, my head on his chest. I drew in a deep breath, memorizing his scent, every nerve in my body waking up from a long hibernation.

I want to give in to it, this new, strange, delicious desire, but I can't.

I can't.

Fun is great every once in a while, but I live in the real world. And here, in the real world, there are jobs to be done and decisions to be made.

Big decisions—like, what am I going to do with the rest of my life?

"Sorry to disappoint you," I tell Daisy as I leave the room. "But we really are just friends."

"Don't you want to know if I kissed Louie?" She follows me.

"No," I say. "I walked in on you guys kissing, don't you remember?"

"Oh, right." She giggles. "Sorry about that."

"It was like two seals fighting over a grape," I joke.

She laughs. "Yeah. It got pretty intense there. He's a really good kisser. You wouldn't think it, but he does this thing where—"

I hold up a too-much-information hand in the air as I walk into my bedroom and start pulling clothes from my dresser.

"We made out like we were teenagers!" Daisy calls from the other room. "I love kissing."

"That's gross and I don't want to hear any more!" I call back, half teasing, half serious.

I want to ask her why she's not more concerned about all the things that could go wrong dating a coworker, but I don't.

I can't be the one to rain on her parade.

I walk into the bathroom and get dressed, aware that the melancholy is back in the hollow part inside me. Am I . . . jealous?

Of course I want Daisy to be happy, the same way I want my friends back home to be happy. But why does their happiness leave me feeling like the last kid picked for the badminton team in gym class?

I'm weighing what I have against what other people have and coming up short. Why do I always come up short? And why does this matter so much?

It's not a competition, Rosie.

Besides, I don't have time to sit with any of this right now. These feelings are not why I'm here. I'm here to direct a show.

I grab my things, pack up a bag, and head out to the theatre.

....

I spend the next several days diligently working on the show.

I meet with Ginny and talk through the costumes, explaining what I want for each character. She barks back at me when she doesn't agree, but ultimately we come up with a plan. It's obvious that making the costumes gives her a sense of accomplishment, and I feel good about leaving them in her hands.

Veronica and I talk through the musical numbers, and while she tries to insert tap numbers all over the show, I'm able to successfully steer her in a more traditional direction.

And then there are rehearsals.

Our schedule is fairly intense, given how soon the show is coming up, which means that every afternoon we are blocking scenes (a fancy name for telling people when and where to move), learning songs, or teaching choreography. The cast starts doing that thing casts do—falling into a rhythm, becoming friends.

And I pay attention. Because this is another thing I love about theatre. By the end, if I do my job right, these people will feel like family.

Dylan starts to put together a list of backstage volunteers, and every night after rehearsal, Booker shows up to work on the set, basing it off the many photos I emailed him.

I took shop class in college—you had to in order to graduate—but I require a refresher before I'm any help to him at all.

We haven't talked any more about the non-date at Buster's, and that's just fine with me. I can't come up with words for any of the things I'm feeling at the moment.

I just know that the summer will be short, and I don't want to waste time not being around him, no matter what logic and reason say.

Friday, he shows up at our cottage with Louie and a pizza, and I think the extra couple will get me out of Friday questions. But at the end of the night, I walk him outside, and he asks me, "Do you want to have kids?"

It's dark, and he can't see my wide eyes. "Wow, you're playing hardball." And then, lightly, I add, "I guess these are the things you think about when you get to be, you know, your age."

I can feel him smiling, and I decide that if I could be the cause of that smile every day, I'd be okay never making anyone else laugh again.

"But yeah," I say. "I do want kids."

He nods, and we both lean against the porch railing. "What happened to your parents?"

He stiffens beside me.

"Too personal?"

He draws in a breath. "No, it's fine. My dad was never in the picture, and my mom gave me up when I was almost two. She was young, and she couldn't handle it. My grandma—my dad's mom—she was the one who took me in. And Bertie helped. When Grandma died a few years later, Bertie didn't hesitate for a second." He shrugs. "Just adopted me like that was the only thing to do."

I go still.

He bumps my shoulder with his own. "I don't see that as a sad story, if that's what you're thinking."

I glance over at him. "You don't?"

He shakes his head. "I see that as a gift. Yeah, my parents didn't want a kid, and I guess I could dwell on that. But I guess I'd rather be thankful that my grandma and Bertie loved me."

I reach over and take his hand, marveling at this attitude because, really, it's pretty incredible.

"And they're the ones who taught me that a lot of life is about how you see it."

It's just life, Rosie.

The words burrow down deep inside me and start to take root, and I hope I remember to water them because I really want to see what they grow.

CHAPTER 26

SUNDAY AFTERNOON, AFTER A FULL week of rehearsals and meetings and show-related work, I need a distraction, so I hop in my cart and drive over to the theatre.

When I arrive, I see Arthur and Bertie sitting on a bench under a big oak tree. There's a picnic basket on the bench between them, and as I park and get out of the golf cart, realization settles. They're on a *date*.

I quietly let myself into the theatre so I don't disturb them. The space is empty on Sundays, and I stop in the lobby for a moment, just to inhale it all. To remind myself that I'm here, getting paid to work in the theatre.

Booker was right—directing is a *lot* more responsibility than being an actor. The show is mine, and I want to do right by it. It won't lead to more jobs or notoriety or my name in lights, but I've always been a person who takes pride in my work.

No matter where that work is located.

I pull open the door of the auditorium and step inside, instantly struck by the scene in front of me. While I'd helped Booker in the scene shop, nothing we were building took any shape—until now. In the center of the stage is a large curved staircase, with a platform that stretches the width of the stage on either side. It has ornate pillars, entrances and exits underneath, simply perfect for a palace—and as I look at it, I can see the way it will come to life.

I stare and beam and appreciate.

I can't believe those seemingly unrelated pieces came together to create this.

I pull my script out of my bag and immediately start envisioning the staging for multiple scenes. Slowly, I make my way up the stairs and start walking through it, speaking lines and writing down the movements that feel natural to me. We have another blocking rehearsal tomorrow, and this is so inspiring.

I walk through two more scenes this way, eventually growing more and more comfortable being up here. And while the desire and love for performing hasn't disappeared, I do note how good it feels to be the one to decide where and when the actors will move and stand. I make notes about inflection and motivation, all things we'll discuss as we run through the scene.

And when I'm finished, there's that light feeling again.

Happiness.

Huh.

I go back to the first scene I blocked, walking it one more time to get it in my head, and when I'm almost finished, I hear the stage door open. I freeze and wait, unsure who else would be here on a Sunday, but when I see Arthur, I can't help but smile.

He doesn't smile back.

"What are you doing here?" he barks.

"I'm the director, buddy," I crack.

He grumbles something that I can't hear. Despite all my best efforts, he is a nut I haven't been able to crack. Not that I'm giving up.

"I came to get some work done," I tell him. "The set looks amazing."

He barely looks at me as he walks across the stage to the fly lines. "Electric coming in!" I can tell he says this because he was trained to say it when bringing in one of the lines, and not out of courtesy to me. Still, I respond with, "Thank you," to acknowledge that I heard him, and step out of the way.

Once the row of lights is lowered, Arthur stops the rope, clamps the brake, and steps out from the wings. He's holding a gel and a few tools, and as he gets to work replacing the old gel, I stand there wondering if I should leave.

I don't leave, choosing instead to make things awkward.

"So you and Bertie seem to have hit it off."

It takes 0.3 seconds for me to realize this was the wrong thing to say.

Arthur stops moving and glares at me. "*That*"—he points his crescent wrench at me—"is none of your business."

My instinct is to apologize and run away, but I've noticed that Booker was right when he told me to dish it right back. Arthur doesn't respond well to the people he intimidates.

He does, however, respond well to Bertie.

And she doesn't take his crap.

"It is, sort of," I say. "I mean, I was there when you two met."

If he's surprised by my response, he doesn't let on. "That doesn't make it your business."

I watch as he goes back to fiddling with the lights. "I think I know why my song made you emotional."

"Your song was mediocre at best," he says.

"It wasn't, but okay."

Even though he doesn't respond, his puckered face communicates plenty.

"You think you can make it better?" I pause. "Professor?"

He stops moving, but only for a moment.

"I googled you," I say, as if that simple sentence was enough to fully encompass the amount of research I'd done on Arthur. Once I finally got back to my search, I couldn't stop—what I found was fascinating.

"Turns out, you were kind of a big deal once upon a time," I say.

"And look at me now!" The words drip with sarcasm, and I go still.

"You taught acting and directing at NYU," I say, because it was one of the first things I'd discovered.

He rolls his eyes. "Are you just going to stand there and tell me things I already know?" He holds out a wrench. When I don't move, he says, "Hold this."

I take the wrench and press a bit further.

"I think the song reminded you of that life," I say. "Of the way it felt to train up the next generation of actors and directors." Another pause. "I also know you directed *Funny Girl*." That one took a bit more digging to uncover.

He yanks the wrench out of my hands without so much as a glance in my direction. "You don't know what you're talking about."

"I know you're brilliant," I say. "I read countless reviews of plays you directed. I think you're the first person in the history of theatre to never get a bad one."

I think about my own miserable reviews, and I'm even more in awe. Because I know how hard it is to get a critic to like you. Arthur didn't seem to have that problem.

All of the critics seemed to agree on one thing: Arthur Silverman was brilliant.

"Why did you stop?" I ask.

He tightens a fixture, ignoring my question.

I hug my script to my chest, my gaze trailing to the stage floor. "This is the first show I've ever directed."

"Obviously," he says, annoyed.

The barb irritates me. "Just because I haven't done as much as you or know as much as you doesn't make me bad at it."

He pauses working on the light, and his eyes flick to mine, and I realize that I have an opportunity to learn from one of the greats. And I want him to teach me. I'll soak it all up—whatever he'll share. I'll take anything. Lighting, directing, acting, anything.

Except how to be a colossal jerk.

I'm just not sure how to get him to agree. Teaching hardly seems like a priority for him right now.

"You think I can do better? You think I need help?"

He raises his eyebrows as if to say, *"You really want me to answer that?"*

I lift my chin and stare straight at him. "Fine. Make me better."

He moves down the row of lights. "And why would I do that?"

I'm not sure what I'm going for here, but I push on.

He thrusts another tool in my direction, and I hold it until he motions for me to give it back.

"Out of the goodness of your huge bleeding heart?" But my attempt at humor falls flat. I go still. "Don't you miss it, Arthur?"

A sigh. A chink in the armor.

"Life is much simpler now," he responds.

He keeps working on the final light fixture for several seconds without acknowledging that he heard me.

"Tell me about directing *Funny Girl*," I say. "Why did my song make you emotional?"

"You're pushy." He holds out his hand, demanding the tool back. "And you ask too many questions."

My shoulders slump, and I begrudgingly hand it back.

He takes it, walks back into the wings, and calls out, "Electric going out!"

"Thank you." I don't shout it. I don't even say it loud enough for him to hear me.

He's right. I do ask too many questions.

But I still have so many more left to ask.

CHAPTER 27

"I REALIZED I MIGHT NOT have been clear in my intentions."

I'm standing in the doorway of my cottage, at the end of my Sunday with Arthur and the lights, and Booker is back on my porch.

With a pizza.

And those eyes.

"Oh?" I try to tell myself to stay strong, arm's length, aloof, but I feel my resolve crumble the second I see him standing outside. I'm like a giddy teenager the second I step onto the porch.

And when he says, "I want to date you," all bets are off.

Never mind the way it sends my pulse racing, the way I could easily lose all sense of reason. It's like the part of me that cares about that decided it needed a nap.

"You want to date me," I repeat, looking down at the pizza box, then back at him. I have to keep this light or else I'm going to get lost. "And feed me more pizza?"

"Yes." He smirks. "You seem to really like pizza."

"I'm leav—"

"Leaving at the end of the summer," he cuts in. "I know, I know. But I like you, Rosie." He takes a step closer. "I'll take whatever time I can get."

It's not late enough for it to be dark outside, but I almost wish it were. I'm certain my face is showing every single emotion I'm trying not to have. I assumed that the night at the bar was just a glitch because this whole past week we'd hung out and talked and had our second Friday questions—and it really seemed like he'd backed off of the whole idea.

"I was kind of waiting for your cue, but you're hard to read," he says.

"I know," I say, because I could've easily been straight with him.

"I think there's something here," he says. "I had fun with you. It's nice. We can keep it casual."

"I don't really do casual," I say.

"Neither do I." He leans against the doorjamb and smiles down at me.

"Then why would we start dating?" I ask lightly.

"Because we're trying new things this summer?" He smiles—a *casual* smile—and I don't know why I'm bothering to pretend. I'm going to give in. I'm going to agree to dating him against all logic, and that should concern me more than it does.

Because I have a feeling I won't be able to say no to this man. Because I had fun with him too. And also because I like him. I like that he feels safe. That he knows a few things about me that nobody else knows—and he doesn't seem to mind that I'm full of flaws.

I like that I actually want to tell him all of my secrets, even though wanting it terrifies me.

And I really like that he's a grown-up. No games. He just says what he feels. That's hard to find.

I shake my head. "This is a really bad idea."

His smile is slightly wicked. "My favorite kind."

He takes a step toward me, and I draw in a slow, deep breath. It's been a while since I kissed anyone, and honestly? The only thing I'm thinking about is trying to remember how to do it. Is it like riding a bike? Will muscle memory kick in? What if I'm way out of my league and Booker is so much better at this than I am?

What if—but my inner monologue is silenced by his lips on mine, dashing away all my fears.

He *is* good at this, and while I want to hold up my end of the kissing bargain, I also want to close my eyes and let myself get swept away for once, even though it doesn't make sense.

He drops the pizza box onto the porch and pulls me closer, hands at my waist as I wrap my arms around his neck. His lips are soft but firm and fully attentive to me. I lean in, our bodies pressed close, savoring each sweet movement as his mouth sweeps over mine. There's a fluttering inside my rib cage, like the release of a thousand happy butterflies. It's a rush of excitement and nerves and an endless desire that awakens something inside me. Something I'm not sure I've ever allowed myself to feel.

It's a heady, intoxicating kind of kiss. So intoxicating, in fact, that when he pulls away and searches my eyes, I go up on my tiptoes for more.

A wave of worry washes over me. I could fall for him. The thought scares me, and yet, that fear is exactly what makes this so exciting.

I'm not sure how to reconcile that.

I don't know how much time passes, because passion doesn't wear a watch, and when I finally pull back, I let my gaze fall to his chest because I feel like I've revealed more of myself than I intended.

"Yep. I knew it," he says.

I try to silence my pounding heart, but I'm sure people can hear it down the block.

"Knew what?"

"Kissing you would be amazing."

I draw my eyes to his. "Oh . . . you've thought about it?"

"Not a ton," he says with a flirty shrug. "Only every single day since I picked you up at the bus station."

I press my lips together to try to conceal a persistent smile. "But why? I only had eyes for Roberto."

He laughs and tucks my hair behind my ear, his hand lingering on my neck. "And for the record, there's nothing casual about the way I feel about you, Rosie." He steps back, pushing a hand through his hair. "I know that probably freaks you out. It kind of freaks me out too. I know all the reasons this doesn't make sense . . . I shouldn't like you this much already."

"I know what you mean." I take a step away, letting the door of my cottage close. "But . . . I'm still leaving."

He steps toward me. "Can we pretend?"

"I don't want to pretend. Not with you." I screw my eyes shut because all at once I'm afraid they might give me away.

He takes my hand and gives a gentle tug. I don't resist, mostly because I like the way it feels to keep him close. He kisses me again, this time so sweetly it makes me want to cry. Because this is what I want. Isn't this what everyone wants?

To love and be loved? To share life with a person who knows all of the things you don't say out loud and chooses you anyway?

But—and I remind myself of this again—Booker is not that person for me.

Booker isn't going to suddenly decide to leave Bertie and move to New York. And as much fun as I'm having, directing shows for senior citizens in Wisconsin isn't my dream.

The thought assaults my mind and I pull back.

"Can we just . . . see?" he asks.

"Or maybe we go back to being friends?" This shouldn't be that hard. I've only known Booker a few weeks. Never mind that it only took days for me to realize he was different.

"Uh . . . I don't think I can."

The air between us is charged.

"Yeah," I half laugh. "That was a stupid thing to suggest." My shoulders slump at the realization that we're at a crossroads and I don't want to choose a path. I just want to sit here with him for as long as I can.

"Maybe we don't need to figure it all out right now," he says. "Maybe we just keep hanging out and see where it goes?"

"Like, live in the moment?"

He shrugs as if to say, *"Might not be the worst plan."*

But I'm not so sure. Actors are trained to stay *in the moment* in classes and in scene work. Can I do that in my real life, even though it goes against my nature? I've always been a person who operates with a plan. This—me and Booker—wouldn't have a plan. But it would have an end date. Normally, knowing that would make me run the other way. Better to protect my heart from what I see coming for it.

So why do I hear myself say, "We can try?"

"Okay." He smiles. "I'm all for trying."

And as he leans in to kiss me again, I note that Booker Hayes is under my skin, on my mind, and pushing my buttons. Not in an annoying way. In an "I'm not sure I can keep my hands off him" kind of way.

And it's a disaster. A *delicious* disaster.

CHAPTER 28

OVER THE NEXT FEW WEEKS, my life settles into a pattern, though not a predictable one. In the way it always is with theatre, every day is different. Every rehearsal brings a new challenge.

Last week, we had to pause a scene because Evelyn's teeth fell out. And yesterday, a man named Sal nearly choked on a salami sandwich, which I'd already told him he couldn't have onstage.

I eat breakfast with Daisy in the dining hall, then go straight to the theatre. If we aren't rehearsing, we're painting set pieces or collecting props. Ginny roped me into sewing (straight lines only), and Grace has come in twice for extra help on her songs because she's already so nervous.

Booker is always waiting after rehearsals, proving he was serious about getting as much time as he can with me this summer, and I won't lie . . . I don't hate it.

We raid the Commons after hours and watch reruns of *The Office* with Daisy and Louie. We attend cooking classes and show up for swing dancing because Daisy begs us to. We make root beer floats and kiss under the stars on my back patio.

And all of these moments spent with a man I'm trying desperately not to love become the ones that matter most of all.

They are the moments that make up my life.

Maybe *this* is all I need to be happy.

Kissing Booker has become my favorite pastime. He's good at it. *We're* good at it—well on our way to getting great at it.

I've mostly kept up with the group chat and contributed to choosing peacock blue as the color for Maya's bridesmaids' dresses. Taylor is kicking around the idea of naming her baby Nellie, which I personally love, even though Marnie is violently opposed, thanks to old reruns of *Little House on the Prairie*. And maybe I still haven't caught them up on everything, but they're a part of my life.

And that feels good.

And then there's the show.

Even that is going well.

Yes, Belinda is still the diva, and the Margies often have to leave the stage mid-scene due to a bladder crisis, but after a month of rehearsals, I'm actually starting to see it take shape.

The members of the cast eat and play pickleball and do Zumba classes together. They're friends. And I like them.

And I like being here.

I even like working with Dylan, who is maybe the biggest surprise of all. She anticipates the things I'll need before I even ask for them, and it's possible that my favorite part of this whole experience has been watching her come to life.

She's still Dylan—all angst and eye rolls—but honestly, that's come in handy, considering how many times she's wielded them on Belinda. Watching the two of them face off is like watching a nineteenth-century duel. Or a haphazard game of table tennis, depending on the day.

I also notice that she's the first one at the theatre and the last one to leave. Part of me thinks it's because she doesn't feel like she really has a home, but I wonder if it's something more.

Like maybe she loves it.

I want to know what the plan is for Dylan once the school year starts, but even the tiniest bit of probing leads to her clamming up, leaving, or pulling out her phone and ignoring me, so for now I don't push.

We eat lunch together in the dining hall as a cast, which is a truly wild experience. It turns out theatre people are pretty much the same, regardless of age. Loud talkers, big personalities, obnoxious laughter, and spontaneous sing-alongs, even in public places. Of course, there are also the introverts, who perform for the love of performing and not because they want to be the center of attention.

Grace falls into that category, which makes her and me fast friends.

Daisy and Louie join us most days and manage to fit right in with the rowdy crew.

And so do I, which I never could've predicted.

In addition to teaching the music, I block scenes and talk to the cast about character and inflection and diction and projection. These actors might not be professional, and they're all much older than I am, but I realize early on that I do have things I can teach them. Most of them haven't done theatre since high school, if at all.

The great thing is that most of them listen. They care a lot about this show, and they've all taken ownership of their part in it. They want it to be good, not only because they also know what's riding on its success, but because they take pride in their work. And several of them had to work up the courage to do this after years of wishing they would.

I admire that. They make me want to be brave too.

When I get stuck, I somehow always seem to get help from the most unexpected—and most qualified—person in the room.

Arthur.

And he helps in the quietest, most unassuming way.

Once, last week, Connie was really struggling in one of her scenes. I don't like to do line readings—I feel like they can insult an actor, taking away their ability to do their job—but after five straight minutes of conversing *about* the scene, Connie still wasn't getting it. I even tried using examples from movies or TV shows, hoping she could mimic them, but it was still so robotic.

"Why don't we take a minute and we'll come back and tackle it again?" I'd said, backing away from the stage because, honestly, I didn't know what else to try to get through to her.

Arthur casually walked over and sat down in the row behind me. "What are you trying to get out of her?"

I frowned. "She's playing the character too stiff. Too serious. I wanted the fairy godmother to feel like a cozy, quirky grandma."

He was quiet for a long moment.

Then, thoughtfully, he simply said, "Ask her how she is around her grandkids."

I actually *saw* the light bulb over my own head. Here I was, a supposed actor who has been taught to draw on my own life experiences to connect with a role, and I didn't even think of it.

It worked. Easily. She changed in an instant.

I turned toward where he was sitting to give him all the credit, but he was gone.

It seems that underneath the grouchy exterior, there's still the heart of a teacher.

One thing Arthur doesn't save me from, though, is Belinda.

She seems to live for every opportunity to make this whole process as difficult as possible. It's challenging to have one person in the cast who seems intent on ruining the show for everyone else, and I know this is something I have to handle. I'm just not sure how.

Anytime I offer a thought or give her any direction, Belinda responds with either an excuse or an inane reason why she didn't do it that way in the first place, or why she simply *can't* do whatever I suggest. It's been going on for several weeks, and now, halfway through the process, I see it's affecting the others.

Evelyn and Sadie both questioned my blocking today in front of the rest of the cast, and I can feel the overall vibe of the show shifting.

One evening, I'm packing up my things when I notice Arthur

standing nearby. There are a few volunteers painting sets in the scene shop, but everyone else has gone.

"Sorry, I'm hurrying."

He makes a grunting noise and waves a hand in the air. "It's fine."

I frown, and then I remember that usually, after rehearsal, Arthur makes himself scarce. It's almost like three hours is too much *peopling* and he needs to get away from everyone.

So, I reason, if he's standing out here while I'm packing up . . .

"How did you think it went today?" I offer, hoping to open the lines of communication.

"It's your show," he says, shrugging. "How do *you* think it went?"

I'm inclined to steel my jaw and snark back some comment, but I resist. Because the longer I stand here, the more certain I am that he has something to say.

I know that Arthur has a lot of knowledge and experience locked up in that head of his. In addition to teaching at NYU for years, Arthur has directed at least thirty professional shows. He's script-doctored more than a dozen. His name appears in various roles—director, producer, designer, consultant—on more shows than I can count.

I'm assuming they offered him this position at Sunset Hills ages ago, and I'm also assuming he turned it down. Oddly, I don't think he turned it down because he thinks it's beneath him, even though an argument could be made that it is. I think there's another reason.

I just don't know what it is.

The mystery remains.

"If it were your show, how would you feel about it?" I ask, wanting honesty, not flattery.

He stops and looks at me. I can see the gears turning, as if he's deciding to even deign a response.

He draws in a breath. "Connie needs to stop giggling after every line," he says. "Evelyn needs to learn her choreography. The scene with the stepsisters drags—the pacing needs to be much tighter, because that's where the comedy is. The timing just isn't right. Edgar doesn't open his mouth when he talks—there's no way the audience will hear him." He stops when he sees me glance at the open notebook on the table next to my things.

He nods to it as if to say, *"Go ahead."*

I grab the notebook and pull the pencil out of my hair, scribbling in an unreadable shorthand to try to record his every thought. He has notes for everyone, including Veronica, who isn't going to want to hear his criticism of her choreography, so I add a separate note to myself to sandwich the critique between compliments so it's easier to digest.

"And, lastly . . ." He pauses, waiting for me to look up from my notebook. "You need to deal with your Belinda problem."

I frown. "Yeah, I'm not—"

"You're in charge, Rosie. And a good director knows she can't have an actor going rogue. She needs to know she can be replaced."

"I mean, I don't take her suggestions," I say weakly.

"But you do let her give them, right in the middle of when you're talking."

I wince. "And that's bad."

He shrugs as if to say, *"Well, duh."*

"Look, Rosie, you're a good performer."

I go still, because whatever he's about to say next feels important.

"But if you want to be, you could be a great director." He draws in a breath. "You have options, is all I'm saying. And all of it helps make you better."

I can see he's uncomfortable giving me a compliment, so I try my very hardest to keep my face neutral, to pretend that his words aren't potentially the most meaningful anyone has ever said to me. To my shock, he's not finished.

"You're good with people," he says. "That's key. A lot of directors are like dictators, and while they might put the fear of God into their actors, they create a hostile work environment."

I begin to see a softness at his edges, and I wish I'd known him back when he was teaching. "What kind of director were you?"

His face shifts. "Contrary to what I'm sure is current popular belief, I was . . . fun." He draws in a breath and sits down in an aisle seat next to where I'm standing. So I sit across from him, anxious for him to go on. "As long as Annie was there."

I watch Arthur but try not to stare, because I can practically see all the memories stored in the wrinkles of his skin. And I have a feeling those memories are the kind he keeps for himself.

"She calmed me down," he says, voice tinged with nostalgia. "She was the one who made me believe I could do more than just perform. You know, they always say, 'Those who can't do, teach,' but the truth is—teaching was hard. It *is* hard. And I'm sure you've had bad teachers who proved that not everyone can do it. Not well anyway."

At that, I wince a knowing smile. "I absolutely have."

"There are teachers—great actors, mind you—who tear their students down because it makes them feel smarter or special," he says.

"Professor Castle," I say, surprised by this unexpected connection.

"Professor Hall," he says.

I smile. *Common ground.*

"I wasn't going to be that kind of teacher or director," he tells me. "And if I ever hinted at letting my ego in, well, my Annie kept me on track."

"*My Annie,*" he said.

Nothing feels the same as when you belong to someone, held in their hearts and resting in their minds.

"She never let me get away with anything, least of all thinking I'm more important than anyone else." He smiles, and for a moment, he's lost in the memory.

I don't dare interrupt because the memory looks like a beautiful one.

"I still can't believe that woman loved me," he says wistfully.

"Oh, I don't know," I say, hopefully lightly enough. "I'm sure you were lovable once."

He looks over at me, and when he meets my eyes, he actually laughs. It's the first time I've even seen him smile, and it stirs something inside me.

Happiness.

I'm starting to see the common thread of what has made me happy this summer, now that I've really tuned in. It's the one thing I've continued to push away—other people. Relationships. Connection. The real kind, where I admit to the ugly parts of my life and let the chips fall where they may.

The one thing that scares me the most is the thing that's been missing all along.

I've let my own embarrassment keep me so isolated, and now I wonder if that's been the problem all along.

I don't wonder. I know. It *has* been the problem.

I've built myself a lonely life.

I press my lips together, unsure how to ask for clarification on something I don't think he wanted to talk about in the first place. "Why do you think I could be a great director?"

His thin eyebrows shoot up. "Didn't peg you as one to go compliment fishing."

I laugh to myself. "I swear I'm not. I just . . . never really thought of myself as a director."

"Your ego told you that you wanted to be the one getting all the applause," he says, not unkindly.

"No, I—" But I stop myself. Because maybe he's right. Was it pride that has kept me isolated?

"Maybe," I admit. "I mean, I love the work, but I think . . ." One glance at him, and I know he's listening. And oddly? Not judging.

I cross one leg over the other and scoot back in the chair. "I've always wanted to perform. For as long as I can remember, that has been my dream."

"And now?"

I shake my head and shrug. Because now? I have no idea.

An odd sense of peace comes over me when I entertain the idea of pivoting. Or at least being open to the idea of pivoting.

"Annie always said I had a superpower." He rests his hands on his lap, and his head bobs ever so slightly, perhaps involuntarily. "But she made it clear I do *not* look good in capes."

I smile at that. "I wish I'd known her. She sounds so wonderful." I pause, then add, "And anyone who could put up with you must be a saint."

"That's a fact." He chuckles softly.

"So, what is this superpower?" I ask, genuinely curious.

He tilts his head and looks at me. "She said I can see things in people they can't see in themselves." His smile turns a bit rueful. "You have that same gift."

I laugh off the comparison. "Oh, come on. We're so far apart from one another, you may as well compare apples and car batteries."

He meets my eyes across the aisle, and I try not to let myself get caught up in how unexpected—and wonderful—this conversation is. "Nobody else wanted to cast Grace as Cinderella, but you saw something in her. And you were right." He points at me as he says this. "She's a beautiful Cinderella. And Dylan! Everyone thought you were crazy for bringing her on board, but look at how she's blossomed."

And then, eyes going serious again, he says, "I've also noticed that, like me, you don't share much about yourself."

"Perceptive."

He taps his nose. "Superpower."

"Maybe you hold back because you're a deep thinker," he says. "And a deep feeler."

I've never thought of myself as either . . . but now that I hear someone else say it, it makes sense.

I think about the Friday questions and how difficult it's been to share with Booker. I want him to know me, but for some reason I resist.

The third Friday, he went easy on me and asked about my family. I gave him the quick rundown, telling him about my mom and John—my stepdad who adopted me and gave me his name and loved me like his own, blah, blah, blah.

But the next week, he asked about my real dad, and that was a much more difficult discussion. In the end, I stuck to the facts, answering the questions as if the answers didn't make me feel anything at all. When really, they made me feel everything.

Last Friday, Booker changed direction completely. His question was, *"What's your favorite way to be kissed?"* which required me to show him my answer, multiple times, for lengths between thirty seconds and eighteen minutes.

Simply telling him wasn't effective.

For his part, Booker had shared so openly I almost wondered if he'd ever had a hard time sharing feelings at all. I now know that he once spray-painted the equipment shed at his high school's baseball field because he was mad at the coach (and got away with it). I also know his last serious relationship ended amicably when he and his ex-girlfriend, a professional marathon runner who was every bit as intimidating as that makes her sound, realized they were better off as friends.

"She's married now," he'd told me, as if that could steal away my insecurity.

But this thought that I keep to myself because I *feel* too deeply? I don't know . . . I glance at Arthur. "You think I'm a deep feeler?"

"Just putting it out there," he says. "Maybe you avoid emotions because you feel them all a little more deeply than other people. And that's overwhelming." He shifts in his seat.

I sit with it, like it's a cat that's curled up on my lap. Something about the words resonate.

"Professors always want you to relive the bad things," I say.

"And you don't want to do that," he says—a statement, not a question.

I shake my head.

"Then you can't use it."

I look away, trying not to let the words penetrate the wall I've built around myself. Because some part of me—a part I buried way, way deep down—already knows this. "It's my life, Arthur. Not fodder for a future character."

He stills. "That's your job, Rosie. If you ever hope to make anyone feel anything, you have to let yourself feel it first."

An unexpected knot forms at the back of my throat, and I will myself not to cry. "I can't. It hurts too much."

There's a beat, and I work to keep my emotions in check.

But then Arthur says, "It's supposed to hurt. It's life."

"Well, then," I say, half laughing, "life sucks."

"And that means you're alive." Arthur leans in, and I see a glimmer of something new in his eye. "That's part of the adventure. If everything was good all the time, you wouldn't appreciate any of it. It's the hard stuff that makes the good stuff so much sweeter."

I pause for a long moment, then decide it's okay to confide in him. After all, hundreds of other students have probably poured their hearts out to this man. "I don't like reliving it."

"I understand, Rosie." He scoots back in the chair, still studying me. "But *this* is what's holding you back."

CHAPTER 29

MY CONVERSATION WITH ARTHUR HAS me contemplating things I don't normally think about—things I don't *let* myself think about. The truth is, I had a relatively normal childhood. My dad left, and it nearly destroyed my mom. Big deal.

Feelings shouldn't be this hard for someone who wants to act. I should be able to call them up whenever I need them, then put them away when I don't.

Why doesn't it work that way?

"You know, you're good at this teaching stuff." I shift back into the chair even farther, like I'm settling in for a long chat, even though I'm certain he's about finished. "You should do it more often."

He waves me off. "I'm old, Rosie."

"You're old," I say. "But you're not dead."

He scoffs. "I've made my contributions to the world, young lady. Quite a few of them, in fact. It's your turn now."

"If that were true, then you wouldn't be sitting here with me, now, would you?" I say in a scolding tone.

He squints over at me, then stands. "You're right. I don't know what I'm doing here."

I stand, facing him in the aisle. "Why are you telling me all this? You don't even like me."

"That's true," he says. "I don't."

I react with a shocked "Ha! Rude!"

But then he smiles, the wrinkles around his eyes and across his forehead deepening. And it's a beautiful thing—proof that, once upon a time, there were things that made him happy enough to smile, even laugh. "You want the truth?"

"I do," I say, even though I really want to make a joke in an attempt to make him laugh again.

"I talked to Annie yesterday." He holds up both hands in front of him. "Before you say it, I'm not crazy—I know she's gone. I'm not seeing ghosts or hearing her voice or conjuring her through some kind of candle or crystal or something." His expression shifts. "She would've reminded me that teachers not only teach, they encourage, and if I saw something in you, it was my duty to tell you." He starts to walk away. "So, do whatever you want. It's not my problem anymore."

For some inexplicable reason, I jump up and run after him, blocking his exit. And then I throw my arms around him in a tight hug that I hope conveys everything I need it to convey—that his words, so simple for him to say, have caused everything inside me to shift.

I *do* feel deeply, and I don't want to feel deeply. Because when I let it all in, it hurts.

I've never viewed this as an asset in my life or my relationships or my work. But what if it is? What if feeling deeply *is* my superpower because it's the thing that allows me to connect with other people?

And this? This feeling of overwhelming gratitude? This I have to let in. Because it just might be the thing that gives me the courage to change my life.

When I pull back, I see tears in the old man's eyes.

"You big softie," I say, smiling.

He grunts and waves me off.

I drop my hands to my sides but don't move. "Do you think I'm crazy to keep pursuing this?" I ask.

He draws in a breath, and it occurs to me that I'm only seeing a fraction of his wisdom right now. How much more could I learn from this man?

"I think you have to ask yourself what it is you want most," he says. "And you have to be okay if what you want most isn't what you thought. Or if your dream has changed. Or if what you want is different now." He pauses. "Our priorities shift as we get older. And you can still love the things you love, but maybe in a different way. Maybe a different city. Or a different aspect of the dream. Or maybe something entirely new. You could be a goat wrangler in Mexico—who knows?"

I meet his eyes as the hint of amusement flickers away.

"It's your life, Rosie. Only you can decide what's best for you. And if you don't want to quit, maybe you just pivot. Keep your eyes open. Opportunities are everywhere."

I laugh. "Okay, now you're just speaking in fortune cookie."

"I'm leaving."

He starts to walk away, and I call after him. "Arthur?"

"I'm not stopping this time," he says without turning around.

"I just wanted to say thank you."

He lifts a hand to acknowledge he's heard me, and I can't be sure, but I think . . . maybe . . . he smiles.

MAYA: Rosie, we need an update on Love Match. Full disclosure, I'm still logged into your account and saw you turned off notifications and haven't responded to a single message.

MARNIE: Are you logged into my account too?

MAYA: I'm invested. I set them up. Marnie, Greg G. looks promising!

TAYLOR: I don't think it's the best idea for Rosie to get involved with someone who lives in Wisconsin.

MAYA: She doesn't have to marry the guy. She can just have a little fun!

MARNIE: Maybe casual hookups aren't Rosie's idea of fun.

TAYLOR: Casual hookups definitely aren't Rosie's idea of fun.

MAYA: Well, how is she ever going to meet anyone if she doesn't put herself out there?

I send a photo of me and Booker.

ROSIE: I'm doing just fine ;)

TAYLOR: ROSIE WATERMAN, WHAT THE . . .

MAYA: THIS IS THE MOST BEAUTIFUL CREATURE I'VE EVER SEEN!

(Except for Matty, of course.)

MARNIE: Rosie! I thought we were in this together!

ROSIE: We're trying to keep things casual. But, you guys . . .

I send a photo of Booker smiling.

ROSIE: It's a rough go.

....

MOM: It's been a little while since I've heard from you. What's new?

ROSIE: Oh, nothing, really. Just work, work, work!

CHAPTER 30

ANOTHER WEEK GOES BY AND the show is starting to feel like a show. We're a little less than three weeks from opening night, and while there are some nervous jitters, there are also a lot of great things happening.

Veronica has finished teaching the choreography, I've taught all the music and blocked the entire show, so today . . . we'll attempt our first run-through.

I affectionately call it a Stumble-Through and Stop-and-Fix.

I arrive early to get things prepared, entering through the scene shop because, yes, I happen to know that Booker is already here, working on his day off. And because I really want to see him.

I walk into the large space behind the stage, and there he is, putting the finishing touches on Cinderella's house. I watch him for a few seconds, mostly because he's very nice to look at, but also because I'm keenly aware my time here is coming to an end.

And because I really, *really* don't want to say goodbye.

The door closes behind me, and at the sound of it, he turns, smiling when he meets my eyes. "Hey."

"Hey."

I walk over to him, and when I'm a foot away, he reaches for me. Letting myself step into his arms is the easiest thing in the world.

He kisses me, and I can tell the intention is for it to be a simple hello, but it quickly becomes something more.

I savor it. Every time I kiss him, I savor it, because I know it's all fleeting and soon he won't be so accessible to me.

When he pulls back, I see he's frowning.

"What?"

"You're in your head," he says, and I'm struck by how strange it is that he knows things about me already. Things nobody else has bothered to pay attention to. "What are you thinking about?"

I shake my head, not wanting to admit it because I know how pathetic it sounds. Because I knew this going in. I said it out loud. Told myself over and over what a bad idea this was. But I ignored my own warnings.

"Rosie?"

"I was just thinking"—I step back—"I'm only here for a few more weeks."

The frown deepens. "So, in your head, you're already saying goodbye?"

"No, I'm just . . ." But I *am* already saying goodbye. I'm already thinking about *lasts* when I should be thinking about *firsts*.

"We still have a few weeks," he says. "Don't get sad yet. Live in the moment, remember?"

Right. In the moment. You miss out on so much if you dwell on the past or try to predict the future. I draw in a breath, as if to cement the reminder in my mind, and then because I can't think of anything else to say, I smile. "I told my friends about you."

He inches back. "Ooh. This is a big moment. What did they say?"

"That you're a beautiful specimen of a man." I pump my eyebrows.

"So you're telling me they're smart women," he jokes. He grins, then leans down and kisses me again, then moves back toward Cinderella's house. "Are they coming to the show?"

I'm caught off guard. "Oh. Uh, I don't think so." I white-knuckle the strap of my bag. "I don't think they can make it."

He watches me. He's reading me. That's what he does. He can see straight through me, past all the things I'm not saying.

"You didn't tell them."

I heave a big sigh. "I told them about you," I offer.

"Rosie."

"And they know I'm directing a show," I say lamely. I find his eyes. "They just don't know *where*. I think it would be . . . hard to explain."

"Why? Are you embarrassed by us?" asks a voice from behind me.

I turn and find Evelyn, Sadie, and Ginny all standing in the doorway that leads to the dressing rooms downstairs.

"No! Of course not!" I protest, though I'm not sure it's true. "I'm proud of you all. Impressed, even."

"But not enough to invite anyone out to see it?" Ginny practically grunts. "My transformation dress alone is worth the price of the ticket."

"It *is* a beautiful dress," I say, and I mean it. The costumes *are* beautiful. The set is beautiful. And the acting and the music are all really impressive, especially considering where we started.

But this is not what my friends think I'm doing up here. It's not what I've led them to believe.

"Why haven't you invited anyone, Rosie?" Sadie asks. "You know our ticket sales are low."

"And you know how important it is that we have a successful run," Evelyn pipes in. "We should all be inviting everyone we know!"

"Do you not want people to come see the show?" Sadie asks as all three of the women stare at me.

"I—" I shrug. What do I say? Deep down, maybe I do know why I still haven't told my friends and family how to get tickets when they've all asked. Because I'm still too proud? Because I still care too much what people think? Because I'm still a jerk?

And here I thought I was growing up this summer.

In the wake of my nonanswer, the three women turn to one another, looking hurt, and walk off.

The message I just sent them? That I'm ashamed and embarrassed by what we're doing here—that all their hard work isn't good enough. I sigh. I feel awful.

I turn and find Booker watching me. His eyes are kind, but I feel like I've even let him down.

"I'll invite them, I swear," I say, sounding like a cheating husband promising it was just one time and it'll never happen again.

He squints at me. "Where do your friends think you are?"

"Where I told them. The Sunset Playhouse." I slump to the floor, back against the wall. "I just didn't correct that when I found out where I would actually be working this summer."

"*Are* you embarrassed?" he asks.

I don't look at him. I can't.

I feel ashamed. Ashamed that I *do* feel embarrassed. When I shouldn't. Which makes me feel even more ashamed.

As much as these people and this place are winning me over, I've still chosen to keep them a secret.

He sits against the opposite wall, facing me. "Rosie, if they're really your friends, they won't care what you do or where you do it. You could be unemployed living in your parents' basement or a Broadway star. Real friends don't care."

I want to ask if he'd stick around if I was unemployed and living in my parents' basement, but he goes on.

"So are they real friends or not?"

"Yes," I say without hesitating. "They are the best friends." I've never doubted that for a second. The problem is not with them. It's with me. It's always been me.

"Then you should tell them the truth," he says. "All of it."

All of it.

He has no clue how difficult that is for me. I don't look at it as lying either. Not really. Just withholding some parts that aren't as pretty as others.

This is what's holding you back, Rosie.

And Booker wants me to tell them all of it? Even the part about being a failure? Even the part about not knowing if I want to go back to New York? Even the part about worrying I've wasted all this time pursuing a dream that simply does not want to come true?

I thought I'd made so much progress in being honest and sharing my feelings, but now I'm not so sure.

Booker must sense that my defenses have gone up.

"Hey," he says, a bit softer. "I'm not trying to tell you what to do."

I feel stupid for feeling this way. I know the right thing to do—I even know all of reasons to do it. It's just that when I come up to that point of admitting my failures, I have an overwhelming desire to hide.

I know it's not a huge deal, and I also know that my cast is full of very dramatic senior citizens who act a whole lot like very dramatic teenagers. Still, the thought that I might've hurt them in any way stings.

"I know," I say. "I *am* working on it."

"Oh, I know," he says, smirking. "Every Friday." And then, because he's kind, he adds, "I think you're ready."

I look up at him just as I hear something crash.

A metallic *crunch* followed by another woody *boom.*

"What the—?" Booker jumps to attention, and we both race toward the noise.

There are voices, frantic voices, getting louder and more frantic as we get closer, and then—an alarm starts blaring.

Booker and I burst through the scene shop door and onto the stage.

It's raining.

Inside the building.

Which is impossible. My brain is having trouble reconciling what I'm seeing when I hear Arthur's voice from above me.

He's in the rafters, near one of the fly lines, and the few people who had already arrived for rehearsal are running around, covering their heads and calling out for help. Who they're calling for, I'm not sure.

"Rosie!" Arthur hollers at me from up above. "We've had a flyaway!"

It takes a second for me to access this term, but when my mind finally finds the definition, I flash hot with panic.

In a theatre with a fly system—rigging and ropes and counterweights to fly in set pieces, backdrops, or lights—a flyaway is when the counterweights become unbalanced, sending either the heavy steel bar that the pieces are hung from careening to the ceiling, or the opposite, where a set piece comes crashing to the stage floor.

I wipe the smelly, brown sprinkler water from my face and look. There's no line on the stage, so it must've shot toward the ceiling.

Arthur calls out again. "One of the brakes failed—the line snapped a sprinkler head up here. Go find the shutoff valve!"

"The shutoff valve? Where is that?"

"Scene shop, left corner! The fire department is on their way!"

I'm frozen. I'm watching in horror as the sprinkler system is dumping hundreds of gallons of water on our set. On the stage. On me.

"Rosie! *Go!*"

I snap into focus. I do as I'm told, racing into the scene shop, wide-eyed and frantic, looking for and quickly finding the shutoff valve, which is, of course, locked behind a fence with a chain and a padlock.

I let out a frustrated groan.

All I can hear is water and the violent monotonous blaring of the alarm.

I desperately look around and find a five-foot length of pipe, and start to pry back the fence where the chain joins it.

Booker comes in behind me, grabs the pipe, and we both pull it open enough where I can reach in and pound the shutoff button.

The alarm continues to blare, and the water slows to a dripping halt. Booker looks at me and says something like, "You good? You okay?" but I don't answer. He leaves, running back to the stage.

I stand, shaking. Then I start to whimper.

I drop the pipe with a clang, and slowly, apprehensively, move out of the scene shop toward the stage.

I'm immediately hit with a dank, musty, wet smell. There is still water coming from above, but as I look up, I realize it's not coming from the sprinklers anymore.

It's the curtains, now sopping wet with brown water. They're dripping in steady streams, slowly starting to lower. The brakes on the lines are straining under the hundreds of gallons of added water weight.

Pools of water are everywhere on the stage, and I can see where some are starting to soak into the wood floor and the storage room beneath.

Where all of the costumes, props, and set pieces are stored.

I . . .

I can't . . .

I see Booker move over to the set pieces, most of which were stored on the stage or in the wings. He begins to assess the damage.

Arthur is down from the rafters, and he rushes toward me.

"Rosie. Rosie, you need to get ahold of Connie. Tell her what happened."

I stare. "Everything is ruined."

He hesitates. "We don't know that yet. I need you to focus, Rosie."

I shake my head, trying to clear it. Yes. Call Connie. Mobilize people. Move.

I phone Connie, willing my voice not to shake as I relay what has happened. "We need fans and towels and . . . just . . ." I shut my eyes. "Everything is ruined."

She apologizes, but then I hear in her voice she's leaping into action, letting me know she'll contact everyone she knows.

I hang up the phone and turn to face the stage.

I see Arthur, soaking wet, directing a few people to start moving things. I see Booker, sweeping off swathes of water from the castle set. Sadie and Evelyn are standing off to the side, stacking what looks like towels or blankets, and Ginny is stage right, assessing what appears to be the loss of a whole rack of costumes.

I feel anger and pride rise.

No, I think.

Not like this.

I didn't—*we* didn't—work this hard and come this far to have it end like this.

I feel my spine stiffen and my jaw clench, and I know, as the director, what I need to do.

I walk to the center of the stage.

"Everyone!" I call out. "Everyone, listen up. This is probably the worst thing that could've happened, but this is *not* the end of this show. We work together. We figure it out, and we find a way."

"We open in less than three weeks," Belinda says sourly. "How are we going to do that now?"

Her Evil Stepmother energy hovers in the air, thick like a storm cloud that really wants to dump rain all over this stage—as if it's not wet enough.

I spin around and glare at her. "We're going to figure it out.

We're going to clean it up, and the show is going to go on." But I feel my resolve waiver even as I say the words. Because this is an actual disaster. There's a very good chance that even if the sets and costumes are okay, the stage and fly lines aren't.

"Really," Belinda scoffs. "It's cute that you think *you* can fix this." She waves a hand in the air. "On the plus side, you won't have to tell anyone in your real life how you stooped so low you directed this embarrassing little show with all of us old people all the way up here in Door County."

I glance over at the three women who confronted me earlier. They all avoid my eyes.

"It's not like that," I say. Shame and a sense of being overwhelmed vie for equal footing at the back of my mind.

But Belinda and the others harrumph and walk off. As they reach the stage door, I hear Belinda say, "This musical is *canceled*."

I clench my jaw, angry at this ridiculous situation, angry at myself for not truly seeing how important this show is to me until now, when there's a chance it might not happen.

Booker and Arthur work to soak up as much of the water as they can, and after a few minutes that feel like hours, three firefighters come in.

I wander out to the center of the stage. The main drape drips thick, wet, discolored drops of water onto my head. I turn a slow circle, looking around at the absolute mess.

All the work we put into the show—ruined.

Unless God grants us a small miracle, Belinda is right—the musical will be canceled.

Which means the whole Sunset Hills theatre program will be canceled too.

Rosie Waterman fails again.

I mentally sing a slowed-down, pathetic version of "Don't Rain on My Parade"—the same lyric playing on a loop in my mind.

The words mean something completely different in light of our current situation.

I glance up and find Booker watching me. Beside him, Arthur looks desperate, almost guilty.

It dawns on me that he might've been next to the lines when the brake failed.

I turn away.

I finally understand that these people have somehow become everything to me. I'm not embarrassed by them. I'm proud.

They are what's been missing all along.

Slowly, Arthur makes his way out to center stage. When he reaches me, he stops. "I . . . I should've checked the—"

I cut him off. "No. This isn't your fault. It's not anyone's fault."

His shoulders slump in relief.

I stare out over the empty auditorium, now muggy and thick with a mildew odor. Only yesterday, I'd imagined people in these seats. I'd imagined their applause, their laughter, their awe at the way this cast brings a classic fairy tale to life.

Now I can only imagine silence.

"What do we do, Arthur?" I feel the desperate resignation in my throat.

"I don't know, Miss Director," he says. "What *do* we do?"

It feels like a challenge from a teacher who isn't willing to spoon-feed me the answers. But I'm not equipped to handle this. This is a nightmare.

I toss him a look. "Belinda might be right."

He shrugs. "If that's your decision, then I'll support you."

In the silence, I feel that anger and pride rise again. "I don't want to quit."

He nods. "That's a start."

I sigh, looking at the stage. "But this . . ." I turn to him. "What would you do?" I want him to write me a game plan because I have no idea where to begin.

He puts a hand on my shoulder. "I wouldn't quit either." He smiles. "I know you'll do the right thing."

When he walks away, I search the wings for Booker, but he's gone back into the scene shop to talk to the firefighters.

I break into the bridge of "Don't Rain on My Parade," turning back to the imaginary audience and moving downstage, closer to where, somehow, some way, in three weeks' time—there will be a real audience full of people ready to cheer for my cast as they open a surprising, magical production of *Cinderella.*

My cast.

My show.

My mailbox.

I just have no idea where to begin.

CHAPTER 31

MORE CAST MEMBERS BEGIN ARRIVING, many of them already aware that something has gone wrong before they even walk in the door.

The fire truck and small crowd outside are a dead giveaway.

Arthur, Booker, and I are all working on mopping up the water, wringing it out in buckets, carting it off to a utility sink in the scene shop, and repeating the process.

I feel like the guy in Hades who has to push the rock up the hill, because when I return after emptying the bucket, the puddles have all filled back up again. The water will surely ruin the stage floor, and we've already had to haul the main drape out to the dumpster.

Connie rushes in through the scene shop door with a man who is carrying a big fan.

When she looks around at all the water, her face falls. "Oh no. Rosie, what are we going to do?"

The man doesn't wait to be told where to plug the fan in. He moves it to the front of the stage and turns it on, then walks over to Booker, who points him toward a stack of mops and several Shop-Vacs. The maintenance crew collected every mop they had and dropped them off about twenty minutes ago.

Connie walks over to stand by my side. "That's Danny, my husband. Sorry, I should've introduced you," she says absently, obviously overwhelmed by the scene in front of her.

"No, it's fine," I say. "Did you happen to put out a call for fans or towels or . . . help?"

She nods. "We sent out a text blast, so hopefully we get a good response. Most people around aren't . . . well, let's just say they aren't in the best physical condition to help with this kind of cleanup."

She places a hand on my arm. "But, Rosie, what about the show?" Her gaze snags on something behind me, and she gasps. "Is that my dress?" The words come out in a wail as she makes her way over to the rack of costumes. Ginny is laying pieces out flat on a square of dry floor, trying to dry them with a hair dryer she must've gotten from home.

Connie picks up the pink fairy godmother gown, which looks anything but sparkly in its current state. Everything is not only wet, it's dingy. Brown. Gross.

Connie spins around and looks at me. "We're going to have to cancel, aren't we?" The question is laced with meaning. She was counting on the show to buy the theatre program more time. Without it . . .

Grace, Dylan, and Veronica have all come in through the back door and now stand a few feet away, eyes full of worry. Another small group has gathered at the front of the stage. Everyone is looking at me for guidance, and while I feel every bit as hopeless as the rest of them, I also know I'm the one they're looking to for answers.

I'm not quitting. I've already made that decision. I'm about to tell them all we will make it through, we'll figure it out, we'll band together . . .

. . . when Belinda strolls back in.

The smug look on her face and the small group trailing behind her make me think of the mob song in *Beauty and the Beast*. They may as well be wielding pitchforks and torches.

I think about Arthur's advice—"*You need to deal with your Belinda problem*"—and I draw in a deep breath.

Now's as good a time as any, I suppose.

I don't feel compelled to say anything to put her in her place, though. Better to show her. She assumes I'll fold under the weight of this. Heck, I assumed I would too.

But I won't. I can't. My cast is depending on me.

"The show is not canceled," I say firmly. "The show *will* go on."

Belinda scoffs. "Out on the front lawn?"

"If need be," I counter.

I can feel others starting to gather around us, like a fistfight in a schoolyard.

I pause, gathering myself. "You know what I love best about theatre?" I say, loudly enough that the whole group can hear me. "It's a community. It's a group of people coming together for a common goal." I draw in a breath. "Before I got here, this theatre was struggling, but it was well loved. Here at Sunset Hills and in the community. People care. *I* care."

Belinda laughs. "*You* care?"

I take a step toward her. "Yeah. I do."

I look at their faces—these people who've come to mean a whole lot to me in a very short time.

"I care about this place even more now than I did when I got here, and I'm not about to throw in the dingy, wet towel just because of a setback."

Belinda scoffs again, looking around to make sure she's not the only one who isn't buying this.

"All that matters is how we respond to it. You have all worked so hard and come too far to quit because of a little water."

"Um, it's more than a little water," Edgar says, just as a perfectly timed drop hits him in the head. He wipes it away.

"Fine, yes. It's a lot of water. It's a big, fat mess. But you know what?" My eyes meet Booker's for a split second, and then I go on. "So am I."

I feel the rush of that admission.

"And so are you. We're *theatre people*, for crying out loud—we're as messed up as they come!"

A trickle of laughter and acknowledgment at that.

"We are all in various stages between brilliant and crazy—and that's what it means to be alive." Now I look at Arthur. "Someone a lot smarter than me taught me to embrace the hard stuff because it makes the good stuff that much sweeter. Well, you guys, this is about as hard a situation as I've ever had to deal with during a show." A quick scan of the crowd tells me they're with me. Most of them anyway.

"But this mess is going to make opening night that much sweeter. It's going to make having an audience that much more special. If we can get through this, nothing can stop us, and our show will be stronger for it."

"This show you're embarrassed by?" Belinda says, eyes hooded under a raised brow.

"Let me correct you there, Belinda." I face her, and at this rare show of strength, her expression shifts.

Good.

"I'm not embarrassed," I say honestly. "I'm proud to be here. Proud of all of you and of what we've accomplished. You all have reminded me what it means to be a part of something amazing. We make each other better, and that's why I believe we can still pull this off."

"But how?" someone says.

"By adding a synchronized swimming part to the ballet sequence," I quip.

A ripple of groans and laughter.

I smile.

"I will tell you that it won't be easy," I say. "We'll have to roll up our sleeves and get a little dirty." I look around, trying to catalog everything that needs to be done. "The floor will have to be pulled up and repainted. The set pieces will need to be dried out.

Some of them repainted. The costumes—" I meet Ginny's eyes. "We can start by dry-cleaning them, then see what needs to be remade."

Others look at her, and she gives me a firm nod, as if to let me know she's on board. I feel a surge of confidence just from that one small gesture.

"And the show?" Connie asks. "We haven't even done a full run-through yet."

Right.

The show.

"We can practice in the dance studio down the hall," Veronica says.

"Yes!" I turn toward her. "Good idea. We'll tape off the floor to the size of the stage and use whatever furniture we can find to mimic the set pieces." I look around the circle and see that more of them have gathered. "The word of the day is *flexibility*."

"I'd say the word of the day is *disaster*," Belinda muses.

"No." I look at her, and it's obvious from the look on her face that no one has dared stand up to her in a long time. "I'm done looking for the worst in every situation. That is not who I am, and it's definitely not who I want to be. If we stick together and stay positive, we can get through this."

I look around the group, which has continued to grow as word has spread. They're all focused on me, waiting for me to lead them. It's a strange, wonderful feeling because I actually think what I'm saying is landing.

For them *and* for me.

"I may be the director," I tell them. "But this isn't *my* show. It's yours. It's *ours*. And it's important—you all know what's on the line. So if we want to save the Sunset Players, then it's time for all of us"—I let my gaze linger on Belinda—"to stop whining and start helping."

Belinda looks like she wants to roll her eyes, but when the

chatter among them is overwhelmingly positive, she resets her face to neutral.

"Where do we start?" Grace asks.

"We need to call in reinforcements," I say. "Reach out to anyone in the area and see if they want to help us clean up a disaster."

"If word gets out about this, nobody is going to come see the show," Evelyn says.

"Let me worry about that," I say, fresh resolve blooming inside me. "I have a feeling *everyone* is going to want to see this show now that this has happened."

Because it's not only time to tell *my* people what I've been doing the past month and a half; it's time to tell everyone. The people who love you are meant to share everything with you—the highs and the lows. The joys and the disappointments.

Revelation is a great thing.

I start divvying up jobs for all the willing helpers as a few others trickle in the door. Spouses and neighbors of cast members, other residents who got Connie's text alert—many with towels or fans or heavy-duty Shop-Vacs—all here, all willing to help, contrary to her initial worry that some of them might not be able to handle it.

Once everyone is situated, I pause and look around.

I take in the scene.

I watch for a brief moment as this group—some of them with no vested interest in the success of our show—work to clean up the mess. The fire department has gone, leaving all of us here to sort through everything in hopes of sucking up enough water and drying things enough to make them usable again.

There are a lot of people I've never seen before, alongside people like Daisy and Louie, who've shown up without being asked. *Theatre is a community*.

A beautiful community that I'm proud to be a part of. Whether on a stage in New York City or right here in Wisconsin.

I catch Booker's eye across the stage and see the way he's assembled a small group to help move the set pieces out onto the loading dock to dry in the sun. He gives me an encouraging nod, and I hand a mop to Grace's husband, David, who tells me he took the day off to do what he can to help.

"This show has been so good for Gracie," David says, taking the mop from me. "She's singing around the house again! She never sings anymore, and boy, I love to hear her voice. We moved here so I could be closer to my dad. She left her friends back in Omaha, and"—his eyes trail across the stage to where Grace is helping Ginny sort through dripping-wet costumes—"she's happy again. This show and these people—you—mean everything to her."

I go still because I understand how being a part of something can change a person's direction. It can change their life.

But it's been so long since I was a part of anything that changed mine.

He's giving me more credit than I deserve, and it hits me sideways, right in the deep part of my big feelings. It almost makes me cry.

He pushes the mop across the stage, then stops. "A lot of people stop doing the things they really love when they get older." He brings his eyes to mine. "I'm not sure why. Those things are what keep us young. So thank you for giving Grace a place to do that. And for reminding her what it feels like to be happy."

The nerve endings in my body tingle at that because it dawns on me that I should never be embarrassed by doing something good, of being a part of something wonderful. This isn't what I set out to do or who I set out to be.

It's so much better.

CHAPTER 32

AN HOUR LATER, THE DOORS at the back of the theatre open, and I see Bertie walk in. She makes her way to the stage, and I meet her near the stairs, giving her a hand as she walks up the steps.

Once she's standing next to me, she faces me and squeezes my hands. "Booker told me what happened. Are you okay?"

Her kindness makes me want to collapse, to be honest and let all my feelings out.

"Not really, if I'm honest." Tears sting my eyes, but I blink them away. "But we have a lot of help."

"I made muffins," she says. "Baking is my love language."

I laugh through the emotional drain. "That was so kind of you," I say. "Thank you."

I look around, marveling at all the people who've come out to help. Booker has started removing the ruined top layer of the floor, which is painful to watch, and a few of the others stand by to help him. Who knows what it looks like underneath that layer—it will need to be dried and painted and the staples pulled out, but hopefully the damage doesn't make the stage unusable.

"I wish the accident was the only problem we're facing," I say sadly.

"What do you mean?"

I tell Bertie about the low ticket sales and the importance of this show turning a profit. "I know I won't be here after this summer, but I can't stand the thought of this group losing their theatre program." And I really can't stand the thought that I could be the one who couldn't save it.

Bertie squeezes my arm. "You really care about them, don't you?"

I look around the space again. *This* is community. This is the adventure. It's not traveling or seeing the world—or starring in a huge show on Broadway. It's simpler than that. It's people.

It's always been people.

"Yeah. I really do."

"Then let's put our heads together and figure out how to fill this place," she says. "What have you tried so far?"

I shake my head. "Nothing. I haven't even invited my friends or my parents yet."

She frowns. "Why on earth not?"

I give her a half-hearted shrug.

If she's disappointed, she doesn't let on. "Well, we should fix that immediately." She pauses. "Do you know anyone at the local news station?"

I shake my head. "I don't know anyone local at all." But then I remember something . . . "Wait. Wait a second. One of my best friends just took an anchor job in Milwaukee . . ."

Bertie's eyes light up. "Call her!"

"I doubt she knows anyone all the way up here," I say, really not wanting to ask for this favor.

"Milwaukee stations cover Door County news sometimes," Bertie says. "It can't hurt to ask."

I chew the inside of my cheek, trying to imagine what I might say to Marnie, one of my best friends who has no idea what I've been doing up here. Or really, since I moved to New York.

"Call her." Bertie squeezes my hand. "She might actually be able to do something here."

I give her a nod. "I will."

She smiles, but I notice that smile fades when she sees Arthur, who takes one look at us and walks the other way.

I frown, turning back to her. "What's that about?"

She tries to wave me off, but I can see the hurt behind her eyes. "Oh, it's nothing."

"I thought you two were getting along."

"We were," she says wistfully. "He's a wonderful man."

"I'm surprised to say I agree with you," I say.

She sighs. "But he made it clear he doesn't want to see me anymore." She hands me the basket. "Too much baggage, I guess. Old people stuff." She says it as a throwaway.

I start to ask another question, but she cuts me off. "Here, you take these and make sure to pass them around. I don't want to be in the way."

As she turns to go, I glance back over my shoulder and see Arthur standing off to the side, working, but looking like he's trying very hard to pretend not to notice Bertie is here at all.

After a long moment of me glaring at him, he finally turns and walks out the stage door and into the scene shop, leaving me standing onstage with a basket of muffins and a whole lot of questions.

CHAPTER 33

"YOU HATE THE PHONE. WHAT'S wrong?"

I laugh at Marnie, who picked up on the first ring. "Hello to you too."

I can practically hear her frowning. "I mean, I love that you're calling me . . . but are you okay?"

"I'm good, I promise," I say, though I'm not sure it's true. It's not like I've stopped to take stock of my mental state. I'm still running on caffeine and adrenaline, and I'm sure I'll crash later. "I mean. I'm okay."

"You have some explaining to do," she says. "You send a picture of a hot guy, and then you leave us hanging!"

"I know," I say. "I'm sorry about that. Things around here are pretty busy, and being in charge of everything, it's . . . it's a lot, that's for sure."

"Well," her voice brightens, "I love that you're calling *me* and not Maya or Taylor."

I grin at the playful fake competition. "Yeah, feel free to lord that over them for a while."

"So, what's up?"

Hmm. What's up? Where do I begin?

"It's just . . ." I'm standing in the back of the theatre, watching as volunteers work to make the stage usable again. "This job hasn't exactly been what I expected." I chew the inside of my lip. "Turns out, I'm not just part of the creative team. I'm the director."

"Oh!" She sounds impressed. "Fancy."

I groan a little to myself. "Not really."

"Why?" There's confusion in her voice.

I pause for a beat, and then—"It's at a . . . retirement community?" My voice goes up at the end, like a question.

Marnie is quiet.

"Marnie?"

"Sorry . . ." I picture her, perfectly made up without a hair out of place, trying to make sense of what I'm saying. "Did you say 'retirement community'?"

I clear my throat. My skin feels prickly, and I'm totally uncomfortable. "Uh, yeah. Yeah. It's a whole campus—there's a golf course and a fitness center and . . ." I search my mind, which only comes up with, "Pickleball! Do you know it's the country's fastest growing sport?"

"You play pickleball?" she asks.

"I mean, I don't," I say. "But I could, you know, if I . . . had a paddle."

Another long pause.

"So . . . you're directing a production of *Cinderella* with a bunch of old people?"

"Yes?" I wince.

"Rosie, that's amazing," she says, and it takes me by surprise.

I stand a little straighter. "Wait . . . it is?"

"Yes," she says emphatically. "That's really cool! I didn't know there *were* shows for senior citizens. My grandma would love that."

"There are in Door County," I say, smiling. "Only . . ." I hate the thought of using our friendship to ask for a favor.

"Only . . . ?"

"I'm actually calling because I need a favor," I say, pacing a circle.

"Name it," she says.

"This morning, we had an accident that flooded the space."

"Oh no! What happened?"

I briefly tell her about the flyaway, about the broken sprinkler heads, and the people now working to mop everything up and dry everything out.

I can hear her concern. "Oh my gosh, Rosie, are you okay? What's going to happen to the show?"

"Well, that's just it. We're in power-through-it mode, making it happen because the show must go on and all that, but ticket sales haven't been great, and they're in danger of losing the theatre program."

"You want me to do a piece on you?" she asks without an ounce of hesitation.

A lump wells up in my throat. Of course she is reacting this way—why did I ever expect anything else?

"No, not on me," I say. "But I was hoping you know someone up here who might be interested in doing a piece on the theatre. Like the actual program here at Sunset Hills."

She pauses, and I can hear her clicking around on her computer.

"What are you doing?"

"Googling . . ." She's distracted. "Sunset Players you said?"

"That's us," I say, realizing there's no trace of embarrassment left.

"I thought you were at a regional theatre this summer," she says absently.

"I thought so too," I tell her. "I was a little surprised when I arrived."

"It does look like a thriving community," Marnie says, obviously still scrolling the website. "What made you stay when you discovered it wasn't what you thought?"

Surprisingly, the list that pops up in my head is long, and I choose to tell the truth.

"Well," I say, "a couple of things. I didn't have any other prospects. And everyone here said it was a great place to work."

"Is it?"

My eyes scan the space, full of diligent volunteers. "Marnie. It's great. I never would've thought so . . . but it really is."

"And they're counting on the show to help save the program," she says.

"Yes." I explain that they've struggled to get audiences in. And now, the accident and the flood are major setbacks. "Whether I knew it or not, they brought me here to save this program. I can't let them down."

"Okay, give me an hour. I'm going to pitch the idea to my producer."

"Wait, seriously?" I ask. "I thought you were in too big of a market now—"

"We sometimes cover things that happen up there," she says. "Between the flood, the senior-citizen-slash-feel-good angle, and you coming from New York to do this show, there are some great stories here."

"Really?"

"Really," she says.

"That is amazing," I tell her. "You are amazing."

"I know." I can hear the smile in her voice. "But you know you're amazing too."

I swallow the lump in my throat.

"You sound genuinely excited about something again, Ro," she says. "It's good to hear."

"What do you mean?"

"I don't know," she says. "The last few years, we've been worried about you. You haven't really seemed like yourself."

I shake my head and walk out into the lobby and stare out the window. "Things haven't been going very well for me in New York."

"Yeah, we kind of guessed as much."

I frown. "You did?"

"We kept waiting for you to talk to one of us about it," she says. "But you always said you were fine. Things were good. No complaints."

"Yeah, I was"—I feel the irony—"acting."

"You're good at it," she says, laughing. "But not with us."

"I'm sorry, Marnie," I tell her honestly. "I should've been straight with all of you."

"Yeah, you should've." She sighs. "But it's okay. You had your reasons. And you're telling me now."

"Yeah. I am."

"Nobody needs to go through the hard stuff alone."

I sigh. "I know. And it's been a lot of hard stuff."

"It's the hard stuff that makes the good stuff so much sweeter." I look around, and I understand what Arthur meant.

"When we come see the show, you can catch us up on all of it," she says. "The real story."

"Okay, but let's not tell Taylor and Maya about the"—I search for the right word—"unique aspect of this show."

"You mean don't tell them it's a bunch of old people?" she asks dryly.

"Yes," I say. "I want them to be surprised. You guys are going to love my cast. Seriously, they're amazing."

"I can't wait."

"Thanks for this, Mar," I say.

"Are you kidding?" she says. "That's what friends are for."

I bust into off-key singing, something we did all the time growing up.

"Keep smile-linn', keep shine-ninn' . . ."

She laughs, and then I laugh, and then I wonder how I got so lucky to find such good friends and how I got so stupid that I thought I needed to keep myself from them.

....

MARNIE: Producer LOVES the idea. She's sending a reporter to Door County to interview you tomorrow!

ROSIE: What?! For real? Marnie, you are the best! Thank you!

MARNIE: I'm happy to help. But promise you'll be better with the updates.

ROSIE: Deal. I owe you!

Marnie sends a GIF of Dionne Warwick.

ROSIE: You're my favorite. Don't tell the others.

....

MARNIE: I got us all tickets to see Rosie's musical on opening night.

TAYLOR: Can I have an aisle seat? This baby is Riverdancing on my bladder 24/7.

MARNIE: 👍

MAYA: Backstage tour, Ro?

ROSIE: Of course. But, guys, this show might be a little different than what you're expecting . . .

MARNIE: This show is going to be beautiful because our talented best friend directed it.

TAYLOR: And we can't wait to see it!

MAYA: I'm going to cheer so loud they're going to have to have me removed.

ROSIE: You're all nuts.

And I love you.

CHAPTER 34

AN HOUR LATER, I FIND Arthur in his tiny office off the back of the scene shop. To everyone else, it probably looks like he's working, but I see this for what it is—hiding.

"You've been in here for a while—is there really that much paperwork?"

"You want to open on time, don't you?" His bark is back, and I wish I knew why.

"What's going on?" I ask quietly, knowing he probably won't give me an answer. "Bertie said you told her you don't want to see her anymore."

He barely acknowledges me.

I dare a step toward him, looking around the small, dank space. "It's depressing in here."

"It's peaceful." He looks at me. "At least it was."

I glare at him, but he doesn't notice because he's gone back to clicking buttons on his computer. "I'm not scared of you anymore."

He makes a face at me.

"And I want to know why you told Bertie you don't want to see her." I move a stack of books off the only other chair in the space and sit.

His muscles tense. "None of your business."

"You like her, Arthur." I lean in. "And she likes you. What's the problem?"

"The problem!" He spins toward me but snaps his jaw shut the second his eyes meet mine. I see hurt nesting there, the threat of unshed tears pooling in his eyes. "I don't want to talk about it."

I nod. "I understand. As you know, I don't like to share my feelings either."

"Good, because I don't want you to." He turns back to his computer, but it's obvious he's not really seeing the screen.

I cross one leg over the other and force myself not to shy away. Because Arthur told me I have the ability to connect with people—on a personal level. And right now, I think I'm supposed to connect with him.

"You know"—I lay it on a bit thick—"a *very* wise man told me that I'm a deep feeler. He said I avoid emotions because I feel them more deeply than other people."

Arthur stops pecking on the computer keys.

"He also told me that in order to make anyone else feel anything, I have to feel it first." The second the words are out, my gaze drops to the chipping paint on my toenails.

If I look at him, I'll lose my nerve. And there's something I need to tell him.

"When I was six, my father left," I say. "I still don't really know why. When you're older, and you think back to when it all happened, your brain sort of . . . makes up all kinds of things. I know he and my mother were too young to try and raise a child. I guess I give him credit for lasting that long."

I wring my hands, then force myself to set them in my lap. "My mother didn't handle it well—his leaving. I remember she got really depressed. The house was always dark. I ate a lot of peanut butter and jelly sandwiches. And . . . I spent a lot of time alone."

He glances over at me, but his eyes don't linger.

"I had big feelings back then too," I say softly. "But I knew that sharing them wasn't good for my mom. So I learned how to mask them. Cover them up. Mostly with humor, which came easy to me. Making people laugh. I would pretend to feel other things, and I got so good at it—the acting—that it turned into a whole career." I chuckle, mostly to myself.

He shifts in his seat and folds his hands on his lap.

I continue, "I stuffed the real feelings down, and I did everything I could to make my mom smile. I was intent on not being a burden—I didn't want her to leave me too, you know?"

"And these are the memories you don't use in your work," he says, more of a statement than a question.

I nod. "I never have. And I've had professors and teachers, heck, even friends, recognize that I close myself off. But until you, nobody made it make sense." I pause. "I'm afraid of my big feelings. I don't like that everything seems deep and difficult." I half laugh. "I want to be the joy. I just want things to be easy."

"Things are *never* easy. Not the things worth anything anyway," he says.

"True," I agree. "But if I'm not the happy, upbeat, funny one, then who am I?"

"Be happy and upbeat and funny when it suits," he says. "But sometimes, you might be quiet and thoughtful—and honest."

Honest. It's hard hearing that.

"I want people to like me." I shift in my seat. "And sometimes I find fiction easier than reality."

He meets my eyes, questioning, and I'm not even sure why I said that. Except that . . . I sometimes find fiction easier than reality.

Easier to escape into someone else's story than to face everything in my own.

But that's not what I tell Arthur. Instead, I say, "I made a promise to my mom not long after my dad left."

"What kind of promise?"

"That I'd get a big dream and go after it. Never let myself be swayed or deterred or stopped. Not by a guy, not by circumstance, not by anything. I think she sometimes wishes she hadn't gotten sidetracked." I think but don't say, *Hadn't had me.*

"So the whole pursuit of this dream—it's all been for her?" he asks.

"I didn't think so. I *don't* think so." I shake my head. "Actually, I'm not sure."

"Rosie." He leans forward. "Why do *you* want to be an actor?"

His simple question confounds me.

Because I can't answer it.

I don't know.

When I meet his eyes again, I can see him read through all the things I'm not saying.

He goes still for a long moment, and then he says, "The first time I ever met my Annie was when she came to audition for *Funny Girl*."

My shoulders drop, and I go still.

"She was the most beautiful thing I'd ever seen," he says, looking off, and I imagine him picturing her. "In a quirky, sort of oddball way." He leans back in the chair and seems to go somewhere else. "When she sang that song"—his eyes flick over to me—"the same song you sang, I remember thinking, *Where has this girl been hiding?*"

My gaze drifts past him to a framed photo next to the computer.

"When you sang it that day in the dining hall"—he looks away, then shrugs—"you reminded me of her."

"I'm sorry, Arthur," I say. "I didn't know—"

He holds up a hand to silence me. "The thing is, Rosie, she made me better. Without Annie, I don't know how to exist, let alone work. That superpower she told me I had? I don't want it anymore. I don't *want* to connect with people. Or to understand them. I don't want—"

"The big feelings," I say quietly.

He nods, and it's like placing the last piece of a puzzle I've been working on for weeks. Arthur changed when Annie died. They were a team, and he doesn't know how to function without her. So he doesn't even try.

"Do you know when I met Bertie, I felt something I hadn't felt in a long, long time."

"That's good," I say.

He shakes his head. "It feels like betrayal."

I understand even more how deeply he loved her.

"She's not my Annie."

"No, Arthur, nobody can replace Annie," I tell him with more authority on the subject than I have. "But I don't think that's what she's trying to do."

He's very still for a beat, and then says, "She kissed me, you know?"

My eyes go wide, and I try very hard *not* to picture that, but I fail.

And now the imagined image of Bertie and Arthur making out on the park bench outside is burned into my brain.

"She kissed me, and I liked it," he says.

I manage not to wince and shudder and run home and shower myself off with steel wool, though it takes all my energy. "Isn't that . . . good?"

"I felt so guilty," he says. "Because I made a promise to Annie. To love her forever."

"To love her until death do you part," I say gently.

"But I still love her, Rosie." His voice breaks. "I always will."

"I know."

Then realization hits me. If things don't change, if *I* don't change, I'll never have a love like Arthur and Annie's. And I want one. A love of my own. It's never been a priority. I always played it safe. Focused on my career. Avoided the big feelings. And I told myself it was enough.

I told myself I didn't want to lose myself in some guy. Or to let anyone or anything pull me off course.

But this summer has cracked me open and made me see that there's so much more to this life than the singular pursuit of a dream.

"Arthur," I say. "I believe that our hearts are made to hold a lot of love. Different kinds. Different sizes. For a lot of different people."

I do believe that, don't I?

"It's not a betrayal to let yourself enjoy someone's company," I tell him. "And I have to believe that if Annie had a say, she'd want you to be happy. She'd want you to live the years she didn't get to live. Do you really think Annie would be happy to see you pushing everyone away? Not teaching when there are so many of us who could learn so much from you?"

"No, she would not." His smile is sad. "Annie would tell me to get my head out of my rear and do what I was born to do." He brightens a little. "Only she'd use more colorful language."

I smile. "Ooh. I like her."

"You two would've been peas in a pod," he says, shaking his head slightly.

We sit in the quiet for a moment, and without meaning to, I stumble upon the answer to his earlier question. "You know, I didn't go after this dream only because of that promise I made. I know why I want to be an actor."

"Oh?"

I shake my head, letting the revelation form because it's there, but it's foggy, like it needs time to completely slip into place.

"I love to perform. I love that feeling of connecting with a character so much that I almost slip on her skin and bring her to life." I let myself remember it, all the times I'd been onstage, under the lights, sharing a story in a way that no other medium allows me to do. I close my eyes. "I miss it when I'm not up there. It's not about the crowds or the applause or anything like that. It never has been. It's about creating something from nothing, doing the work, then expressing it in a way that allows people to see themselves up there, on the stage. Or allows them to get lost in the story I'm telling . . . I know it sounds crazy, but I feel like . . ." Why am I embarrassed to say this out loud? It's not a secret. "I feel like this is what I was born to do."

His steady expression remains. "So it *is* your dream."

I nod. "It is. In spite of everything that happened with my mom . . . I think it always was." I go still. "But maybe, at some point, it became about the promise I made. Maybe I forgot all the reasons I wanted it in the first place. Maybe I forgot that this is the thing that makes me feel alive."

He sets his hands in his lap but doesn't meet my eyes. "Sometimes I think we can convince ourselves that a dream has to look a certain way." Now he glances at me. "Part of the fun of this stuff is staying open to the unexpected."

"Like working in a retirement community?" I quip.

"I bet you took this job thinking you were just punching a clock." He chuckles to himself.

"I definitely didn't think I'd learn anything." I sigh. "But I can honestly say, it's been one of the best experiences of my life.

He nods. "It's amazing what you discover if you hold the dream loosely." He holds up a hand. "I'm not saying you quit on it. Just maybe . . . reimagine it. You can pursue this dream in a million different ways. Maybe it's not the dream that needs to change but the method of making it come true."

I frown, trying to wrap my head around it. "I wouldn't know where to begin."

"Rosie, my dear, I think you already have."

CHAPTER 35

THE SHOW, PERHAPS, MAY ACTUALLY go on.

After a full day of working on the space, most of the volunteers go home, weary and exhausted but with an against-all-odds sense that we're going to be okay.

That the show is going to be okay.

In the evening, Dylan took the cast to the dance studio to run through the show, and while I wanted to be there, I didn't feel like I could leave the cleanup efforts. Afterward, she returned and gave me a full report, and I think maybe she was proud of herself for running things without me.

I was proud of her too.

I thanked her and told her to go home and sleep, to which she replied, "I'll sleep when I'm dead."

Good to know the Dylan I know and love is still in there somewhere, even if she sometimes hides behind the face of a responsible person.

The stage is still damp in spots, but we cleared it in time, and it doesn't look like the water will render it unusable, so I'm taking that as a win.

This has been one of those days where you're in one place, focusing on one thing for so long, the concept of time is lost. I think it's probably dark out, and I know I need to go home, but when Booker walks in with a pizza, I realize I'm not going anywhere until it's been completely devoured.

"Oh, you beautiful human," I say.

He grins. "Hungry?"

"Starving."

He hands over the box, then spreads a tarp out on the stage. The work lights are on, but they're dim, and the longer I stand there, the more I can mentally turn this setting into a romantic one . . . despite the disaster of the day.

I walk over and set the box at the center of the tarp, then go back to the scene shop and grab two bottles of water from a small refrigerator in the corner.

When I walk back out onto the stage, I slow down, studying Booker when he's unaware. It's one of my favorite pastimes—people watching—but watching him, admiring him . . . it's a different experience. Transcendent somehow. He has an effect on every part of me.

It's still early, but I really think there's something here. I think maybe, it's possible, under different circumstances, that I could . . . you know, love this guy.

And more importantly, if I let him, I think maybe he could love me back.

He glances up. "That was quite a day." He takes a bottle of water from me, and we both sit, the pizza box between us.

We're quiet for a long moment. The adrenaline of the day is still sloshing around inside me, but thankfully I can start to feel it ebb.

"Quite a day," I repeat.

He opens the box, and we each take a slice of what I am certain will be the best meal I've ever had simply based on how hungry I am. "I can't believe I survived."

"You did more than survive. You were amazing. I think your cast respects you even more now."

I shake my head. "They think I'm embarrassed by them."

"I feel like you proved how important this show is to you." He takes a giant bite of pizza, closes his eyes, and lets out a moan that's practically rated R.

"Do you want me to give you a minute?" I laugh. "Or a room?"

He half finishes chewing. "I just realized I haven't eaten since this morning."

"Me either. I didn't even have time to feel hungry."

I look around. Compared to this morning, the stage looks a million times better. I know we still have a lot to do, but it's progress. And a lot of it happened because of him.

"Thank you for your help."

"I'm glad I was here," he says. "You're good in a crisis."

"Ha!" I laugh. "I hid my panic well."

We eat and talk about what else needs to be done. I tell him about Bertie and Arthur, which, it turns out, he already knew about, and it's . . . nice. This casual familiarity that's developed between us is something I've grown to love.

It's strange—people talk about romance like it's all flash and sizzle. Heck, musicals are the worst for romance. People fall in love within the span of one act. Unlike Sarah falling for Sky after one trip to Havana, or Maria falling for Tony's fire escape falsetto, I'm finding the quiet, simple things stick with me longer. I still want to spend a fair amount of time kissing him, but this—the conversation, the getting to know each other—is the good stuff.

This is the stuff I'll carry with me when I go.

When I go.

The thought attaches itself like a cinder block tied to my ankle.

"You know . . ." He throws a crust into the box.

"You're a heathen," I say, thankful for lighter thoughts. "That's the best part." I pick up his crust and eat it.

He smirks at me. "It's Friday."

I swallow the bite and shake my head. "I don't even know what month it is."

He chuckles. "If you're not up for it, I get it."

I shake what's left of his crust at him. "Bring it on. I'm not scared of you."

"It's not exactly a question," he says. "It's a request."

"This is supposed to be about sharing *feelings*," I say.

"Do you really want to dig into your feelings after the day you had?"

"Fair point." I take a drink. "So, what is the *request*?"

He brushes crumbs off his hands, then leans back on his elbows and looks at me. "Would you . . . sing for me?"

I stop mid-swallow and nearly choke. "What?"

"I didn't get to see your performance in the dining hall," he says. "Some of my patients told me about it. I feel like I missed out. And I think I deserve a personal concert."

"Oh, you do? Why?"

"Because I'm an excellent kisser." The corner of his mouth turns up.

"That's true." I set my water bottle down and crawl toward him, but not in a sexy way because I know the second I *try* to be sexy, I'm probably going to end up looking like a newborn giraffe. I move into his orbit, stopping right in front of him, our lips barely an inch apart.

I stare into his eyes, and I hear his breath hitch. The words that wander through my mind cannot be spoken aloud, but it's taking everything inside me not to tell him exactly what I'm feeling. Even though *these* feelings are big and complicated and messy. All I can think is, *I love you.*

"I have a Friday question," I say, without moving a muscle.

"Okay," he breathes.

"Do you see any way that this ends well?"

I feel him stiffen. "I thought we agreed not to say goodbye until we had to." He brushes his lips gently across mine, and I pull away slightly.

"You know we have to think about it."

"I don't want to think about it." He sits back. "I want to live in this moment, here, with you, on a tarp on this damp stage, eating pizza and drinking water. Can we just leave the future out there for a little while longer?"

I wish I could. I wish I could freeze time, or at least stretch it out, but it's there, the end, waving a red flag at me, whether I want it to or not.

I kiss him, and his hands sweep up into my hair. I shift, sitting sideways on his lap, and he holds me so close, I feel safe in a way I've never felt before.

I love you. The words are back. They scare me, and yet they feel absolutely right. So I choose to take Booker's advice, to give in to the moment and stop dwelling on what happens tomorrow or next week or next month. I'm leaving, but maybe there's a solution we haven't thought of.

Either way, I don't have to figure it out now. *It's just life.*

And yet, this feels like a lot more than *just life*. It feels like a precious, tangible treasure I can't fathom losing.

I'm not good at expressing my feelings like normal people, so instead of blurting out something I'll regret later, I back away, sitting cross-legged on the tarp across from him. I draw in a breath and start singing "When You Say Nothing At All" by Alison Krauss. I get through a verse and a chorus before Booker silences me with another kiss.

This kiss leads to another kiss, which leads to another kiss. And finally, he pulls away. We're both breathless, and I'm dizzy, feeling drunk on something that's so much better than alcohol.

"Oookay . . . I need a minute," he says through a smile. "To calm down."

We both lay back on the tarp, staring up to the rafters overhead.

After a minute, he looks at me. "Your voice is amazing."

"Thank yo-ou." I sing the words—badly.

He laughs. "And you're still so weird."

I let my head rest on his chest, and he wraps an arm around me, holding my hand with his free one. We lie like that, in silence, right out in the center of the stage, and I think but don't say, *I'm exactly where I'm supposed to be. This is where I belong.*

I'm so comfortable that I let my eyes flutter closed, and then the world fades to black.

CHAPTER 36

WORDS SWIM AROUND IN THAT foggy space between awake and asleep.

"Are they dead?"

"No, I can see them breathing. Look, their chests are moving."

"Thank God they're not naked."

"I think it's a crime Booker isn't naked."

"Evelyn!"

"We're old, not dead."

"What do you suppose happened here? Do you think they . . . ?"

My eyes pop open and the four women standing over me let out a collective gasp. "What's going—" I glance to my side and find Booker. Asleep.

"Rosie!" Sadie says. "You're awake."

"Looks like you had a great night, *if you know what I mean*," Evelyn cracks.

"This is *not* what it looks like," I say, willing my creaking muscles to work. A tarp on a stage isn't a mattress.

I give Booker a shake and try to sit up straighter.

"Well, that's a shame." Evelyn looks genuinely disappointed. "Unless you're just saying that."

I shake Booker again. "Booker, wake up." Then, to the Nosy Nellies: "I'm not just saying that."

"What do the young people call this?" Sadie asks the others. "A walk of shame?" Back to me: "Rosie, walk around so we can officially tell everyone you did a walk of shame this morning." She giggles.

Evelyn is staring at Booker. "Rosie, did you get to see him with his shirt off?"

I shake Booker a third time. Geez, this guy sleeps like the dead. He stirs, eyes fluttering open, confusion in all of his features. "Rosie? What's wrong?"

"He even looks good in the morning," Evelyn whispers.

"Sorry the same can't be said for you, Rosie." Sadie winces and the others shake their heads in agreement, like a brood of chickens.

Booker sits up. I can see him bring the scene into focus. "Oh. Uh . . . we fell asleep."

"Looks like you had a good night, though," Evelyn says.

Sadie giggles.

I'm about to stand when the door to the lobby opens and Bertie walks in. She lifts her hand in a wave, but her smile fades when she spots us, still positioned center stage, on a tarp, where we've clearly spent the night.

She turns and glances behind her, just as someone else follows her in: a woman wearing a very nice royal-blue suit and sporting a very specific kind of newswoman haircut, followed by a man carrying a camera and a tripod.

"Oh my gosh," I say, jumping up. "Oh my *gosh*," I repeat, because what else do I say right now?

"What?" Booker says. "What's wrong?"

"Are we going to be on the news?" Grace's eyes go wide.

"Shoot, shoot, shoot. They never told me a time, and—" I start swiping at my hair like there are bees in it.

Sadie grimaces. "That's not going to help."

Bertie is staring at the stage, and I see the moment she realizes that Booker and I are both here, spread out on a tarp, like we just had an indoor camping excursion. She glances at the reporter trailing behind, then back to me, eyes wide.

I smooth my hands over my leggings. I can smell my armpits. Beside me, Booker stands. "You have an interview?"

"Yes, but they didn't tell me . . ." I stop myself from repeating. It isn't going to change the fact that they're here. *Now*.

"Obviously, *you* distracted her," Evelyn says.

Bertie has reached the stage now, and she gives us a tentative smile. Her eyes flick from me to Booker and back again. "Things here look . . . interesting."

"Oh, this?" I'm about to spiral, I can tell. "This is not what it looks like."

"Methinks she doth protest too much," Sadie mutters.

I choose to ignore her. "We were working late, with the accident, everything was still wet, so the tarp, and the pizza. I didn't eat all day yesterday, so . . . yeah." I turn off the open fire hydrant that is my mouth. "We fell asleep." I helplessly shrug, and then, as if I haven't said enough, I add, "We *just* slept."

"Fully clothed," Evelyn says, then adds, "unfortunately."

Sadie swats her across the arm.

"It's my fault." Booker runs a hand through his hair, making it even messier—and my goodness, sexier—than before. "I showed up with pizza."

"And really, how could she resist?" Evelyn gives Booker a once-over, and it's clear she's not talking about the food.

Bertie walks up onto the stage. "I just happened to bump into this lovely woman, looking a little lost over by the clubhouse." Then, quietly, she adds, "I'm sorry, Rosie, I should've called."

"No, it's good." I step forward and look at the reporter. "I'm so sorry. I'm Rosie Waterman. The director."

The woman smiles. "It's really nice to meet you. I'm Deirdre. Your friend Marnie and I went to school together."

Marnie. Just the mention of her name makes my heart squeeze.

"Are you able to talk with us on camera? About the accident and the show and this whole program?" Deirdre asks.

I look around the stage, and a million newsworthy stories come to mind. "Oh my goodness, yes. Yes, of course. There are *so* many stories here to be told." I look over at the small group of women, still standing on the stage. "Grace, she's our Cinderella. She moved here from Omaha and found happiness again simply by becoming a part of this show." In the wings, I see Arthur's shadow. "And did you know the theatre manager, Arthur Silverman—he's a renowned director and former NYU theatre professor. A true legend." I run my hands through my hair. "The accident, the flood, the way everyone came together—I think we might actually still open on time, and that's a story worth telling."

Deirdre's smile looks practiced, her teeth whiter than they should be. "That's so sweet! But, Rosie, we're here to talk about you."

I frown. "Me?"

"Yes," she says. "We'll get to all of that—the others—but *you* are the story. Marnie told us you live in New York?"

I look around the stage, and I see them all watching me, Booker included, and I freeze.

I press my lips together. "I really don't think I'm the most interesting thing here."

"A young woman leaving a thriving career in New York to direct a musical for senior citizens?" Deirdre is holding a microphone, and I notice there's a flashing red light on the camera. "That was quite a sacrifice."

I shake my head. I feel caught somehow. Like I'm on the stand. "No, it wasn't. It . . . isn't."

"Can you elaborate?"

I press my lips together. "New York is great, and my career"—I pause—"is fine . . . but these people? And this musical? It's taught me so much. About myself, about life and community, and what it really means to be happy." I meet Booker's eyes, and his slight nod encourages me to continue.

"And what *does* it mean to be happy?"

"Hold on!" Belinda hollers from the wing, stepping out onto the stage.

I didn't even know she was back there. At the interruption, I pause, worried about what she might say to embarrass me.

"Belinda, they're filming," Sadie hisses.

"Rosie, I will not allow you to go on television looking like that." She extends a hand, as if to usher me toward her.

I'm frozen.

"Come on," she says, and then to Deirdre: "Give us five minutes."

"She's going to fix *that* in five minutes?" Evelyn says under her breath.

"She's a miracle worker with the makeup," Sadie says.

I glance at Deirdre, who gives me a kind nod, and I rush off toward Belinda.

"I'm not sure what you can really do," I say. "I fell asleep on a paint tarp."

"Yes. We all saw that."

There's a noted change in her voice. It's not . . . harsh.

"You might've cast me as the Evil Stepmother, but today I'm your fairy godmother." She starts toward the stage door that leads downstairs to the dressing rooms. "I've got makeup downstairs. You'll look, well, *alive* at least, in no time."

I rush behind her, trying to keep up and finding I'm getting surprisingly out of breath. I wonder why, out of everyone who lives at Sunset Hills, I'm the one in the worst shape.

Once we're downstairs, Belinda opens the door to one of the small dressing rooms and pulls a bin off the shelf. She points to a chair and flips on the bulb lights around the mirror. "Sit."

I do as I'm told, watching as she starts pulling makeup from the bin. "Why are you helping me?"

"No talking," she says. "Down here, I'm the one in charge."

I press my lips together to conceal a smile.

She pulls out a bottle of foundation and starts dotting it on my face with a sponge. "I was impressed with how you handled things."

My eyes flick to hers, but she doesn't look back. "You were?"

"Every show has its challenges. I've been in more than a few, as you know."

It *feels* like she's trying to be nice, though she still seems to be handing me her résumé. I wonder if this is insecurity and choose to give her the benefit of the doubt.

"But a flood in the theatre? That's a new one." She pulls blush from the bin. "Especially for a first-time director."

She dots the brush into the powder and starts swiping it on my cheeks.

"But you took charge," she says. "I believe in giving credit where credit is due." She reaches into her pocket and pulls out a breath mint. "You need this."

Something about her bluntness mixes with my embarrassment, and I have to laugh. "Thanks." I unwrap it and stick it in my mouth.

"I've been hard on you," she says, sighing and still fussing over my face. "But calling your friend and getting the news here—that took guts. You're really going to let them do a story on you?" She swipes eye shadow over my eyelids.

"If it helps the show, then yes," I say.

She inches back, and I open my eyes. "You surprise me, Rosie Waterman."

I smile ruefully. "You surprise me too."

"Good." She clicks a compact shut. "I'd *hate* to be predictable." She adds a few finishing touches, and then she's done.

I sit back and admire her work. She hands me a comb, which I run through my messy waves, and when I'm finished, I almost feel like I didn't sleep on a hardwood floor.

I stand, and Belinda gives me a quick once-over. "I suppose that's as good as it's going to get."

"Just when I thought you were nice."

"You look thirty-foot pretty." She quirks a brow, then explains, "Pretty from thirty feet away."

I shake my head, but she's not done.

"Hopefully the camera won't add ten pounds. Now go out there and tell them how amazing I am."

CHAPTER 37

THAT EVENING, WE TAKE A break from rehearsing in the dance studio to watch the news segment on one of the televisions in the lobby, usually used for sharing Sunset Hills' announcements.

When I show up on the screen, everyone cheers, which is oddly overwhelming. All I'm doing is what I should've done from the start—taking ownership of this show.

Across the lobby, a phone rings.

"What is that?" I ask.

"Do you really not know what a phone is?" Sadie asks. "Young people." She rolls her eyes.

"I didn't know there was a phone in the lobby."

"It's the box office," Grace says. "Do you think someone wants tickets?"

"Should we answer it?" Veronica asks.

"Of course we should." Belinda bustles over to the box office and picks up the landline, then proceeds to give the person on the other end a full rundown of where the theatre is located.

Dylan glances up from behind her laptop. "We just sold fifty-eight tickets."

"And the segment isn't even over." Connie looks at me. "Rosie, you are a genius."

At that, I smile.

And I don't stop smiling all the way through rehearsal.

The thing that threatened to close the show completely, actually brought everyone closer together.

As I sit back and watch my cast walk through the second act, a thought hits me. Maybe I don't need Broadway or a big movie career or a national tour to be happy.

Maybe I just need to do what I love with people I love.

If this summer has shown me anything, it's that dreams shift and change. They grow and evolve. The life I'd always imagined for myself wasn't the one I was living. And now, because of this place and these people, I wonder, for the first time in, oh, forever, if my dream could look different.

There's just one problem. I still love acting. I still love being the one on the stage.

Am I ready to give that up in favor of a different kind of life?

The thought looms like a creeping storm in the west.

Once we finish rehearsal, I give the cast my notes, thank them for being amazing, and send them on their way. I watch everyone go, noting the way they interact with each other, and soon I'm left in the seats with only Dylan.

She looks at me, then quickly looks away.

"What?"

She shakes her head.

"Dylan?"

"It's just . . ." She picks at a hangnail, and I don't prod her to talk because I know teenagers hate that. Instead, I go still, giving her space to figure out how and what she needs to say because there's obviously something on her mind. "It was, I don't know, easier before you got here or whatever."

"Oh." My shoulders drop. "Like, better, or . . . ?"

"No, not like that. I mean . . ." She lifts her chin, then sighs. "It was easier to ignore everyone."

I nod.

"People left me alone."

"I mean, you kind of gave off a vibe."

She glares at me as only Dylan can.

"I haven't had a lot of luck, you know"—she looks down—"caring about other people."

I watch her, but she won't meet my eyes. I want to tell her I haven't had a lot of luck with that either but decide it's best if I just listen.

"I shouldn't have done this show because now"—she looks up at me, struggling—"now you're going to leave, and it's . . ." Her lower lip quivers, and she pushes the heels of her hands into her eyes. "So *stupid*. I hate crying."

"I don't really want to leave either," I tell her. "I've learned a lot here. And I've grown to really like—"

She looks at me. "Booker?"

I laugh. "A lot of people." I pause. "Including *you*, you nerd."

"Whatever, boomer."

I laugh. "Boomer? I'm not even thirty!"

"Whatever. You're old."

I shake my head and laugh.

"For what it's worth," she continues, "I think a lot of people have grown to like you too."

We sit in silence for a few long seconds, and then I announce, "You know, I've been thinking a lot about my life choices."

I don't have to turn to know I have her attention.

"I've been chasing this big dream—my dream—for a long time. Forever, really."

She looks at me. "To work with old people?"

I chuckle. "No. That is not the big dream. Shocker, right?" I take a breath and lean back in my chair. "To perform. To be in front of a camera or an audience."

She shrugs. "So go do that." She says it like it's easy.

"There's no stability in it. Only rejection. So. Much. Rejection."

Is it weird that being honest with a teenager comes easily to me when being honest with almost everyone else in my life doesn't?

"Huh," she says. "I think that would suck."

I nod. "It does suck. It sucks the life right out of you." I pause and feel like I'm learning this as I'm saying it. Because while I know something needs to change, I haven't worked out the what or the how. "I guess I'm just trying to figure out how to keep doing what I love without sacrificing my happiness." I go still. "I *really* want to be happy again."

She leans back in her chair, matching my posture. "Happiness is overrated," she deadpans.

I turn to her. "Tell me your life isn't happier since you've started on this show."

She shrugs. "Whatever."

I nod. "Yeah. Uh-huh. I'm right." I make an explosion with my hands. "Boom. Drop the mic."

She stares, trying not to laugh. "Don't ever do that again."

I shimmy my shoulders. "I just might. I'm cool. I'm with it."

She rolls her eyes, shaking her head.

I sigh. "I don't know. I guess I need to figure out what to do."

A long pause, and then she says, "I don't think you should quit on your dream. You're good."

"Thanks," I say dryly. "I don't *want* to quit on it. I think maybe . . . I just want to reimagine it. Maybe the dream just got away from me. Maybe I idealized it a little? Convinced myself there was only one path when really there might be a hundred."

And then, I'm lost in thought again. Thinking about how different I am now than I was when I first arrived at Sunset Hills. "I've changed, I think."

Even the simple act of speaking hard things out loud changed me. Maybe it took the fear out of using real emotions in my work *and* in my life? I don't know . . . but I want to find out. And I want to do that without the desperation I've been lugging around on my shoulders all this time.

"I didn't know you before, so I can't say," she says. "But I guess you're pretty cool, for an old person."

I feel the slow smile creep across my face. "You're pretty cool too, I guess, for a bratty teenager."

She grins. "I have to go. My grandma is forcing me to eat full meals instead of grabbing Pop-Tarts on my way to bed."

"That monster." I stand, stretching.

She stands. And she lingers.

"Yes?" I quip, keeping the banter going. "May I help—"

She stops me midsentence and pulls me into a fierce hug. It's tight, and I can feel her heart beating, fast.

I'm suddenly aware of exactly who Dylan is. And why. It doesn't take a heart-to-heart for me to fill in the blanks about her life. A teenager only ends up living in a retirement community as a last resort. Which means that Dylan and I have something in common.

I wrap my arms around her and hug her back.

I want to tell her I understand, even without knowing all the details. That I only came here because I didn't have another choice.

But I say none of those things. This isn't about me.

"You're so special, Dylan," I say quietly. "You're smart and creative and strong." I pull back and look at her, but she avoids my eyes. "Don't forget that, okay?"

She dries her cheeks with the sleeve of her sweatshirt and nods.

"Promise?"

Now she looks at me. "Shut up."

"Close enough."

As she goes, I draw in a breath, feeling like maybe for the first time in my life I've made peace with the fact that this big dream isn't going to happen for me, and also for the first time in my life—I'm okay if it doesn't.

CHAPTER 38

OVER THE NEXT TWO WEEKS, all my spare time is spent on the show. There are so many last-minute odds and ends that suck up every minute of the day, making it nearly impossible to see Booker as much as I want to.

When he's not working, he's at the theatre, helping backstage, bringing me dinner, and reminding me to stay hydrated.

The ticket sales, thanks to a joint effort from the entire cast and the news story, are booming.

Our cast feels more like a little family than ever with so many of us spending every spare second at the theatre, taking care to get the show ready.

I'm looking over a few of the remade costumes with Ginny when Connie bustles in through the scene shop door. "Rosie!" She rushes toward me. "Do you have a minute?"

"You are my boss." I point at her.

She giggles. "That's true, though I feel like over here you're *my* boss."

I smile. "Also true. Sort of."

She pulls me away from Ginny, who, I am certain, is eavesdropping as best she can with her bad hearing. "I didn't want to say anything before because, well, it wasn't a for-sure thing, but with ticket sales going gangbusters and the way you handled this little flood crisis, it was easy to convince the board."

"Convince them of what?"

"To offer you a full-time job." She snaps her jaw shut, widens her eyes, and lets out the faintest squeal. "Here. As the director of theatre arts."

"There's a full-time position here for the director of theatre arts?" I didn't even think that was an option.

"There is now," she says, her accent a little more pronounced than usual. "They realized"—she leans toward me—"thanks to me, that a volunteer was *never* going to be able to make a real difference with this program. Between the ticket sales, the endowment, and new donations that have come in over the summer, we have enough to hire someone full time." She squeezes my arm. "You'd also have to work in the box office and take over the social media marketing, but compared to a flood, that's all easy peasy, right?"

I give the space a quick cursory glance. This isn't something I ever dreamed I would do, but I can't deny that a part of me is at peace here.

My mailbox is here.

Booker is here.

I'm not too far from my friends back home—is this how my dream is supposed to change?

"Can I think about it?" I ask.

Connie's smile holds. "Of course you can. We aren't going to offer it to anyone else until we have your answer. We don't want to lose you, Rosie."

"Okay, wow." I push a hand through my hair. "That's . . . that's actually really flattering." If I did stay here, the decision would be final. I'd have to give up on the big dream because there's really no way I could be available for auditions from here. And if this was my job, I wouldn't be able to take even a short run anywhere else.

"I know it's a lot to consider," she says. "You have your life in New York."

Are we really calling that a *life*?

"Let me know what you decide." Connie pats me on the shoulder and walks away.

When I turn, I find Booker standing in the wings, hands stuffed in his pockets. "I didn't mean to eavesdrop."

I tilt my head sarcastically. "Uh-huh."

"Okay, fine, maybe I did," he confesses.

"How much did you hear?"

He takes a couple of steps toward me. "Enough."

I tuck my hair behind my ears, certain that if he asked me to stay, I would.

Just like my mother did.

Just like I promised her I wouldn't.

Somewhere, an apple doesn't fall far from a tree, hitting the ground with a thud.

Conversely, I think of Arthur.

The conversation with him planted a tiny seed deep down inside me.

Why do I want to act?

The answer was so clear. It still is. It's the thing that makes me feel alive. The thing I was born to do.

For me.

Not for my mom.

I'd been so certain. Does this change that?

"What are you going to do?" Booker asks.

I chew the inside of my lip, aware that I'm nervous, and also aware that I really do not want to have to say goodbye to this man.

But that was always the plan, wasn't it? I knew that going in.

"I don't know yet," I say, turning it over in my head. "Steady work would be nice."

He nods.

"And, you know," I say comically nonchalantly, "you're here. I guess that's a perk."

I can practically feel myself shouting: *"I'll stay with you forever!"*

But then he says, "I don't think I should factor into this decision."

I frown.

"Not like that," he says. "It's not that I don't want to be a part of your decision; it's just that I don't *want* to be a part of your decision."

"Oh, well, yeah, that's crystal clear."

He smiles, moving closer to me. "I don't ever want you to give up on your dreams because of me."

"I get it," I say, taking his hand. "You don't want me to resent you."

"Exactly." He gently pulls me toward him. "No matter how much I don't want you to go."

When he kisses me, all I can think is that I don't want to go either. I could stay here, even endure winter in Wisconsin, if it meant I could be with him.

But if I did that, what happens to that part of my soul that comes alive when I perform? Does it simply disappear?

CHAPTER 39

PRO/CON LISTS AREN'T REALLY MY style.

Usually, I trust my gut.

But right now, my gut is only thinking of Booker.

So I made a list.

It didn't help.

At the end of the day, this isn't the kind of decision a simple list can make for me. The pros and cons are all super important, but equally so. Which means this is the kind of decision I have to make for myself.

This is my life. What do I want it to look like?

The thought makes my stomach tumble.

A few days before we open, we break for dinner, and as I sit down to eat the pasta Daisy picked up from the dining hall for me, I check my email for the first time today.

I'm bulk deleting the junk mail without paying much attention when I see one with the subject line: Audition Request.

I blink.

It's still there.

Audition Request.

I click on it.

Dear Miss Waterman,

Your headshot came across my desk, and I'd like to see you for a part in a new production of *A Doll's House* at The Majestic. We're a regional theatre based in Chicago. This is a professional credit. If you could send in a self-tape, we'd like to hear you read the attached pages for the part of Nora. You can use an off-screen scene partner.

If cast, rehearsals will begin in early September with a two-month run, seven shows a week, Mondays and Tuesdays off. If you're unable to audition at this time, please let me know; otherwise, we'll need your tape back by the end of the week.

Sincerely,
Britta Shockley

I read the email again. It's the kind of email I always wanted to get. They want to see me. For a professional role.

This is my dream.

I guess my propensity for bulk-submitting paid off—although I sent those before I came here, and like with this job, I have no memory of submitting for this.

It doesn't really matter.

It's *A Doll's House*.

I first fell in love with the play in college when I spent a summer in New York and saw the revival on Broadway. The entire experience moved me, and I related to Nora. I still do. It's why her monologue is part of my portfolio.

I take note of the bubble of nerves in my belly as I type out a reply:

Dear Miss Shockley,

I will happily submit for this role, and I'll have my tape back to you by the end of the week.

Thank you for your consideration.

Sincerely,
Rosie Waterman

I resist the urge to add: *PS, Nora has been a dream role for me ever since the day I saw the show on Broadway. But I'd happily play any role or be the person who gets the director coffee, which would definitely be a step up from 98 percent of the jobs I had when I lived in New York.*

After all, adding too much personal detail in a business email is frowned upon.

And would probably make Britta Shockley think I'm a weirdo.

"You're smiling."

I'm sitting cross-legged on the floor, a plate of uneaten pasta in front of me, while I hit Send on the reply to Britta Shockley. I look up and see Booker standing beside me, amusement playing behind his eyes and his baseball hat turned backward.

I'm a sucker for a guy in a backward baseball hat.

"You've hardly eaten." He sits down next to me.

I hand over my phone and twirl some spaghetti onto my fork while he reads the email. When he's finished, my mouth is full, and his eyes go wide, excitement on his face.

"This is a big deal, right?" He hands it back to me.

"Not really." I lay it on thick. "I mean, it's just a dream role at a professional theatre in a major market . . ."

"Congratulations!" He picks up my garlic bread and takes a bite.

"Well, I haven't gotten it yet," I say. "I still have to audition."

He lets out a *pfft* sound. "Details."

If only I were as confident in myself as he is. Never mind that he knows nothing about theatre or acting or auditions. It's still nice to have someone tell me I'm great.

I stare at the words on my phone. "I never thought about Chicago. Seems too close to home. I mean, I never really considered anywhere but New York, but they do have a huge theatre community there. *Tons* of shows premiere there before going to New York."

He swallows his bite. "One of the many things to admire about the city." Then he winces. "Their football team, however . . ."

I pick up my plate and take another bite. "I'm going to audition. I already have the monologue memorized. I just . . ." I think about the last time I performed it for the renowned coach who held the master class I attended a few years back.

The performance was followed by probing questions, the kind that sent me running from the room.

But I don't want to run anymore.

"Booker, do you think I could tell you my life's story?"

He's mid-drink, but my question stops him. He coughs as he takes the bottle away from his mouth. "Uh, sure?"

"It's just . . . I need to let myself feel some things before I record this performance, and I think it'll help."

He takes my hand and squeezes it. "I would love to hear your life's story. When?"

"Tonight?" I ask on a wince because it's already dinnertime and we still have to finish rehearsal.

He lets go of my hand and picks up the other half of my garlic bread. "And to think . . . it's not even Friday."

. . . .

I know that cutting my heart open and gushing all over the stage isn't a requirement for this audition—but I think I need to do it.

It's time that I finally—*finally*—let myself connect with the hard feelings.

And also? I really do want to open up to Booker. More than facts and details. More than tarps and pizza.

I want him to know me. Warts and all.

That may be foolish and misguided, given the fact that our summer romance will end with the season, or maybe that's why he feels safe.

Dump it all, then leave. Clean.

I know in my heart that's not true.

So I tell him. Unprompted. Unfiltered. And unabridged.

"Booker Hayes," I say, sitting in a chair at the center of the stage. "Welcome to my life."

I tell him about my dad leaving and what it did to my mom. I tell him what that in turn did to me. I tell him about the nights I slept on the floor outside her bedroom because I was worried she'd leave me in the middle of the night. I tell him how I've spent years chasing after a dream, but I didn't really know until a few days ago that I'd been chasing it for the wrong reasons. That I've been so worried about pleasing other people that I forgot to check in with myself and figure out who I am and what I want out of this one life I get to live.

I tell him I feel like this summer has been an awakening. I've opened myself up to possibilities. I've begun to see all the ways I'd closed myself off. I've woken up. Just like Nora at the end of *A Doll's House*. Her monologue is a realization that she's lived to please other people but that she is equal to her husband, who only ever treated her like a doll. A plaything.

When I'm finished sharing all of these things, when the feelings are right there, poking through the surface, I ask Booker to record my performance.

It's a monologue I could recite backward and forward. I could do it in my sleep. Without thinking. I've had it memorized for so long, with choreographed gestures and manufactured emotions.

I throw all of that away.

Instead, I think about Nora. And I think about me. I think about how it felt to be left behind by someone who was meant to love me forever. I think about growing up too fast and making sure my actions pleased as many people as possible. Of playing a part, even in my own life.

I think about holding myself back because I was afraid. Of standing in my own way.

And I use Nora's words to communicate all of those feelings.

When I'm finished, I look at Booker, who stands a few feet away, recording. His eyes are wide, and for a second I'm worried he thinks that was terrible. But then he shakes his head, an impressed disbelief on his face.

He clicks the video off. "Wow, Rosie, what was that?"

"That was my monologue," I say. "Was it okay?"

"I mean, I'm no expert, but—"

"I am," Arthur calls out from the catwalks.

And I want to hide. I look up into the darkness, but I don't see him. "You saw that?" I call out.

"I did."

"Can you come down here? This is like talking to the Almighty," I joke.

He chuckles. "Maybe I like it that way."

A few seconds later, Arthur appears at the top of a winding metal staircase that leads from the catwalks down to the stage.

I freeze like a person on trial, waiting for the judge to issue a verdict.

Arthur walks over to me, slowly, like he's got all the time in the world, and I realize that his opinion means more to me than getting the actual part.

He stops in front of me and sticks his hands on his hips. "What's the monologue for?"

"An audition."

"For Nora?"

"Yep."

Then he narrows his eyes, as if summing me up one more time before sending me off to the gallows. "I don't believe in flattery."

"Did you flatter Annie?" I straighten.

"Not onstage," he says seriously.

I smirk.

"I only give compliments when they're earned."

"Like the Paul Hollywood handshake?" I ask, but it's obvious by his expression that Arthur is not a fan of *The Great British Bake Off*.

Booker says, "I think that performance more than earned a compli—"

Arthur holds up a hand that shuts him right up. "Like you said. You're not an expert."

The old man turns his gaze to me. "I've seen this monologue performed a million times. Usually those performances are closed off and stiff and"—he scrunches up his face—"act-y. Maybe a little like you would've been."

I give him a firm nod, letting him know I can take it.

"What you just did here?" He points to the stage. "Was none of those things."

I force myself not to smile, but I feel the compliment wash over me.

"You were thoughtful and measured and, Rosie"—he leans in and quietly says—"I believed you."

Warmth crawls from my belly up to my neck and all the way to my cheeks. I press my lips together, holding in a smile, but the tears in my eyes give me away.

But Arthur isn't finished. "I don't know what the director is looking for, but if this were my show, I'd cast you in a heartbeat."

At that, a tear escapes.

Arthur glances at Booker, then back to me. "Feelings aren't the enemy, Rosie. Let yourself feel them. Those are your tools. The joy and the elation. The hurt and the despair. They all go together, working in tandem to become the memories that matter most of all. For work and for life."

It takes me a second to pull myself together, but once I do, I say, "That's good advice, Professor." I reach out and squeeze his shoulder. "For both of us."

He waves me off, his face returning to its usual gruff and craggy expression. "Yeah, yeah." He turns to go, but I call after him.

"Arthur?"

He glances at me over his shoulder.

I start bouncing to a song that's playing in my head and burst out into the chorus of "Wishin' and Hopin'" by Dusty Springfield, which I used to perform in my bedroom using the choreography from the opening credits of *My Best Friend's Wedding*.

I change "him" to "her" and hope Arthur understands I'm talking about him showing Bertie how he feels about her.

To my utter shock, Arthur doesn't grunt and storm off. He actually starts dancing in a goofy little circle, which makes me giggle so much I stop singing, and Arthur has to pick up the music.

I regain my composure and we finish the chorus duet-style.

"Think she'll talk to me?" he asks when the song is finished.

"If you sufficiently grovel, I think she might consider it," I tell him.

He points a finger upward. "Right." He starts for the door, then turns back. "Are flowers a good idea?"

"Always," I call after him.

Another upward point, and then he's gone.

I spin a circle on my heel and find Booker smirking at me. "You two theatre geeks are adorable."

I smile. "He's a great teacher."

"And you're a brilliant actor." He holds up the phone, where the video is paused. "You ready to send this?"

I walk over, take the phone, and open a new email. Without thinking or doing another take, I type out a quick note in reply to Britta's email, upload the video to Google Drive . . .

Then I hit Send.

CHAPTER 40

I LEARNED IN SCHOOL THAT where auditions are concerned, the best thing to do is to go in, do your best, and then forget about it.

That method has never worked for me. I tend to dwell and wring my hands and worry, desperate for news about the parts I really want.

But after I send Britta my video, I forget about it. Not because I don't care, but because things are so busy with the show—the prep, the last-minute checklists. So two days later I realize I never even told Daisy about it.

But maybe it's better that way.

I like this novel idea of taking a less desperate, more measured approach to my career. It's like I've made my peace with all of it, and if this one doesn't work out, something else will. For the first time in a long time, I feel like I have options.

We're on a ten-minute break during rehearsal, and I glance up and find Grace and Connie walking through the transformation scene. The costumes have all been repaired or replaced, thanks to Ginny's recruitment efforts, which basically consisted of knocking on every single door in Sunset Hills and asking if anyone knew how to sew.

We now have eight new seamstresses, all of whom said they had so much fun they can't wait for the next show.

Somehow, word got out that I've been offered a job here, and while I'm still mulling it over, most of the cast and crew have let me know their feelings on the subject.

Belinda said, and I quote, *"Well, it wouldn't be the worst thing in the world, I suppose."*

I've thought about it a lot. I've thought about how I could be happy here. I like the people, and the conditions of my employment are next-level amazing. Not many jobs offer room and board and late-night kitchen raids as perks.

But then I think about how it felt to film that audition. I think about the prospect of performing in a play I've wanted to do since I was eighteen. I think about how it felt to tap into what that character was *really* feeling during that speech.

Evolve my dream in Sunset Hills.

Rekindle my passion in Chicago.

It's the age-old question that The Clash sang about in the eighties. Should I stay or should I go?

....

Three days later, I wake up with nervous jitters in my stomach and a beautiful bouquet of roses on my counter.

I'm about to see if there's a card when Daisy pops out of her room. "They're from Booker," she singsongs.

I smile. "Was he here this morning?"

"He had to work early, so he dropped them off on the way," she says. "I canceled all the events for the weekend and have two big groups doing dinner and a show." She shrugs her shoulders in perky excitement. "I cannot *wait* to see all your hard work pay off!"

I scrub a hand down my face and pour myself a cup of coffee.

"Have you . . . thought any more about what you're going to do? About the job offer?" Daisy asks tentatively.

I pour cream into my cup and take a drink. "I've thought about it a lot actually."

"And?" Her eyes are hopeful.

"And I still don't know." I sigh. "Stability is appealing. But so is acting. I love it here, but I also love being on the stage. I'm not sure I'm ready to give that up yet." I can tell something is shifting, like I'm on the cusp of a big change—I just don't know what that looks like.

Daisy leans against the counter. "Your housemate is ah-mazing," she croons. "That's in the pro column, right?"

"Absolutely."

She grins. "Really, Rosie, whatever you decide, I'm going to cheer you on."

"Thanks." I study her as she sits down and pulls on her shoes. If I do go, I'll really miss her. In just a few months, she's become a real friend to me.

"I'll see you tonight." She rushes out the door, and I laugh as I hear the tires squeal when she peels away. I can't imagine what that girl is like behind the wheel of a real car.

I stand in the living room, holding my coffee and staring out over the common space. It's peaceful—a calm before the opening-night storm. All of the details have been taken care of. Everything we could've done has been done.

The theatre has been as repaired as it's going to get, though we're now performing on subfloor without a curtain in the middle of the stage.

All that's left to do is show up and deliver a speech that builds confidence in my cast, many of whom are undoubtedly full of nerves today. And once that's finished, I'll get to sit back and watch as the hours and days and weeks of hard work finally pay off.

My phone buzzes, and I find a text from Connie.

CONNIE: Rosie! We are all sold out for the entire run. No tickets left at all! I hope everyone you know already bought their seats!

My eyes go wide just looking at the words. We're sold out?

ROSIE: For real?!
CONNIE: I guess we'd better do a good job, huh? 🤞

We're sold out.
It's almost like it's real now.
A new wave of excited terror washes over me.

CONNIE: You did good, Rosie. I hope you celebrate!

I shower and get ready, and a little before noon, there's a knock on my door.

I rush out to it, pull it open, and find my three best friends standing there, all of them looking like they're holding their breath. We erupt in a wild fit of excitement, screams, hugs, maybe a few tears, all of us talking at the same time.

"I'm so glad my instructions made sense!" I say, hugging each one of them.

"Yeah, no, they didn't," Maya says. "We had to stop at the desk in that clubhouse. This place is fancy."

I go to hug Marnie, but she holds up a hand. "Still not a hugger."

"I don't care." I hug her stiff body anyway. "I've missed you. And that favor you called in saved our show. I just heard we're sold out!"

"Sold out, Rosie, that's amazing!" Maya says.

"Can I use your bathroom?" Taylor has one hand on her protruding belly, the other on her back.

"You've, uh, grown," I say, moving out of the doorway so she can come in.

"I know. I'm as big as a barn. And I have to pee every forty-five seconds."

"You can watch the show from the back with me," I say.

"Bathroom?" She looks like she might actually burst.

"Down the hall." I point, and she rushes off.

"This place is adorable," Maya says. "And you get to stay here for free?"

"It's a perk of the job," I say. "Crazy, right?"

I show them my room, the patio, the common area, and a photo of Daisy and Louie that's stuck to the fridge. "She's my housemate. You guys will love her."

"As long as you don't love her as much as you love us," Maya says.

I grin, and the smile drops off her face.

"I'm serious," she says.

"Nobody could ever replace you three," I say. "Let me give you a campus tour."

We decide to walk over to the dining hall to get some lunch, and I show them all the highlights along the way. I tell them about line dancing and point out the park bench where I found Dylan sitting a couple of days after I arrived. I even take them to the spot where I ran the cart off the road and into the mud, explaining that Booker pulled me out, which Maya finds terribly romantic.

We reach the dining hall, pick up trays, move through the line, and once we sit, I glance up to find my friends looking at me. "What?"

Taylor smiles. "It's like you're back to your old self."

I frown. "What do you mean?"

"Come on, Ro, you didn't think you were fooling us, did you?" Maya asks. "You haven't been yourself for a while."

I meet Marnie's eyes, remembering our phone call. I should've known I couldn't fool any of them. They all know me too well. I don't ever want to take their friendship for granted again.

"It's just good to see you happy." Taylor reaches over and squeezes my hand.

"Why is everyone here old?" Maya asks, and not quietly.

Beside us, a table of ladies shoot her a look.

"Maya," Marnie says.

"Sorry." Maya widens her eyes unapologetically. "But seriously, Rosie, why?"

I check my emotional pulse, then say, "It's a retirement community."

Maya is mid-drink and chokes on her Diet Coke. "What?"

Taylor frowns. "You spent the summer living in a retirement community?"

Marnie smiles at me because, of course, she already knows this.

"I spent the summer directing a show for senior citizens." I pop a french fry in my mouth.

"So Cinderella is . . . old?" Maya winces, as if this thought has left a sour taste in her mouth. But I'm not offended because before I saw Grace, I was doubtful too.

"She's . . . seasoned," I say. "And brilliant. Voice like an angel. You're going to love her."

"I think it's awesome," Marnie says. "There was a big flood in the theatre, and Rosie handled it like a champ. Rallied the troops and got the local news out here to do a story on the production."

"I've learned so much being here." I look at them, one at a time, and I remind myself that these three believe in me. They want to cheer me on. They're *for* me—maybe more than anyone else in my life.

"The truth is, when I got here, I was pretty close to quitting," I say.

"Quitting what?" Taylor takes a bite of her sandwich while Maya crunches kettle chips beside me.

"Auditioning. Performing. New York." I shrug. "Everything."

A double take from Taylor. "Really?"

I nod. "It's hard when your *big dream* doesn't come true." I go quiet for a moment. "But I think I was thinking too small."

"You never think small," Marnie says. "You've always been the world conqueror."

"But I haven't," I say. "Not really. I mean, I *wanted* to be. I tried to be. Even pretended to be. But it turns out, I couldn't do it. Not that way at least. Thinking that there was only one way to make my dream come true was silly. This place showed me I can be happy anywhere if I'm doing what I love *with people* I love."

"Like your boy," Maya says.

I shake my head. "No, like my *man*."

We erupt into giggles then, but once the laughter falls away, I'm left in the middle of an admission I should've made years ago.

"You guys, I've been pretending. A *lot*," I say. "I didn't want you to worry about me, but I also didn't want anyone to think I was a failure. I didn't want to admit that I was struggling, especially when you are all doing so well. I mean, coming back and seeing everyone was so, so good. But it really reminded me how far behind I am."

"You're not behind," Marnie says. "It's not a race."

"But it feels like it sometimes," Maya says, like she understands.

"You want to know the truth?" Taylor sets her sandwich down.

"The truth is always best," I say, a reminder to myself.

"I'm not sure I can do this," Taylor says.

"Do what?" I ask.

"The baby thing," she says.

"Uh, Taylor, I hate to tell you this," Maya says, "but you're doing it."

Her eyes turn glassy as her gaze falls to her lap. "I know."

I reach over and take her hand. "What's wrong?"

Her words all come out at once.

"Babies don't come with instruction books. And am I losing all of my independence by becoming a mother? My body, my time, my life—they'll all belong to this baby now. And what if I'm bad at it? What if Aaron comes home from work and I'm covered in baby puke and the house is a mess and we're eating ramen for the fifth night in a row because it's all I can handle making? Or what if the baby won't sleep or poop or I don't have milk or I have to put cabbage leaves on my boobs?" She's fully crying now.

"Okay, *so* much to unpack there," Maya says.

"The cabbage leaves are just an old wives' tale," Marnie says, but then tosses me an I-don't-know-what-to-do-here look.

Taylor is near a full-on meltdown. "I didn't just hear it from Mrs. Copecki. I read about it in a book!"

"Hey, hey, hey," I say, putting a hand on hers. "It's scary. And unknown. And life-changing. But you're not alone. Let's start with the fact that Aaron is all in," I say. "You're partners, Taylor. He's going to help with the cooking and the diapers and the . . . cabbage leaves." I steal Marnie's expression and volley it back to her.

A tear slips down Taylor's cheek, and she wipes it away, then sniffs so loudly it prompts Marnie to hand her a napkin.

"Taylor, it's normal to be scared about big life changes," Marnie says. "You don't think I was scared to move to Milwaukee and start a whole new job?"

Taylor turns toward our friend. "You were?"

"Yeah, we're not all brave like Rosie," she says.

I freeze at the comment. Me? Brave? They're not around to see my hands shaking almost every single day, to watch me pep talk myself in the mirror when I get ready because otherwise I'll never survive. "You think I'm brave?"

"Duh!" Maya's eyes go wide. "You're so brave, Rosie. Nobody else had the guts to leave. To move to New York City. That's wild."

"And inspiring," Taylor says. "Who cares if it isn't exactly what you thought? You're really out there doing it."

"Yeah, I think you sort of inspired me to dream bigger," Marnie says. "I wouldn't have applied for that Milwaukee job if it weren't for you."

I frown.

"You're totally fearless," Marnie says.

I sink a little in my seat under the weight of humility. "Some people would call it stupidity."

"Well, we aren't those people," Taylor says. "We think it's amazing."

"Does it change your perception if I tell you how hard it's been?" I ask. "That I've barely been getting by?"

"No," Marnie says. "It makes me feel a little better actually. Because I'm only two months into this job, and the anxiety has not gone away. I could really mess this up. And chances like this don't come along every day." She pauses. "What if I fail?"

What if I fail? The question taps me on the shoulder, begging for my attention.

"You won't fail," Maya says. "You were born for this."

"You really were," Taylor agrees.

I sit there, listening to them, these three amazing, smart, and strong women. I'd spent months comparing myself to them, assuming I knew the feelings behind their fearlessness, but the truth is, I didn't.

And I didn't ask.

I held myself back from them, when actually we're really all the same.

"I'm terrified to be a mayor's wife," Maya admits. She takes a long drink of her soda through a straw. "Politics aside, people are just brutal to public figures. I know it's a small town and everything, but that makes it even worse. I mean, everyone knew me before Matty. Will any of them take me seriously?"

"I can't believe this whole time I thought I was the only one," I say.

"I can't either," Taylor says. "I've been freaking out since I found out I was pregnant."

"You're all scared too," I say, marveling at the revelation.

"*Everyone's* a little scared, Rosie," Marnie says. "Even the people who seem like they know what they're doing all the time."

"Somehow, I convinced myself I was the only screwup," I say.

Maya laughs. "Do you even know me?"

"You own your own business," I say.

"That Matty helped me buy." She looks a little embarrassed.

"Look, Rosie, it doesn't matter anyway," Taylor says. "Because the truth is, you can tell us anything. Even if you *were* the only one who was a first-class disaster, which you are not, we would love you because of who you are."

"That's what friends do," Marnie adds.

I've been so stupid. I was so worried about what they would think. So worried I was letting them—everyone—down, and so embarrassed by my own situation that I let it all keep me isolated. Lonely.

Now I see all the ways my friends and I are alike.

Battling fears and worries. Navigating joy and hurt and disappointment and excitement. Moving through each chapter of life as best we can.

None of us have it figured out.

Maya is right. In a way, we're all pretending. Not because we want to keep ourselves hidden, but because we just don't know yet who we're supposed to be. Or maybe we're afraid of change.

"I'm so sorry," I say quietly.

They all look at me.

"For what?" Taylor asks, her mascara a wet line of sludge underneath her eyes.

"For not trusting you guys with the truth," I say. "I was too embarrassed to admit I'm not perfect."

They all burst out laughing. "Uh, we always knew you weren't perfect, Rosie," Maya says.

I laugh with them, aware that there's a lump in my throat

that's going to demand some attention, and as I do, my phone dings with a new email alert.

I look down and see it's from Britta Shockley.

"Everything good, Rosie?" Marnie asks.

I tuck my phone away and choose to stay in the moment. "Everything's great." I smile.

"Now that we've fully established that we're all making things up as we go . . ." Taylor sets her fork down. "Where's the bathroom?"

CHAPTER 41

OPENING NIGHT JITTERS ARE TOTALLY normal.

But these jitters are different.

If I'm the one acting, there are things I can control. My performance. My breathing. My heart rate.

Kind of.

Here, once the curtain goes up, this show is out of my hands.

And that's exactly what I tell my cast. It's like a moment, a ritual, of handing our hard work over to them. Of letting it rest solely on their shoulders.

It's their show . . . and it's a good one. And not a good show for a bunch of old people.

It's just solidly *good.*

I stand in the back, listening and not listening as Dylan calls the show. I look and don't look as my cast takes the stage. It's like peering through my fingers at the part of the scary movie you don't want to watch.

But you look anyway.

Edgar drops a few lines, and Sal accidentally chokes and spits part of his turkey sandwich straight into Belinda's corset, but her ad-libbed reaction—"Sunset Hills cooking, my dear boy?"—gets a laugh.

But it's Grace's transformation dress that steals the show.

It seamlessly, perfectly transforms her from peasant to princess, and it goes off without a hitch. I run backstage to celebrate with Ginny and find her in the wings.

"I'm so relieved it worked," she says, laughing through tears.

All in all, the show is beautiful. The audience is wonderfully loud. The cast is superb, and when it's all over and I stand to applaud their hard work, I'm overcome with emotion and the absolute certainty that this will forever go down as one of the most special memories of my life.

Afterward, while the cast mills around, I hand out "congratulations" and "I'm so proud of yous" like I'm on a parade float tossing Tootsie Rolls to kids. Everyone is buzzing and chattering about the show, including my friends, who practically tackle me the second they find me in the crowd.

Screams, hugs, and all of the oh-my-gosh-ing I can stand. It's overwhelmingly sweet, and I soak up every second.

"Rosie, it was *so* good!" Maya raves. "I decided I want my wedding dress to be a transformation dress. Can you make that happen?"

"We're so proud of you, Ro," Marnie says. "It turned out perfect!"

I'm chatting with them when I spot Bertie down near the front of the space. She's holding a program and looking around like she's waiting for someone.

"I'll be back," I say. "I just want to say hi to someone."

I make my way through the crowd, moving toward Bertie, and my heart squeezes when I see Arthur emerge from backstage, look at her, and then walk down the stairs to where she's standing.

I stop moving and watch, wishing I could hear what he says. I assume it's something kind (hopefully that he's sorry for being an idiot) when she smiles shyly and looks away.

There's something extra sweet about a second chance at love.

Then, from behind me, Dylan's voice. "Hey, um, Rosie?"

I turn to find Dylan standing with a woman dressed in a simple black pantsuit. She's striking, sharp, and put together. And she looks like . . . Dylan.

"This is . . . um. This is my mom."

The woman extends a hand. "Miss Waterman."

I'm utterly shocked. I had filled in Dylan's backstory with a mom that looked *completely* different.

I take her hand and grasp it warmly. "Yes! Dylan's mom."

"Margaret," she says. Her curt smile is hard to read.

"Margaret. It's a pleasure." I pull my hand back and look at Dylan. "You have an incredible daughter. She's basically the glue that held this whole show together."

I can see the visible shock on her face as she slowly turns to Dylan, who responds by shrinking a bit and looking at the floor.

"She . . . was?" Margaret doesn't hide her surprise.

"Yes," I gush. "I've worked with stage managers in New York, and I can safely say that she's as good, if not better. Detailed, patient, caring—"

"Caring?" She cuts me off. "Are we sure we're talking about the same girl?"

I pick up a bit on the dynamic here.

"I'm not sure what she was like before I met her, but we could not have done this show without her. She was utterly amazing."

Three of the cast members pass by us, wave at me, and give Dylan huge hugs from behind, pulling her close, messing her hair. She looks uncomfortable—classic Dylan—and she turns bright red. The women leave, waving to others and making their way across the room.

"I'm . . ." Margaret clears her throat and straightens her blazer. "Well. We have a lot to talk about, don't we?"

Dylan, still wearing her embarrassment in the form of red cheeks, says, "Uh . . . yeah. I think I know what I might want to do, for my, like, life."

Margaret looks at me, dumbfounded, and I wink at Dylan.

She rolls her eyes.

"Mom? Is it cool if I talk to a few people before we go?"

Margaret shakes her head, still in disbelief. "Yes. Go."

Margaret and I watch as Dylan mingles, congratulating and joking with cast members, clearly part of this team.

Her mom looks back at me. "What have you done with my daughter? She's a completely different person."

I smile, putting a hand on her arm. "I take no credit. She did it all herself."

I turn toward the crowd, and my eyes fall on someone I instantly recognize.

My mom.

She's standing next to John and my friends, all chatting and smiling, and she looks over and catches my eye.

We share a moment across a crowded room, and she gives a tearful slight nod.

I don't think she knows what an impact a few words, spoken in a desperate time, had on my entire path. She tried to protect me from the pain of heartbreak, not realizing it's not possible. Life has good and bad. And I really do believe the bad makes the good sweeter, just like Arthur said.

Maybe I was always supposed to learn that lesson this way.

John reaches over and takes my mother's hand, and I see that her heartbreak is long gone. She moved on. She dared to love someone again.

She changed. And so have I.

There was a point this summer when I considered talking to her about all of this, but now it seems unnecessary. I understand why she said what she said back then—but I also understand that my promise to her was never meant to last forever. It was never meant to hold me hostage.

Sometimes dreams shift and change and grow, and changing along with them isn't failing. Pivoting isn't quitting. Happiness isn't linear, and seeking it isn't selfish.

Margaret thanks me again, then heads off to find Dylan, and I turn and see Booker standing in the aisle.

Like the scene in the gym in *West Side Story*, we're Tony and Maria, and everyone else disappears for a moment as we move toward one another.

I want to run to him, of course, but I'm also hesitant. Because this morning, separate from anything Britta's email says or the rush of goodwill I'm feeling tonight, I made my decision.

And it wasn't easy.

He eyes me for a long moment once we reach each other, and then, as if we've communicated telepathically, he says, "You've made up your mind." A statement, not a question.

"I have." I take a step toward him. "And it was difficult."

"Did you—?"

I shake my head. "I don't know yet about the part. She emailed me, but I wanted to wait to read it. I wanted to give the show my full attention." I look away, worried he won't understand my choice. "I might get that part. I might not. But either way, I've realized I'm not ready to quit. And while I've loved directing and want to do more of it in the future, I also want to perform. I just . . . need to figure out a way to do that while also having a life." I look up into his green eyes, afraid if I stare too long, I'll change my mind. "Because I've also realized I really, really want to have a life. Outside of a floundering career."

"Can we . . . ?" He tips his head in the direction of the door that leads outside. I nod, and he reaches for my hand, leading me out into the warm air.

I look up at the dark sky, marveling at how bright the stars are. "I'll miss this sky." A knot forms in my throat, and I hope he hears what I'm not saying.

"I think this sky will miss you."

We stand face-to-face. I try to memorize everything I can about him. The way he smells. The way his eyes see straight through every wall I try to put up. The way his hands rest at my hips, firm yet gentle. And especially the way he always seems to pay attention to what I need.

I know he's not perfect—nobody is—but he might be perfect for me.

But he can't leave.

And I can't stay.

I step into his embrace and let him hold me, aware of how good it feels to fold myself into him.

"For what it's worth"—he kisses the top of my head—"I'm glad you're going."

I look up. "You are?"

"Oh, I'm not glad you won't be here anymore," he says, brushing a stray hair away from my face. "That part is terrible. But I *am* glad that you're going to go for it."

"It seems foolish to keep pursuing something that hasn't gone well up until this point," I say thoughtfully. "Do you think I'm crazy?"

"Definitely," he deadpans. "But not for that."

He leans in and kisses me. When he pulls back, he searches my eyes. "When did you decide?"

"Well." I think about it. "I did a lot of soul-searching, and the answer finally came to me earlier today. I don't want to quit, because I love it too much. I remember now why I want to act. Not because I promised my mom or myself, or because I want to be rich and famous. I really don't care about that stuff."

I really don't. It feels so good knowing who I am and what I want, and it makes this incredibly clear.

And incredibly difficult.

"I want to create characters. Tell their stories. Make people feel something. Remember what it's like to be alive. I want to walk in someone else's shoes and study the human condition and close the gaps between us and show that we're not so different. That all of us humans essentially want the same things.

"I don't need to be on Broadway to do that. I don't need to be working with big-name talent to do it. But I *do* need to be performing. And that's not what this job here is asking me to do."

He tucks my hair behind my ears, taking a slow breath and letting it out. "So, what now?"

I shrug. "Now, I finish out the show, and I start looking for jobs in Chicago."

"Acting jobs," he says.

"And other jobs," I say. "Acting adjacent. I think working in the theatre would be good for me even if I'm not the one on the stage." I toss a quick glance back toward the theatre. "Who knows what a job will lead to? Who I'll meet . . . what I'll learn . . ."

A rush of memories whirls through my mind, like a montage in a movie.

Booker. Arthur. Dylan. The flood. The community. My friends. Bertie. The sound of the crowd. Performing. Connecting. Being alive.

I never would've expected any of that to happen here, but it did, proving that there's life worth living out there if you're willing to let go of what you think it's supposed to look like.

"Well, look at you, growing up."

"I'm a late bloomer."

His smile is bright as he leans in to kiss me.

I memorize that too.

CHAPTER 42

IT'S THE DAY OF THE last show.

Tomorrow, my contract is up.

Tomorrow, I'll be leaving. And I'm full of emotions.

The temptation to shove them all away, to force myself not to feel any of it, is notable, but I resist. And when I arrive at the theatre, I take it all in. Every ounce of the experience that I can safely say has changed me.

I'm not the same person I was when I arrived.

I wonder if every performer feels the same about an empty stage, an empty theatre. Like it's an invitation to sing without judgment or worry.

And so I sing.

It's like I can't help myself, and the words to "For Good" from the musical *Wicked* flow out of me, perfectly fitting for the way I feel about this whole experience and these people.

When I reach the end of the first chorus, I'm surprised by a second voice, coming from the wings, and when I turn, I see Dylan walking toward me.

Shut up.

Dylan can sing?

My eyes go wide, and I blink back tears as she sings the entire second verse, and then I join her on the chorus. We end in a flourish, possibly in a different key than we started in, and I have to wipe my cheeks dry when she is the one who reaches out for a hug.

"This feeling-all-the-feelings thing kind of sucks," I say into her shoulder.

She laughs and draws back. "You know, you leaving here is actually good for me."

"Oh?"

"Because I'm going back to my mom's, and even though she's talking about doing all kinds of mother-daughter crap—thank you for that, by the way—I'll actually still be able to see you. If you end up in Chicago, I mean."

Dylan knows about the audition, but she doesn't know my plan is to live and work in Chicago, regardless of what Britta's email says.

The email that's still sitting there unread. Yes, it's been nearly impossible not to open it. Yes, it's been tormenting me. But I made a promise to myself to stay in the moment here. Never mind that I've done plenty of research about Britta Shockley, about this production, the director, The Majestic. It's been very . . . enlightening.

I smile at Dylan. "I'm glad for that too. Not the 'still seeing you' part, but for sure the lame mother-daughter crap."

She laughs, and it's so genuine that tears prick the corners of my eyes.

"Are you two finished being sappy?" Arthur's voice calls down from the catwalk.

I smile up into the darkness. "Lord, is that you?"

"Funny." I can hear him harrumph.

I draw in a breath. "One more show."

"I need to go check the props table," Dylan says.

"Isn't that someone else's job?" I ask.

"Yes." She starts toward the door. "But I just want to be sure."

As she walks out, Arthur appears in the wings. He seems to have no intention of stopping to talk to me, so I trail behind him. "Did you know Dylan could sing?"

"Nope." He leaves the backstage area and walks into the scene shop. "Nice voice, though."

I follow him into his office and sit down on the only open seat. "You should clean this place."

"I call it creative chaos." He sits behind the computer.

"I call it a disaster."

"Good thing you're leaving then." He tries to hide his smirk, but I catch a glimpse of it before he turns away.

"Saw you with Bertie," I say, probing.

He looks up at me. "Don't make it a thing."

"I'm really glad you're talking again," I say, but the request for more information is evident in my tone.

He shoots me another look, and I begrudgingly take the hint.

I look around his office. "So . . . I've been thinking."

"That's a first." Arthur clicks around on his computer, barely acknowledging me.

"Okay, first, nice dig, and second, I went back through my submissions. I have a tendency to randomly panic-submit for jobs I'm *technically* right for. And some I'm really not right for. I mean, that's how I ended up here."

He squints over at me. "Is that what happened?"

I ignore him. "And I started to think about Britta Shockley."

"Am I supposed to know who that is?"

I fold my arms. "She's the casting director who asked me to audition for *A Doll's House*."

He shrugs, remaining disinterested.

I watch him, letting my pause grow a bit, just to see if he reacts.

He doesn't.

He's good.

"So I went back through my submissions." I chew on the inside of my cheek, leaning forward a bit, looking for a rise, a flinch, anything.

Still no reaction.

"And I've never submitted anything to Britta or her company or to The Majestic Theatre before."

Arthur flips through a few folders on his desk.

"But you know who *did* work at The Majestic Theatre?"

Ha! There it is.

He stops shuffling the folders and pulls his hands into his lap. He stares blankly at the screen in front of him and seems to be purposely avoiding my eyes.

"You."

He draws in a deep, slow breath.

I go on. "*And* the artistic director was one of your students." I pull up the theatre's staff page on my phone, still open from last night's deep dive, and read the pertinent information. "'Harold Lowe was a longtime assistant director and student of Arthur Silverman. Together, the pair brought more than fifteen productions to The Majestic stage before Arthur's retirement in 2021. Harold hopes to continue the Silverman tradition of teaching, encouraging, and using theatre to bring people together.'"

I look at him. "You sent them my information."

He turns but doesn't fully meet my eyes. "You have no proof."

"Arthur!" I wait until he finally looks up. "Why would you do this for me?"

He finally relents. "All I did was get you the audition. You still have to get the part yourself."

I pause, then say, "I got the email on Friday."

His eyes widen. "And?"

"I haven't opened it yet," I say.

"Why not?" The lines in his forehead deepen with his frown.

"I was trying to make sure I was, you know, in the moment."

He only stares.

"For the cast," I say. "They deserve my undivided attention."

He holds the silence for a beat, and then, as if it's a line in a play, he says, "Well, that's the stupidest thing I've ever heard."

Now I'm the one frowning.

"Open it," he says.

"Now?" I ask, but what I really mean is, *"In front of you?"*

He quirks a brow.

I typically don't love to share my rejection, as evidenced by, well, the last seven years.

But maybe this will be good for me. Still, I hesitate.

And still, he stares.

"Fine." I click over to my email, scroll to Britta's name, and open it. My heart is racing with nerves as I scan the words that come in and out of focus on the screen.

"Well?" Arthur leans closer. "What does it say?"

My eyes jump to his, but I don't let my expression give anything away. "Do you really not know?"

"I really don't," he says. "I floated your name and that's all."

I hold his gaze for a three count, but after that, I can't keep the smile from spreading across my lips.

"You got it," he says, and I get the sense he's having trouble keeping his own smile away.

"I got it," I say.

He neutralizes his expression. "Well. Yes. Good." He clears his throat. "That's great news, Rosie. Congratulations."

I smirk, but he's not looking at me anymore. "Why did you do this for me?"

"I didn't—"

"But you did," I cut in. "I hear you when you say I got the part, but you opened the door." I pause. "Why?"

He leans back in his chair and looks at me. "I could say because it's what Annie would want me to do." He stops, like he's trying to find exactly the right words. "But the truth is, I see something in you. As long as you stay out of your own way, I think you're going to be"—he squints—"exceptional."

I feel myself brighten at this. Like a flower turning toward the sun. "You really think so?"

"Don't go fishing for more compliments. You get the one, that's it." He starts shuffling papers on his desk but then stops again and looks at me. "And remember, you can be exceptional anywhere." He gives me a little nod, as if to punctuate the sentence, then stands, walks over to a shelf, and picks up a small box. He opens it, and for a moment, he's lost to whatever memory he finds inside.

When he turns back to me, I stand, but I don't say anything.

"This was Annie's," he says. "She didn't believe in good luck. She believed in making your own. At least she said she didn't, but she never did a show without wearing this." His hand shakes a little as he picks up a gold chain with a small butterfly charm hanging on the end of it. "It's the first gift I ever got her." He smiles down at it, then holds the necklace out to me. "I want you to have it."

I hold my hands up. "I can't take that."

"*Annie* would want you to have it."

"Arthur, you can't give that away," I say.

"Why not?" He pulls his hand back. "Annie's not in this necklace like some Horcrux. She's here . . ." He taps his chest, then sets the necklace back inside the box. "We never had children, Rosie. And the thought of passing this on to someone who reminds me so much of her, well, that makes me happy."

I look at the necklace, then at him. "You're sure?"

He nods and holds it out to me.

Slowly, I take it, feeling how precious it is. "I'm going to make you proud."

And that feels like exactly the kind of promise I can carry with me into the next chapter—whatever it holds.

"Good," he says. "Now get out of here and let me do my work. I have to figure out what show I'm directing in the fall." He plops back down in his chair, leaving me standing there, mouth ajar.

"What?"

"Connie offered me the job when you turned it down," he says. "I decided to give it a go."

I do nothing to hide my smile, and he must sense it because he waves me off and orders me out of his office.

I turn to leave, but when I reach the door, I glance back, and that's when I see him wipe a tear from his eye. And I think this precious, bristly, gooey-centered genius has changed my life forever.

CHAPTER 43

WHEN THE CURTAIN FALLS ON the final matinee performance of *Cinderella*, it's like the emotional floodgates fail, sending torrents of joy and love and sadness spilling over everyone's banks.

I don't even try to sandbag the feelings, which means by the time the crowd has dispersed, I've cried off my mascara and have a red nose and an armload of flowers—gifts from people I'm going to be so, so sad to leave.

The cast and crew mill around on the stage, where we've decided to meet for a small celebration, my chance to give them all a proper goodbye.

But it's Belinda, not me, who gets everyone's attention. "People! People! I know it's almost five thirty, so most of you are out way past your bedtime." Good-natured groans and hollers and boos ensue. "So let's get this started."

There's a murmur of quiet laughter, and she waits for complete silence before going on.

"As most of you know, I wasn't thrilled when we found out our beautiful production of *Cinderella* was going to be directed by"—she slides her stink eye over to me—"a child."

I give her a playful eye roll.

"But I have to say, Rosie, you changed my mind about that." Belinda straightens, her shoulders back, her head held high, poised and graceful the way she always is, but she pauses for a long moment, and I wonder if something is wrong. Her chin lowers, gaze landing on the stage below, and then she steels her jaw, regaining her composure.

"I know how hard it is to direct a show," she says. "I did it—unsuccessfully—which is why they had to bring you in. To clean up"—her voice falters slightly—"my mess. To save this wonderful program." She waves a dramatic hand in front of her, as if to include everyone and everything on this stage. "I regret that I made things so difficult for you. Especially because you proved to be more than capable. Creative and encouraging." Then, as an aside, "Even when dealing with the likes of me."

More laughter and murmurs, mostly agreeing with her.

She shoots the rest of them a look but manages a smile. "I am nothing if not self-aware."

A voice from the back. Evelyn. "Does this mean you'll be nice now?"

"Not on your life," she shoots back without missing a beat.

More laughter.

"Rosie, we wanted to send you off with a token of our appreciation, so . . ." She turns and Sadie hands over a large gift, wrapped in brown paper and tied with a red bow. "We all chipped in to get you this."

I walk toward her and give Belinda a hug, choked up over this whole thoughtful scene. "Thank you."

She hugs me back but pulls away quickly, pushing the gift into my arms. I think I've gotten about as much emotion from her as I'm going to.

And I'll take it. Winning her over is perhaps my greatest accomplishment to date.

I hold the large gift and look around the group. "Do I open it now or . . . ?"

A chorus of "Of course you do!" and "Definitely" rings out. So I set the gift on the floor, kneel down, and pull off the wrapping.

Inside, I find a large shadow box the size of a poster.

Center-mounted inside is a miniature version of the transformation dress. Surrounding it, a program. A ticket stub. A blue piece of . . .

"Is that a piece of the tarp we fell asleep on?" I shout.

Eruptions of laughter and applause.

There's the fairy godmother wand and candid photos—ones I had no idea were being taken—of me directing, talking, pointing, smiling.

There's one photo that catches my eye, and I have no idea how anyone captured it.

It's Booker, up on a ladder working on the set, and me staring right at his rear end.

It's foam-mounted, so it sits higher than the rest, with a big, red sketchy heart drawn around it.

And then it hits me.

"This is just for me."

"Dylan, you little . . ." I shoot her a look, and she waggles her eyebrows at me.

More laughter.

At the bottom is a glossy print of the cast photo we took on opening night. And littering the white cardboard backing that everything is mounted to are signatures. Notes. Hearts. Messages.

"We all signed it," Sadie says, beaming.

"You can hang it in your new apartment," Grace adds. "If there's room."

"So you don't forget us," Evelyn adds.

I pick it up and stand, holding it out in front of me, unable to keep the tears at bay. "I could never forget you."

I look around, doing my best to carve each face in my memory. "You all have helped me so much. You helped me remember why I love theatre and why I can't give up on it yet. This community and the way you all give of your time and your talent—it's so special."

The reactions are quiet, emotional, meaningful, honest, and I let myself feel it all.

"We would've loved to keep you here with us, Rosie," Connie says, "but there are dreams yet to be chased." She points a finger toward the ceiling as if to make a point.

I nod, gaining a bit of composure back. "Yes. There are. And I'm going to chase them a little differently this time. I'm going to chase the joy and leave all the desperation behind." I scan their faces. "And even though I'm sad to go, I'm excited that I'm leaving you in the most capable hands."

Quiet chatter filters through the group, and I realize they don't know yet.

"When I got here, I had no idea you were hiding a true theatrical genius in this theatre, but the more time I spent with Arthur Silverman, the clearer it became."

Arthur tries to duck behind the man in front of him, obviously not wanting any part of this unsanctioned announcement.

"He is more capable, more renowned, and more decorated than I could ever hope to be, and he has agreed to take the position," I say. "Doing more of what he was born to do."

The applause is tentative, but when I force Arthur to come stand next to me, the cheers pick up, and soon he's waving a hand to make them all stop.

"I run a tight ship," he says. "But I've seen how much talent I have to work with, so I'm not going to go easy on you."

"But you are going to have fun," I prod.

"Yeah, yeah," he grumbles. "Fun too. Maybe."

I wrap an arm around his shoulder and squeeze. "I can't wait to come see your shows."

He doesn't exactly smile, but his frown loosens the wrinkles in his forehead. "And I can't wait to come see yours."

....

After the party, Booker drives me back to my cottage and walks me inside. "I want to show you something."

I must look suspicious because he smiles and adds, "Trust me." He reaches for my hand, then leads me through the cottage and into the backyard—the part that feels secluded and hidden away.

On the grass, there's a big blanket, and in the center of it, a wooden board under several lit candles flickering in the darkness.

"It's our last night together," he says. "I wanted it to be special." He stuffs his hands in his pockets, looking adorable and sweet, and I wonder how in the world I'm going to walk away from this man.

"I wasn't sure if you'd eat after the show, but I picked up sandwiches from this great little deli in town. And there are chips and fruit." He leads me over to the blanket and shows me the picnic basket, full of all the things he mentioned. "And I brought chocolate." He pulls out brownies. "There's frosted and unfrosted. I wasn't sure which kind you like. People have strong opinions about frosting."

"I love frosting," I say as seriously as I can.

He stuffs the unfrosted ones back in the basket. "Frosted it is."

"Did you make them?" I ask.

"Louie helped," he says, and then he adds, "I made sure he didn't accidentally drop anything in them."

I smile as heat rushes to my cheeks. "Nobody's ever half made me brownies before. Nobody's ever half made *anything* like this for me before." I sit down across from him, and he hands me a sandwich—chicken salad, my favorite—and then a bag of chips.

We're quiet for a few minutes while we set up makeshift place settings, then unwrap and open our food. He pulls a bottle of champagne from the basket, pops the cork off, and pours us each a glass. Then he holds the glass up in the air and says, "To the success of this show and the success of the next one."

I hold my glass up and say, "To you not being Roberto," and he laughs.

Oh, how I'll miss that.

There's a quick pang of sadness at the thought.

He drops his arm slightly, and his gaze catches mine. He sets the glass down on the wood plank. "We haven't talked about long distance," he says. "Chicago isn't New York." A beat. "Should we try it?"

I want to say yes. I want to tell him that FaceTime and the occasional in-person dates will be enough, but I know better.

When I don't respond, he shakes his head. "I know it won't work."

"I think we'd try it and it would end badly," I say. "And I don't want anything to ruin"—I motion toward him—"this."

He holds my gaze. "So, what then? We just say goodbye?"

"You're kind of like a drug for me," I admit. "I think it's better to quit cold turkey, don't you?"

He presses his lips together and looks away.

I set my glass down on the wood plank next to his and crawl toward him. He reaches for me, and I let him hold me, savoring the way his strong arms draw me close. "I'm not sure how to let you go," I whisper.

He kisses me then, and I get lost in it, certain if I could bottle up the way it makes me feel and carry it with me, it would be enough—at least for a little while. When I finally pull back, it's because there are fresh tears streaming down my cheeks.

He uses his thumbs to gently wipe them dry, then tilts his head slightly. "Friday questions?"

"It's Sunday."

A soft shrug. "Oh, right. Maybe let's pretend."

I nod. "Okay."

"Now that you're heading off to this new life," he says, "are you going to forget all about me?"

I'm so still I'm not even sure I'm breathing. "There's no chance I will ever, ever forget you, Booker Hayes."

And when I kiss him again, I know that this is really it. *This* is goodbye.

And while I wouldn't trade my time with him for anything, goodbye really, really hurts.

CHAPTER 44

SEVEN WEEKS LATER

OPENING NIGHT JITTERS ARE TOTALLY normal.

But these jitters are different.

This time, the play *is* in my hands. Mine and the hands of this wonderful new cast.

It's not a large group, but they are talented and generous and kind, and because of them, I've settled into Chicago like I've lived here all my life. I have a small apartment without a roommate, which is slightly unheard of, but the older woman playing the nanny in the show offered it to me at a steal. Turns out it was her mother's and she doesn't have time to deal with putting it on the market.

That, or she really is a kind soul.

That kindness allowed me to save the money I made this summer, and I was able to send my old roommate Ellen most of what I owed her in unpaid rent, with a promise to pay the rest as soon as possible.

I finally feel like I'm starting to grow up.

My entire approach to this role has been different. The desire to make people like me creeps in sometimes, but it's easy to swat it away. I remember the things I learned from Arthur, the things the cast at Sunset Hills taught me, and I pour myself into playing Nora in a way that makes sense to me.

It's so freeing. And natural. And honest.

Tonight, I ritualistically take the reins of this show from our director, imagining it being evenly distributed among my castmates and myself, and I know we are ready.

When the curtain goes up and the play begins, I'm lost in the world we've created on the stage. I *am* Nora. I'm on a journey of self-discovery, the same as her, and from the second the first line is spoken until the curtain falls at the end, I don't let my mind wander once. I am fully in the moment, something I learned all those years ago in school and only now understand applies to my real life too.

There is no feeling like it.

It's utterly incredible. Like a game of tennis between two people who are perfectly, evenly matched. The volley between me and my scene partners is riveting.

When the show is over and it's time to take a bow, I close my eyes backstage and think about all the events that have brought me here.

The good *and* the bad.

Arthur was right—the hard stuff, the stuff that led me here, has made this payoff so much sweeter. Because this moment, this role, this cast . . . this dream . . . wouldn't matter as much to me if I hadn't almost given up.

I'm the last to bow, and when I walk out, there's a loud, raucous cheer from the third row. I expect to see my mom and John and my friends, but they're on the other side of the space. This crowd is a noisy, rowdy group of old people.

My cast.

They're all cheering and clapping, three rows of them, and I instantly start to cry.

They cheer for so long they get everyone else on their feet, and our cast has to do a second bow—something you don't see often with plays these days.

And it doesn't escape me that in the sea of faces I've memorized and grown to love, one very important one is missing.

Cold turkey means cold turkey.

There have been a few scattered texts over the last seven weeks, along the lines of, "Hope things are good," or "Good luck with the show," but I haven't responded.

It's too hard.

I know I shouldn't expect Booker to be here, even if Bertie and Arthur are, but I'd be lying if I said I wasn't just a bit disappointed.

Daisy has sent the occasional update, sometimes including his latest news—mostly, "Booker still isn't dating anyone," or "He won't even go out with us. All he does is work." But I've tried not to let myself dwell there because the hardest part about leaving was letting him go.

I miss him. More than anything. And it's true what they say—absence does make the heart grow fonder. Because seven weeks away has only made me think maybe I do believe in soulmates.

And maybe mine is living in Wisconsin.

Finally, I take a step back, and the curtain falls. I attempt to dry my cheeks, but my mascara has gone rogue.

The cast mills about, all of us hugging and congratulating each other, and I don't want to rush through this moment, but all I can think of is getting out to see my people.

My people.

A picture of a sage-green cottage with an adorable mailbox flashes through my mind.

I rush down to my dressing room to change, and when I walk in, I gasp.

Booker is sitting at the vanity, back to the mirror, facing the door. He's wearing black dress pants and a black button-down, and at the sight of him, everything inside me melts.

My hand covers my mouth, and I close my eyes, opening them again to find him standing. "Are you real?"

A smile peels across his mouth slowly. "I think so."

"Did you see—?" My voice catches, and I point up toward the stage, hoping he understands the question.

He nods. "You were brilliant."

We stare at each other for a few more seconds, a cord of electricity pinning us in place. Finally, I rush toward him, throw my arms around him in a tight hug, the kind of hug I've been missing and dreaming of for weeks. "What are you doing here?"

He pulls back and looks at me, and I can see in his face that he's missed me as much as I've missed him.

"I couldn't miss this, Rosie," he says. "It was too important."

"But we're not supposed to— Oh, who cares?" I go up on my tiptoes and kiss him. I can't help it. Within seconds, we're right back where we were on my last night in Door County. Lost in each other, like we're the only two people in the world.

I pull away, breathless, our foreheads pressed together. "I've missed you."

He kisses my forehead, holding me close. "Yeah. I've missed you too."

I reach up and touch his face, relishing the way his skin feels under my fingers. "I can't believe you're really here."

He turns and kisses the palm of my hand.

"It's going to be so, so hard to say goodbye again."

"I've been thinking about that." He takes a step back, reaches into his pocket, and pulls out his wallet. He opens it and produces a small white card. "It took some time, and a few conversations with Bertie, but"—he hands me the card—"you're looking at the new physical therapist for the Chicago Comets."

"Wait. What?" I take the card and stare at it. "For the Chicago . . ."

"Yep."

"Does that mean you're moving . . . ?"

"Yep."

There, in bold black letters, is Booker's name next to the logo for Chicago's professional hockey team. Underneath it, the words *Physical Therapist.*

He shrugs. "You inspired me."

"I did?" I ask. "To go after your big dream?"

"Yeah, but also . . . to get a new dream."

I frown. "What do you mean?"

"It's you, Rosie," he says. "You're the new dream."

And there's that swoop in my stomach again.

I grin. "I've never been anyone's dream before."

"You're about to get weird, aren't you?" He grins back.

"Probably." I stare at him for a few long seconds, still trying to process the fact that this isn't the end. "Why didn't you tell me you were thinking about this?"

"In case it didn't work out," he says. "I started looking a couple weeks before you left, but I didn't want to make any promises."

"Before I left?" I ask.

"After I recorded your audition," he says. "I knew you'd get the part." Then, after a beat, he adds, "It's okay, right?"

"Are you kidding?" I laugh. "It's so much more than okay."

His smile almost looks relieved, and I have to wonder if he is unclear how deep my feelings for him really are. If so, I need to change that.

Because I have big feelings for Booker Hayes.

"What about Bertie?" I ask. "Won't she miss you?"

"She practically forced me to leave." He laughs. "Told me if she's the only reason I'm at Sunset Hills, then I'm an idiot, especially when it's keeping me from the woman I love."

My eyes go wide. "The woman you love . . . ?"

"The woman I love," he repeats, as if to assure me he did not misspeak. He leans in and kisses me, and I mark the moment in my mind.

This is the *good*, good stuff, and I want to hold on to it.

"You love me," I say, pulling back. My eyes jump to his, and he smiles. There's a lump at the back of my throat, but I still manage to whisper, "I love you too."

Our kiss is interrupted by a forceful rap on the door. I pull away just as Belinda pushes through, followed by Sadie, Evelyn, Grace, Ginny, and several others.

"Enough hanky-panky," Ginny hollers as everyone rushes into the small dressing room, including my mom and John; Marnie; Maya; and Taylor, who is wearing her new baby, Aaron Jr., across her body via a cloth-bag-like contraption.

All that fighting over girls' names and, surprise! The doctors were wrong. Taylor had a boy, and he is perfect.

I glance past everyone and see Arthur standing in the hallway.

I make my way through the crowd and meet him outside my dressing room. "You don't want to come in?"

"It's a little crowded."

I toss a quick peek over my shoulder. "It's a lot crowded."

"Probably a fire hazard."

I smile.

"You did good, kiddo," he says.

My face flushes, heat rushing to my cheeks. "Yeah?"

He nods. "Really good."

I smile. It doesn't matter one bit what any critic says about this show. To me, this man's opinion is the only one that matters. "I'm going to hug you, Arthur."

"Please don't."

"Doing it." I move toward him, and he grimaces, but it all feels like an act. Because he hugs me back instantly, and I hear him whisper, "I'm proud of you."

I pull back and smile.

Arthur winks at me.

The noise in the dressing room kicks up a notch, and the room is like a visual representation of the way my heart feels in this moment.

Loud and noisy and filled to overflowing with people I adore.

People, it turns out, really are life's greatest adventure.

That, and a production of *Cinderella* at a retirement community.

Who would've ever guessed?

THE END

AUTHOR'S NOTE

Dear Reader,

I first discovered my love of theatre in grade school when I got the lead in our school's Christmas program. It was like a light bulb went off and I realized "this is what I love . . ." probably because being on stage didn't require me to do anything with a ball.

An athlete, I am not.

That passion for theatre only grew as I got older, and I pursued it heartily, certain that this was my future. I auditioned and acted in as many shows as I could throughout high school and college. I studied in New York at Circle in the Square Theatre and graduated from Bradley University with degrees in theatre and journalism.

And then I had a bit of an awakening. The life of an actor is hard. It requires a thick skin and an ability to take rejection in stride. It's uncertain and grueling, and it wasn't until I was preparing to pursue that life that I started to think maybe I didn't want it after all.

I wasn't scared to try—the trying excited me. But when I imagined the days, the weeks, the months—the life I would be creating for myself, it just didn't suit my personality. I sensed that I was supposed to go a different direction, I just wasn't sure what it was.

Now, all these years later, I see that I didn't give up on that big dream. I just reimagined it. I rebranded it. I let it grow and change.

I allowed myself to think, *What if I wasn't right the first time?* and *What if the dream still stands but it looks different than I thought?*

Now, my husband and I own a performing arts studio and youth theatre in Northern Illinois, and theatre has been a constant part of my adult life.

In all these years of writing, I've only included theatre in my books once. It's hard to think that the things you deal with on a daily basis will be interesting to read about, but with *Rosie*, I wanted to write a little bit of a love letter to the stage.

And I wanted to write a story for the dreamers. I wanted to let you know that changing course isn't giving up. That it's okay to walk away from something good if your gut says to walk away. That life surprises us, and the good stuff is waiting in the surprises.

I suppose what I'm trying to say is . . . dream big dreams, beautiful soul. But be willing to let yourself reimagine them every once in a while. It's the only way to make sure you don't miss out on what God has for you . . .

Courtney

PS: That flooding in the theatre before the big opening night? That actually happened. And no, writing about it wasn't cathartic—it was sort of traumatic. LOL

PPS: I always love chatting with my readers! Feel free to stay in touch through my website, www.courtneywalshwrites.com, or find me on Instagram @courtneywalsh.

DISCUSSION QUESTIONS

1. Sometimes Rosie sugarcoats things to make her life sound better than it is. She tells herself she's doing this so she doesn't worry the people who love her, but it's possible that the real reason has more to do with her own pride. Has your pride ever made you do the same?

2. Rosie gleans great wisdom from the senior citizens at Sunset Hills. Do you have an older, wiser influence in your life who has done the same? Are you able to be an older, wiser influence in someone else's life?

3. Rosie set out to make a big dream come true, but the reality of that dream isn't at all what she thought. How hard is it to shift your thinking to embrace your own dreams in a new way? Can you give an example of a time you've done this?

4. Have you ever given up on a dream? Do you feel like it was the best decision, or do you have regrets?

5. Rosie is able to see something in Dylan that other people don't see. Talk about a time when someone surprised you (in either a good or bad way).

6. Which of Rosie's relationships do you think was the most impactful on her life? Which of your own relationships have been the most impactful on yours?

7. When Rosie first arrives at Sunset Hills and realizes her mistake, she considers leaving, not ever thinking this might be exactly where she belongs. Have you ever misjudged a situation in your own life and almost quit before giving it a chance? What would you have missed out on if you'd walked away?

8. One surprising benefit of Rosie's being a part of the Sunset Hills community was having a real life impact on people around her. These days, it's easy to focus on building an online presence and to feel like we're connecting with people through our screens. How important is it to you to show up in real life, and when was the last time you were able to have a human connection outside of your immediate family?

LOOKING FOR MORE GREAT READS? LOOK NO FURTHER!

ABOUT THE AUTHOR

COURTNEY WALSH is a novelist, theater director, and playwright. She writes small town romance and women's fiction while juggling the performing arts studio and youth theatre she owns with her husband. She is the author of thirteen novels. Her debut, *A Sweethaven Summer*, hit the *New York Times* and *USA TODAY* bestseller lists and was a Carol Award finalist. Her novel *Just Let Go* won the Carol in 2019, and three of her novels have also been Christy Award finalists. A creative at heart, Courtney has also written three craft books and several musicals. She lives in Illinois with her husband and three children.

Connect with her online at courtneywalshwrites.com
Instagram: @courtneywalsh
Facebook: @courtneywalshwrites
X: @courtney_walsh